I'll Leave
You With
This

KYLIE LADD

I'll Leave You With This

HODDER

First published in Great Britain in 2023 by Hodder & Stoughton
An Hachette UK company

This paperback edition published in 2023

1

A CIP catalogue record for this title is available from the British Library

Paperback ISBN 978 1 399 72035 9

Printed and bound in Great Britain by Clays Ltd, Elcograf S.p.A.

Hodder & Stoughton policy is to use papers that are natural, renewable
and recyclable products and made from wood grown in sustainable
forests. The logging and manufacturing processes are expected to
conform to the environmental regulations of the country of origin.

Hodder & Stoughton Ltd
Carmelite House
50 Victoria Embankment
London EC4Y 0DZ

www.hodder.co.uk

For Nikki, my sister by blood and by luck.
For Piers, my brother, organ donor to five recipients.

And, just a little bit, for Taco, queen amongst dachshunds.

Cerney (1993) argued that to understand the response of the donor family to specific aspects of their bereavement, one should understand their previous functioning.

Dicks, S. et al. (2018) An exploration of the relationship between families of deceased organ donors and transplant recipients: A systematic review and qualitative synthesis. *Health Psychology Open.* Jun 25;5(1).

Prologue

At first he thinks it's fireworks, a quiet popping in the distance. Daniel is heading into the city, sweating slightly as he walks up the hill, the harbour at his back. He could have taken an Uber but he needs the exercise – too much time hunched over his laptop and sewing machine, too many long lunches like this one will be, God willing – and it's a glorious day, why wouldn't he walk? It was only twenty minutes. Morgan had laughed when she saw him setting out, told him he was crazy, but then Morgan never walked anywhere. Couldn't, in those stilettos. He'd suggested once that she wear sneakers to work, even Ugg boots if she wanted to – there was nobody at the studio to appreciate her Manolos – but she'd winced as if he'd slapped her and told him to have her committed if he ever saw her wearing Uggs.

It is spring. The dappled sunlight through the plane trees is warm on his shoulders, and he stops to remove his jacket, folding it carefully across his arm. He'll put it on again before he enters the restaurant, and he doesn't want it creased. That would hardly give the right impression. Daniel checks his watch and sets off again. Plenty of time. It really is a lovely day, the sky a blue dome above him. He's booked his usual table at Sake, but maybe they could sit outside, on the deck. If the pitch goes well, he might even linger, make an afternoon of it looking out over the water with a beer and a smoke. How long has it been since he's done that? He should have told Morgan he might be back late, or not at all. She wouldn't be impressed, but who gave a shit? All work and no play, right? It'd been ages since he'd had a lunch of no return, and the last collection had really taken it out of him.

Daniel rolls his shoulders reflexively, feels their aching, endless tension. His own fault for still insisting he make everything by hand, both the samples and the actual garments they sent down the runway to be applauded and ordered, but how else did you *know*? All these years in the business, all those sketches, everything he'd produced, and he still couldn't tell if, or even how, something would hang together unless he sat down and stitched it himself. It drove him nuts. It drove Morgan nuts too, no doubt about that; she'd sigh and roll her eyes whenever he pulled his stool up to the Singer, bitching that they could hire a graduate for that, that his job was to design. He agreed with her in theory, but it felt like cheating, somehow, to dream something into being, then hand it over to an underling to figure out how to make it up. That's what creativity really was, wasn't it? Not just the dream, but the execution too. The vision, then the work. And Daniel isn't a shirker.

His phone pings and he reaches for it without breaking stride. There is a text from Joel: *Good luck Danny boy. You've got this!* Daniel smiles, but he pushes the mobile back into his pocket without replying. Joel could wait. He always waited.

A teenage girl lurches past wearing a t-shirt emblazoned with the name of Bridie's film. Bridie's big film, the one that made her an overnight success after fifteen years of graft. Seeing it gives him a kick like it always does, a gratifying hit of dopamine. He wants to stop the girl, with her mauve hair and wobbly eyeliner, and tell her, 'Hey, that's my sister! She made that!' A few years ago he would've snapped a photo, with or without permission, and sent it to Bridie, or told her the next time he saw her. The last time he'd done that, though, she'd just shrugged and said that those t-shirts were everywhere, probably made in China, nothing she could do. It had astonished him. She was no longer elated that her film was, if not quite yet a cultural touchstone, still well-known enough to rip off and flog to the masses. She wasn't even annoyed that that t-shirt had been bootlegged somewhere and she was losing the merchandising revenue. She was simply resigned. Worse, she was blasé. Blasé! That level of push-through, and Bridie had only shrugged. Maybe it was because she's older, forty-two to his thirty-five, but still. Daniel can't imagine a time when seeing something of his in the street wouldn't make his breath catch, his spine straighten. Can't imagine ever wanting less than everyone in the world to be wearing his clothes, truth be told.

Why not t-shirts then? The idea crackles like electricity, as the best ideas do. Daniel has always eschewed t-shirts – too sloppy, and his is not a sloppy brand – but he could do something tailored, maybe, with the discreet DOS logo over one breast. His main game is suits, impeccably constructed, effortlessly stylish without ever being flashy, but the market for suits is shrinking. T-shirts though . . . who doesn't wear those? A fitted t-shirt, bucking the trend – none of that oversized stuff – and definitely not cotton. Something luxe, something you wouldn't expect, but would long to touch. Tencel? Could he get away with velvet? Velour? His fingers are itching to sketch.

He pulls out his phone again to make a few quick notes, automatically checking his hair in the camera app before turning it off.

Perfect. He has good hair. He has *great* hair, actually; it has its own Instagram account. Bridie had been the one to alert him to it and they'd laughed together at a family lunch. Allison hadn't got it; she didn't know what Instagram even was, never mind why anyone would want to dedicate an account to her kid brother's hair. Bridie had tried to explain but neither of them could stop laughing at the absurdity of it, and Allison had thought they were laughing at her and made a show of picking up her wine and turning to talk to Emma instead.

Poppoppop. There's the noise again, like champagne corks, only louder. It can't be fireworks though, Daniel finally computes. It's the middle of the day. Now he hears a siren, but there are always sirens in the city, most of them false alarms. He is hungry and pays it no heed. What entrée would he order, the kingfish or the popcorn shrimp? It was good manners to let the client – *potential* client – select the main, but the entrées were his. Maybe he'd suggest both.

The pops are closer now, strident. Daniel turns a corner and confronts a scene of carnage. There is a figure on the ground, others sheltering behind benches and advertising boards set out on the footpath . . . over there, a woman on her back, lying still, one arm thrown up as if to shield her eyes from the sun. A splash of crimson pools beneath her . . . Is it her jacket? Blood?

A bang now rather than a pop, a sharp sound that he has only heard in the movies. Daniel wheels around, startled and staring. Is that what is happening? Is someone making a film? There should be lights and a boom mike, a catering truck somewhere subtle but not too distant. He knows this from visiting Bridie on set, and searches for it earnestly. A catering truck will make it all okay. But instead there is a second bang, and this time he sees, actually sees, another woman fold in two like a wallet and slump to the ground.

A movie, right? It has to be a movie. Daniel's heart is racing, so loud in his ears it silences anything else. People are running towards him and he freezes, a leopard caught in a stampede of wildebeest. He has never been one to follow the herd.

And that is what does for him. A masked figure with a gun advances – a real gun, not a prop; he knows this in his bones. Face covered, clad all in black. Daniel notices these things. The buttons on the shirt are mother of pearl. A nice touch against the dark material. He must remember that, but the figure is facing him now and raising his arm . . . The world erupts and then contracts once more, caving in around him. He thinks of Bridie again, then Allison, Clare, Emma, all his sisters; he hears his mother's voice and his father singing; he sees the quadrangle at Central St Martins and realises he won't be having the kingfish after all, not today, and the sun has gone behind a cloud; that's what must have happened because the light is waning, the bright green leaves of the plane trees leaching into olive, into the colour of mud, the pavement surprisingly warm against his cheek. Shoes, he sees shoes. Why do people wear such cheap shoes? Velcro fastenings on sneakers have always offended him. They signify indolence, giving up. What was so difficult about laces?

Daniel closes his eyes in disgust and can't seem to open them again. There's something wet in his hair, his hair that has its own Instagram account. The thought makes him want to laugh even now. Should he post a shot to it, or was that uncool, to acknowledge you even knew about it or were, God forbid, actually following yourself? Pain now, sudden and chilling, like a bucket of water thrown over him. The ice bucket challenge for charity that Joel had talked him into, to use his profile for good instead of simply selling shirts. 'Come on, Danny boy,' he'd cajoled. 'Surely you'd want to support this?'

Daniel's teeth are chattering. Joel. He reaches for his phone but he can't feel his fingers, his body distant, absent, missing somehow. He's cold now, so cold, and for the first time afraid. He wishes, as he dies, that he'd replied to Joel's text.

Part One

Part One

Allison

September 2018

By the time Allison arrives home she can smell herself. The sweat is crusted in her hair and under her arms; the blouse she put on fresh that morning – a lifetime ago now – is stuck to her back and clings damply around her neck. She could have had a shower at the hospital, but she'd forgotten to replace the fresh change of clothes she usually kept in her office and didn't want to go home in scrubs. There had to be a boundary. The hospital needed to stay the hospital, her home, her home. Blurring the lines between them was sloppy, dangerous. It meant she could never truly leave one or the other, and each needed her total focus, no distractions, when she was there.

As she climbs out of the car she notices blood on one of her shoes and winces, stooping with a hastily wetted index finger to rub it off. Blood is part of the job, inevitable, especially in the sort of scenario she's just dealt with, and somehow it gets everywhere, no matter how much protective gear she wears. It doesn't bother her, but she doesn't want the boys to see it. Eliot particularly is squeamish, goes white if she has to remove a splinter or he stubs his toe. Allison has little patience with it, not with the trauma she witnesses on a daily basis, not after all she's lost, and she's noticed he turns to Jason now, who clucks and coos like a woman when he takes his son in his arms.

She sighs. Too bad. It was good, she reminds herself, that she and Jason refused to let their genders define them. It was important that the boys saw that daddies could give kisses and cuddles and tuck them into bed every night while mummies did the work and earned the money. It wasn't how she'd been brought up, but the world had changed, was still changing. And boy, did this mummy work.

Jason turns from the stove to greet her as she comes into the kitchen. 'You're late,' he says, but without judgement or rancour. 'Big day?'

He is wearing an apron, she notices, a frilly, flowery affair that Marty bought her earlier in the year from the Mother's Day stall at school. When she'd opened it she'd had to fight the impulse to laugh and Marty had noticed, but wasn't offended.

'It was that or soap,' he'd said, shrugging. 'And the soap smelled *disgusting*.'

She had laughed then and hugged him, proclaiming it the best apron ever while already mentally consigning it to the back of the linen press.

Now here it was around her husband's still-trim waist. 'Nice apron,' she says, arching one eyebrow, longing, despite all her gender-neutral self-talk, to tear it off him and make him a man again.

Jason turns back to the stove. 'Yeah, well, the sausages were splattering oil everywhere. Eliot suggested it. He didn't want me to get my clothes dirty.'

'You could have turned the gas down,' she says, 'or done them under the grill.'

He gives her a *back off* look and smiles, though not with his eyes. 'Let's start again, shall we? Big day?'

Allison swallows and pushes it all down: the fear, the fatigue, the adrenaline, the ridiculous spurt of repulsion that had gone through her when she'd seen the apron. 'Yes,' she agrees. 'A very big day. Touch and go in a delivery this afternoon. Uterine rupture.'

Jason nods as if he understands exactly what such an event has demanded of her. 'But it was all okay? The mother survived?'

Allison exhales. 'She did. And the baby. We were lucky. It could have been bad.' The expectant father's face as they worked to resuscitate his wife suddenly comes back to her, his incomprehension morphing into terror. The breath she draws in is shuddery.

'Hey,' Jason says, setting down the spatula. 'Hey. That sounds awful.' He pulls her into his arms and she sinks against him gratefully, closing her eyes. 'Drink, or a shower first? Dinner's almost ready, but it can wait.'

'Drink,' she mutters, then changes her mind. 'No, shower. I stink. Thank you.'

Eliot looks up from where he is seated at the kitchen table with his iPad, seemingly only just aware that she is home. The *Bluey* theme music rings tinnily from his device.

'Mummy!' he exclaims. 'Can we go to the park now?'

Her face must betray her, for his own immediately contorts in disappointment.

'You promised!' he whines.

'I did?' She genuinely can't remember.

'You did!' Eliot insists. 'Yesterday, at dinner. You said you'd take us to the park when you got home from work.'

Maybe she had, but that was yesterday, she wanted to tell him. She thought she'd be home by three, not six; she didn't know she'd be literally wiping off another woman's blood as she walked in. Her hands clench into fists, the car keys that she has yet to put down biting into her flesh. *Run.* The impulse surges through her. *Get back in the car. Drive. Escape.*

'Mummy's pretty tired, mate,' Jason intervenes. 'What about tomorrow?'

Tears well in Eliot's pale blue eyes. Jason glances at Allison nervously, as if anticipating a scene, and their expressions make her immediately contrite.

'Maybe a quick trip after dinner. It should still be light enough. But only if you eat all your peas.' She can't resist making her surrender conditional. There has to be something in it for her.

'I will,' Eliot declares earnestly, as if he were in court. 'Every single one. I promise.'

He jumps from his chair to rush to his twin with news of the victory.

Jason drops a kiss on her forehead and murmurs, 'Good on you,' before returning to the sausages.

Yes, Allison thinks, trudging up the stairs towards her ensuite, the pile of laundry that had been left at the bottom in one arm, the files she still has to write up tonight under the other, good on her. She is a good sport. She is a good girl. Good, good, good. She is the classic oldest child who always does what is asked of her, but the thought brings her only a sort of hollow pride, no real satisfaction, no joy.

She turns the shower on, deliberately making it a little too hot, all the better to wash the afternoon away. Her patient today was a relatively young woman, Maya. She already had two children. Two boys, like Allison. Maybe this third pregnancy had been an attempt at a girl. Who knew? Allison hadn't had a chance to talk with her, had only been paged when the tear had been discovered and Maya was already unconscious, haemorrhaging life. Allison had stepped into the delivery suite and, as if on cue, Maya's monitor had flat-lined. 'We're losing her,' someone had cried at the same time as a nurse announced, 'I can't get a foetal heartbeat.' Every eye had turned towards Allison.

She winces as she recalls it, and makes the shower even hotter. They'd all looked to her to tell them what to do, to fix things, to make it all better. And she'd pulled it off. But if she hadn't? Those two little boys would have no mother tonight. That husband would have no wife. Maya's parents would have lost their daughter, lost a grandchild. There would be a rend in that family that could never be repaired, and it would have been her fault. Not entirely – there was bad luck too, the roll of the dice – but her failure would have played a part. She'd pulled it off, but only just. Only just. Allison reaches for the shampoo, and bursts into tears.

Dinner eaten, she checks her watch while herding the boys into the car for the trip to the park. There is only an hour of light left, which at least limits how long she'll have to stay. The thought prompts both relief and guilt. This is her only real alone time with her sons all day. Can't she at least embrace that, be present for it, not wishing it gone? Lean in. That's what all the self-help books advise, or is it the parenting ones? She wonders vaguely if she's even read a book since she was pregnant.

Eliot, still small at seven, insists on buckling himself into his car seat, but the minute it's done, remembers he's forgotten his football.

'I'll go get it, Mum,' he says, working carefully to undo the harness he's just done up.

'Do you have to?' Allison sighs. 'Can't you just . . . run around or something instead?' But he is already gone, hurrying up the path towards the house. His gait isn't quite right. Allison leans forward in her seat, watching him now with a clinician's eye. Is he limping?

'Marty,' she says, 'did Eliot fall over at school or something today?'

He shrugs. 'Dunno. Can I get my footy too?'

She shakes her head. 'One's enough.' At this rate they won't even get out of the driveway before it is dark. The front door opens, but instead of Eliot, Jason emerges, a squirming dachshund under his arm. He'd offered to come with them, but she'd selflessly refused. This was her duty – and hopefully he'd clean up while she was gone. One less task for her before she got to the files.

'Can you take John Thomas?' Jason asks. 'Sorry. I haven't had a chance to walk him today.' He opens the door of the Volvo and hands the dog to Martin without waiting for her answer.

'Seriously?' she mutters but is drowned out by the dog's excited barking. Jason only works half days in his physio practice, spending the rest of the time running their household, getting the twins to and from school, doing the shopping and the laundry, making the beds and the lunches and then dinner. Yes, it is a great arrangement – her friends and colleagues constantly remind her of that – but it's what they'd agreed on. He had the flexibility, she had the income. It made sense. And it worked well. But he could have walked the bloody dog.

'Ready!' Eliot has reappeared, brandishing his beloved red and green football.

'Is your leg okay, El?' Allison asks as he does battle once more with the car seat.

'Yes?' he says, pausing as if it is a trick question. Eliot aims to please. 'I think so?'

'You looked as if you were limping when you went inside just then,' Allison says, reversing into the street. She catches a glimpse of grey roots among her sandy hair as she checks the rear-vision mirror. God. So soon? Six weeks came around so quickly!

'It sometimes does that,' Eliot says, reaching across the back seat to rub John Thomas's ears. 'It's like it has a mind of its own.'

Despite everything, despite her day and the rupture and the work still waiting for her at home, the park trip is a success. Eliot and Martin are thrilled to have her to themselves and show off excitedly, hanging from the monkey bars, scrambling up the big slide, incessantly imploring her to *watch, Mummy, watch*. She showers them with praise, relieved not to have been made to join in some sort of kicking drill, while John Thomas trots beneath the swings, wagging his tail and trying to eat discarded cigarette butts. The dog would eat anything. How many lollipop sticks and chip packets had she had to pull out of his ever-ravenous maw on previous park trips, how many times had she found him with his head in one of the boys' discarded school bags, scarfing down a forgotten banana or half a ham sandwich? Bananas, for God's sake. He ate them with the skin on.

'You crazy mutt,' she says when he approaches her bench, sniffing furiously, and he looks up and practically smiles at her, mouth agape, tail a black blur. Her heart lurches. This is all she has left of Daniel. Allison scoops him onto her lap and buries her nose in his velvety fur, his body warm against hers like a newborn. 'Crazy, crazy, crazy,' she mutters as he squirms with delight. A dog hadn't been part of the plan when he'd first come to them, almost two years ago, when the boys were still in preschool and she'd just been made head of the department. They'd had their hands full, but Sophie, Clare's partner – Clare's *wife*, she reminds herself, the idea that her sister was married to a woman still a little surprising to her – was allergic and they couldn't have him anymore.

'It's getting worse,' Sophie had said, sniffling, when she and Clare had handed John Thomas over. 'My eyes, my nose – everything runs. It's awful. I feel so bad about it.' She'd glanced across at Clare, who was teary but bit her lip and attempted to smile.

'I'll miss him so much,' Clare had said, 'but I'm so glad he's going to you, that he'll still be in the family. Daniel would have liked that too.'

John Thomas had belonged to Daniel, her brother killed almost three years ago in a shooting in the city. Their brother – hers and Clare's, and Bridie's and Emma's too – number four of the five of them, the lone son among all those daughters. It was still hard to think of him gone, so most of the time Allison pretended that he wasn't. Daniel had bought John Thomas as a pup and treated him like a child, the dog spending his days at the studio napping at Daniel's feet, sharing his sushi or attempting to get into the bin in the tiny kitchen. Clare had volunteered to have him that terrible October, once it was clear that Morgan, Daniel's business partner, would be selling the studio and had no desire for his pet. Sophie's allergies had declared themselves soon afterwards, but the couple had hung on for a year before asking Allison to take him.

Jason had been reluctant. 'Why us?' he'd asked. 'We're busy enough as it is. Can't Bridie have him, or Emma?'

'We've got a house, and kids. I guess that makes us the obvious choice,' she'd replied, adding placatingly, 'He won't be much work. He's such a little dog. How hard can it be?'

How hard, indeed. Allison sighs and sets him back down on the grass. Such a little dog, but one who seems to require constant maintenance. He is always devouring socks or needing walking or tracking dirt through the house after digging in the garden. Most of that work – all of it, in truth – falls to Jason, who has never warmed to John Thomas. He had been particularly frosty since a five-hundred-dollar trip to the vet's for the removal of an avocado pit from the dachshund's behind.

'He ate an avocado?' Clare had shrieked down the phone when Allison had told her. 'A whole one?'

'It wasn't that big,' Allison had said defensively. 'The pit, anyway. I don't know how he even got the avocado out of the fruit bowl. One of the boys probably fed it to him.'

'Big enough to get stuck.' Clare was laughing, snorting through her nose.

Allison had smiled despite herself, imagining Clare's whole body shaking, her head rocking back and forth. Clare had such a vigorous laugh. 'Yeah. We only noticed something was up because he was off his food, and John Thomas is *never* off his food.'

'How did the vet get it out?' Clare had asked between snorts.

'I don't know,' Allison had said. 'Jason took him. Vaseline and rubber gloves, I imagine,' which had promptly set Clare off again.

'Mum, will you come on the seesaw with us?'

Martin is tugging at her sleeve and she acquiesces, knees creaking as she rises from the bench. 'You sit down one end and me and Eliot will go up the other.'

'Eliot and I,' she corrects automatically, gingerly lowering her spreading bottom onto the splintered wood. The fit is not flattering. 'What now?' she asks, anchored to the ground, knees awkwardly at the level of her chin. 'How are you going to get on?'

'We'll climb,' Marty declares, and the boys shimmy up the steep incline like twin monkeys, blond heads bobbing.

'Be careful,' she calls out. Was this safe? It was so rare to even find a seesaw at a park anymore, most having gone the way of the dinosaur, of the flying fox, of playing tennis on the road after school, as she and Bridie had done when they were girls. Other parents complain about the creeping infantilisation of children's play areas, but she isn't among them. The world is a risky place, she sees that every day. Why give it any more chances to kill you?

'Push, Mummy!' Eliot implores from the top of the seesaw, arms wrapped around Martin's waist. She does as she is told, but remains stolidly earthbound.

'Harder!' Martin says. Allison tries again. Still the seesaw won't budge.

'I think she's too heavy,' Eliot tells Martin. 'We need another kid up here.'

'Yeah, or maybe Dad.'

'I can hear you, you know,' Allison calls back, tempted to stand up and let them both bump to the dirt. 'It's not going to work this way. Martin, you come down this end and just do it with Eliot. Slowly!'

Once the boys are established she goes to round up John Thomas. The shadows are lengthening; it is time to go home. She lingers, though, in the dusk and considers her own shadow, distinctly fuller than it was ten years ago. But that was to be expected, wasn't it? She'd had twins; she is Chief Obstetrician at a major teaching hospital, with no time to exercise. Some days it feels as if she barely has time to urinate. In the last year or two she'd become a regular blood donor at the centre up on level four, claiming it was to inspire her staff and other employees to do the same. But really it was just so she could lie down for an hour without looking lazy. Her hands sneak to her stomach. Still relatively flat, and her boobs are in good nick, but there is no doubt she's getting heavier through her hips and arse, the Irish peasant genes that her father had been so proud of well and truly asserting themselves. Menopause isn't going to be pretty.

They are almost home when Allison realises that John Thomas, who yaps enthusiastically throughout any car trip, is unusually quiet.

'JT's in the back with you boys, isn't he?' she asks. 'We didn't leave him at the park?'

'Yeah,' Martin says.

'He's right under your seat,' Eliot adds, the helpful one. 'I think he's chewing on something.'

Allison goes cold. 'Can you see what it is?' *A cheese stick*, she prays. *A muesli bar*. The boys were always leaving snack foods in their wake.

Eliot leans forward. 'It's a box. A shoebox? He's chewed right through it. Naughty John Thomas!'

Allison pulls to the side of the road without signalling and slams on the brakes, but by the time she has undone her belt and twisted around to extract the dog it is already too late.

His muzzle is grey and flaky; he sneezes as she thrusts him at Martin, admonishing her son to hold on tightly and not let go. Then, taking a deep breath, she climbs out of the car, opens Eliot's door and bends to inspect the damage. The cardboard box has indeed been chewed through. So too has the wooden lid on the eco-friendly urn inside, scattering all that was left of Jason's elderly aunt across the black carpet of the footwell.

'Fuck!' she exclaims.

'You owe twenty cents to the swear jar,' Eliot tells her, while Martin cranes forward.

'What's *that*?' he asks.

'Nothing,' Allison says, trying to sweep the ashes back into the urn with her hand. They are fine and gritty, like dirty sand, though now she looks more closely she can see bone fragments among the dusty powder, pearlescent and jagged. Her airway narrows. She fights the impulse to gag or to cry. Death, again, always in her face. She was so tired of death.

'That's not going to work, Mummy,' Eliot tells her. 'You'll need a vacuum.'

The image saves her, hauling her back from hysteria. She could call in at a service station before they got home, she thinks, starting to giggle. Jason would never have to know. It was his fault, anyway. He'd left the box there, in the back seat of the family car, what – three, four months ago, after the funeral home had contacted him to collect it? Jason hadn't been close to Aunt Tanya, had barely known her in truth, but he was her oldest living relative and thus bequeathed with her remains. Afterwards, he and Allison had made desultory plans to scatter them somewhere, and then promptly forgot, swept along by her work, by his work, by the boys, by the dog, by the house, by his practice, by the lawn that needed mowing and the weekly swimming lessons, by the endless stream of school newsletters and CPD seminars and supermarket runs. Life had overtaken them, and the box had been forgotten. It must have fallen beneath the seat, out of sight and out of mind. It was a wonder John Thomas hadn't got to it before now. *Sorry, Aunt Tanya.*

Shame wrestles with exhaustion, but exhaustion wins. They were always so busy, too busy. It was why they never had sex, that and things like the apron. She straightens up, goes back to her seat and starts the car. Jason can deal with it later. She has had enough of looking after people for one day, living or dead. She just wants to go to sleep.

Bridie

'I'm sure it must be there somewhere,' Bridie says hopefully, craning her neck to try to see the list. 'O'Shea. Bridie O'Shea.'

The usher checks again, but comes up empty-handed. 'I'm sorry,' she says. 'I don't have that name.'

'You must,' Tom insists. 'Next to me. Can you check, please? Tom Flanagan.'

'Of course, Mr Flanagan.' The girl, Bridie notices, can't resist a sneak peek at her husband before she does. Tom is forever drawing second looks and backwards glances, even here it seems, surrounded by actors and celebrities at the AACTA awards. Normally it doesn't bother Bridie, but right now she itches to snap at the usher. *Hurry up.* There are other nominees starting to bank up behind them.

'You're here, Mr Flanagan,' the young woman says finally. 'Row B, seat sixteen, right next to Sam Neill, and, uh, Shane Jacobson.' She giggles and bats her eyelashes. 'Lucky you. Lucky them!'

Bridie doesn't attempt to suppress her sigh. 'But not me. His wife. Is that right?'

The girl has the grace to look embarrassed. 'I'm sorry,

Mrs Flanagan. You're probably in the balcony, with the other part-ners. I'll get one of my colleagues to take you up, if you like?'

'O'Shea,' Tom says. 'Her name's O'Shea, as in Bridie O'Shea, director of *Black Box*.'

Gratifyingly, the usher's eyes widen. 'You made that film? I *loved Black Box*. I had a huge poster of it on my bedroom wall right through high school – oh, and I went to Comic-Con as Cassandra in my first year of uni. You should have seen me! I even had my hair dyed, just for the day. Indigo, like hers . . .'

Tom pulls Bridie away. 'Bird, I'm so sorry. What do you want to do?'

'Do? Nothing. It's fine. I'll go take my seat with the other partners.' She can't quite keep the edge from her tone.

'We don't have to. We can just go home. It doesn't matter.'

He means it, she realises. It's his big night, but he wants her to be okay. This lovely man, this biggest stroke of luck in a lucky life. She feels herself soften. So she'll sit in the balcony. So what?

'Don't be silly,' she says, but lightly; she is lighter now. 'We're not going home. I'll meet you straight afterwards. Good luck. Break a leg.'

He leans in and kisses her, breathes *thank you* against her lips. Another usher steps in to guide him to his seat and she watches him go, standing at the edge of the aisle. Broad shoulders, dark hair, slim hips. A classic matinee idol and hers, all hers. Sam Neill holds out his hand and the two men shake. Tom says something, and Neill throws back his head in laughter. They are deep in conversation as Bridie makes her way back to the foyer.

Her glow lasts until she is following yet another usher into the nosebleed section of the balcony. No one here, she can't help but notice, is dressed like her. No one else expected to be seen. At five eleven, with abundant gold hair and a figure kept rigorously in check by Pilates, kickboxing and a personal trainer who screams at her if she so much as thinks about a cupcake, Bridie needs no gimmicks. Her scarlet evening gown is almost spartan in its simplicity. No sequins for her, no frills or flounces, not even a hint of sideboob. She is positively demure compared to some of the women she'd stood alongside on the red carpet, but there was no getting away from it: she looks out of place in the balcony. People mutter to each other as she sidles past them to get to her seat, and she imagines what they're saying. Who does she think she is, with her Balenciaga dress, her statement jewellery, her uncovered shoulders?

The houselights dim and she sinks back, cheeks burning. It wasn't so long ago that Tom was *her* plus-one on the award invites, at the premieres, the galas. When *Black Box* took off, people had fallen over themselves to have her in their front rows . . . but things have changed. Try as she might, there hasn't been another feature film with her name on it, not as the director anyway. She's been mentioned once or twice as a consultant, which is a polite way of saying she was attached to the project because someone thought involving her and her Leone d'Argento would bring in funding or clout or both. Did it work? Bridie can't even remember. All she knows is that she hasn't made a film in over a decade, and it is killing her.

A round of applause. The first award is announced, but Bridie doesn't hear it, isn't interested anyway. Her career has stalled. She's been fearing it for a while, but tonight is proof. The balcony is proof. Oh, her family wouldn't think so, but they're still glassy-eyed at the success of *Black Box*. Most of her friends, too, but she was thirty-three then. The age Christ was crucified, she muses to herself. Well, he made a comeback. Maybe there's hope for her yet. But she fears not. She is forty-five now, and the industry is pulling away, leaving her behind. If it wasn't for Tom, she probably wouldn't have been invited tonight.

What had gone wrong? She'd been engaged for plenty of features post-*Black Box*, but they'd all fallen over for one reason or another. It happened; it wasn't her fault. Directors often went years between films, particularly in the early stages of their career, and hers had taken a while to get going. Twelve years, though, raised question marks, raised red flags brighter than her dress.

Bridie's palms are sweating and she takes care to wipe them on the seat rather than mark her clothes. The gown has to go back tomorrow. It isn't even the money that bothers her. They have plenty, thanks to Tom's years on *Neighbours* and her cult film. Thank God she'd elected to take a percentage of profits rather than a flat fee. *Black Box* was a decidedly odd film, a spec-fic fantasy about a group of teenagers who, realising they are immortal, band together for protection against a government agency that is hunting them down, one by one, to mine their DNA. *Sex, Lies and Vivisection*, Daniel had quipped after he'd first seen it, which Bridie had conceded was an apt description. It had garnered only two reviews on its release, the first calling it 'quirky', while the second went straight for 'weird'. No one had ever expected *Black Box* to turn over a tenth of what it had, a hundredth even, but Bridie had had a hunch. The royalties were still coming in – not a lot, but enough. Tom had suggested she set up her own production company, but she isn't interested in that. She doesn't want to spend her days in meetings or unravelling red tape. She wants to be on set, knee-deep in the work, creating the magic, not just overseeing it. She doesn't want to buy her way in. She wants to be there on her own merits, but right now her own merits can't even get her a decent seat at a second-rate award ceremony.

Daniel would understand. A hit of pure loss goes through her, more potent than heroin. It has been almost three years now. She has mostly learned to live with it, has days, even, that she passes through without thinking of him, but every so often the grief finds her again, ambushing her as completely as it did in the first weeks after the phone call.

It was Clare who had rung her. Afterwards that felt strange. Clare is the sibling she is probably least close to, despite their proximity in the family line-up – Bridie at number two, Clare number three. Even so, there are five years between them and, more than that, whole oceans of temperament. Bridie is creative, driven, ambitious, was the first to fly the nest and is always the last to know what's going on with any of her sisters. Clare is solid, reliable, practical, no-nonsense, the one who organises Christmas and remembers birthdays. They have little in common other than their surname. They don't even look like each other: Bridie tall and toned and leonine, Clare more like an aardvark or an armadillo, head down, barrelling stolidly through life. At Daniel's funeral, Bridie kept glancing over at Clare, who was weeping openly, and felt an irrational anger. *You shouldn't have told me. It wasn't your place.* But who, then, would she have allowed to bear the news? Of all of them, Daniel was her confidante, but he was up by the altar, lying in a casket with the lid closed because the bullet that had killed him had also blown away part of his face.

Strange that they'd been so close. Daniel had been the fourth-born with seven years between him and Bridie. When she was starting high school he was starting school, period – just a kid with a *Masters of the Universe* lunchbox and a bowl haircut. *Masters of the Universe* wasn't even his thing, she recalled. It had been bought on a whim by their mother, who, after three girls, was only guessing what a boy might like. But Daniel had never been a particularly predictable boy. He had preferred to draw rather than run or climb and had never liked being dirty. He'd also made far more use of the dress-up box than Allison or Clare. 'It's my fault,' their father had opined on more than one occasion. 'He's seen me poncing around on stage too much. He wants to be like his dad.' Privately, Bridie didn't believe her father's devotion to the local musical theatre troupe had anything at all to do with it, and she certainly didn't see it as a fault. Daniel was just Daniel, unique, complete.

They'd grown close after Emma was born, when the family home, which had once seemed so spacious, finally ran out of bedrooms. Emma cried a lot and couldn't be bunked in with one of her sisters. With their mother still in hospital, their father had decided that the two next-youngest, Clare and Daniel, should share a room, freeing up Daniel's for the baby. To everyone's surprise though, Daniel had requested that he move in with Bridie instead. She had recently started her period and discovered pop music and that she liked it when boys looked at her. A five-year-old in her personal space should have been anathema, but there was something about the way that he asked, so certain, so sure, the way he chose *her*, not smarty-pants Allison or good-girl Clare . . . She'd agreed to a trial period, and three years later, Daniel was still there, until the extension was built.

They'd had fun, Bridie thinks. By then she was a teenager and he was in grade two, but still they'd had fun. Daniel had loved lying on her bed, poring over her *Dolly* magazines with her; they learned the steps to the Locomotion together and walked like Egyptians. 'Do you like girls or boys?' she'd asked him once, as they were filling in a quiz on finding your perfect match. 'Girls AND boys,' he'd replied without missing a beat, circling a response. Years later, when he came out as bisexual, she'd remembered that conversation. 'He's gay, isn't he?' her mother had said. 'He's just pretending he likes girls too to make us feel better.' But Bridie had believed him. There was no subterfuge in Daniel. He was perfectly content with who he was and what he liked, and felt no need to hide it.

As he grew older, it became more and more apparent that one of the things Daniel really liked was clothes. Fabric, cut, colour, style – he appreciated it all. He *understood* it all. She was at AFTRS by now, the Australian Film, Television and Radio School, and modelling on the side for cash – TV, when she could get it, rather than print, so at least she'd be near a camera. Daniel styled her for go-sees and casting calls, somehow instinctively knowing how to make her stand out or be exactly what the client was looking for. Their own tastes in fashion were similar, classical verging towards the severe, but he never let that get in the way when sending her off to an audition.

As the work rolled in and her bank balance grew, Bridie's innate liking for him blossomed into a deep respect. Daniel was no longer just her little brother, he was her collaborator. They were exclusive members of a secret society of two, flamingos in a family of wrens. No one else ever got it, Bridie thinks. Not Emma, in her churchy skirts and floral blouses; not Clare, always in scrubs; and certainly not Allison, with her preference for sensible shoes and washable fabrics. Because of her job, she would argue, because of the blood and the shit and the amniotic fluid she was constantly in danger of being splattered with, but really, Bridie knows, she has just grown lazy. She'd wear a tracksuit to the shops, for God's sake, and think nothing of it.

Irritated, she shifts in her seat. She wished Daniel had been there to dress her tonight. She wished they had worked together, seriously, as adults and equals. It was something they had always intended to do. On her next film, she'd promised, after *Black Box* broke through, and he'd smiled, and said *cool* and *no hurry*. They had all the time in the world, until they didn't.

Applause again. Lots of applause. Bridie starts, jolted out of her reverie. Was that her name? She peers towards the stage, and Tom is there, brandishing something crass and shiny. He's won, Tom has won, and she has missed it.

'. . . my beautiful wife,' she hears him finish, 'who I couldn't have done this without – I couldn't do anything without.'

The people in her row are nudging each other and shuffling forward to get a look at her, but Bridie barely notices. She is flushing, crimson, delighted despite herself. Maybe it had been worth coming after all.

Clare

October 2018

As she leaves work, Clare is feeling good. The shift has gone well – no deaths, no codes, just the straightforward clinical care she enjoys so much, plus she had a chance to actually chat with some patients and their families for once. That didn't always happen – the ward could be so busy – but it made such a difference. To the way she was able to care for them, certainly, once she knew them as people, not just bed numbers, but to their recovery time too, or so it seemed at least. Someone, she muses, should do a study on that – the correlation between personalised nursing and patient outcomes. The availability of personalised nursing though, that was the issue. And patient outcomes, or patient throughput? In her experience the research grants were skewed towards the latter, all about getting bodies out of beds as quickly as possible so they could be invoiced for and replaced with fresh ones, rather than actual quality of care. But that wasn't right. Maybe *she* should do the study, show how much good nursing mattered. It could be her Masters. She'd always intended to do one . . . but not right now. Right now she has her period, which is the other reason she is in a good mood.

It's funny, she thinks, climbing into her car. Normally her period is cause for tears, despair, the sign of yet another month lost, another child not conceived. Today though, when she first felt the cramping during her shift, she experienced a surge of hope instead. Finally! She'd been waiting for it since her last miscarriage, the fourth, almost six weeks ago now. Her specialist had wanted to wait two cycles before making another IVF attempt, ideally, but time was ticking on. They'd agreed Clare could come back after one.

She starts doing the sums in her head. Today is, what – 9 October? She'll be finishing her period in five days. If she calls the clinic as soon as she's home she can probably get an appointment for late next week to have her bloods done and get the meds started again. They still have one embryo in storage, so she can go straight to a frozen transfer, not have to mess around with ovarian stimulation and retrieval . . . She could be pregnant by November, by Christmas.

Goosebumps lift her flesh and a little shudder of delight runs through her. It would be too soon to tell her sisters at the family lunch, but she'd have to refuse any drinks, of course. Maybe they'd guess. Allison would be straight onto something like that, given her job, and then everyone would toast her and Sophie, and she'd sit at the table, glowing, with one hand over her stomach, even though there wouldn't be a bump there yet . . .

Clare is picturing it so clearly as she arrives home that it takes her a second to realise Sophie's car is already there, tucked into the garage. She checks her watch. It's 3.30, about the usual time she gets home after the morning shift, but Sophie should still be at work. A lawyer at a city firm, she is never back before six at best.

Great, Clare thinks, *I can tell her straight away*. But something keeps her in her car, even after she has pulled the keys from the ignition. She gazes at their house, admiring it. Just a simple brick terrace, but so pretty at this time of year, with the wisteria blossoming across the railing of the upstairs balcony and the espaliered pear coming into bloom in the pot by the front door. Not strictly their house, though, unfortunately. Four rounds of IVF had put paid to saving for a deposit, even on Sophie's salary, so it is only a rental – but it's secure, Clare reminds herself. They have a great landlord, an older gay man who loves them and calls them his girls and hasn't once raised the rent in all the time they've been living there. He'd come to their wedding earlier that year and toasted the legislation that had finally allowed them to marry after a decade together, then made a joke about who was going to carry whom over the threshold. At least, he'd thought it was a joke, but Clare had been inspired.

They'd left their reception for a simple honeymoon in the Blue Mountains – the IVF costs again – but when they returned a week later, Clare had surprised Sophie by scooping her up before she got her keys in the door. Clare was the heavier of the two; it made sense for her to do the lifting, but she wanted to mark the occasion too. Sophie had giggled and kicked, protesting that the tradition was only for true newlyweds, not middle-aged lezzies like them, but Clare had kissed her until she stopped talking, until they were safely inside, the world shut out behind them.

Afterwards, they lay in bed together as the setting sun came through the leadlight and stained the walls pink, turning Sophie's bare skin into one rosy blush, and Clare had thought, with surprise, how she'd never been happier. It was perfect. They were perfect. Except for just one thing.

She gathers herself and gets out of the car. Maybe Sophie wasn't feeling well, has left work early because of that. She'd had a lot of headaches recently. Maybe she has taken herself to bed, or is having a bath . . . But no. As Clare makes her way down the hallway, she hears Sophie call out from the dining area at the rear of the house.

'Clare? Can you come in here?'

'I'll get changed first,' Clare calls back, butterflies sprouting in her stomach. This is weird. Home early, no *hey baby*, just a summons to the dining room.

'No, don't,' Sophie says. 'I need to talk to you.'

Clare puts her bag down, swallows and enters the room. Sophie is seated at the table, a wedding gift from her parents they rarely use, preferring to eat together on the couch in front of the TV or at the kitchen bench. There is half a glass of wine in front of her.

'Bit early for that, isn't it?' Clare jokes, trying to make light of the situation. Suddenly it dawns on her. 'Oh God – did you lose your job?'

'What?' Sophie's brow creases. 'Oh. No, no, I didn't. I had some overtime owing, so I took a half day to come home and talk with you. This'—she nods towards the wine—'is so I don't lose my nerve.'

Clare sits down opposite her. It doesn't feel like home, it feels like a job interview. 'What do you want to talk about?'

Sophie looks away, out the window, into their tiny courtyard. When her eyes return to Clare's they are filled with tears. 'I'm sorry,' she says. 'I can't do it anymore. The injections, the stress, your moods . . . all that hope every time, then all the disappointment.'

'I got my period today. We can do a frozen embryo transfer this cycle, maybe in a couple of weeks. We've got one left, remember? It will be much easier.' Clare knows this is the wrong thing to say even as the words leave her mouth, but she is unable to stop herself. 'Maybe this is the one. I have a good feeling about it. Some of the research I read said there's a better chance than with a fresh cycle, because the uterine environment is more natural and . . .'

'No,' Sophie says, bowing her head. Her hands are clasped in front of her on the dining table. She looks as if she is praying. 'No more.'

'No more?' Clare echoes.

'I can't do it,' Sophie repeats, face still averted. 'I'm not going to sign the papers. Don't ask me to.'

'We could have a break, maybe leave it until early next year?' Clare suggests. Her lungs feel as if they have shrunk, as if her childhood asthma has suddenly returned; she can't get enough air in. 'Maybe you'll feel differently then. You just need a breather. We both do, probably.'

'No!' Sophie cries, and this time her voice is angry rather than sad. 'You don't get it, do you? I can't do *any* of it. Not just the IVF – you, this, us, the whole shebang. I'm leaving.'

'Leaving?' Clare wheezes. Sweat slickens beneath her arms, between her buttocks.

'It's not working. All you ever think about is babies, babies, babies. Taking your temperature and doing your bloods and when we can try again, and if that cramp means you're ovulating or implanting or miscarrying. It might just be fucking gas – have you ever thought of that?'

Sophie's eyes, finally looking at her, are cruel, scornful. Clare shrinks from their fury.

'Six years I've sat through it, because I thought you'd let go eventually. Four miscarriages, for God's sake! When will you give up? What's it going to take?' Sophie slowly shakes her head, answers her own question. 'You're not going to give up, I've realised that. You'll keep going until there's nothing left, no love, no money, until you've destroyed yourself with hormones and procedures and yearning. You've already destroyed us . . . so if you won't give up, I will.'

'You're leaving?' Clare asks again. She can't keep up. Nothing is sinking in. Sophie reaches across the table and takes her hand. Her anger is suddenly gone, a balloon that has just been popped.

'I have to,' she says gently. 'This relationship isn't about us anymore, hasn't been for ages. I can't keep going along with this, this . . . obsession of yours. I never even wanted children. I was only in it because it meant so much to you, because you insisted. You know that.' Tears are caught in her ginger eyelashes and she reaches up to brush them away. 'I tried. Don't hate me.'

'I love you!' Clare wails, tears streaming down her own face now. 'I'll stop. I'll give it up. I'm kidding myself anyway. You're right. Four miscarriages. It's clear my body can't do it. Please don't go.'

Sophie shakes her head. 'You say that, but I know you. Another month or two and you'll be itching to get back to it, just one more try, or looking up international adoption sites on your laptop and forgetting to clear your search history.' She sighs. 'It used to kill me that I wasn't enough for you, that you couldn't just be happy with us, but I finally understand it isn't personal. You won't be happy with anyone. You won't be happy until you have a baby, and I don't know if you ever will, and I can't bear to hang around watching that, hoping you'll notice me again. That's why I have to go.' Sophie withdraws her hand and takes a shuddery breath. 'I'll move out. I know you weren't expecting this.' Her laugh is a bark. 'That says it all, doesn't it? I've been planning to go for weeks, and you had no idea. Never even noticed.' She collects herself. 'The rent's paid until the end of the year. It's up to you after that.'

'Where will you live?' Clare asks, weeping.

'It doesn't matter,' Sophie says, rising from the table.

Clare howls then, throws back her head in grief. Sophie turns at the sound as she is walking from the room, retraces her steps and stands behind Clare, who prays that she's changed her mind. But she hasn't. Sophie touches her lightly on the shoulder then leaves again. Five minutes later Clare hears her car reversing out of the garage, idling briefly, then driving away.

She doesn't know what to do next, so she does what she had planned: gets changed, has a quick shower and cooks dinner. Every few minutes she calls Sophie's mobile, but Sophie doesn't pick up. Clare's meal is eaten mechanically, without taste or pleasure, standing at the kitchen bench, and afterwards she washes up, including Sophie's wine glass, retrieved from the dining room. There are leftovers, of course, and Clare perfunctorily scrapes them into a plastic container for work the next day. *Work.* The thought makes her crumble. How can she go to work? She needs to be here, at home, in case Sophie returns. *I will beg*, Clare thinks; *I will fall on my knees and plead with her, bargain, cajole, implore.* Sophie is a kind woman. It was one of the things that first attracted Clare to her, that and the figure she cut on the pool deck: the swoop of her back, her sinewed, capable arms. Sophie is kind, and will not let her suffer. Surely she is just trying to teach Clare a lesson, snap her out of her baby-lust? Sophie will come back . . . but the hours tick past and Sophie stays gone.

Eventually Clare goes to bed. What else can she do? She lies there, unable to sleep, listening for the front door, for Sophie's keys in the lock. The pillow smells of her, as do the sheets, and Clare gulps them in, inhaling the comforting essence of her wife until she abruptly panics that she might somehow use it all up, and stops. She closes her eyes and concentrates on breathing in through her nose, out through her mouth, just as she has instructed patients overcome with anxiety. Sophie is only trying to make a point, to give her a scare. Sophie will be back. Sophie will be back. Sophie will be back.

The mantra almost lulls Clare to sleep, but then her eyes fly open. What if she isn't? What if she's gone for good?

The wardrobe, Clare thinks. She needs to check the wardrobe, the drawers. If nothing much is gone, if Sophie's suits and jeans remain, this is simply a test, an ultimatum. And that would be fair, wouldn't it? Clare had given her one, after all. She rises from the bed and flings it open, hands shaking on the knobs. Sophie's side is empty, coat hangers jangling, bare and spare as a rib cage. Clare flies to the tallboy in the corner of their room, yanks at a drawer, but that is barren too. All of Sophie's underwear is gone, her gym gear, her jumpers, even her winter scarves. It is only mid-spring. If she has taken her scarves, she is never coming back.

Somehow Clare sleeps, but only fitfully. She dreams of John Thomas and wakes up thinking, *Well, at least I can get him back now*. That would be a comfort, to have the little dog around again, a piece of Daniel in her home. It dawns on her, though, that it probably won't remain her home, and who knew if her next landlord would allow pets? Besides, he is Allison's dog now, he belongs to Eliot and Martin. It would be cruel to take him from them.

She dozes again until startled from sleep. Her heart is hammering against her skin as if trying to escape her body. She sits up in bed, clutching at her chest. It hurts. Oh fuck, it hurts. Is she having an MI, or is her heart simply broken? Is this what people meant by the phrase? Sophie has been her only serious relationship. She has no experience in being left. She rocks back and forth, willing the pain to subside. No wonder Daniel always kept things casual with his partners. Who could survive this more than once?

She forces herself to get up and stumbles to the kitchen, not allowing herself to understand why until she is there. It is pitch black, the middle of the night, but she leaves the lights turned off, does everything by touch. Second drawer down at the left of the stove. The utensils. The knives. Clare feels around until she has the one she wants, lodged right up the back. A carving knife, brought out only at Christmas or on special occasions. Will it be sharp enough? She tests it against her forefinger. The skin eases apart, surrenders, gifts her blood. Clare sinks to the floor, her back up against the oven. She has not long turned forty. She has no wife, no home, no child. The carving knife will ease all that, negate it. She slides it against her left wrist, feeling the dull throb of the vein beneath; it increases as she bears down. Up her arm, not across it, she suddenly recalls. Her stints in the ER have taught her that at least.

She shifts the blade, holds her breath, applies pressure . . . but nothing. The steel nestles into her arm, cushioned by flesh, and she can't bring herself to push any harder. *I'm too fat,* she thinks. *I'm a failure. I can't even get this right.* The knife falls to the floor and she is crying again, debased, humiliated, though a tiny part of her is glad that she hasn't succeeded. *Drugs,* she thinks. That will do it. Much easier. She can't fuck that up. She'll steal some from work during her next shift. The thought calms her, finally slows her thundering heart, and while she isn't able to sleep again she finds she can lie there, unmoving, on the kitchen floor, watching while the ceiling shifts from black to grey to light.

Emma

'Would you like a drink while you're waiting?'

'Yes, thank you,' Emma says, smiling at the waitress. A drink would be good, would give her something to do with her hands and settle her nerves. 'A glass of the house white, thanks. Chardonnay, if you have it.'

The young woman nods and turns to go, and Emma suddenly panics. Is wine okay? Does it send the wrong message? It's part of the church, she tells herself. It's in the parables and the wedding at Cana; it's one of the sacraments. But wine, drunk alone, in a restaurant while waiting for someone she's never met before, somebody she has connected with through a Christian dating site . . . maybe that looks a bit sad, or a bit worldly.

'Actually, I've changed my mind, sorry,' she calls after waitress. 'Just a mineral water instead, please. Thank you.' Better to be safe. Maybe this Brad person would be a teetotaller. Or maybe he'd like a wine too, and then they could choose a bottle to share together. Relieved, she settles back in her seat, trying not to watch the door. Why is she so nervous? She's dated before. She's thirty-three, of course she has. She's done online dating too, though only eHarmony and RSVP, never anything as specific as Christian Connection, but that should make things better, not worse. Her faith was important to her, the cornerstone of her life. *Do not be yoked together with unbelievers . . .* She knows this now, to her cost, and wishes she had never forgotten it. Not only was it decreed in the scriptures, but it made perfect sense. How could she ever love anyone who didn't also love God? Marriage, any partnership, had to be based on shared values, and that was her most important value of all.

The mineral water arrives and she sips it slowly, discreetly checking her watch. Brad is late. Only five minutes so far, but she wishes he'd hurry up. She hates sitting here alone, so conspicuous. Solitude defines her, it so often seems. She fights to keep it at bay, but it creeps back again and again, like a virus she just can't shake. In her family, at work . . . but this is crazy, Emma thinks, pulling herself up. Not just crazy; wrong. She has God in her heart and in her life, the source of all love. How could she ever be lonely? She needs to work on that – more prayer, less self-pity. It was just that you couldn't touch God, couldn't feel His arms around you, and, oh, there were days when she longed for arms around her.

She'd confided in Daniel once, she remembers with a smile. That Christmas, her first after leaving the orchestra, when she'd fled back home, her life in tatters, one enormous throb of hurt. He'd picked her up at the airport and noticed straight away, enfolding her in a hug. 'You okay, Emmie?' he'd asked, and she'd shook her head no, fighting back tears, face mashed against his chest. 'I'm so alone,' she'd choked out in the car, and he was kind and sympathetic, and then later that night had sat her down and loaded Tinder onto her phone.

Such a Daniel move, she thinks fondly, without judgement. Just hook up with someone and it will all be better. She didn't want to tell him – couldn't bear to tell him – that she was still a virgin, had no interest in casual sex. Tinder was never going to be right for her anyway, all that swiping based purely on looks, when what she was interested in was a man's heart. Still, her curiosity had been piqued, and she'd eventually summoned the courage to accept a few dates on some of the more conventional sites. But those men hadn't been right either. They didn't have Jesus in their life; they got twitchy and started looking towards the door as soon as she told them about Crossfire . . .

So Christian Connection it was. The images on the home page had soothed her immediately. No hairy-chested men posing with their shirts off or draped across a car, like Tinder; just soft-focus pictures of wholesome, smiling couples, many in wedding apparel. The testimonials, though, had sealed the deal. Anita and Michael: *God brought us together*; Samantha and Kevin: *It was His divine will*. Jeremiah 29, verse 11, Emma thinks to herself, not for the first time. '*I know the plans I have for you,*' declares the Lord, '*plans to give you hope and a future.*' If God had a plan for Samantha and Kevin, surely He could spare one for her too.

'Emma?' The man standing at her table is older than he appeared in his profile photo, and distinctly balding.

Bland, Emma thinks instantaneously, disappointed in both her date and herself. Hearts – she was supposed to be interested in hearts, not looks.

He holds out his hand and she rises from her seat to take it, as seems only polite. 'Oh, you're tiny,' he remarks. The comment burns. Emma has heard it before, many, many times. No one would dare comment if she was fat, though, or ugly, so why was her stature up for grabs?

'Yes,' she says simply in reply. She is. She has to stand on a box when she conducts the choir at Crossfire; she often buys her clothes from the children's section at Kmart. It is easier that way, not having to get them taken up or in, and today's tweens at least have far wider fashion choices than when she was growing up. 'You must be Brad?'

'I am,' he says, sitting down. 'Sorry I'm a bit late. Got caught up at work.'

'You're a teacher, right?' Emma asks. That had appealed to her when she read it in his bio. It was one of the reasons she had responded to his 'wave'. Teachers were kind and patient, teachers served. Leadership was overrated in Emma's opinion. Too many people wanted to rule, to oversee; not enough were prepared to actually roll up their sleeves and do the work. She'd pictured him gently guiding a class of innocent five-year-olds through their first reader.

'Yeah,' he said. 'The Year Tens were feral today. Had to keep half of them back for detention.'

Emma blinks, takes a swallow of her mineral water and wishes it was wine. Brad signals for the waiter, then asks in turn what she does. *It's in my profile*, she wants to reply. *Surely you read it?* Though maybe he was meeting up with lots of women and had trouble keeping them straight. 'I'm the music director at Crossfire,' she says instead, with some pride.

'Crossfire?' He wrinkles his brow. 'I think I've heard of it. That's one of those megachurches, right? Like Hillsong?'

'Well, sort of . . .' Emma begins, but Brad speaks over the top of her.

'I went to Hillsong once, just to see what all the fuss was about. They had car parking attendants! Unbelievable. Most churches don't have enough members to arrange ushers, yet they had a whole platoon of guys in high-vis waving their arms around.'

Crossfire did too, Emma wants to tell him, but thinks better of it. When there were fifteen hundred people all turning up for a service at once it was only logical, surely – it kept things running smoothly. And it wasn't as if the attendants were paid. They all volunteered their time, then joined the worship as soon as they were done. 'I guess God calls everyone to different ministries,' she replies instead. 'Shall we order?'

Brad selects a steak and a beer and turns back to her. 'Music director, huh? So you actually work for the church. That's pretty impressive. And Godly.'

Emma feels the first faint stirrings of warmth towards him. Maybe this will be okay after all. 'Yeah. It's a pretty big job. I've been there four years now, though I was only promoted to director last year.'

'Do you play an instrument?'

'The cello,' she says. 'I used to be in the MOO. The Melbourne Opera Orchestra,' she amends as he frowns again. 'Not much call for it at Crossfire though. It's all synths and electric guitar.'

'Yeah, I can't stand that stuff. It's just pandering to the masses, trying to be cool.'

Emma sits back as if he's slapped her. 'Well, I guess, but if it brings people to the Lord . . .'

Brad ignores her. 'Speaking of masses, what are you doing on Christian Connection? There must be heaps of blokes somewhere as big as Crossfire. You could have your pick.'

She flushes. Was that a compliment? She hopes so. She's due one after his previous comment. 'I suppose. I've thought about it, but it's not a good idea. I don't want anything to distract me from my ministry.' Or, she thinks, a messy break-up that might cost her her job. Again.

'No fishing off the company pier, eh?' Brad asks. His steak is set down before him and he attacks it with gusto, then abruptly stops mid-chew. 'Sorry, would you like to say grace?'

Throughout the main course they talk about him: his childhood, the church he attends, his favourite NRL team. Emma knows nothing about rugby but listens politely, toying with her carbonara.

'South Sydney,' he tells her. 'Best team in the league. Oldest, proudest, loudest.'

'Is that the Rabbitohs?' she asks, not because she cares, but simply to have something to say. 'My brother followed them.'

'Smart fella.' He lifts his second beer to his mouth, slurping appreciatively. 'But what do you mean *followed*? He didn't give them up, did he? I hope he hasn't gone across to the Roosters.'

'Oh no,' Emma says, staring at her plate. She hates this moment, cannot bear the way that everything shifts whenever she has to explain about Daniel. 'He died. Almost three years ago now. He was thirty-five.'

Brad lowers his cutlery. 'I'm so sorry,' he says, sounding sincere. 'How awful for you. Cancer?'

She shakes her head. 'He was shot. In . . . in the city. The papers said it was ISIS, a terrorist attack, but it wasn't really. Just some guy with a gun and a mental illness.'

Brad is visibly appalled, mouth hanging open, and she shrugs in an attempt to make less of it, as if Daniel's murder is something she has to smooth over.

'The Lindt Café siege?' he asks.

'No.' Emma still can't look up. 'That was a year earlier. People always get them mixed up. The inquest found that this one was probably some sort of copycat event, but it was over much more quickly, so there wasn't the protracted coverage. Three people were killed.'

'I think I remember now,' Brad says, as if that's the important thing. 'Near the Rocks?' He picks up his knife and fork again. 'Your poor parents. How awful, to lose a child like that.'

'Thankfully they never knew.' Emma pushes her pasta away. She won't be finishing it now. 'They both died years ago, when I was still at school.'

'Wow.' Brad regards her with genuine sympathy but also intrigue, as if she is some sort of freak. 'Your mother, your father *and* your brother? That's just nuts. I hope they knew the Lord.'

Emma does not respond; she cannot risk watching him condemn half her family to eternal damnation if she reveals that they most definitely did not. 'Yeah,' she says instead, as if describing a bout of stomach flu. 'It's been pretty rough. Crossfire were fabulous though. We held Daniel's service there.'

It wasn't the most appropriate choice, but they'd needed a big venue – Daniel had lots of friends – and none of her sisters had come up with any other ideas. He would have laughed at the cheek of it, she'd thought at the time, being laid to rest by the sort of fundamentalist types who would have recoiled in horror if he'd actually turned up at a service. But he probably would have liked it too. Daniel had always thumbed his nose at convention.

'And have you got some other siblings?' Brad asks.

'Three sisters,' Emma replies, relaxing. They are much easier to talk about.

'That's a lot. So five of you all up? Are you sure you're not Catholic?' He smiles, trying to lighten the mood, and she is grateful.

'Well, my father was Irish, so close. And there were actually supposed to be six of us. Mum and Dad wanted a large family, but they had a plan: three lots of two, with gaps between them. So my oldest sisters are not much more than a year apart, then they had a five-year break before having another two – my third sister and my brother, Daniel, the one who died. The idea was to spread the load, and that each pair would be playmates for each other.'

'So where do you fit in?'

'Number five,' Emma says, holding up her hand, fingers outstretched. 'Born five years after Daniel. They were very methodical, my parents. Even named us in alphabetical order – A, B, C, D, et cetera – to make labelling everything easier. But something went wrong during my delivery. Mum had a haemorrhage and had to have a hysterectomy, so I never got my playmate.'

She has been the odd one out right from the start, she thinks. It was nobody's fault – she had been planned, wanted, loved – but she didn't quite fit in. She made the whole family lopsided, somehow.

'Bummer,' Brad says. 'I bet you got spoiled though.'

Did she? Emma wondered. Maybe. She has dim memories of Allison and Bridie dressing her up, painting lipstick on her tiny mouth, carrying her around like a doll. But she also remembers being shut out, left behind, doors closing on her as her older siblings retreated to their rooms to study or talk on the phone, or left to go to school.

When she doesn't answer, he pushes on. 'Tell me about them, your sisters. Are you close to them?'

She loves them, Emma thinks, but they're not close. They remember her birthday, they phone and check in occasionally, but they barely know anything about her day-to-day life – who her friends are, what she does at work, the TV shows she watches, or even if she watches TV at all. The age gap was part of it – Allison was thirteen years older than her, Clare seven – but it was her own fault too, those bad years when she'd pulled away from everyone. Plus they were all partnered, settled, Allison with Jason, Bridie with Tom, Clare with Sophie. They had other priorities. Higher priorities.

'Allison's the oldest. She's an obstetrician. Crazy smart, good in a crisis, a bit scary. I wouldn't want to be one of her students. Then Bridie. She's gorgeous, really tall and blonde – we're all blonde, except Clare.' And Daniel, she thinks. Daniel had amazing hair, dark and glossy, falling in a perfect flop over his forehead so that he was always raking it back with his fingers. But there was no point talking about Daniel.

'Clare's a nurse. She's solid, dependable. Down to earth. Doesn't really care about what she looks like, unlike Bridie.'

Brad smiles. 'Kids? Do you have any nephews and nieces?'

Emma finds herself warming to him after all; she likes that he is taking an interest. Maybe she should order dessert. 'Allison has twin boys, Marty and Eliot, seven years old. They're gorgeous. Bridie doesn't want children, I don't think. Clare does though. I'm sure she and her wife would love to have some.'

Brad stiffens. 'Her *wife*?' He spits out the word as if it is something distasteful.

Emma lifts her chin. 'Yes. They were married earlier this year, but they've been together for ages. They were just waiting for the legislation to be passed.'

'So she's a homosexual?'

What a stupid word. Clare was just Clare. 'I suppose.'

'But you know that's an abomination in the eyes of the Lord?'

Emma sighs. She hasn't told anyone at Crossfire about her sister's wedding, didn't pass the photos around the office. She knows it is complicated at the church. Clare loves a woman, but so what? Jesus still loves Clare, she is sure of it. And what could Emma do about it anyway?

'It's none of my business,' she replies. 'I leave it up to God. He can work it out.' And God is love, she nearly adds. Love, and love entirely. The whole of Jesus' ministry was built upon it, loving God, loving your neighbour as yourself. It was what had led her to Him, truth be told, unconditional love at a time when she was all alone in the world. But would Brad understand that, or was he the sort of believer who favours rules over love?

The answer is clear. He is signalling for the bill.

They leave the restaurant ten awkward minutes later. Emma had offered to pay her share of the cost, and he hadn't refused.

Brad holds out his hand, as he did not much more than an hour ago. 'Nice to meet you, Emma.' He clears his throat. 'I'm going to pray for God's guidance as to whether we should see each other again. Maybe you'd like to do the same.'

She nods her head demurely, the good Christian woman assenting to the man, but she has no intention of doing so. She already knows what God will say, and she's okay with that.

Allison

1998

When Allison was twenty-six, her mother fell over. It shouldn't have been a big deal, but her mother was only forty-seven and this was the third time. Allison had missed the first two, had only found out about them when she asked about the bruising, but there was no missing this: one moment her mother was carrying in groceries from the weekly shop, the next she was sprawled on the hard grey slate of the driveway, mouth twisted in surprise, wrist bent back beneath her.

'I just lost my footing,' Barbie protested as Allison assessed the damage and called for her father, for Clare, for Daniel to help get her up and back into the car so Allison could drive her to hospital. 'I just lost my footing,' she told the triage nurse, and the attending, and the X-ray technician, and anyone who would listen, and they all nodded and her mother probably even believed it, but Allison kept an eye on her after that. How could she not? She was the eldest child and a freshly minted doctor. Both made her honour-bound to do the watching.

Two months went by, three, and nothing. Allison began to relax, and then one night her mother was passing Emma the gravy boat at dinner when it slipped out of her hand. Emma was the first to react, quickly looking around the table and calling out, *It wasn't me I didn't even touch it,* the only child in a family of adults and accustomed to feeling inadequate. Clare had shushed her and gone to get a cloth; Daniel, ever-practical, had used his fork to scoop the brown sauce from the tablecloth and onto his chicken before she returned. Allison ignored the mess and asked her mother to hold her hands out, to grasp hers, and to squeeze. There was distinctly less pressure from the right one.

'I think you should see someone,' she told her later when they were alone, stacking the dishwasher. 'Get that looked into. It's not right.'

'Oh, it's nothing,' her mother said, wiping her hands on a tea-towel. 'That was the wrist I broke. It probably got weak, all that time in the cast. And I've always been a bit clumsy.'

But her mother *hadn't* been clumsy. She had been an air hostess juggling laden trays in a tiny galley back in the days before they became flight attendants, and she'd brought up five children without ever dropping one of them.

'The cast was only on a few weeks,' Allison said, and contacted one of her past professors to get a referral.

'You're overreacting.' Her mother sighed as Allison wrote the date of the appointment on the family calendar. 'Tell her, Fionn.'

'Yes, tell me,' her father said, turning towards her, blue eyes crinkling at the corners. They all had those eyes, or some variation of them, Irish eyes that he was as proud of as his surname: navy in Bridie and Daniel, paler for Allison and Emma, a startling cornflower in Clare's otherwise unremarkable face. 'Are you overreacting? Is this a little knowledge being a dangerous thing?' He gestured floridly towards her. 'Physician, heal thyself!'

Allison's smile was thin-lipped. Trust her father to turn this into a production. 'There've just been a lot of . . . incidents. Mum's too young for all that. It doesn't hurt to get an opinion. A baseline. Hopefully I'm wrong. But Clare agrees with me.'

'Of course she does,' her mother scoffed. 'She's on an oncology rotation. She probably thinks we all have leukaemia or something.'

'She wanted to practise listening to my heart the other day,' Fionn mused. 'Told me she thought it sounded enlarged, but I asked her how it could be otherwise with such a beautiful wife and abundance of children?' He beamed at Allison, who didn't know whether to believe him or not. Clare was twenty and only halfway through her nursing degree. Surely she wasn't up to diagnosing cardiomegaly with just a stethoscope? Her father, she decided, was exaggerating, as usual.

'What does Bridie think?' her mother asked, but Allison hadn't consulted her next sister down. Bridie had moved out of the family home over a year ago, the first of them to do so, and was always on location somewhere, or so it seemed.

'This isn't a vote,' Allison replied. 'You're going. Just humour me.'

The specialist didn't make a diagnosis.

'Mostly normal, Mrs O'Shea,' he told her.

'Barbie,' her mother said, and turned to Allison. 'See? I told you. Now let's go have lunch. Your treat.'

Allison ignored her. 'Mostly?' she asked.

The specialist shrugged, looking back at his notes. 'A few irregularities. But everybody's different, and the CT looks good. I can send her for a lumbar puncture though, if you feel that's best, Dr O'Shea?'

Allison blushed. He was making fun of her, probably thinking, like her father, that her brand new prefix had gone to her head. Stuff him. For all his certificates, all the letters after his name, she knew her mother, knew her better than almost anyone in the world, and she knew that something wasn't right.

'That won't be necessary,' she replied, standing up, 'But I think that if things are only *mostly* normal, a review in one year is indicated, yes?' She hooked her arm through her mother's and steered her through the door before he had a chance to reply.

The slurring started not long afterwards, *champagne* emerging as *shampan*, *cheese* defeating her mother entirely. Barbie started dropping her scissors while attending to clients in the small salon at the back of the house that Fionn had had built for her, then gave up hairdressing altogether after twenty years of running the business.

'I'm just not up to it anymore, love,' she told Allison. 'It's a young woman's game, being on your feet all day.' *Hyoung womansh game.* But her mother *was* still young, was barely forty-eight, and while only eight months had elapsed, Allison knew it was time to take her back to the specialist. This time he didn't brush her off.

That night Allison called a family meeting. Thankfully Bridie was in town for once and came over as soon as she got off set, just as Emma was clearing away the plates from dinner.

'You don't have to ring the bell,' Allison said, opening the door to her. 'It's still your home.'

Bridie shrugged and tossed her long hair over one shoulder. 'You sounded serious on the answering machine. I didn't just want to . . . barge in on something, when I haven't been here in weeks.'

'Months,' Allison said, ushering her down the hallway. 'Three of them. What's in your bag?'

'Wine,' Bridie said, rummaging through her oversized tote to produce two bottles. 'Left over from the shoot. Nobody's going to miss it.'

'You brought wine?' Allison was incredulous. 'It's not a party. It's about Mum.'

'I know,' Bridie said, placing the bottles on the sideboard as she came into the back lounge, eyes darting around the room. She was looking, Allison knew, for Daniel, and he, hearing her voice, thundered down the stairs. 'There's another one in there,' she said, handing her bag to Allison just as Daniel caught her in a bear hug. 'I don't know what this is about, but I thought we might need them.'

Motor Neuron Disease, Allison told her family. She was standing in front of the fireplace, though it hadn't been lit, feeling, ridiculously, like a lecturer gazing out to see if her students were paying attention. Daniel and Bridie were sitting side by side on one couch, Clare still at the table, fiddling with the saltshaker, Emma curled on her father's lap. She was fourteen, far too old to be on anyone's lap, but so slight that she seemed about nine and often behaved accordingly. Their mother hovered in the doorway to the kitchen behind them all, out of their line of sight. 'You tell them,' she'd asked Allison as they sat, stunned, in the car after leaving the specialist. 'You understand it all much better than I do. You can answer their questions. I'm just a hairdresser.'

'Oh, Mum,' Allison had said, taking her hand. She wanted to cry, but what message would that send? 'You're not just anything. You're amazing.' When her mother hadn't replied Allison swallowed, then asked, 'So what do you understand?'

'That I'm going to get worse.' *Worsh*. 'That I won't be able to walk. Or talk, or one day breathe. And after that I'll die.'

'We're all going to die,' Allison had said stupidly. 'And some people with MND live for years and years and years. There's a really good chance you could be one of them. I'll make sure of it.' She'd squeezed her mother's hand, but there was no responding pressure.

Afterwards, what she most remembered of the evening was her father weeping. Fionn was prone to big emotions – joy, surprise, anger – and they had all seen him crying at some time or another, though usually over airline commercials or as he sat with his eyes closed in his favourite chair near the stereo listening to *Madame Butterfly* or *La Traviata* or even *South Pacific*. This was different though. Those tears had been an indulgence, an enjoyment, but as Allison broke the news, talked the rest of the O'Sheas through what Motor Neuron Disease was and did and meant, his face collapsed, his shoulders fell and he wept so furiously Emma's hair was wet with it.

Allison tried to embrace him, but it was only Barbie that he wanted, almost tipping Emma to the floor as he reached for her when she moved across to comfort him. They remained like that for ten, fifteen minutes while Bridie and Daniel peppered Allison with questions, and Clare extracted Emma, taking her to the kitchen for some ice cream, Barbie's bird-like arms wrapped around the heaving bulk of her husband, her unsteady voice soothing and shushing him as if he were the one condemned, not her.

'Will she have to go into a home?' Daniel asked. The colour had washed from his skin; he blinked repeatedly. Daniel was almost twenty, but Allison could see again the boy that he'd been not that long ago.

'Hopefully not,' she said, 'or not for a while, anyway. It's hard to predict the course of these things, but we'll try to keep her at home. That would be much better if we can manage it.'

'I'll nurse her,' Clare said, returning to the lounge. 'I can drop out of uni. Or defer. I know what to do. Some of it, anyway.'

Allison shook her head. 'No. No dropping out. I've thought about it, and it should be me.'

'You?' Clare asked. 'But you're starting your specialist training in, what – four months? You worked so hard for that place. You can't do both.'

'I know. I'll defer it if I have to. Neurology can wait. Mum's more important.' Allison took a deep breath. She'd rehearsed this bit. 'I'll just keep working at the hospital after I finish my residency, or do some GP locums, or both. That way I can choose my shifts, work around what Mum needs. But I think she needs one of us.' She glanced over at their parents where her mother cradled her father, face buried in his hair, his own face in his hands. They weren't listening to her. 'Look, Dad won't be any good. We all know that. The first time she wets herself he'll call triple zero.'

'She'll wet herself?' Bridie said, her mouth a moue of repugnance.

'Yep. And soil. Eventually she's going to lose all muscular control. She'll have to be fed, showered, dressed, toileted – and you'll be on set, Emma's too young, Dad's too hopeless, Clare and Daniel are both in the middle of their degrees . . . It has to be me.' No one argued with her, for which she was both grateful and incensed. But that was what she had intended, wasn't it? 'Neurology can wait,' she repeated, convincing them, convincing herself. 'Or I'll start it, but put it on hold if she deteriorates. Who knows how it's going to go?'

'Well, if you insist . . .' Bridie murmured.

Allison's hands curled in anger. It was all right for Bridie. She'd just go back to her life, back to her house and her job and her boyfriend as if nothing had happened, nothing would happen. A flash of hatred shot through her, as unexpected as it was violent. Selfish, that's what she was. Bridie always put Bridie first. Allison opened her mouth to rail at her sister, then closed it again. She *was* insisting, wasn't she? This was her decision, her plan. No one had forced her. This was why, when it all came down to it, she was a doctor in the first place: not simply because she wanted to look after people, but because she felt obliged to do so. It was what she had been doing ever since she could remember, and even before. It was all she knew.

Bridie had been deposited into her life when Allison was only one and of course she had no memory of it, yet she had grown up knowing that she had to watch out for her younger sister, take care of her. She was the big girl, after all. Her mother had told her so, struggling to get Bridie's shoes on as she wriggled and kicked, imploring Allison to manage her own. It was her very first memory. She was the big girl who could wash her own hands, blow her own nose, who could keep an eye on the baby while her mother had a shower or talked on the phone. Then, during Allison's first year at school, Clare arrived, swiftly followed, or so it seemed, by Daniel. There were babies everywhere, a conveyor belt of infants, always someone needing to be picked up or distracted or entertained.

To be fair, her mother had never actually expected this of Allison, but she was so thankful, so full of praise whenever her eldest daughter helped out that Allison happily fell into the role. It felt good to please her mother. It felt good to be the big girl.

By the time Emma was born, Allison was an old hand. And just as well, because the delivery had been complicated and her mother had taken weeks to recover. Once she was out of hospital and back on her feet, Allison, at thirteen, was perfectly adept at changing Emma's nappy, making up her bottle, soothing her to sleep. It felt, in fact, to her, that it was she and her mother who had co-parented her youngest sibling that exhausting first year, while her father blew in and out from work and the other children played around their feet.

And she loved it, she loved almost every minute of it. Emma cooing and reaching her tiny arms out for Allison over anyone else, Emma favouring her with her first smile, her father calling her a natural, her mother's gratitude. When pressed to think about her future in her final year of high school, medicine had been the logical progression. Allison looked after people. It was what she did.

'Well, I'll still help,' Clare said. 'You can't do it all yourself.'

'Cheers to that,' Bridie said, opening a bottle of wine.

Barbie's condition was stable for the next few months and Allison wasn't needed as much as she had expected. She put off deferring her neurology traineeship, began to hope that maybe, just maybe, her mother would be one of the outliers who lingered for years with the disease, incapacitated, sure, but alive, still alive. Then, on Christmas Day, Barbie stood up from the table, thanked Clare for cooking the roast and promptly crumpled against the sideboard, her arms grabbing wildly but her face impassive. The gash on her forehead required seven stitches. She was tucked into bed by mid-afternoon and never really got up again.

Soon came the weight loss, the wasting, the dysphagia. Barbie could no longer manage a knife and fork, so moved to a spoon, grasping it clumsily in her fist like a toddler. Another six weeks and even that was impossible. Mealtimes became an hour-long struggle of bibs, of drool, Allison holding her breath with every mouthful she fed her mother in fear that she would choke. Barbie cried some-times, laughed at others, slumped in her seat. Fionn started skipping breakfast and leaving early for work. Allison knew it was due to a surfeit of love, not a lack, that he simply couldn't bear to see his wife of almost thirty years in such a condition, but still it irked her. For better or worse? He sang to Barbie, plumped the pillows behind her in bed, rubbed her always-cold hands, but left the feeding, the washing, the changing to Allison.

So did everyone else except Clare, who was quick to assist when-ever she was home. Bridie's visits, though, became more and more infrequent, Daniel was always out and Emma retreated to her room. She could hardly blame Emma, Allison thought – the girl was six-teen now, in her final years of high school. She should be with her friends or studying, not wiping shit from her mother's atrophying arse. But Bridie and Daniel made her blood boil. 'Just call them,' Clare snapped at Allison once when they were working together to manoeuvre Barbie into the bath. 'Tell them they have to step up. She's their mother too.' But Allison wouldn't. This was what she had insisted on, wasn't it? This was what she had asked for. And if she, a doctor, had days where she struggled to care for her mother, for her lovely, loving mother who had always cared so well for her, how on earth would Bridie and Daniel manage? She wouldn't do it to them. She wouldn't do it to Barbie.

Because she did struggle. The tears came more quickly now, two and a half years after that fall with the groceries. Allison welled up whenever her mother moaned in pain as her limbs twisted and con-torted, she cried throughout the shower she took last thing at night until she was so exhausted she could sleep.

When Barbie, her mind slipping, called Allison Aisling – *Shashlin* – she wept so loudly that Fionn rushed in to see what was the matter.

It was her birth name, the choice of her proud Irish father, but Allison, who never liked to stand out, had hated it almost from the moment she started school. No one could pronounce it. No one spelled it correctly. In a classroom full of Jennifers and Lisas and Michelles, Aisling was an anomaly, an abomination. By grade two she insisted that everyone call her Allison instead. Fionn had argued, pouted, but Barbie had been the first to comply. And not only that, but to go out and buy Allison a necklace with the name on it, a new doorplate for her room. She had always taken her eldest daughter seriously, never doubted her judgement, and in so doing had instilled in Allison a similar self-belief.

But now her mother didn't know her anymore. Now she was Aisling, a stranger, and her mother, not quite fifty, was drifting away from her, slithering through her fingers like sand.

It terrified her. Allison was a doctor, had seen death in all its forms, or so she thought, but this was something else. This was someone she cared about, loved deeply, and the shock of losing her, the sheer injustice of it, shook her deeply. Her mother was dying. There were only so many more breaths she would draw, only a finite number of times her eyes would turn to Allison as she came into the room. Allison, who had taken leave from her GP work, whose social life had already been significantly curtailed, stopped going out altogether. There were only weeks left now, and she would not miss a moment of them.

Once, in the middle of the night, washing her hands after changing and settling her mother, she caught sight of herself in the bathroom mirror and was surprised. Her cheeks were still smooth, her skin unlined. Allison leaned closer. How could that be, when she felt so old? Yet her eyes were bright blue, her ash blonde hair fell wispily around her face, her breasts beneath her nightgown were high and full. How long had it been since she'd noticed them, since someone else had noticed them? How long had it been since she'd had sex? She had a sudden hot memory of losing her virginity in her first year of university to a fellow medical student she'd met in her anatomy class. Allison hadn't expected much, had gone along with it more because she was nineteen and it felt like a milestone she should have ticked off by now rather than out of any unbridled lust, but oh, the sweet shock of pleasure when he'd unexpectedly knelt before her and kissed her stomach, her navel, his head dipping lower and lower and . . . Allison straightened up, cupped her breasts beneath her hands, felt something stir between her legs, and then her mother cried out, so she left the bathroom and turned off the light.

Part Two

Part Two

Clare

October 2018

Clare is the first to arrive. She is almost always the first to arrive – Allison is often dealing with some crisis or another, and Bridie has a notoriously relaxed relationship with time, at least when it comes to her family – but Clare has made a particular effort today. It is the anniversary of Daniel's death, three years since he was killed, and she is meeting her sisters and Joel for lunch to mark the occasion, as they do every year. To be late would be disrespectful to Daniel, so she ensures she is at the restaurant ten minutes early.

But she has another reason too. Her brow dampens, thinking about it, and she swipes her hand across her face before remembering that she is wearing make-up, which she has now somehow transferred to her skirt. Fuck it. She'll be seated by the time the others arrive; no one will notice. Hopefully she won't have sweated through the fabric under her arms by then.

'Good afternoon. Do you have a booking?' The young woman greeting her is so perfectly put together that Clare automatically runs her tongue over her teeth before returning her smile, wary of traces of lipstick. She isn't used to dressing up. She isn't used to places like this, fancy restaurants in the Rocks where the staff look like film stars and the carpet feels so expensive that she's fighting the urge to remove her shoes, just in case she marks it. Daniel had been coming here on the day he died. It had astonished her, the opulence, at that first anniversary gathering. Oh, she knew places like this existed, of course – the CBD was riddled with them – but for a work lunch? On a Wednesday?

Bridie had laughed when Clare mentioned it, didn't even look up from studying the menu. 'Tax deduction,' she'd declared, flicking over to the wine list. 'Daniel had been hoping to snag an investor. He needed to look the goods.' Clare had peered around open-mouthed. When she was at work she ate her lunch in the hospital cafeteria, or on a bench out the front of the path lab if the weather was nice. That her brother, her younger brother, had spent even some of his lunch hours in a setting like this had made his death seem even crueller, somehow. Someone average, someone unremarkable, should have died instead. Someone like her.

'Yes, we do, thank you,' Clare tells the hostess. 'O'Shea, at one pm. There's five of us.'

The young woman checks her screen, nods, and motions for Clare to follow her.

'You're the first to arrive,' she says, seating Clare at a round table by the window. 'Is it a special occasion?'

'Oh, well, yes . . . No, not really,' Clare stutters. How to explain it? *My brother was killed on his way here three years ago today, so my family come here to remember him.*

The venue had been Bridie's idea initially, and was now a habit they had fallen into. Daniel had been cremated, his ashes scattered into Sydney Harbour from a ferry, the same one he'd caught almost daily to work or to party. The house they'd all grown up in was long sold; there was nowhere else to meet and mourn him. The restaurant was the most appropriate place anyway, Bridie had asserted. Daniel had loved going out, loved seeing and being seen, delighted in fine dining. They should have the meal that he'd been denied, raise their glasses to him in a place that he'd loved. No partners, no children, just the four of them, all that was left of their family of seven. Plus Joel, of course. You couldn't leave out Joel.

Allison looms into view, ploughing across the restaurant like an ocean liner, saving Clare from answering the question. She is on time, Clare notes, not up to her elbows in some patient's uterus for a change.

'You've done well,' Clare remarks as her oldest sister sinks into the seat beside her. 'No trouble getting away?'

Allison leans over and briefly pecks her on the cheek, smelling faintly of Miss Dior, the same perfume she has been wearing since she was sixteen. That probably made birthdays easier for Jason.

'Oh, I took the day off,' Allison says. 'Didn't want to risk getting caught in surgery, plus I had some errands to run.' She settles herself, stashing her handbag under the table, then attempts to fluff up her hair, which, despite her words, looks as if it has spent the day under a scrub cap. 'Very nice it's been, too. My husband better watch it. I might ask for his job. Send him back out to earn the money.'

'As if.' Clare smiles. Her sister was born to work, gets irritable on holidays.

'Would you ladies like to order a drink, or will you wait for the rest of your party?' A waitress has materialised, even younger and prettier than the woman who had led Clare to the table.

'We'll wait,' Clare says at the exact moment that Allison replies, 'Gin and tonic, please. Tanqueray, preferably. Oh, and could you get me a bowl of water?'

'I'm sorry?' the waitress asks.

'Just an ice-cream container, something like that, with water in it.' Allison turns to Clare. 'John Thomas is in the car. Don't ask. It was a last-minute decision. I'm parked in the shade, but, you know, in case he gets thirsty.'

'You brought the dog? Why on earth?'

'Shhh,' Allison cautions. Clare follows her gaze and sees Bridie approaching, Joel tagging behind her. Their second sister is wearing a skin-tight black leather dress and elegant stilettos, somehow managing to look both rock chick and haute couture at the same time. Of all of them, she is the only one the restaurant would want to employ. Other patrons look up as she sails towards their table.

'Clare!' Joel exclaims happily. He towers over her, a genial giant. She stands to embrace him and then, a little more stiffly, Bridie. By the time she sits down again Emma has arrived, slipping soundlessly into her seat without anyone noticing. In the hubbub of hellos and greetings Allison furtively intercepts the plastic bowl full of water and disappears briefly back out to the street. Bridie orders champagne in her absence.

'This always feels a bit weird,' Emma says as it is being poured. 'Like we're celebrating something, instead of, you know . . .'

'We are,' Bridie interjects. 'We're celebrating Daniel's life. Much better to do that than sit around wailing. Otherwise the fucker who killed him wins.' She raises her glass. 'To Daniel.'

'To Daniel,' Joel echoes, and the rest of them join in.

Clare gazes around the table as she lifts her glass to her lips. The scene reminds her of the portrait that her parents had had painted of their children, which had hung, gently fading, over the fireplace in the living room for the duration of her adolescence and many years beyond. Emma had still been little, she remembers. Littler, anyway. She has never been big. Was she three? Four? That would have made

Allison seventeen, herself eleven, Bridie and Daniel filling the spaces on either side.

The artist had initially arranged them in two rows, like a tiny choir – the O'Shea family singers – then changed his mind. 'You stand in the middle,' he'd directed Daniel, then positioned the girls around him, petals flanking his central corona. Clare had always thought it was a strange decision. Why put Daniel there, the number four child, at the heart of the painting? Why not Allison, the oldest, or Emma, the tiniest, or even her, the true middle of their line-up? She could only imagine it was because Daniel was a boy, the sole male in a thicket of girl children, which made the picture more striking, or more balanced. For years she'd vaguely resented it, Daniel right in the centre like that. As if he didn't get enough attention. Now though, as she sips her champagne, she offers a silent apology. Daniel had been short-changed, ripped off, snuffed out, as the tabloids had said, in the prime of his life. She was glad he'd had the spotlight while he'd lived.

'What's everybody having?' Allison asks, returned from her hydration mission.

'The kingfish is great,' Joel says. 'Healthy, too.' Is it Clare's imagination, or has he slimmed down somewhat since Daniel has been gone? Grief would do that, and Joel had definitely grieved. Not that they were together at the time of Daniel's death, of course, not for years and years, but they'd remained close. Very close. In some ways, Clare thinks, they'd never really stopped being partners. Lovers, she amends. Lovers, but without the sex. That was the correct word, because they'd loved each other, even if they no longer lived in the same house, even if they sometimes went months without meeting face to face. Not all of her sisters had understood that. Oh, the look on Allison's face when the will had been read!

'He left Tideways to Joel?' she'd hissed on the pavement outside the solicitor's office. '*Joel?* But that was, like, half a decade ago.'

Clare had understood it though, understood and applauded the decision. Daniel hadn't had a lot to leave. The business was successful but still growing, still needing profits ploughed back into it, and half-owned, anyway, by Morgan. Tideways, Daniel's bolt-hole on the Central Coast, was pretty much the only thing he possessed outright, that and a hell of a lot of suits. It wasn't a large property, just a three-bedroom cottage near the water, and while Allison seemed to think that Daniel should have willed it to his sisters, Clare didn't see how that would have worked. Try to share it? There were too many of them; things would have got messy. Sell it and divvy up the money? But then it would be gone, one of the few pieces of Daniel they had left. Big burly Joel had cried when he learned of his inheritance, broke down and sobbed. Daniel, Clare knew, was the one who had left the relationship, who had broken Joel's heart. Tideways, she guessed, was part peace offering, part memento. It was kind, and it was right, no matter what Allison said.

It is not until the main course is done that Clare works up the courage to clear her throat. She coughs once, then again more loudly, and when that doesn't work she resorts to tapping on a wine glass with her bread knife. Their faces turn towards her: her blue-eyed sisters, bearded Joel, surprised and interested by this interruption to their meal.

'There's something I want to say,' she begins, sweat beading again on her upper lip. Clare raises her serviette to her face and dabs at it, her foundation bleeding onto the starchy cloth.

'Speech!' Joel urges, smiling.

She smiles back weakly. 'Not a speech . . . I've made a decision. Something I want to do, something I hope you'll all join me in.'

Bridie's eyes flick to Allison. They are the matriarchs of the family now. *Do you know about this?* the glance asks. Allison frowns in reply, already disconcerted.

Clare takes a deep breath, teeters on the edge of the high board, aims herself at the water far below before she can lose her nerve. 'I've been in contact with the New South Wales Organ and Tissue Donation Service – the agency who managed the transplants after Daniel died. I want to find his recipients, make contact with them.'

Nobody says anything. Emma looks at Joel, who looks at his lap. Bridie and Allison are both scowling now, mouths twinned in disapproval.

'Why?' Allison finally asks. 'Why on earth? He's dead, for God's sake. What does it matter?'

Clare knew this was coming, has practised her response – in the shower, as she goes about her duties at work, on the upper deck of the train that had brought her to Circular Quay two hours ago. 'It's something I've been thinking about for a while,' she says. 'I nursed a guy who'd had a kidney transplant a while back. Maybe that's what got it started. It just made me wonder about Daniel's'—she hesitates; she is not expressing this as well as she had hoped—'organs and where they ended up.'

'*Ewww.*' Bridie's stately nose crinkles in distaste.

Clare tries again. 'For three years all we've thought about is his death, right? And that's been dreadful, awful. It still makes me want to cry. But what about all the lives that he's changed? That he's *saved*. The people who are still here because he died. There must be quite a few of them . . . his kidneys, his liver, his heart, his lungs, they were all used.' She appeals to Emma, to Joel, ignoring her older sisters. 'Doesn't it make you feel better, that they're out there? Wouldn't you like to know that they made a difference, to talk to the people who received them? I would. I feel like it would all make a bit more sense, I guess, that what happened wasn't a complete waste. Wasn't purely tragedy.'

Emma's eyes are glistening, her body bent towards Clare. Joel still has his head down, but Clare senses he is with her too, that her words have moved him. Allison, though, remains unconvinced.

'How will you do it?' she snaps. 'Is it even ethical? Did you think about that? You can't just go blundering into somebody's life, ask them, "Hey, how's that lung working out for you?" and then wander off again. What would it *mean*, even if you did? It's just flesh. It's not Daniel.' She swivels to Bridie, enlisting her. 'Don't you agree?'

Bridie shrugs. 'I'm not against the idea, but I don't really get it either. I miss Dan every single day. But meeting someone who has his – what, liver? – won't change that. And just say I don't like them? Do I ask for it back? Demand a rematch?'

'Now you're just being ridiculous,' Clare says, fighting to keep her voice steady. In the two weeks since Sophie had ended their marriage, this plan, this idea, has been the one thing keeping her tethered to the earth, preventing her from returning to the knife or the drugs or simply driving her car into a tree on the way home from work. There hadn't been a transplant patient. That was a ruse to try to sell this to her family. Instead, the scheme had arisen as a way of distracting herself, of playing a tug-of-war with death – her death.

Sophie was gone. Their four babies had died. She would never have her own child, not now, not alone and broke and especially not at her age. In the face of all that, the only thing that had thus far stopped Clare from killing herself was the nagging unease that to do so would be unfair to Daniel, who hadn't had a choice about his own death. She wasn't religious, not like Emma, but just say there was an afterlife and she had to explain herself to him? The idea was preposterous, but she somehow couldn't shake it. He would be so disappointed in her for throwing away something he would never willingly have surrendered.

The plan had come to her soon after that. Find Daniel's recipients, keep him alive, keep herself alive too. It has given Clare a focus, a goal, and a small, creeping hope – that maybe, just maybe, by assuaging this earlier loss she can lessen, even live with, the more recent one. Divert her grief, channel it, be able to look Daniel in the eye should they ever – she cringes at her own idiocy – meet once again at the Pearly Gates.

Now, though, she feels foolish, the proposal derailed, as she might have expected, by exhibit A and exhibit B. Her older sisters intimidate her, always have. They are so competent, so accomplished. If they think she is crazy, who is Clare to disagree? Their derision deflates her. She sinks in her seat and pretends to sip some water, when really she is swallowing back tears.

'Well, I think it's brilliant. Daniel would have adored it!' Joel claps his hands together like a child, eyes alight. 'Can't you just imagine? He'd be fascinated, and *soooo* self-important. He'd be walking around with his chest out, posting it all on Twitter, loving himself sick. Look what I did! Look who I helped!' Though bald, Joel flicks a pretend quiff out of his eyes and Clare can't help but smile. He has her brother down to a tee.

'I'm with Joel,' Emma says. 'It's a sort of reconciliation, really, isn't it? It might be good for all of us. How are you going to get started? Can we help?'

Clare wants to hug them, a cautious optimism seeping once more through her veins. Instead she sits up straight, squaring her shoulders. 'The Organ and Tissue Donation Service would have to initiate contact with recipients, see if they're amenable to us getting in touch.' She avoids glancing in Allison and Bridie's direction, speaking only to Emma and Joel. 'Then, I guess, I'd prepare a letter or email asking if we can speak. Some might not want to, but even if they don't, just to hear about the impact the donation has had – at the very minimum that it's worked – would be wonderful.'

'It really would,' Emma says. 'I'm in.'

Clare reaches across the table and squeezes her hand in grati-tude. They are not a demonstrative family, but right now she wants to scoop Emma into her arms, or jump up and down in glee. Joel places his own giant palm over both of theirs and the three of them grin together, conspirators.

Bridie coughs. 'Dessert, anyone? Or just coffee?'

'Definitely dessert,' Clare replies. She shouldn't, she is always watching her weight, but too bad. She is, for the moment, happy. Happy! That in itself is cause for celebration.

'I'm going to have a Dragon's Egg,' Joel says. 'They're amazing. Remember?'

'Good choice,' Clare says. 'Maybe I will too.' And then she adds, to no one in particular, 'Oh, and by the way, Sophie and I have separated. She's moved out.'

Allison

For a moment Allison fears that she will not be able to get her pantyhose down in time, clawing at the gusset so frantically that it ladders. With her other hand she hoicks up her skirt – can't risk stopping to unzip it – and sinks onto the toilet seat, grateful that the lid is already up and she hasn't had to negotiate that too. Her bowels open. She leans forward, eyes closed, consumed with relief and shame and nausea.

It takes a few minutes for her breathing to return to normal. When it does she wipes, flushes, flushes again just to be sure, but sits back down on the toilet. Her stomach is still cramping; she has no desire to return to the restaurant where her sisters and Joel are eating dessert. Dessert! How can any of them even think about dessert after what Clare has suggested? Something about the plan has turned her stomach, sent her fleeing to the bathroom. Allison knows about surgery, about dissections, has watched on as chests are cracked like crab shells and the skin peeled back from the mottled flesh beneath. As Clare was speaking she'd had a vision of Daniel on the operating table, technically dead but kept alive by machines, a surgeon hovering above him, trying to decide where to cut first, then slicing at random. First his eyes, then his lungs . . .

Allison shudders. She knows she is being irrational. It doesn't work like that; there are separate teams for every organ and each procedure is meticulously scheduled and then executed. Daniel – Daniel's body – would have been treated with the utmost respect throughout. Still, the image has unsettled her. As she smooths down her skirt she notices that her hand is shaking. Panic ricochets through her. A tremor. But it's just shock, surely? It's not something else, something like . . .

'Allison? Are you in here?'

The voice interrupts her thoughts, brings her back to herself. Was it Bridie? The echo from the tiles makes it difficult to tell, but nonetheless Allison is compelled to her feet, yanking her stockings into place. She has been gone too long.

'Just a second,' she calls out, tucking in her blouse, flushing a third time to buy herself another few seconds. When she finally emerges from the stall it is Emma who is waiting for her. 'Oh, it's you,' Allison says, moving past her youngest sister to wash her hands at the basin.

'Are you all right?' Emma asks. 'I was watching you at the table. You looked so pale.'

'I think it was the sushi. It didn't agree with me.' Allison reaches into her handbag for her lipstick and reapplies it, staring carefully into the mirror, not meeting Emma's eyes.

'Do you feel any better now? Can you come back to the table? The others have nearly finished. I think they'll be leaving soon.'

'What are they talking about?' Allison asks.

Emma looks surprised. 'Well, everyone asked about Sophie, of course. Clare's not saying much, but it sounds like Sophie left her.

I don't know why. I can't quite believe it. They haven't been married a year, and after all that time together . . .'

Allison recaps the lipstick, allows Emma's words to wash over her. She had barely registered Clare's announcement in her scramble to get to the bathroom. 'Seriously? They've split up?'

Emma nods, her small face sad. *Is she going to cry?* Allison wonders. She hopes not. She doesn't have the energy to comfort her just now.

'Uh huh. Clare's still in their house, but she said she'll have to start looking for a flat. It must be awful for her.'

'God, Clare's full of news today. First the stupid recipient idea, then that bombshell. No wonder she's not thinking straight.' Allison knows she is being awful, that she should be worried about Clare, should be rushing back out into the restaurant to put her arms around her or at least offer her the spare room, but she can't hold her tongue. 'It's just nuts. Chasing down Daniel's organs, I mean. It's mawkish and it's sick and what does it achieve? Nothing. And it's rude too! If the recipients had wanted to be in contact with us they would have arranged that themselves.' She can't help it. She is getting worked up again and feels another spasm flit across her stomach.

'I guess,' Emma says, taking a step backwards. 'I haven't really thought about it – I was so upset by what Clare said next.' She peers closely at Allison. 'Are you sure you're okay?'

Allison turns back to her handbag, ferrets out her brush and attacks her hair. The ash-blonde strands fall obediently into place, though her scalp tingles with the force.

'And I don't have any time!' she protests, glaring at her reflection without seeing it. 'I've got my job and the boys, and there's grants I need to apply for and student evaluations to be written up . . .

I don't know how Clare expects me to fit in looking for bits of Daniel as well.'

Emma winces but reaches out, putting a hand on Allison's forearm. 'She doesn't. You don't have to. Joel and I will help her. No one else has to get involved if they don't want to. We all know you're busy. You do so much, Allison. I don't know how you manage it.'

Emma's kindness, undeserved and sincere, brings tears to Allison's eyes and stills her manic brushing. 'I'm sorry,' she says, finally facing her sister. 'I don't know why I'm being such a bitch. I was up half the night with Eliot. His asthma was playing up, and he only wanted me . . . and it just shook me, Clare's suggestion, I don't know why. The whole day has been a trial – getting parking, and the dog, and then Bridie turning up dressed as if she's going to the Oscars. Her breasts! Did you notice them? How could you not? For a memorial lunch! Do you think she's had them done?'

Emma giggles. 'You do seem a bit overwrought. And I think Bridie looks gorgeous. But then she always does.'

Allison pulls a face, but allows Emma to steer her towards the door and back to her family. 'Black leather at her age? She's forty-five, not twenty-five. And honestly – don't you think she's had a boob job?'

Goodbyes are being said as Allison rejoins the table, Clare hugging Joel while Emma waits her turn. Bridie remains in her seat, busy with her phone, and Allison takes the opportunity to swoop down next to her. 'Hey,' she says, 'do you want a lift home?'

Bridie doesn't look up. 'It's okay. I'm just booking an Uber.'

'No, don't.' Allison places her hand across the screen. 'I'll take you.'

She has Bridie's attention now, her eyebrows arched in suspicion. 'But it's completely out of your way. You'll get caught in traffic. What gives?'

'Can't I just want to spend some time with my favourite sister?'

'You could have done that in the last half hour instead of decamping to the bathroom. What the hell were you doing in there for so long? Cocaine? Texting a lover?'

Allison forces a laugh. 'Hardly. I just wasn't feeling well. But you're right. There is something I want to talk to you about.'

'And we can't do it here?'

Allison shakes her head. Clare, she notices, has left without acknowledging her. She pushes the sting of guilt aside. Too bad. She'll call her later, talk her round, make her see reason. Poor Clare. Sophie's desertion has clearly unhinged her.

Bridie returns her phone to her clutch and stands up. 'Fine. You've intrigued me now. Lead on.' They farewell Joel and Emma, who are still chatting, and leave the restaurant. Allison blinks as they emerge into the sunshine. It is a beautiful spring day. How has she not noticed? She must have had her back to the view.

'So,' Bridie asks, 'what's this big secret you've got to share with me?' She hooks one arm through Allison's as they cross the road together. Allison softens, touched by the gesture. At least Bridie still likes her. *Thick as thieves, you two*, she hears her mother saying, decades ago when it was just Allison and Bridie, before all the others arrived.

'Do you remember how Mum used to dress us in matching outfits?' she asks, suffused with nostalgia.

Bridie's lips purse. 'Ugh. Don't remind me! Those culottes, and the terry-towelling jumpsuits. Hideous!'

'I thought it was sweet,' Allison replies, deflated.

'It didn't last though, did it?' Bridie says. 'We couldn't be more different now.'

Yeah, Allison thinks. *Only one of us might be mistaken for a dominatrix*. She doesn't say anything though, suddenly nervous as they approach the car. 'So here's the situation,' she begins, but Bridie is striding ahead of her, is already at the passenger side door.

'Oh, you brought John Thomas!' she exclaims, peering in through the window. 'I'd forgotten how cute he is. It's good to see him again.' She taps her fingers on the glass, makes little yapping sounds in response to the dog's frenetic barking, then appraises Allison across the Volvo's roof. 'But it's pretty warm. Why didn't you just leave him at home?'

'I couldn't. Jason won't have him anymore.' She swallows. 'So I thought you might. Actually, you have to.'

'Me?' Bridie jumps back from the car as if electrocuted. 'No way. I don't do dogs. Give him to one of the others.'

'I can't! Emma's in that tiny flat. She doesn't even have a garden, and Sophie's allergic, remember? They already passed him to us.'

'Sophie's gone though, allegedly.' Bridie is eyeing the dog through the glass as if he were a tiny bomb about to explode.

'But she could come back. Who knows? This is the first we've heard of it – it might not even be serious. And if it is I can hardly saddle Clare with a dog if she's getting over a break-up and has to move.' She could hardly ask Clare for a favour full stop, she thinks, not after the scene over lunch.

'But what about the boys?' Bridie persists. 'Marty and Eliot? Aren't they devastated? John Thomas is their pet.'

Allison unlocks the Volvo. Hearing the beep, John Thomas leaps into the driver's seat, tail wagging furiously, breath misting the glass between them. Despite herself, Allison's heart contracts. 'Jason promised them a trampoline instead. Said there'd be more room in the garden without a dog. And maybe a pool.' She opens the door and the dachshund dives into her arms.

'And they fell for it? Heartless little souls. What are you raising in that house? Robots?'

Allison wants to protest; she buries her face in John Thomas's scruff to stop herself. The twins had cried for a day when Jason broke the news, but once he found out about the ashes her husband had been adamant. The dog had to go. 'He promised them lizards as well. They've always wanted water monitors, for some reason, but JT would have eaten them.'

'Lizards, a trampoline *and* a pool.' Bridie looks sceptical. 'What did the dog actually do? Crap in his shoes?'

I wish, Allison thinks. She could have dealt with that. Devouring his aunt's remains though, that was harder to negotiate. 'Nothing!' she lies. 'Jason just didn't have the time to walk him, not with running his practice and driving the boys all over town for soccer and ju-jitsu and what-not. The poor dog was always being left on his own. Plus I think Jason really does want a pool.'

'I don't have time to walk him either!' Bridie protests. 'I'm always on set, when I'm working, or away. You know that.'

'Yeah, but Tom's home a lot, isn't he? When he's not doing a film, that is. He'd love JT. For company. And you've got that huge yard. You've practically got acreage! It's perfect. Or you could take him to work with you, like Daniel used to do. He'd be good. He's used to it – I can't though, obviously. The hospital would never allow it.' The dog is licking her neck now, but she hardens her heart and walks around the Volvo, pushes him towards Bridie.

Her sister struggles to hang on, taken by surprise, and Allison holds her breath, praying the dog's nails won't mark Bridie's leather dress.

'There!' she says, sounding far more confident than she feels. 'He suits you. You look great together.' John Thomas, she is relieved to see, is now licking Bridie, completely indiscriminate with his affections.

'For fuck's sake,' Bridie exhales, but Allison can see she is wavering. 'He is pretty cute. But I'm not making any promises. I still have to check with Tom.'

Allison relaxes. Tom is a pushover. How did Bridie get all the luck?

'Hey, I thought you two left ages ago?'

Allison starts. She hadn't seen Joel approaching, focused as she was on willing Bridie to take John Thomas off her hands.

'We did,' Bridie replies, 'but Allison had something she wanted to share with me. For good.' She holds up the dog, who immediately squirms towards Joel.

'JT! My man!' Joel bends down to fondle John Thomas's ears and is rewarded with yet more licking. Honestly, Allison thinks, she may as well have left the animal on the street. He clearly doesn't care who he lives with. 'I thought I'd head down to the memorial before I go home,' Joel continues. 'I'm not in the city much. It's a good chance to visit. I was going to see if you wanted to join me, Bridie, but you took off too quickly.'

Just Bridie, huh, Allison thinks. She sure wasn't making any friends today. 'Actually,' she says, 'I was about to drive Bridie home. I've got all the dog's stuff with me – his bed and bowls, and one of those huge bags of kibble.'

Bridie tucks the dachshund under her arm and bends to speak to him. 'Wow. She was pretty confident about offloading you, wasn't she?' Then she turns to Joel. 'That's a great idea. I'd love to come. And from what I'm told, this one'—she nods towards John Thomas—'could use the walk.' Finally, she addresses Allison. 'If you could still drop everything off that would be great, so it's there by the time I get back. Maybe just give me his leash now.'

Allison does as instructed. How can she argue? She remains by the Volvo as Joel and Bridie walk away, John Thomas scampering between them. The dog goes readily, doesn't even look back, but then again why should he? She's just given him up and, though she should feel grateful, melancholy arcs through her. Clare is wrong with all her morbid organ talk. John Thomas is the last living piece of Daniel, and it hurts to see him go. Still, she tells herself as she climbs into the car, she'd had to let Jason win this one. Marriage is a balancing act. She wears the pants in their relationship, they both know that, but she also knows it can't become a dictatorship. Jason doesn't put his foot down very often, but when he does it's better if she accedes. Pick your battles: the first rule of matrimony.

Allison closes her eyes and sinks back against the seat, still mourning the dog. He is a funny little thing, full of personality – but it is better this way, she chides herself. They haven't been looking after him properly, don't have the time to give him the attention and exercise he needed; he is left all alone most of the day, and she only really loved him when he was asleep on one of the boys' beds, not unearthing her petunias or forever yapping to be let in or out. John Thomas will be happier with Bridie. He can go to shoots with her, though she doesn't seem to have been on one for a while, or dig all he likes in that enormous North Shore garden.

The car is warm. It is making her drowsy. She should get going to Bridie's, beat the traffic across the bridge, but instead she nestles further into the soft leather seat. The day has taken it out of her: Clare, the dog, the constant tightrope of work and family, family and work. She should get going, but within seconds she is asleep.

Bridie

'So,' Joel asks almost as soon as they are out of earshot, 'you weren't expecting that, were you?' He nods towards John Thomas, who is pulling at his leash with his nose up, sniffing, inhaling the many scents of Circular Quay.

'I was not,' Bridie confirms. 'I'm still not actually quite sure how it happened.'

Joel laughs. 'The perfumed steamroller. Who was that? Margaret Thatcher?'

'Jana Wendt,' Bridie says. 'But Thatcher's a better comparison. She and Allison would get on brilliantly. God, Tom's going to kill me.'

He won't, though. She knows that. He'll groan a little, make the same sort of remarks about her older sister as Joel, but then he'll find a spot for the dog bed and probably walk John Thomas around the garden a few times to acclimatise him. Tom is a softie. It still surprises her that he looks like an action hero yet emotes like a rom-com lead. He *should* be angry though, she thinks. Somebody needs to stand up to Allison. Usually it's her, but today is proof that she could do with some back-up.

'Oh, what a gorgeous dog! I love dachshunds. Is he a standard or a miniature?'

A passer-by has stopped to pet John Thomas. Bridie has no clue what the woman is talking about.

'He's a middie, actually,' Joel answers for her. 'His mother was a standard and the father a miniature. It's a nice mix. He shouldn't have the back issues that bigger dachshies have, and he's not yappy like the minis.'

'Oh, he's perfect!' The woman is squatting on the pavement, almost eye level with the dog, her underwear riding up above the back of her jeans. Bridie looks away. 'How long have you had him?'

Two minutes, Bridie wants to say.

Joel answers instead. 'Since he was a puppy. He's almost five now.'

'Five! I thought he *was* a puppy. Who's a gorgeous boy?' She scratches the dog under the chin and he arches his neck in return, relishing the attention. 'What's his name?'

'John Thomas,' Joel replies.

'John Thomas!' she repeats, standing up. 'That's a big name for a little man. Adorable! You make a lovely family.'

The woman thinks they are a couple, Bridie realises. If only she knew. Joel with his Greenie beard and crumpled chinos is so not her type, just as she clearly isn't his. He is her brother's ex, after all.

'Thank you,' she says, trying to keep a straight face while she slips her hand into Joel's. 'Come on, honey,' she says to him. 'We need to get going.'

'You're a shocker,' he says fondly after the woman has moved off. 'And, God, if she thinks we're adorable, imagine if she saw you with Tom? But then I guess if you were with Tom she wouldn't have noticed you.'

Bridie drops her hand and punches his bicep. 'Rude! She's right, though. It is a big name. Why do you think Daniel chose it?'

Joel stops walking. 'You don't know?' Bridie shakes her head. He laughs, rubbing his chin. 'It's from a book. *Lady Chatterley's Lover*. You've heard of it?'

'Of course,' Bridie says. 'But I haven't read it. Is John Thomas one of the characters?'

'You could say that.' Joel seems to be choosing his words carefully. 'It's what the groundsman, Mellors – the one who sleeps with the lady – calls his . . . penis.'

Bridie splutters. 'Seriously? I did think it was rather formal, but I assumed that had to do with Daniel's time at Central Saint Martins, the way he liked to pretend to be British.' She studies the dachshund. 'But it's because of the shape, right?'

'Sort of,' Joel says. 'Plus Daniel really liked cock.'

They are still giggling as they turn into Bent Street. Bridie is glad she has come, is happier to see the anniversary out with Joel rather than Allison. Than with any of them, really. It was strange. Losing their parents while they were all still young – that should have brought them closer, shouldn't it? Bridie was yet to hit thirty when her father had died from a heart attack just eighteen months after her mother, effectively orphaning her; Emma was only seventeen. You might have expected the five of them to turn to each other, to prop each other up, but instead the reverse had occurred. Daniel had returned to CSM almost straight after the funeral, Allison had buried herself in her obstetrics training, Emma had moved to the Con to take up her scholarship. Granted, all those plans were already in place, but couldn't they have talked more? Texted, called, met up for lunch as a family now and again rather than just at Christmas, and only then because Clare cajoled them all into it and organised the whole thing so nobody had any excuses?

Was that grief, Bridie wonders, or were they just not the sort of family that she'd grown up watching on TV – the Brady Bunch, the Waltons, *Full House*? Families who were forever sitting down to chat about their issues over a plate of cookies, who hugged things out . . . But TV wasn't reality, it was designed, constructed, edited. She'd bet those three Brady girls had *hated* having to share a room.

'Here we are,' says Joel, stopping in front of a bench at the edge of the footpath. Bridie blinks; she would have walked right past. She has been here only once before, when it was first unveiled a year after the shooting. There is a small plaque in the footpath just in front of the bench, and she bends to read it.

In Memoriam
Rebecca Henderson
Daniel O'Shea
Olivia Nguyen
October 26, 2015
'*Come to me, all you who are weary and burdened,*
and I will give you rest.'
Matthew 11:28

Bridie sighs. She remembers being disappointed with it when she first saw it, and she is disappointed again now. Maybe that's why she hasn't visited. The Bible verse irks her. It has nothing to do with her brother, but one of the female victims had been religious – she can't remember which now – and it had been her family who had lobbied for the memorial, maybe even funded it. It had probably made Emma happy at least. Bridie straightens up.

'It's no Martin Place, is it?' Her tone is whiny even to her own ears. It wasn't a competition . . . though in truth only two civilians had died there, not three.

Joel reaches down and traces Daniel's name with his finger. 'The Lindt Café was the first time that sort of attack happened here. I think people thought it would be the only one. The event that killed Danny . . . maybe that was embarrassing. Awful, but embarrassing for authorities, for it to happen not even a year later. The inquest certainly got a whole lot less publicity. What a waste.'

He is referring to her brother, she knows, not the inquest, and she places her hand on his shoulder, bows her head in their shared pain. When she looks up again John Thomas is sniffing at the bench, then before she can stop him he lifts one short black leg and urinates on it.

'John Thomas!' she cries, yanking at the leash. She glances across at Joel, afraid he will be upset, but to her relief he is smiling.

'That wouldn't have happened,' he says, 'if Allison was still in charge.'

There doesn't seem much point in lingering after that.

'Do you have to be anywhere?' Joel asks and when Bridie says she doesn't he buys two takeaway coffees and they head back towards the Quay, putting the depressing bench behind them. 'It's really good to see you,' he says as they settle on a patch of grass in the sun near the Museum of Contemporary Art.

'Likewise,' Bridie replies, and means it. 'We should do it more often. Why haven't we?'

'You've always been too busy,' Joel chides her with a smile. 'Jetting from Cannes to Berlin to Sundance, making your block-busters. I've been free.'

'Blockbuster,' she says, emphasising the singular. 'And that was years ago.' She has a sudden memory of Daniel and Joel at the premiere of *Black Box*, a tiny event barely worthy of the name and almost solely attended by contacts of the crew and cast. Nonetheless, Joel and Daniel had prepared as if they would be walking the red carpet in Hollywood. Joel had worn a tuxedo and top hat; Daniel had gone one better in white tails, brandishing a cane. Her heart had swelled with both love and embarrassment when she laid eyes on them outside the cinema in Newtown hosting the event. 'It's only a little indie pic,' she had cautioned, to which Daniel had replied, 'Darling, it's *your* little indie pic, which means it's huge. We shall celebrate commensurately!'

Looking back now, she was glad they had. *Black Box* may have been just a little pic, pulled together on a budget of under two million, but Bridie had been sure it was the start of something. Of her career, of premiere after premiere in the years to come, of reviews in *Variety* and invites to film festivals. Wrong. Oh, the latter, at least, had materialised during *Black Box*'s slow burn from obscure flick to cult film, but even they had dried up in the last few years. Her presence hadn't been requested anywhere of note for ages, but then Joel would hardly know that. They'd only seen each other a few times since Daniel's funeral, at the anniversary lunches and occasionally for a drink before Christmas. She should have made more of an effort, Bridie thinks. 'Sorry,' she mutters. 'You're right. I've been slack.'

'Nah, it's fine,' Joel says, affable as always. 'I really do know you're busy. God, you're a film director! I love boasting about that. I'll tell anyone who will listen.'

'Really?' Bridie says, touched and a little mortified. Was she still actually a film director? There had been yet another knockback that morning via email from a production company she was desperate to work with. She'd deleted it, but the words still echoed in her brain: *We've decided to go with someone with a few more runs on the board, all the best in your next venture.* She'd snorted. There *was* no next venture. 'Are you telling anybody in particular?' she asks in an attempt to change the subject.

'Do you mean am I seeing someone?' It is Joel's turn to prevaricate. He rubs his bald patch, shoos John Thomas away from a discarded fish and chip box that the dog is threatening to devour. 'Nup. No one special. No one at all, to be honest. Danny's a hard act to follow. Plus I can't really be bothered, you know? Grindr, Meetup – it's all too much work at my age. I'd really like someone to simply turn up on my doorstep, with kids if possible, but you can't advertise for that.' He amends himself. 'Well, you can, I suppose, but I'd be wary of the results.'

Bridie laughs. 'At your age? You're hardly over the hill. Have you even turned forty yet?'

'Nope, still thirty-nine,' Joel says. 'And planning to remain that way.'

'Good call. Wish I was. How's Tideways? Have you been there lately?'

Joel's eyes sparkle. 'Oh yeah. Most weekends. It's my favourite place in the world. I've just repainted it, actually. I was telling Clare at lunch that she should come for a visit and see it. You too.'

'That would be great. Let's do it soon, before summer and all the crowds.'

'You're on.' Joel lies back on the grass, shielding his eyes from the sun. A seagull squawks overhead and John Thomas yaps in reply. 'Every day that I was working on it I was thinking how I wish I could show Danny. He'd be amazed at the transformation. He'd let it go a bit, you know – not his fault,' Joel quickly adds. 'He was busy too. It's the curse of the O'Sheas. His label was really taking off, wasn't it? It's sad that Morgan shut it down.' He rolls onto his stomach, looking away from Bridie, his gaze following the Manly ferry as it chuffs across the harbour. 'You weren't keen on Clare's suggestion, I take it?'

Bridie tugs at John Thomas's leash, buying herself time as she pulls him onto her lap. She hadn't seen the question coming. 'I just don't get the point of it, I suppose,' she says at length. 'But you do?'

Joel nods, an abrupt gesture, his face still inclined towards the water. 'I miss him, Bridie,' he says quietly. 'I miss him so much. Danny dying like that . . . it still upsets me, if I let myself think about it. It's all so arbitrary. He was just in the wrong place at the wrong time, and snap'—he clicks his fingers—'he's gone for good. But maybe this would make a bit more sense of it, somehow. Give me closure, whatever that is.' He pauses. 'And Clare . . . I'd like to do it for her too. She clearly needs it.'

Bridie's fingers twine themselves in John Thomas's fur. 'Clare?' she repeats blankly.

Joel nods again. 'Yeah. She looked terrible at the restaurant. Didn't you notice? Done in, exhausted. As if she was in pain.'

Bridie hadn't noticed. She'd been a bit tipsy if she was honest, using the champagne as a poultice against the morning's rejection. 'Do you think something's wrong with her?'

'What, apart from her wife leaving her, and the anniversary of her brother's death?' Joel scoffs. Bridie has never heard him like this. 'You four chicks. Do you even talk to each other?' He exhales, takes a deep breath and starts again. 'No, I don't think she has cancer, if that's what you mean. But this is clearly important to her, so I want to help. She was the one who introduced me to Daniel, after all.'

'She was,' Bridie says, chastised. She is spared from further discussion by an elderly woman who is hovering above her, leaning on her stick.

'What a dear little dog,' she interrupts. 'May I pat her?'

'Him,' Bridie replies automatically, clambering awkwardly to her feet, proffering John Thomas. It is the most attention she has had in ages. Maybe she should give up directing, or trying to, and become a professional dachshund walker instead. The idea is intoxicating. No more rebuffs, no more chasing after things she isn't given. No more disappointment . . . But no, she thinks, she is only forty-five, still too young to give up. There are no lifetime achievement awards handed out at her age, not unless she dies. Even then she should probably have done so five or six years ago, when *Black Box* was at its peak. An ache goes through her. She wishes she could talk to Daniel. Daniel would understand. At that moment Bridie misses him more than she has all day.

Emma

November 2018

Emma gazes out the window as the woman behind the desk goes through Daniel's file. Beside her, Clare is leaning forward in her seat, one foot tapping the carpet. She thrums with impatience. *Relax*, Emma wants to tell her, *it will be okay. We'll find out what you need to know,* but she is afraid that will only irritate Clare or, worse, sound patronising, so she keeps her mouth shut. She is thirty-three and still can't always read her sisters. Oh, she can tell when Allison is uptight about something, which is a fairly regular occurrence, or when Bridie isn't paying attention, but Clare is often a mystery to her. Sophie, for example. That had been a surprise. Who knew that Clare was into women, or anyone for that matter? Allison and Bridie had had a constant stream of boyfriends while Emma was growing up. Daniel too, as it turned out, plus the occasional girl, but Clare had been different. She had always been single, appearing perfectly content as such, married, if anything, to her work, particularly once she transferred to the Children's Hospital in Randwick.

Then one year Emma had arrived at Clare's flat for Christmas and there, out of the blue, was Sophie, blushing and dimpling when Clare introduced her as 'my partner', the two of them holding hands between courses and announcing over the pudding that they were going to move in together. Sophie's recent departure had been equally as abrupt. It didn't make sense, Emma thought. They'd been together a decade. They'd seemed so happy. Clare had even alluded, a while back, to them starting a family. But now Sophie was gone and Clare was hunting for somewhere else to live and Emma hadn't seen any of it coming at all. It unnerved her. How could she know so little about her sister, about her own flesh and blood?

'Ah! Here we are.' The woman behind the desk pushes her glasses back up her nose and peers at a piece of paper. 'Donation record, Daniel O'Shea.' She falls silent as she scans the page. Clare tenses at the delay and Emma reaches across and places her hand on Clare's knee, gratified when Clare takes it in her own.

Daniel had taught Emma to drive. She remembers it suddenly, waiting for the woman to speak. He had flown back to Sydney from Central Saint Martins after their father had died, as shocked and distraught as the rest of them, but so much more grown up than when he had first left for London a little over a year before. They had never been particularly close – of all the sisters, everybody knew that spot was reserved for Bridie – but the day after the funeral he knocked on her bedroom door, jangling the keys to the family's old Cortina, and called to her to get up, that they were going out. *Out*, it transpired, was to an industrial estate a few kilometres from home and deserted on the Saturday, where he pulled over and told her to take his place behind the wheel. Emma was seventeen and suddenly orphaned, her future still hanging in the balance.

'What?' she'd asked, and Daniel had replied, 'I'm going to teach you how to drive. You'll need to know for uni. Dad taught the rest of us, but . . .' He'd begun crying, tears rolling down his face, and so she had too. When they'd dried their eyes, he taught her how to adjust her mirrors, the importance of checking blind spots and to always signal before pulling out from the kerb. He was a patient and gentle tutor – far more so, Emma later reflected, than her blustering father would have been – and determined to have her confident with the basics before he had to return to the UK in a week. They practised for hours together every morning. Daniel told her about his life at college, the friends he had made, the pubs, the subjects he was enjoying; Emma confided in him that she had applied for the Con.

'Good for you!' he exclaimed, startling her while she was attempting a roundabout. 'Honestly, Emmie, that's fabulous. That's just brilliant. Dad must have been so proud.'

She hadn't told their father, she'd had to admit, eyes fixed on the road. He'd been too distracted since their mother's death, too morose. But she'd tell him if she got in. Then she started to cry and Daniel had had to take the wheel to get them safely through to the other side. They cried quite a lot during those lessons, sometimes individually, often together, and when the tears came she pulled over and they sat for a bit, weeping, and then when they both felt better Emma would signal and pull out again.

Daniel was the one she told when the letter from the Conservatory had arrived two days later. He directed her into a McDonald's drive-thru and they celebrated with hot fudge sundaes and more tears, but mostly happy ones.

Emma sighs, recalling it. What was Clare thinking right now? What were her memories of their beautiful brother? They must all remember him in different ways, she imagines. She misses him whenever she does a three-point turn.

'Nine, ten, eleven,' the woman counts. 'Goodness! That must be some sort of record.' Holloway, Emma remembers. That was her name. Marion Holloway, Family Support Co-ordinator, NSW

Organ and Tissue Donation Service. It's all there on the ID badge around her neck.

'What do you mean?' Clare asks.

Marion smiles. 'Your brother, Daniel, was a wonderful donor. Prolific. He must have been in excellent condition. Almost everything was able to be retrieved: his heart, lungs, liver, intestines, both his kidneys . . .' Clare makes a little noise in her throat and Marion looks up, immediately contrite. 'I'm sorry,' she says. 'It's a lot to take in, isn't it? Do you want me to stop?'

Her question is to both of them, but Emma waits for Clare to respond. This is Clare's mission, Clare's baby. Emma is happy to go along with it, but she had volunteered to attend today primarily to support Clare. It wasn't as if Allison or Bridie was going to offer.

'No, not at all,' Clare says. 'I'm just . . . astonished. It's fabulous. I had no idea. I'd thought maybe three, four people might have been helped, but you're saying there were eleven?'

Marion nods, her eyes returning to the file. 'Possibly even more. All the usual organs were harvested, including his corneas – both of them – which may have been used separately, plus skin, too, and bone.'

'Bone?' Clare asks. 'You can do that?'

'Oh yes,' Marion says. 'It can be used in hip and knee replacements, or to heal fractures. Bone can go to quite a few recipients, actually, as can skin. It's possible up to twenty individuals have had their lives changed by Daniel's generosity.'

Twenty. Emma looks away, peering back out the window. They are on the sixth floor. The jacarandas on the street below are in full bloom, creating a mauve cloud beneath her. For years they have triggered a vague anxiety, coming into flower at the same time as she was due to sit her university exams each November, but today they are soothing, restful. She could clamber out of here, over the sill, and fall asleep in their purple embrace. *Twenty*. Oh, Daniel.

'I want to contact them all.' Clare's fingers cling to the handbag in her lap as if it is an animal that might escape.

Marion picks up the file, begins leafing through it. If she is taken aback by this demand her face does not betray it. 'It could take a while,' she cautions, hunting for something. 'We have the contact details for all the recipients, of course, but you'll need to write to each of them, or maybe just do one form letter, and then we'll have to send it on, wait for them to get back to us, if they do . . .' Her voice trails off. 'Okay. Here it is.' She pulls a single sheet from the thick ream of paper, studies it for a moment, then sits back in her chair and smiles. 'But as luck would have it, this arrived just a week or two ago. Something to get started with. It's a letter from a recipient, a man who received one of Daniel's kidneys. You should have been contacted about it?'

'I didn't hear anything.' Clare turns to Emma. 'Did you?'

'Of course not! I would have told you.' They both look at Marion. 'Who exactly was contacted?' Emma asks.

Marion buries herself in the file once more, flicking through its pages. 'The next of kin is listed as a Mr Fionn O'Shea. Daniel's brother?'

Emma shakes her head. 'Our father. He's deceased. Has been for years.' Clearly Daniel had never updated his details once he registered as an organ donor. And why would he, Emma thinks. He'd probably imagined he was immortal, that mundane particulars like next of kin would never be relevant.

'So the address we forwarded this letter to'—Marion reads it out, the familiar refrain of their childhood—'there's no one from the family there anymore?'

'No.' Clare extends one hand across the desk. 'May I have it, please?'

'Technically, I'm not sure what the policy is in these circumstances . . .' Marion prevaricates, then notes the jut of Clare's jaw and hands her the letter. 'But you're here now, aren't you?'

'Read it out!' Emma exclaims, surprising them both, surprising herself. She has come purely to support Clare, or so she thought, but all of a sudden she needs to know about that kidney.

'Really?' Clare asks her. 'Here?' Her tone is nervous, almost afraid. Clare is naturally reserved, has always kept her business to herself. Emma has long thought of her as somewhat aloof, standoffish, but now she sees how much of that is fear, a reticence to expose herself. *Oh*, she thinks, in sympathy, in recognition.

'Yes, go on,' Marion says. 'It's lovely.'

Clare's eyes dart to the page she is holding, handwritten and closely spaced. 'Well, I guess . . .'

Emma knows she would rather be doing this alone at home, or in her car, and feels for her, but it's too late. They are in this now. They are in it together.

Clare coughs a little and then begins.

> *Dear Donor Family,*
>
> *My name is Jeremy and I have lived with kidney disease since I was teenager. Three years ago I was the lucky recipient of a brand new kidney from your family's loved one, and I wanted to write and tell you what an enormous difference this has made to my life.*

Clare halts, draws in a ragged breath. The paper trembles in her fingers.

Before the transplant I had been receiving dialysis for around four years. While this saved my life, it also took a serious toll on my health, activities and relationships. I am married with three young boys all under twelve, but was never able to attend their school or sporting events because I had to be at dialysis for a number of hours three times a week, or felt too tired and unwell between visits. I also had to cut back to part-time work so I had the time to attend dialysis, which created financial strain for my family and stopped me from progressing in my job. I really had no energy to do much at all, and definitely couldn't travel or even get away for the weekend. It wasn't much of an existence and I often felt quite hopeless and depressed, but everything changed after my transplant. I felt better almost as soon as I woke up from the surgery, even while I was still in hospital. Within weeks I could attend my sons' footy matches and after a month or two I could even kick the footy with them in the backyard. I am now back at work full time and my family is planning to travel to New Zealand for the wedding of my wife's sister. I cannot tell you what a huge difference your donation has made, not just to my quality of life, but to that of my wife and sons too. You have given me my life back, a better life.

Tears are streaming down Clare's cheeks, falling onto her lap. Marion passes across a box of tissues. 'I'm sorry,' Clare says, dabbing at her face. 'I don't think I can . . .'

Emma gently takes the letter from her and reads it aloud to the end.

Every morning that I wake up I am just so grateful for this gift, yet I also know that it only came about because of your

own terrible loss. Please be assured that I will never forget
your generosity or your precious family member who made it
possible, who I think about all the time. I hope he or she knows
somehow what an amazing impact they have had.

Thank you for reading my letter. I would love to be in touch
with you if you have any questions or would ever like to meet.

Yours,

Jeremy

All three women are silent.

Emma collects herself before she speaks. 'The date on the letter,' she says eventually. 'October twenty-six.' Clare looks as if she might cry again. 'That's when Daniel died,' Emma explains to Marion. 'We were all together, our family, having lunch to mark it, and Clare suggested seeking out the recipients.'

'That's a coincidence!' Marion says brightly. 'Of all the days that he might have written . . .'

Emma interrupts her. 'It isn't. Coincidence is God showing that He is listening.'

She believes this, believes with all her heart. Emma is not a superstitious woman, but her faith sustains her, shapes her days. This letter and the date that it was penned endorse Clare's decision to seek out Daniel's recipients. She is so glad that she came along today.

'We could meet him,' Clare says, a tissue balled in her fist. 'He said he'd love to.'

'Actually, that's not usually done,' Marion warns. 'The Human Tissue Act prohibits the disclosure of any identifying information of either donor or recipient. That's why the letters you send have to go through us, with your full name removed, and the same for any we receive from recipients to pass on to you.'

'We could meet all of them,' Clare says, ignoring her. Emma watches as the idea takes root in Clare's mind, the widening of her eyes, the lift of her shoulders.

'Well, that's definitely not on.' Marion collects up the papers from Daniel's file, aligns them with three sharp taps on her desk. She is no longer smiling.

'But if he wants to meet us . . .' Clare begins.

'It must have happened before,' Emma says simultaneously. 'People like Jeremy, who've gotten their lives back. Families who've lost loved ones. What's the harm of them meeting? Wouldn't it be beneficial for both sides?'

Marion removes her glasses and pinches the bridge of her nose. 'Ideally, yes.' She sighs. 'But there's no guarantee of it working out like that. Hence the Act. Not every recipient wants to meet their donor's family. They might feel guilty, or beholden, or just want to get on with their lives, put their illness behind them. And the donor family – they could be disappointed in the outcome of the donation, if the organ went to someone of a different race or religion, for example, or if the recipient didn't appear to be sufficiently grateful. Or they might get too attached, have to grieve all over again if the donation doesn't take. Not all of them do.' Marion straightens the papers again. 'And then there's the worst-case scenarios, where donor families have asked recipients for financial support, or can't properly separate, leading to stalking . . .'

'We would never do that!' Clare interjects.

Marion's smile is tired. 'I'm sure you wouldn't. But it's happened, which is why the legislation is in place.'

'Still, some families must have met,' Emma persists. It is not in her nature to challenge authority. She prefers simply doing what she is told, but this, she now knows, is important. God has brought her here for a reason. 'I mean, I understand the law, but if both par-ties request or agree to it, it's not actually illegal, is it? There must have been cases where a donor has sought out a recipient, or vice versa, via Facebook, or getting hold of records somehow, and there's nothing your agency can do about it.'

'You're right,' Marion concedes. 'We would never recommend it, of course, but it does happen.'

'And Jeremy wrote that he would love to be in touch with us,' Clare says, leaning forward once more. 'Those were his actual words. So we could write a letter, with our contact details, asking to do just that, and send it through you, couldn't we? And he can call if he means it.'

'He might not live locally,' Marion says. 'Organ donations can be sent all over Australia, you know.'

'We'd travel.' Emma grins across at her sister. 'We would, wouldn't we, Clare?'

She will remember this moment later that day, as she leads the music at an evening celebration of the eucharist at Crossfire. The joy that goes through her, how light she feels. *This is my body, given for you.* Daniel had been no saint, certainly no Jesus, but the Spirit, in all of its mysterious ways, is working through his death, she is sure of it.

'Very well.' Marion is gracious in defeat. 'Write back to Jeremy and I'll make sure it's sent to him.'

'Thank you,' Clare says, face aglow with delight. 'We will. We'll write to all of them. You're going to be busy.'

Ten minutes later, as they say their goodbyes out the front of the building, Clare hugs her so fiercely Emma is sure it will leave bruises. It feels good, though. So good to be held.

Bridie

2002

'And the winner for Best Cinematography is . . .' The presenter fumbled with the envelope, deliberately building the anticipation. *Just get on with it, for fuck's sake*, Bridie thought, sitting behind him on the stage, though studying her nails as if she couldn't care less. 'Hugh Miller, for *Lullaby*.'

Bridie snorted. Damn. She'd had hopes for that award. Her own short film was deliberately low on dialogue, even plot, but awash with moody wide shots juxtaposed with pensive close-ups. She'd been proud of that as she edited it, careful to ensure that the shifts were seamless, fluid, so the viewer was carried from the wild landscapes she had worked so hard to find to the gradually narrowing interior view of the protagonist, a young man trapped beneath a boulder, his life ebbing away. Maybe that was the problem, she thought. Maybe she'd interpreted that year's Tropfest signature item, *rock*, too literally, and that's why she hadn't yet won an award.

Every year, the short film competition – Australia's biggest, and now making a mark internationally as well – required that entries included a designated signature object or action to ensure the film had been made specifically for the festival. And, Bridie guessed, as a little bit of a gimmick, something to keep viewers and probably judges on their toes. The item didn't have to play a large role, could simply be featured in the background at some point, but Bridie had decided to make hers the central feature. She'd noticed over the preceding years that entrants had tended towards either subtle glimpses or obtuse interpretations of the nominated inclusion. Why not, she'd reasoned, buck that trend, show that she could think outside the box by making her rock the lead character? One of them, anyway – there was also the unfortunate hiker it was slowly crushing to death, alone and terrified, but it was the boulder the camera lingered on, malice evoked through lingering shots of its jagged edges, its immovable heft.

Bridie fanned herself with her program as the next award was announced – Best Comedy, which her film most certainly was not. The rain had finally cleared, but it was still humid. February in Sydney could be almost tropical in its intensity, warm nights dissolving into sweat and sleeplessness. Despite the downpour earlier in the day the Domain was overflowing, its lawns obscured with picnic blankets and beach umbrellas, eskies and prams, the odd tarpaulin hoisted high to keep off the remaining drizzle. All those people, Bridie thought, chest prickling with pride, had turned out to watch the shortlisted films, hers included, more still watching them via satellite in Melbourne, in Adelaide, in Perth – maybe, she'd heard rumoured, even in LA. Last year she had been among them, just a pleb on the grass with her friends and some sixpacks; this year she was selected, exalted. This year she was a finalist, and on her first try too. Russell Crowe would judge her film, Claudia Karvan, Gillian Armstrong! Gillian Armstrong, a director she could only dream of emulating. It was enough, Bridie told herself. Don't worry about awards. Just enjoy the moment.

Bats swooped beneath the fig trees; a gentle breeze lifted the scent of salt and diesel from the harbour. Best Screenplay was declared, and she clapped loudly, smiling.

Best Actor, Best Actress . . . It was getting late now, almost 11 pm. Emma had school tomorrow, Bridie thought guiltily. It was her HSC year; she should be in bed. It had been good of her to come though. Bridie scanned what she could see of the crowd for her father and sister even though she knew she had little hope of spotting them. Her dad's attendance had been a given – he had always been her biggest supporter, right from the moment she had announced that she was dropping out of Year 11 to work on a set – but she hadn't expected Emma to want to come too. They didn't really know each other all that well, to be honest. There were twelve years between them; Bridie had moved out of home when Emma was barely eight. Her baby sister, in fact, was a mystery to her: played the cello, attended church. Church, when none of them had been so much as christened, when the closest either of her parents had got to religion was when her father trod the boards as Herod in the local troupe's production of *Jesus Christ Superstar*. Still, at least she had come, which was more than Bridie could say for her other siblings. Daniel, admittedly, was at college in the UK, but Allison and Clare had no such excuse. Sure, they both had shifts to work, but they could have changed them, couldn't they? They weren't the only public health employees in Sydney. And this was a big deal for Bridie: 723 entries, but only sixteen had been selected. Clare hadn't even called to wish her luck before she left.

'And second place goes to *Crush*, directed by Bridie O'Shea.' Deep in resentment towards her sister, it had taken her a second to realise that her name was being called. Bridie scrambled up so quickly she trod on the foot of the finalist next to her.

'Congratulations, Bridie! Anything you want to say?' A man wearing foundation and an artificially whitened smile was thrusting a microphone in her face and smiling expectantly.

'Um, no. Not really. Thank you, I guess.' *Fuck*, she thought. She'd been so desperate for an award that she hadn't prepared a speech. That had seemed too presumptuous, somehow – would surely turn the film gods against her. Not that she believed in gods, film or otherwise, unlike Emma.

The man with the iridescent teeth wasn't going to let her off so easily though.

'Many of the finalists were comedies, as you would have noticed. *Crush*, though, is a pretty dark film, isn't it? Was there any particular reason for that, or do you just like contemplating death?' He'd got the laugh from the audience he was angling for, but Bridie couldn't join in. *Oh mate*, she thought, *if only you knew*.

She'd started work on *Crush* the month before her mother had died, barely nine months earlier – but of course she hadn't known that when the entire thing materialised whole one day while she was in the bath. At the time, it had seemed magical, divine, but as soon as shooting had begun she had recognised it for what it was: a farewell, a fuck-you, two fingers raised at the particular cruelty of a drawn-out demise. When the finalists had first been announced one of the judges had remarked that he couldn't bear to watch *Crush* to its end, even though it was only the regulation seven minutes long. *Good*, she'd thought. She'd got it right, then, but there was no way she was going to admit all that to the thousands of people watching. Her mother's death was private, sacred somehow. She didn't want to see it quoted back at her in the papers tomorrow.

'No particular reason,' she replied instead. 'I didn't have the money for a large cast, and the boulder worked for free.'

Her turn to get the laughs. She was surprised how much they buoyed her, enhanced the moment. It was all about bringing the audience along with you, one of her lecturers had said during her first year at AFTRS, and she'd never forgotten it. You could make your work as arty, as cutting edge, as meaningful as you liked, but if no one watched it past the opening scenes you were wasting your time. You might as well stick to commercials. They paid better, and you didn't have to worry about box office.

The wind was getting up. 'Was it a difficult shoot?' her interviewer asked, clutching at his hair. Maybe it was fake, Bridie thought. It was certainly lush for his age. 'I must say it looked pretty uncomfortable, out on the side of that mountain in the rain.'

'The rain was actually my brother and father standing just out of shot with our sprinkler from home.' More laughs. She stood up straighter, over six foot in her heels, confidence flowing through her now. She'd won! *Crush* had won. Or come second anyway, close enough. Enough to open some doors, to decorate her CV, to show those who'd doubted her after twelve years of effort that yes, she was actually serious about this movie business. 'They were there for three days straight. Their arms must have been killing them.' She blew a kiss at the camera. 'Thanks, Dad and Dan. And as for the mountain, well . . .'

Before she could finish, a sudden hot squall of air gusted across the stage, tipped over her chair and blew her mini-dress straight up into her face. Bridie struggled to force it back down, acutely aware that her entire bottom half was on display and she wasn't wearing much more than a tiny thong and fake tan. The audience roared, hollering and whistling, and her glow of the previous moment vanished in a wash of humiliation. Bridie wanted to disappear. She brought her dress under control, turned around and returned to her seat, crouching to pick it up. Whatever she'd been saying, no one was listening to her now.

As she straightened up, acutely conscious of not giving the crowd another flash of her g-string, a voice rang out from somewhere in the front rows: *Marry me, Bridie!*

'Bridie! Bravo!' Emma and her father were waiting on the grass as she came off stage fifteen minutes later. The winner had been announced, the sponsors had been thanked, fireworks had exploded and the whole time Bridie had just sat there, praying for it to finish, her trophy stashed underneath her chair. 'You came second! That's amazing!' Emma, who usually shied away from physical contact, rushed forward to embrace her in a clumsy hug.

Bridie returned it awkwardly. Her baby sister was broomstick-thin and not quite five foot, the top of her head tucking easily beneath Bridie's chin. It was like embracing a sparrow.

'Ah, well done, wean,' her father boomed, his accent turned up to eleven in his excitement.

'I'm so embarrassed!' Bridie moaned. 'The wind . . . My dress . . . Everybody saw!'

'All they saw was that you've got fine legs,' her father said, stepping in to enfold her in his arms over the top of Emma, the three of them locked together for a moment like ill-fitting matryoshka dolls. 'Clever *and* gorgeous, that's what they saw.'

'It was lucky you were wearing your good undies,' Emma said, extricating herself.

Bridie had to smile, though still burning with shame. 'I only *have* good undies. Life's too short for ugly ones.'

'Lucky twice over that it was you up there, then,' Emma continued. 'Imagine if it was Allison. Cottontails for miles.'

Bridie hooted in delight. She hadn't known Emma had it in her.

'Now, girls,' her father said, though he was smiling too. 'No more talk of undies. Show us your award!'

Bridie's hands flew to her mouth. 'I forgot it! I was so desperate to get off stage that I must have left it there.'

'I'll go,' Emma said. 'I know where you were sitting. If you show up again everyone might want a repeat performance.'

'Cheeky monkey.' Fionn said, gently cuffing Emma's head.

She disappeared into the crowd. 'Thank you!' Bridie called after her, then turned to her father. 'And thank you too, Dad. For coming, that is. It means a lot.'

'Like I would have missed it, Bridie Kathleen O'Shea!' He embraced her again, and though she was taller than him too, she nestled against him, his little girl once more as he stroked her hair.

'Not just for coming,' she muttered against his chest. 'For everything. You know.' He'd started this, her father; he'd set it in motion. Bridie could still remember the first time she had seen him on stage, unrecognisable as the title role in a production of *The Mikado* at a local church hall. Unrecognisable, that was, until he opened his mouth, the familiar Irish lilt so at odds with his lacquered black wig, his white face, the kimono. She was six, and she had been spellbound. Her father worked in finance, did something in an office all day in the city, but his true passion was musical theatre. His real job left him gruff and rumpled when he got home in the evenings, but up there, under the floodlights, he sparkled, he prospered, he grew another few inches.

'Daddy!' she'd called out, delighted, and everybody laughed, but she'd barely noticed. Her father had beamed at her, then returned to character, sentencing poor Nanki-Poo to death. She couldn't articulate it at the time, but later she realised what had enchanted her so much: her father was having fun. Fun! When did you ever see an adult doing that?

She couldn't wait to try it for herself. All through primary school she was the first to put her hand up for the Christmas pageant, the class play. And she enjoyed it, tricking audiences into thinking she was someone else, a scarecrow or a toad or a goblin, but as she headed into her mid-teens the urge to direct took over. In every production she had been in she had known what to do instinctively. She didn't need any teacher telling her, standing over her. She knew what everyone else should be doing too, and was never shy about voicing her opinions until one day, exasperated, the Head of Drama had said to her, 'If you know so much, Bridie O'Shea, why don't you just take over?' So she did, and it came easily, felt right. Felt perfect, in fact – she could be all the characters now, not just one; she could bring the production alive exactly as she envisaged it. She was no longer just a part. She was the whole.

And that was that. School held no appeal anymore. Bridie had never been academic anyway, not like Allison in the year above her, who all her teachers were forever comparing her to. When the Head of Drama, now her ally, told her about a feature film being shot nearby and suggested she apply there for her work experience placement she did just that. By the third day she'd been offered a position as an assistant in the editing department, and she accepted without consulting her parents or teachers, without a backwards glance. When she announced she was leaving school immediately her mother cried, then railed at her, forbidding it, but Bridie stood her ground. She knew her rights. She was old enough. And her father stood with her, pacifying Barbie, contacting the school, smoothing her way.

When she asked him, years later, if he'd worried at all he'd just shrugged. 'You were in the right place for you. Anyone could see that.' Maybe, she sometimes wondered, there had also been an aspect of wish fulfilment on his own behalf, or maybe he simply knew it wasn't worth fighting about. She was young; she could always go back to study somewhere if film didn't pan out.

But it had, hadn't it? Five years of bouncing from set to set, picking up work wherever she could get it – in lighting, in editing, writing applications for grants. A stint as a third assistant director, then another as a second. Then AFTRS, once she knew that that wasn't enough, that she wanted to be number one, *the* director. Making ads and modelling to pay the rent, helping out on friends' films, networking, always networking, establishing contacts everywhere she could in the hope that one of them might pay off one day. Shooting short films in the moments she had the time and money, seven of them for her show reel. *Crush* was the eighth, but *Crush* was different. *Crush* was better. She knew it in her bones the moment she finished the first scene.

'Tropfest,' her father murmured as if he could read her mind, still cradling her to him. 'It's wonderful, Bridie. You're on your way.' He pulled back and kissed her forehead. 'At, what, thirty? How old are you now?'

'Twenty-nine, Dad.' She laughed. 'That's Allison. She's thirty.'

'Ah, I always mix it up. Too many children. Big mistake!' He grew serious again. 'Twenty-nine. Even better. It's all ahead of you. I only wish your mother could have seen this.'

'Seen me flash my knickers?' Bridie joked, but there was a lump in her throat.

'Seen you becoming who you were always going to be,' her father said, and softly squeezed her arm.

Fifteen minutes later she was on her way to the after-party, trophy wedged into her handbag. Despite Bridie's protests, Emma had insisted on taking photos of her with it, alone and then with their father.

'I'll send them to Danny,' she'd said. 'He'll love them, and neither of you will ever get around to it.'

Bridie had to acknowledge that she was probably right and hammed it up for the camera, cradling the award like a baby and gazing down upon it lovingly. She could feel her spirits rising again, the grin spreading across her face and, when her father announced that it was time to go, only offered to come with them to be polite.

'Don't be daft, wean,' he'd replied, as she'd anticipated. 'It's your night. You should be celebrating, not catching the train with us back to the suburbs.'

She'd embraced them both again, then watched as they left – Emma so tiny, her father growing ever stouter. He had already been a large man, but had put on more weight since her mother's death midway through the previous year. Probably drinking too much, and who could blame him, but what must he be now – 120 kilograms? 130? Bridie made a mental note to speak with Allison – she still lived at home and she was a doctor, surely she could be doing something about it – then promptly forgot. She had a party to go to.

'Hey, hey, hey, O'Shea, good job!' The first person to congratulate her as she stepped inside was an old friend, Julian, from AFTRS.

'Make sure you look me up when you're after a sound guy for your first feature film.' He went to give her a high-five, then when she raised her arm pulled her into a hug instead. Bridie stumbled against him, caught off balance.

The party, held in a marquee behind the main stage, was almost as dim as the now-deserted Domain outside, loud and getting louder. Daniel would love this, she found herself thinking. When she'd visited him at Central Saint Martins over Christmas she'd found he'd taken to wearing eyeliner, even nail polish. This would be just his scene.

'Thanks, Jules,' she said, eyes still adjusting, habitually casting around the room for anyone she knew or needed to know. 'You're on. Are you working on anything at the moment?'

He began to tell her, but she tuned out. That was Gary Maddox over there, the film critic for the *Herald*, interviewing one of the other finalists. She should make sure he spoke to her too, got a quote or even a picture for the paper. Bryan Brown held court at the bar – and was that Gillian Armstrong a bit further along, with her back to him, talking with another woman? Oh God, she'd *die* to meet Gillian Armstrong. And why shouldn't she? Bridie's fingers drifted instinctively to the resin award in her bag. Tonight she had an in; could waltz over, introduce herself, and thank the famous director for choosing her film. They'd get chatting, Bridie envisaged, Gillian would exclaim over her camera angles or the storyline or something – Bridie didn't care what – then tell her to look her up if she ever needed a mentor. Or work. Maybe she would offer her work! Invite her to be her 2AD on her next project, or get involved with the casting, or . . .

'Sorry, babe,' she lied. 'I've just spotted Zac, who played my lead, at the bar. I need to go over and thank him. I know he'll want to see this.' She hauled the trophy into the light, grasping it like a truncheon, like a calling card.

'Oh, cool, yeah, sure. Hey, we should do coffee sometime, or a drink. Can I get your number? I'll give you a call.' But Bridie didn't hear him, had already set off, striding through the crowd, her gaze fixed. She ordered a drink, then lingered purposefully within touching distance of Armstrong, who was deep in conversation and failed to acknowledge her. It was awkward, just hovering there, like she was a child trying to catch the attention of her teacher, but so what? Nothing ventured, nothing gained. Bridie took a sip of her champagne to calm her nerves and mentally practised her opening line.

Another woman introduced herself, complimented Bridie on *Crush*. She was an agent, she told Bridie, and always interested in new talent. Bridie listened as she spoke, flattered, but with only half an ear, still waiting for her chance. Finally the agent moved off, having taken down her number, which was more than Julian had managed, and Bridie dug in once more, prepared to hang around all night if she had to.

'Bridie?' someone behind her asked. 'Bridie O'Shea?'

She turned to see who it was, and as she did a flash went off, a series of them. Russell Crowe being papped as he shared a beer with the winner. Miniature bright white stars danced in front of her eyes, shooting and falling. The noise under the marquee seemed to reach a crescendo; somewhere nearby someone was smoking dope.

'Bridie?' she heard again, and as her vision cleared there was a boy standing in front of her. Not a boy, a man. A boy-man, impossibly gorgeous and taller than she was, dark hair worn long, his slightly damp, slightly small t-shirt clinging to the planes of his chest. She liked his smile. She liked his eyes.

'I thought it must be you,' he was saying, holding out a hand. 'I'd recognise those legs anywhere. Tom Flanagan. I'm an actor. I had a few lines in one of the other finalists' films, but I wish I'd been in *Crush*. That was magnificent.'

She took his hand and held onto it tightly, disoriented, head still spinning. As the room slowed down she suddenly recognised his voice: *Marry me, Bridie*.

Gillian left without speaking to her, but it was no loss, no loss.

Part Three

Part Three

Clare

December 2018

Her blue shirt, Clare thinks, flicking through the wardrobe. There is a lot more space in it since Sophie moved out, but Clare still can't seem to find what she wants. The cornflower blue one with the tiny buttons, the one that matches her eyes. Or so Joel had once told her, and he notices these things. Clare never does. The shirt had fit and been on special, and that had been enough for her, but she can't find it. Maybe her black dress, then?

Clare pulls it from the hanger, fingers slippery. It is loose and flowy, won't give away that she is already sweating, though it is just after nine, too early for the humidity to have kicked in even for December. Nerves. How ridiculous, she thinks, taking a deep breath. This isn't a job interview, or a date. There is no reason for the butterflies in her stomach, the damp palms. She is simply going to meet one of Daniel's recipients. A second one. She's done this before, it was no big deal. She doesn't have to impress anyone, and the recipient, a young man named Paul, had sounded happy to oblige when they'd spoken on the phone.

Clare pulls the dress over her head and turns to appraise herself in the full-length mirror hanging on the inside of the wardrobe.

Maybe it's okay. It skims her hips and thighs, and the loose skin under her arms is hidden by the cap sleeves. Tuckshop arms, she thinks, though she's never done tuckshop duty. Why would she? She has no children, will never have to worry about scheduling parent-teacher interviews or wondering if she can swap shifts so she can attend sports day. Her hands clench at her sides. She would have been so good at all that too. She would have loved it.

Clare turns to the side to check her profile, and there it is – her stomach. Why does she still look so *fat*? Isn't grief meant to strip the weight off you? How many celebrities has she seen plastered over magazine covers, miserable but slender after *their* break-ups? It isn't fair. Nothing is. And the black dress makes her look as if she is going to a funeral. She unzips it and lets it puddle around her feet, careful not to catch a glimpse of her body in the mirror.

Fuck it all. She should be happy. Why isn't she happy? This is what she wanted – to have been put in touch with the people who received Daniel's organs, for them to write back to her and in some cases agree to meet. Two already, and it hasn't even been a month since she and Emma had had their appointment with the Organ and Tissue Donation Service. The first, admittedly, had already been in the pipeline . . . Jeremy, the kidney recipient. He'd been lovely, Clare remembers. He'd welcomed her into his house in Sydney's west, offered her coffee and freshly baked banana bread, still warm. They'd sat at the kitchen bench with his wife while their boys gusted in and out of the room like tiny tornados, questioning, showing, smiling shyly at Clare when Jeremy introduced her as 'the lady whose brother gave me his kidney.'

'He died, didn't he?' the middle-sized one had asked.

'Lachie!' his mother had exclaimed, but Clare said it was all right. Yes, her brother had died, she'd told the child. And that was sad, but wasn't it great how it had made his dad all better?

'So great,' the boy had replied, leaning against his father's shoulder. 'He was always at the hospital or on the couch, and now we can kick the footy whenever I like.'

Jeremy had ruffled his son's hair, eyes wet, a moment so intimate Clare had had to look away. She sighed. It had been like a Disney movie. She couldn't have asked for more, and yet she'd left unsatisfied. Happy for Jeremy and his family, but unchanged in herself. She still misses Sophie. She still misses Daniel. She is still pissed off about Christmas.

Clare steps out of the black dress, kicking it across the floorboards to the side of the room. Maybe today will be different. A kidney is one thing, but would the meeting have felt more significant if it had been something truly vital, like Daniel's heart? Hearts are special, singular. She knows this as a nurse, but feels it as a sister. Clare imagines for a moment meeting the recipient of that organ, placing – with their consent – her hand on their chest, feeling the life force beneath the skin, Daniel's life, still thudding away, beating on and on and on. Or maybe something she can see. Paul, who she will be meeting soon, has received some of Daniel's skin. Will it still look like Daniel's? Will she even recognise it, separated from his body? Daniel had had an olive complexion and tanned quickly. Did Paul too? Would the doctors have even bothered about that? It was skin after all, there to do a job. Paul had apparently had a motorcycle accident and must, Clare assumes, have suffered burns. The transplant was about function, not aesthetics, but still, Clare can't help but wonder if Paul will look a bit like a patchwork quilt or a mended pair of trousers, pieces of Daniel stuck all over him.

She sits down on the bed, still not dressed, disgusted at her own overactive imagination. *Right*, Clare tells herself in her mother's voice, *time to get a wriggle on*. Where was that shirt? She stares into the wardrobe, willing the garment to appear before her, clean and freshly pressed, but the wardrobe is a mess. Jumpers spill from shelves, shoes are littered across its floor unpaired, the underwire from one of her bras pokes above the lip of a drawer. She needs to start sorting it, putting things into boxes. The lease, as Sophie had arranged, expires on 31 December, barely a fortnight hence. Clare will be moving into the spare room in a dingy apartment five suburbs away, the home of a nurse she works with, and far less convenient to the hospital. It's why she can't host Christmas lunch, or at least that's what she's told her sisters. She'll be too busy cleaning and packing, but really it's that she's sick of them. Allison and Bridie, mainly. Emma is okay.

Year after year, ever since the deaths of her parents, Clare has managed Christmas: the cooking, the shopping, the Kris Kringle, making sure there are oysters for Bridie and the beer Jason likes. Sophie complained about the work, but it seemed important, somehow, with their mother and father gone, to keep the rest of them together. Just once, Clare thinks, someone else could have offered. Just once, particularly this year, now she's on her own. She'd been sure they would offer. She wouldn't have said anything otherwise, but Allison and Bridie had announced that they would spend the day with their husbands' families instead, while Emma had apologised and said there was no way everyone would fit in her flat, plus it was her year to help out with the Crossfire lunch for the homeless anyway. No one had asked what Clare would be doing.

Her mobile rings, but Clare chooses to ignore it. She's already running late. Maybe, though, it's Paul cancelling their meet-up, or work wanting to know if she can take an extra shift. That would be handy, with the cost of the movers and the rent she will soon have to shoulder all by herself.

She crosses the room to extract her phone from her handbag. One missed call from Sophie. Her breath catches in her throat. Sophie has rung her. They have not spoken since the day she moved out, two months ago now. Clare had called and called and called in the first weeks, leaving message after tearful message, but Sophie never picked up. Instead she had texted precisely three times: once to ask when Clare would be out so she could come around and gather some of the cookware and linen, a second time to confirm the date, and finally a curt *thank you*. No kiss, no emoji, and Sophie had always been liberal with emojis. Clare had been tempted to skip work and hide in the house on the date they had agreed upon, to surprise Sophie, force her to talk to her, beg her to come back, but sanity had prevailed. Sanity, or some last shred of self-respect.

Lying awake the night of the thank-you text – she never slept anymore – it had occurred to her with a terrible clarity that if Sophie wanted to come back, she would. Begging would achieve nothing; it would only anger her. Clare could almost picture the disdain on her face, or worse, pity. Pity would destroy her. She'd had to get up and walk around the room until her heart rate returned to normal.

The phone is frozen in her hand. No message has been left. Why has Sophie called? Should she ring her back? She's already running late, but it's Sophie, at last. How can she not call? Her fingers fumble on the buttons, her stomach heaves and churns. There is a staticky silence as the connection is made, then it rings once, twice . . .

'Hello?'

'Sophie, it's Clare.' Her voice sounds panicked, ridiculous. She has never had to introduce herself to Sophie before.

'I know,' Sophie says. 'How are you?' Her tone is kind, genuine and takes Clare back to the moment they first met, when Clare had just joined Sophie's water polo team. The coach had briefly introduced her to the other players, then told them all to get into pairs for a warm-up drill. 'Would you like to be with me?' Sophie had asked her, tendrils of carroty hair escaping from her cap, Speedos tight across her full breasts and wide hips.

Clare had glanced over her shoulder, sure that this glorious creature couldn't be speaking to her, then blushed when she realised that she was. 'Great,' she'd mumbled, scrambling into the pool.

For all she looked as if she'd stepped out of a Rubens painting, Sophie had a powerful skip shot and lightning reflexes. Clare could barely keep up with her, but that was partly because she was so distracted. Clare didn't like girls, not in that way. She'd never much been attracted to anyone in truth, male or female, and certainly not since the Joel debacle, so why, at twenty-nine, was she suddenly flushing and flustered when Sophie complimented her on her eggbeater kick?

'Water polo?' Bridie had smirked when Clare mustered her courage and introduced Sophie to her family six months later. 'You met playing water polo? I always thought you might be a lesbian.' Clare hadn't seen how the two things were related, and it wasn't true anyway. She wasn't a lesbian. She'd just fallen in love with Sophie.

And now here they are, eleven years later. Eleven years, ten living together, one marriage, four miscarriages, and Clare's mouth is so dry she can barely answer. 'I'm okay,' she squeaks. 'Busy. Work, Christmas, you know.'

'I know,' Sophie says. 'Me too.'

They are conversing as if they are strangers, not people who have shared a bed for a decade.

'Why did you call?' Clare blurts out, hope, stupid hope, flaring in her chest.

Sophie hesitates.

Clare can hear it down the line, feels the mobile hot against her ear. She holds her breath.

'Look, I hope this won't upset you,' Sophie says, 'but I had an email today from the fertility centre. You remember that all the bills used to go to me?'

Clare nods, not that Sophie can see it. She remembers. IVF on a nurse's salary? Simply not possible, especially once they'd gotten to cycles five, six, seven . . . Sophie had always paid the bills. 'Don't be silly,' she'd protested when Clare had expressed her guilt. 'It's our money, not mine.' But it had come from Sophie's bank account, would never have been possible without all her hours at the law firm.

'Well, I got another one,' Sophie continues. 'For cryopreservation. Embryo storage.'

'Embryo storage?' Clare echoes.

'Yeah. The one we had left. We can donate it if we like, or, um, have it discarded, but there's an annual fee if we want to keep it frozen.'

'Frozen. Oh.'

'And, well, I don't,' Sophie says. 'I'm not going to use it, obviously, but it was your egg and I thought you should know.'

'My egg,' Clare repeats. She cannot seem to do anything other than parrot back Sophie's words.

'Yes. I can forward the invoice on, if you like?'

Clare swallows. Something glistens at the corner of her vision. 'My egg. An embryo. So I could use it? You'd be all right with that?'

'Seriously, Clare?' Sophie's voice is weary. 'Are you for real? You haven't had enough pain? You haven't *caused* enough pain?'

Clare winces, opens her mouth to reply, but Sophie isn't done.

'We were good, you know? We were really fucking good. Meeting you, moving into Hamilton Street, our first few years together – they were the best of my life, they honestly were. I never wanted kids, you know that, but you did, you insisted, so I went along with it to make you happy. Because I loved you. After the first two miscarriages I thought you'd give up, that *we* could give up, because they hurt me too, you know – watching you go through it every time, the needles and the bloating and the endless, awful waiting. How everything revolved around the cycle, you holding your breath, counting the days, almost too scared to move in case you were somehow pregnant and might shake it loose by standing up.' She sighs down the line. 'And the tears! The tears every time the test showed negative or your period started. Tears for weeks, and there was no way I could comfort you, or make it better. Do you have any idea how that made me feel?' Sophie doesn't wait for an answer. 'It made me feel like I didn't matter. That I was barely even there. I'd try to put my arms around you, and you'd squirm straight out of them to ring the clinic and beg for an appointment to start the whole damn thing all over again.'

Clare is shaking, light-headed, cowed by Sophie's scorn. For a moment she thinks she might faint, her bedroom contracting around her as if she has been anaesthetised. She sinks to the floor lest her legs actually buckle and she hits her head. It's true, all true. Baby hunger had lodged in her not long after meeting Sophie, around the time she turned thirty. It was such a cliché that she had been too embarrassed to admit it for a year or two.

No children, Sophie had said when they first got together. No children, Clare agreed, but then her head would swivel to follow every passing pram and her breasts ached when a nursing mother sat next to her on the train. Eventually she'd had to own up. 'God,' Sophie exhaled when Clare sat her down, tremulously announcing she had something to tell her. 'You frightened me. I thought you were going to say that you'd met someone else.' Then her brow had creased. 'But we agreed about children, didn't we?' They had, Clare conceded, but she'd changed her mind. Or rather, her body had changed it for her. The pull to reproduce had overtaken her, tidal in its ferocity.

Sophie was sympathetic, but unbending. No kids. That had been the deal. No kids, because she loved her job and wasn't at all maternal, because they wanted to travel, stop renting, buy their own place. Clare had nodded and let the subject drop, but the yearning never went away.

Three years they'd prevaricated, arguing the issue back and forth, until Clare woke up on the morning of her thirty-fifth birthday and decided it was now or never. Didn't decide; knew. Felt it in her bones. Sophie had given her a gleaming DeLonghi – Clare loved her coffee – and in return Clare gave her an ultimatum: a baby, or it's over.

She'd been good about it, Clare could never deny that. They'd made a deal. If it meant that much to Clare, Sophie would support her, as long as Clare bore the child, was the at-home parent. Clare had been only too happy to agree, had clutched Sophie's hand, dizzy with love and gratitude, through the battery of IVF appointments and investigations. They would use donor sperm from the clinic's bank, they agreed. This child would be theirs, and theirs alone. There would be no third parties involved, Sophie declared, no man making any claims on them. She was coming around, Clare thought giddily. They had celebrated with Moët when Clare fell pregnant after the very first cycle, had fallen asleep in each other's arms as they tried out baby names. Six weeks later, Clare miscarried.

'Clare? Clare? Are you there?'

She deserves this, Clare thinks, Sophie's frustration, her wrath. It had taken three further cycles to fall pregnant again after the first miscarriage, and then she'd lost that one too, this time at nine weeks. Sophie had asked her to stop after that – Clare was thirty-six; they'd given it a decent shot – and Clare had acquiesced, until the craving engulfed her again. She lost count of the cycles that followed. There had been a third miscarriage at thirty-eight, then a wedding when the legislation was passed, a desperate attempt, she knew it now, to hold things together, before her most recent loss just four months ago. And Sophie, who had never wanted children, had hung on through it all, had funded it all, had put up with it all. No wonder she was angry.

'I'm here,' Clare says softly. 'I'm sorry.'

'No, I'm sorry,' Sophie replies, her ire spent. 'I shouldn't have said all that. I'm just worried about you. I can't bear to think of you going through it all again.' Her voice trails away, exhausted, and Clare knows what she is thinking. *You're forty now. You've never yet made it to the second trimester. And I won't be there to prop you up.* Sophie, though, is too kind to speak the words, and for that Clare loves her more than ever. 'Look,' she says instead, 'if you want to use it, be my guest. In fact, you have my blessing. I hope it works out for you, Clare.'

Did Sophie hang up first? Did Clare? All she knows is that she doesn't put down the phone, still doesn't get dressed. Instead, she dials again, a number she knows by heart, and asks Westmead IVF for the next available appointment.

'I'm sorry,' the receptionist says, 'we're closing next week for Christmas. There's nothing available until late January.' Clare's heart sinks, but then the woman corrects herself. 'Actually, though, we had a cancellation this morning . . . yes, here it is. We can fit you in in an hour if you can make it by then.'

Clare glances at her watch, thinks of Paul, but too bad. 'I'll make it,' she says. 'Thank you. See you soon.'

Bridie

'Come on, for fuck's sake.' Bridie twitches at the leash impatiently as John Thomas stops to sniff yet another bush, a bush no different from the four or five he has already inspected on the course of their walk.

She pulls out her mobile, hoping someone has texted in the two minutes since she last looked at it. Nothing. God. Who knew that owning a dog would be so boring? John Thomas needs a decent walk twice a day or else he will follow her around the house whining gently or staring up at her with reproachful eyes but, when she does finally take him out, he spends so bloody long smelling every single patch of the local flora that she could cry with the tedium of it all. Tom hasn't been any use. 'Download some podcasts, Bird,' he'd suggested when she'd complained to him over the phone that morning. 'Call one of your friends and have a chat.' Bridie had barely been able to contain her scorn. Have a *chat*? Who did he think she was, some housewife at midweek tennis? All her friends were working, as they should be. As *she* should be. They wouldn't be hanging around wanting to have a chat with her. And podcasts were okay if she was driving, or, better yet, flying, somewhere, but no podcast can pacify the itch in her fingers when John Thomas is nose-deep in yet another clump of pissed-on grass and she's supposed to just stand there and wait.

The itch wins. She yanks him away from the bush, tries to interest him in the ball she has brought with her. If he could be taught to chase it at least that would give them something to do, but no, the dog is now investigating a clump of fresh droppings some lesser owner has neglected to pick up. Before she can stop him his pink tongue flicks out, tasting the shit.

'Gross!' Bridie cries. He'll probably try to lick her later with that same filthy tongue, like he had when she bent down to clip on his lead before they left the house. Her hand rises to the place on her cheek where he'd smeared his doggy saliva. She must remember to wash it thoroughly when she gets back home, possibly with bleach.

Bridie hurries John Thomas along the path, silently fuming. It's all right for Tom, who is currently in LA auditioning for a movie. Flown there by the studio, if you don't mind. Business class. 'Why don't you come with me?' he'd suggested when her mouth fell open as he told her. 'I could trade it for two economy tickets, or we could just buy you a seat, make a holiday of it. It's not like we can't afford it.' Bridie had been tempted, but turned him down. Tom has never worked with Paramount before, would look more attractive, more leading man, if he turned up fresh from business class without an unemployed wife in tow. First impressions are everything in Tinseltown.

Besides, she has things to do, her own career to get back on track. Any day now, just as soon as she's walked the dog. Maybe, she muses, this is why she had never had kids, never felt the urge: because anything that was routine was unbearable. Children, pets, regular jobs. Those mothers making lunches every morning, doing the round trip of school drop-off and pick-up year after endless year . . . How did they not go crazy? Bridie thrives on novelty, on constant stimulation, and the daily trip to the park is really not delivering. Thank God she only has to do it when Tom is away. He'd better not dream of extending his trip.

Her phone rings and she snatches it eagerly from her pocket, though her enthusiasm dims as she registers the number. Clare. Damn. Bridie has been meaning to call her since that email Clare had sent her, had sent all of them, effectively announcing that Christmas is off. Christmas the way Clare does it, anyway, which is all they have known for the past fifteen years. And who could blame her? Clare is moving, Sophie has left, yadda yadda yadda. Bridie should probably have asked Clare to join her and Tom for Christmas at Tom's parents' place up the coast, but she'd assumed that Allison or Emma would have invited her to theirs. Surely they had. She was closer to them, wasn't she? She must be close to one of them at least.

'Hello?' she answers guiltily.

'Oh, Bridie, good. I'm so glad I got you. What are you doing?'

Bridie relaxes. She's off the hook. 'Not much. Walking John Thomas.'

'Great,' Clare says. 'Can you do me a favour?' Her words are feverish, tumbled together: *canyoudomeafavour*. Bridie can barely make them out.

'Um, maybe?'

'I'm meant to be meeting a recipient today. This morning, actually, but Sophie just called and there's an embryo, just the one, and the clinic can get me in if I leave now so I can't go and see him, but I don't want to cancel – that would be rude – so can you go?'

'What?' John Thomas is snuffling at the nether regions of a French bulldog, who is pretending not to notice. Its owner smiles at Bridie, looks as if she might try to strike up a conversation, and Bridie turns away to discourage her.

'Can you please go and see a recipient for me? He's in the Royal North Shore Hospital.' Clare's voice trembles with barely contained impatience, with the effort she is making to slow herself down.

'In hospital? Why? And what were you saying about an embryo?'

'Never mind. It doesn't matter.' Bridie hears Clare inhale, attempt to steady herself. 'He's a skin recipient. They can store it, apparently. I don't really understand it myself – the Organ and Tissue Donation Service only put us in contact a few days ago, and he wanted to meet before Christmas, but now I can't . . . so would you? Please?'

Skin. Ewww. Just the thought of it is turning Bridie's stomach, which has never been strong. Why would you need to replace skin? She thinks immediately of bushfire victims, of those poor tourists who got caught up in the Bali bombings, of the rows of barbecued chickens at the supermarket, flesh seared to umber. She doesn't think she can deal with skin.

'What about Emma?'

'Emma's at work, I presume. Allison too, not that I'd dare ask her. I haven't spoken to either of them.'

There have been no Christmas invites, Bridie realises. They have all let Clare down. She sighs, swallows. 'What do you want me to do?'

Clare's tone brightens immediately. 'Just talk to him. All of these meetings are two-way. He wanted to meet someone from Daniel's family too. Find out how he's doing, how it's helped. And tell him about Daniel. Then tell me everything.'

'I still don't understand this, you know,' Bridie says.

'I know. It doesn't matter. Maybe you will, maybe you won't. But it's not about you.'

The words are a challenge, a provocation. Clare has never spoken to Bridie like that in her life. Bridie's younger sisters have always deferred to her, as they should. But maybe that moment has passed. They are all grown-ups now.

Bridie stares at the ground as John Thomas noses at her sneakers. 'What's his name?'

'Paul. Paul Rossi. Thank you! Thanks so much. It's lucky you live so close by. You can be there before eleven if you get going now. I'll let them know you're coming in.'

'Okay, Miss Bossy Boots.' Bridie is the director in the family, she wants to remind Clare, but apparently there is no time.

'Good luck,' Clare says. 'I have to fly. Let me know how it goes.'

'I will,' Bridie replies, but Clare has already hung up. Skin, she thinks again with a shudder. Burnt skin, charred, blistered. But she owes it to Clare. It isn't as if she is busy with anything else, and at least now she can end the damn walk.

Forty-five minutes later she is standing at reception at the Royal North Shore, bracing herself.

'Paul Rossi,' she tells the woman behind the counter. 'I think he's in the Burns Unit.'

The woman taps at her computer, pauses and shakes her head. 'No, no, you've got that wrong. Ward 8D, general medical, bed 15. The lifts are just behind you.'

'So he's not burned?' Bridie asks, suffused with relief, and is met with a glare.

'I'm not the doctor. I've no idea. 8D, bed 15. Next, please.'

Paul is indeed not burned, Bridie discovers when she locates him in a private room. He is young, mid-twenties, and sitting up in bed looking perfectly healthy other than a bandage on one fore-arm. There is a frame under the bedclothes, holding them off his lower half.

'Paul?' she asks, suddenly awkward. This is not a situation she has any experience with.

'Hey,' he says, brown eyes crinkling as he grins. 'You must be Clare. Great to meet you.' He holds out a large hand, rough in her grasp, tanned and hairy.

'Actually I'm Bridie, Clare's sister. She couldn't make it. They were meant to tell you. Sorry.'

'Nah, doesn't matter.' He waves at her to sit down, far more relaxed than she is, and Bridie perches on the single chair at the end of his bed. 'Geez, you can come a bit closer than that,' he says cheerfully. 'I'm not infectious. So you're his sister too then, the bloke who loaned me his skin?'

Bridie blanches. She has a sudden vision of Daniel being – what's the word? – flayed, peeled like a banana. 'I'm not sure that it's a loan,' she says, clutching the hard plastic edge of her seat.

'Hey, are you okay? You've gone all white. Want me to ring for a nurse?' Paul leans forward in his bed, concerned, and Bridie recoils instinctively, hating herself for it.

'Sorry. I'm not good with hospitals,' she says.

'Lucky you're not me, then. Three months they reckon I'll be here.' Paul rolls his eyes, but there is that grin again. 'Still, it could have been worse. A fuck ton worse.'

'What happened?' Bridie asks, curious despite herself. 'When I heard it was skin, that you'd had a skin transplant, I assumed you . . .'

'Wouldn't be so good looking, right?' he interjects. 'Nah, the petrol tank didn't go, thank fuck. I came off my motorbike, took a corner too fast. It was a hot day and I couldn't be arsed with the leathers. Hit the road at 80 kilometres an hour.'

'Ouch. God.' Bridie's own skin prickles. She is suddenly intensely conscious of it, holding her together, smooth and unbreached. 'What were you wearing?'

'Shorts and thongs.' Paul smiles wryly. 'Pretty stupid, hey? You can say it. Don't worry, me mum already has about a hundred times.'

Bridie's hand flies to her mouth. 'Your legs . . .'

'Sliced and diced,' Paul replies. 'The doc says I was lucky not to lose them. Lucky too that I was wearing a helmet, and I had my jacket on.' He holds up the bandaged arm. 'It must have ridden up here when I kissed the bitumen. I don't remember. I was out of it for days, thank God. Morphine is a beautiful thing.'

Bridie is trying to take it all in. 'So . . . Daniel's skin is on you? They couldn't do a graft? From your own body, I mean?'

Paul shakes his head. 'Nah, mate. There wouldn't be enough. Thank Christ for tissue banks. The doc explained it to me. When your brother died they removed some of his skin, just the top layer or two from the backs of his legs and his arse, then they stored it in a deep freeze until somebody needed it. Someone like me. They staple it on, can you believe that?' He gives a low whistle in admiration. 'Eventually my body will reject it, because, you know, it's not mine, but in between they'll take some skin from my back, put it in a dish or something and grow it in a lab until there's enough to cover my legs, then use that. The donor skin forms a sort of temporary dressing until then. It's crazy shit! Hectic.' Then he sobers, regarding her quietly. 'I'm really sorry about your brother, by the way. I wish I could shake his hand.'

Bridie stares at the sheets with Paul's legs beneath them, sheathed in Daniel's flesh. 'Thank you.'

'Was it . . . recent, if you don't mind my asking? The organ place wouldn't tell me. Said that was up to you to disclose, but I do know that skin can be stored for up to five years. I did a bit of googling. Nothing else to do.'

'He died three years ago. He was shot.' Paul has been frank with her; there's no reason to beat around the bush.

Now it is his turn to recoil. 'Jesus. That's fucked. I really am sorry. Did they get the guy who did it?'

'He killed himself at the scene.' Bridie changes the topic, forestalling any further questions. 'So you'll be able to walk again?'

'That's the plan. I don't think my legs are going to look very pretty, but as long as they work.'

'What do you do? I hope you're not a professional runner. Or model.' She finds herself smiling for the first time since she has arrived. She likes Paul. Likes his spirit, his utter lack of bullshit. She is glad he has Daniel's skin.

Paul laughs. 'I couldn't blame you for thinkin' that, but nah. I'm a tiler. Roofs, not bathrooms, up and down ladders all day. I read that you get a lot more mobility back with donor skin, more stretch. I bloody hope so. They've got me doing all this physio stuff, every single day. Hurts like buggery, but it will all be worth it. I need to get back to work.' His mouth twitches, a half smile, half scowl. 'Me girlfriend's pregnant. She wants to stay at home when the bub comes, look after it, not put it in daycare. Me too. But I'll have to be bringing in the money.'

'You'll do it,' Bridie says. 'Dan was young and healthy. You are too. You get his years now, as well as yours. That's only fair.'

Her eyes are wet, Paul's as well. It's a ludicrous idea, the most deluded sort of magical thinking, but it is somehow also comforting.

'Hey,' Paul says suddenly, 'do you want to see it? My legs, the skin. You could touch it, maybe. Gently! No nails.'

An hour ago Bridie would have been repulsed at the idea, but she finds herself leaning in. 'Really?' She swallows. 'Why not? If you're up for it. That would be great.' A spark flickers in her brain, ignites. She bends down to take her phone from her bag. 'And Paul, would you mind if I filmed it?'

Allison

January 2019

Allison is planning her funeral. She opens a new document on her laptop, pulls her shoulders back and resolutely types a heading in bold block letters: ALLISON CUNNINGHAM – FUNERAL WISHES. She considers it critically, then goes back to add her title: DR ALLISON CUNNINGHAM. There. That's better. She's worked damn hard for the prefix, thirteen years all up, why shouldn't she use it even once she's dead?

The qualification had cost her all her twenties and most of her thirties, interrupted only by the two years she spent nursing her mother. She hadn't married until just after she'd finished, aged thirty-seven; she had been lucky that she'd had enough residual fertility to conceive the twins at thirty-nine. Still, it had all been worth it, she thinks, hands poised above the keyboard. She loves her job, adores it. She is so proud of what she can do, though she would never admit that out loud lest she sound like a braggart, but every baby she pilots into the world, wet and streaked with vernix, feels like a personal triumph and makes her want to punch the air. *She* did that. She got everyone safely through. If only they didn't have to arrive at such inconvenient hours, or take so long to be born. Honestly, elective

C-sections are underrated, though that's also an opinion she knows she can't voice.

Right. Plans. Location: the church she and Jason were married in, she supposes. St Augustine's, near the O'Shea family home. Allison is not religious, but she is traditional, has no desire to be farewelled in a forest or someone's backyard. A funeral is an occasion. People should dress up, wear proper shoes, show some respect. But she hasn't been to St Aug's for a while, not since she left in a flurry of confetti, in fact. Would it be rude to assume they'd be happy to dispatch her, a non-believer, a non-contributor? She deletes what she has written, types *Crossfire* instead, then just as quickly reconsiders. Daniel had been farewelled there, but Daniel, she reflects with a pang, had not had a choice. Emma's church gives her the creeps. People raising their hands as they sing, probably speaking in tongues for all she knows. Ridiculous! Show-offs. Plus those huge, echoing bleachers – there's no way she'd have enough guests to fill those, even if she died tomorrow. And how would it look in the funeral notice? *Crossfire*. People would think she was being sent off in a nightclub. She backspaces and deletes again.

She'll come back to that. Next: readings. She has already thought about this. Firstly, her favourite poem, 'The Road Less Travelled', which she was introduced to in an English class in Year 10. Okay, it's the only poem she can remember, any other literature having long since been ousted from her brain by the syndromes, the procedures, the entire textbooks she has had to memorise. Still, it's appropriate, isn't it? It is, itself, a kind of epitaph, a reflection on a life fully lived. But it puts forward a nagging doubt . . . *has* she taken the road less travelled, or has she done exactly what she thought she should?

Allison pushes the laptop away, folds her arms and puts her head down on the desk. She is so tired. She is always tired, but today is worse than usual. It is 1 January. She, Jason and the boys had spent the previous evening at a barbecue with their neighbours, who also have young children. Allison had assumed the evening would end after they'd watched the family-friendly fireworks at nine pm, which would have been perfectly sensible given they'd been going since five o'clock, but no, everyone else had wanted to push through to the big show at midnight. She'd murmured something about Martin and Eliot getting ratty and how Marty would no doubt be awake and wanting breakfast at six tomorrow, but Jason had just pulled another beer out of the esky and told her to lighten up, that it was New Year's Eve. *So what?* she'd wanted to shriek. They weren't teenagers anymore. Another year, big whoop. It would be much the same as the last one, and the one before that: work, kids, work, work, school, kids, work. She'd plastered on a smile, not wanting to mar the evening with a fight, accepted another glass of wine and resigned herself to three more hours. That was her limit though. By 12.15 she was gathering up their belongings and calling for the boys; by 12.30 they were all in bed. Jason had followed obediently.

After his late night Martin had slept through until 6.45, which was a small blessing. She is sick of small blessings though. She wants great big gift-wrapped ones. An in-house masseuse, or children who remain in their beds until 10 am on weekends, and only then creep quietly downstairs and make their own breakfasts. Clean breakfasts, simple breakfasts, breakfasts that don't involve honey dripped across the kitchen tiles or the smoke alarm going off because Eliot has tried to put bacon in the toaster.

'Hey, are you okay?'

Allison jumps. Jason is standing in the doorway, still in the boxers he'd worn to bed.

'God. Yes. I must have just drifted off. Big night.'

'Huge,' Jason agrees. 'You must be hungover after *both* your drinks. You should have slept in.'

'I was awake anyway,' she replies, refusing to take the bait. 'Leave them,' Jason had mumbled when they heard Martin jump from the top of his bunk sometime around dawn, and she knows he's right. They're almost eight, plenty old enough to pour some cereal in a bowl and stare at the TV unpatrolled for a few hours while she turns over and snuggles back down. But she can't. She just can't. Part of it is fear: for their safety, for her house – that bacon in the toaster moment – but a larger portion is guilt, the ever-present knowledge that she spends so much time apart from them that the least she can do is be upright when they are.

'What are you doing?' he asks.

'Oh, just making sure all our paperwork is in order. I always go over it on New Year's Day. The wills, the Powers of Attorney, insurance . . . it's good to check it's all where it should be and up to date.'

'Party animal,' he says archly, but moves to stand behind her, hands on her shoulders, gently pushing the study door shut behind him with his foot.

Allison automatically hunches forward, hiding the screen.

'Relax,' says Jason. 'I was just going to give you a massage. Your back looked so tense.' His thumbs knead the flesh either side of her neck, burrowing in gently towards the nubs of her collarbones.

Allison fights the urge to shrug him away – the document she has just created is far too private to share, would incite too many questions – but then the screensaver kicks in and she lets herself slacken, loosening in her seat. Jason knows what he is doing. She closes her eyes. 'Mmm,' she allows, 'that does feel good. Thank you.'

Emboldened, one of Jason's hands slides down her front, beneath her t-shirt, her bra, seeking out a nipple. *Of course*, she thinks.

There is no such thing as a free lunch or, in this case, a free neck rub. Something else always has to be rubbed as well. Nonetheless, it feels good, possibly even better than what he was doing with her shoulders.

Jason leans in, breath warm against her ear. 'Do you like that?' The back of her seat is between them, but Allison knows he has an erection, knows it like she knows the scrubbing-in protocol or the aisle layout at Coles.

'What are the boys doing?' she asks, her last line of defence.

'Watching *Bluey,* of course. The DVD they got for Christmas. It goes for an hour. Best present ever.' Both Jason's hands are on her breasts now and she feels her thighs shift apart of their own volition, the warm seep between them. A small sigh escapes her, born as much of surprise as it is of desire. How long has it been? The last time she can recall was during the Gold Coast trip in the term two holidays, furtively, after the boys had gone to bed, a quick tussle on the sofa while she kept one eye on the door to their room lest a child appear with a sudden pressing need for water. That had been July though, six months ago. Surely she and Jason had had sex since then? But if they have she can't remember it.

'Let's lie down,' Jason murmurs, and Allison allows herself to be manoeuvred onto the floor. Jason stretches himself out beside her, holding her to him: mouth to mouth, chest to chest, even their kneecaps aligning. So it is with marriage, Allison thinks while trying not to notice that the carpet needs a vacuum: your bodies know what to do even when your mind is elsewhere. But then Jason's hands are on her nipples again, caressing, stroking, easing her towards a response, towards a place where there is no carpet and no vacuum and she can't even hear the *Bluey* theme music just down the hallway . . .

She begins to roll onto her back but he anticipates the movement, reverses it and she is somehow astride him, her bra unhooked, those fingers still tweaking and circling, his penis freed from his boxers and lengthening beneath her. Allison moves against him, giving in to it now, and Jason yanks at her pyjama pants, her underwear, until they are skin on skin and she is wet and wanting, guiding him inside. 'Fuck, you've got great tits,' he moans, still cupping them, and she tightens around him at the coarseness of it, at screwing like this in the middle of the day on the floor of her study, at the unexpected basal *want* she experiences. She thrusts herself against him, as engorged as he is, drawing him up into her body. Everything between them is slippery and hot, red-spangled, urgent. *Death*, she thinks, just before she comes. *I was planning my funeral*, and the thought is so antithetical to the moment she is in that it pushes her, convulsing and laughing, right over the edge.

'Man,' Jason says when they have caught their breath, when she is beside him once more, his boxers scrunched between her legs to catch his juices. 'Who knew that checking our wills could be such a turn on? I can't wait until you have to do our taxes.' He leans across to kiss her, skin damp, eyes tender.

Allison reaches for his hand. She loves this man. She forgets it sometimes, but she does. Before she can change her mind, she tells him the truth. 'Actually, it wasn't our wills, or the insurance. I was thinking about my funeral – the music I want, the readings. Who should give the eulogy.'

Jason draws away, the air between them cooling. 'Shit. Why? Is there something you haven't told me?' The skin across his forehead is creased and puckered. Allison notices for the first time that his hair is thinning, ever so slightly, at his temples.

'No,' she soothes him. 'Not at all. I was just trying to be practical.'

Jason pulls her to him and holds her so tightly she winces. 'God. You worried me.' He shakes his head as if clearing it. 'Okay. Your funeral. I know you like to be organised, but isn't that a little . . . morbid? You're only forty-seven.'

Exactly, she thinks but will not say. The same age my mother was when her symptoms appeared, and she died three years later. Then my father too, then Daniel. Death, she wants to tell him, is no stranger to her. She is constantly staring it in the face, in the eyes of every labouring woman she is called to save, in the ashes of Aunt Tanya in the back of the Volvo, in the tremor that had unnerved her at Sake. Even, recently, in her own children. That limp Eliot had had . . . She'd fretted over it for a week – osteosarcoma? A spinal cord tumour, muscular dystrophy? – though in the end it had turned out that he'd simply outgrown his shoes. Still, she had felt death standing beside her yet again, laying one bony finger on her forearm. *Not this time, but don't get complacent.* Of course she wouldn't, she wanted to scream. How on earth could she get complacent with all the loss she'd experienced? And if preparing for it showed that, maybe warded it off somehow . . .

'I just get scared sometimes,' she admits instead. 'People die. None of you realise how many people die. It happens all the time, every single day, and most of them don't even know it's coming.'

Jason strokes her hair. 'Maybe you need a break. From the hospital, I mean. The stuff that you see, that you have to deal with. It's pretty full on.'

Allison is immediately defensive. 'It's not that bad. I'm not an oncologist.' She can't let him blame her job – she needs her job. Her job is who she is. She nestles in closer under his arm, inhaling his scent. Sweat, but the good sort, fresh, hard won. 'It's Clare,' she mumbles. 'She rattled me, that day at Daniel's lunch. Wanting to locate all his organs. *That's* morbid, if anything is. It's creepy. He's dead. Just let him be dead.'

'Yeah,' Jason says mildly. 'I get it though. Everyone deals with things differently. She misses him.'

'I miss him too,' Allison protests – of course she does, not that missing anyone ever brought them back – but Jason has already moved on.

'I actually came in here to talk to you about Clare, about all of your family, before we got side-tracked.' He smiles, kisses the top of her head. 'I was thinking – the boys' birthday, next month. We should invite them.'

'To a kids' party? Why would they want to come?'

Jason relaxes his grasp on her and stretches. 'It was just an idea. I thought it might be nice. You know, given that we didn't see them for Christmas this year for the first time in forever. It's not like Eliot and Martin have many other relatives.' Jason is an only child and has, Allison has often thought, an overly romantic view of large families.

'They don't care,' Allison says. 'They'll be with their friends, running around high on sugar. Plus it's a lot of extra people.'

'It's four,' Jason says, counting them off on his fingers. 'Bridie, Tom, Clare, Emma. No big deal. Maybe Joel too. You might actually enjoy having some extra help with the lunatics. Sometimes it's good to shake things up a bit.' He smirks, reaching for one of her still-bare breasts. 'Like today, for example.'

Allison is about to reply that she is perfectly capable of running a children's party without conscripting her sisters when the door flies open.

'It's finished,' Marty declares.

Behind him, Eliot covers his eyes. 'You're naked. Ewwwww. That's gross!'

Martin deftly shepherds his brother away. 'I'm starving, Mum,' he calls back over his shoulder. 'Can we have lunch? When you've got your clothes on?'

Emma

'Please, Emma, please, please, please.'

Emma fiddles with her earbuds, unsure if she has heard correctly. Bridie never says please, never asks any favours. Bridie just does what she wants.

'Can you please take John Thomas?' Bridie continues. 'He's *soooo* cute. You'll love him! He'll be great company for you.'

Emma moves across the room to her tiny mantlepiece, lifts up the photo frame at the far left. It is the first Saturday in January. She is doing the dusting, not because her flat is dirty but because she can't really think of any other way to pass the hours until the rehearsal, later that afternoon, for tomorrow's services.

'If he's that cute why are you giving him away?' she asks.

'I'm not!' Bridie protests. 'I just need you to dog-sit for a week or so. Tom got a callback, a serious one. They want him to do a screen test with the female lead. He's already left, and I'm going too, just as soon as I sort John Thomas. I'm *desperate* for a holiday.'

Emma rolls her eyes, but only because Bridie can't see her. For most people, living in Bridie's lavish North Shore home, with its pool, its landscaped gardens, its views across the harbour, would be a holiday, like a trip to a resort. Her sister, though, apparently needs to fly across the world to relax. Emma glances around her own home. One bedroom, one tiny bathroom, the kitchen with a washing machine under the sink but no dishwasher, this lounge room just big enough to fit a two-seat sofa and a television. Bridie wouldn't last here five minutes. Still, it's free. It's owned by the church and came with the job, and she's grateful for it. It allows Emma to use her money in other ways: to tithe, to contribute to the women and children's shelter that Crossfire oversees. Possessions aren't important anyway. Jesus never had a mortgage.

'Can't you just put him in a kennel?' she asks.

'I tried, but all the ones around here are booked out,' Bridie complains. 'I should have organised it in October apparently, but I didn't even have John Thomas then! Or know that Tom would get a callback. And Allison's still away, before you suggest that. On holidays, with Jason's family, which must be fun for her.'

'Free babysitting, at least,' Emma points out.

Bridie ignores her. 'And honestly, Emma,' she goes on, 'I don't think John Thomas would cope in a shelter. He needs to be with me *all* the time. Or Tom, or someone. He's like a bloody ghost. Every time I turn around he's there. Often I don't even get to turn around – I trip over him, because he's wrapped himself around my ankles. So I tried shutting him in the laundry for a bit and then he chewed off all the skirting boards.'

'You locked him up?' Emma is horrified.

'He'd had a walk, a long one, and his breakfast,' Bridie replies defensively. 'I just wanted to get some stuff done without his eyes following me around like one of those portraits in a horror movie. He's so needy.'

Emma snorts. Bridie doesn't do needy. Bridie can conjure an entire movie from a script and some actors, but she won't take responsibility for a house plant. She has staff for that.

'Of course he's needy,' Emma says. 'He's been pulled from pillar to post. Ever since he was born he spent the day with Daniel. Now he's been with – what, three different households in three years? You'd probably chew the skirting boards too.'

'As if. They're not paleo.' Bridie laughs, then tries again. 'Please take him, Emma. I really want to go on this trip. Otherwise I might have to lock him in the laundry for a fortnight.'

'You would not,' Emma says, but she can't be entirely sure.

'I'd leave out lots of kibble. Come on, Emmie,' she says ingratiatingly. 'You might even enjoy it. You might enjoy it so much you never want to give him back.'

'That would suit you, wouldn't it?' Emma sighs. She feels sorry for John Thomas, but she can see where this is going. 'Is it fair to move him yet again though? He's only been at your place a few months. He'll be so confused.' And what, she wonders, would Daniel think of this pass the parcel with his dog? Grief ambushes her for both of them.

'You come and stay here then,' Bridie says brightly. 'Perfect! It will be a nice change of scene for you.'

'But I'll have to get back across the bridge every time I go to work.'

'Oh, there's no traffic at this time of year.' Bridie's tone is dismissive, decided. 'You'll be fine. So when can you come over? Today? Today would be good. The sooner the better.'

Bridie looks down at the duster in her hand, at her already dust-free flat. 'You're so bloody pushy,' she says, like a petulant child, like a younger sister. 'I don't know why Tom even married you. But fine. Fine. I'll be there after rehearsal.'

*

Bridie welcomes her later that night with pizza and a bottle of wine. They spend the evening together, just the two of them, something Emma can't remember doing since they were children, if ever. There had always been other people around: their parents, their siblings and later Bridie's boyfriends, then Tom. Bridie instructs her on the care of John Thomas, which takes all of about three minutes, and then they somewhat awkwardly watch a movie together in Bridie's home theatre, John Thomas stretched out companionably on the couch between them.

Emma is busy at Crossfire all of Sunday, working her way through the services – the 9 am, the 11 am, the 2 pm, the five – while Bridie stays at home with the dog, packing for her trip. She leaves the next morning, on Emma's day off. Emma helps Bridie carry her bags to the Uber, then waves her goodbye, the dachshund trotting anxiously after her as she walks back up the driveway towards the house.

That afternoon they take a long stroll together around the neighbourhood and then, after dinner, she brings the dog's bed into the guest suite, so he won't worry that she's left him in the middle of the night. Emma reads for a bit, then turns out the light and rolls onto her stomach, preparing for sleep. In the darkness she can hear John Thomas doing the same, turning around and around, making himself comfortable. He is so little, she thinks, and all alone. Before she can reconsider she switches on the light and scoops him up onto the sheets beside her. Bridie would be furious, but Bridie isn't here. His velvety head immediately burrows against her skin; he contorts himself to slot, like a jigsaw piece, into the crook of her waist. She falls asleep with one arm around him, his heartbeat pulsing against her fingertips.

The next morning, as she prepares to leave for work, John Thomas gives her the eye. A doleful, guilt-inducing eye, then lays his long body, paws outstretched, in front of the door like a miniature speed bump. His message is clear: *Don't go*. Or rather, *Don't leave me*.

Emma, who has risen early to walk and feed him, who has planned to shut him securely in the botanic garden–like expanse that is her sister's backyard, immediately caves and lifts him into her car instead. It is awful to be excluded. She cannot do it to anybody, even a dog. John Thomas thumps his tail and settles happily on the passenger seat, tongue hanging out, almost grinning at Emma. Anger surges through her. How could Bridie have locked him in the laundry?

A sudden flashback, sharp and pungent: Year 9, the girls' toilets at high school. She had been in a cubicle, trying to get out, but someone was holding the door shut on the other side. A number of someones, judging by the laughter. 'Titch!' one of them yelled. 'Midget!' added another. The bell sounded. Emma was starting to panic. She didn't want to be late to class. It wasn't the scolding she feared or a possible detention, it was the way everyone would look up, the scrutiny, their sneers. 'The primary school's that way,' some smart-arse had called out last time it had happened and Emma had sunk into the nearest seat, cheeks burning, head down.

She was tiny, yes. It was bad enough that she was still the size of a ten-year-old when she was, in fact, fifteen, but it was unbearable that it seemed to matter for some reason, that her classmates felt the need to keep calling attention to it. She drummed on the toilet door, then kicked at it, but it held fast. A wet clot of toilet paper was lobbed over the partition from outside, falling with a splat on her shoulder. At that, Emma retreated. She put the lid down on the toilet and sat there, cross-legged, her head in her hands. A meaty odour rose from the sanitary bin in the corner of the stall. Who cared if she missed her class? No one would notice. No one ever noticed. At this time, her mother had been unwell for two years, and was sinking fast.

Eventually, bored by her silence, her tormentors departed, but not without one final assault: when Emma, having waited five minutes, tried to leave the cubicle she found the door was still stuck. There was only a small gap between its lower edge and the dirty linoleum, but her size, for once, was on her side and she managed to slither through it. The handle, she now saw, had been tied to the frame with shoelaces. If she went back to class or out into the playground at lunchtime she could probably identify her persecutor, the girl walking around with her feet sliding out of her Bata Ponytails, but what would be the point? Instead, she took the only revenge she could engineer: untying the laces and dropping them into the overflowing sanitary bin. She hoped whoever shut her in the toilet came back to retrieve them later.

Things had continued that way for the rest of Year 9, then Year 10 and Year 11. The cool girls, the popular ones with boyfriends and highlights and double piercings, had made fun of her because she was short and flat-chested, because it made them feel better, and the majority of her cohort, sensing weakness, had joined in. Or maybe not all had joined in, but they had looked away, hadn't released her from the toilets she was trapped in or offered to help her up after she was knocked to the ground during netball. Hadn't sat next to her in class, or on the bus at excursions, hadn't offered to share their textbooks when honey was poured through the vents of her locker.

Thank goodness, then, that Emma had had music. It was compulsory at the state school she attended for each student to learn an instrument for the duration of Year 7. Her teacher, no doubt thinking himself funny, had initially paired her with a double bass, smirking when she was unable to reach its fingerboard, before pointing towards the cello instead. Even that had been a stretch, but at least she was able to sit down to play it, and when she did, to her great surprise, the first note that she produced as she drew the bow across the glimmering strings was as clear and pure as water. Her teacher stopped smirking after that, his head jolting towards her as if she'd set off an alarm. 'Play that again,' he'd challenged her, and she had, holding his gaze, what she later learned was a perfect C resonating in the air between them like the bell that sounded at the start of a boxing match.

She had sat her Grade One AMEB exam three months later, racing through the syllabus while the rest of the class were still learning what a treble clef was and how to rosin their bows. Her father liked to boast that her musical aptitude must have come from him, and she had glowed and stood taller in the warmth of his praise, but didn't believe it for a second. Yes, he loved to sing in the shower and with the local theatre company, but he had no training, no nuance. Fionn O'Shea was a belter, he valued volume over diction or pitch or any sort of interpretation of the song he was ploughing through, stomach heaving in exertion, face beaded with sweat. Emma, in contrast, yielded to every piece that she played, was dissolved in it, intuitively honouring the music above any thought of performance. She learned to sightread, something her father had never bothered with; by the end of Year 8 she was well on her way to passing Grade Four and had just been offered first chair in the school orchestra. Okay, it was a pretty average orchestra and there was no second chair, but Emma had fallen head over heels for the cello, now taking lessons outside of school as well.

When she picked up her bow nothing else mattered. Music transported and delighted her, it both electrified and calmed. And music was always there, her cello was always there, as her mother began to falter and fade, as Clare and Allison took over her care and Bridie stopped dropping around, as her father became distracted and his songs dried up, as everyone, it seemed, ceased noticing Emma at all.

Emma reaches across to stroke John Thomas, leaving her hand in his fur even as the lights turn from red to green and she accelerates away. She has trained herself not to think about her high school years, to store them deep in a trunk in the attic of her brain, a place she never visits. Something about having the dog beside her, though, is allowing her to go there. She has always been so ashamed of what happened to her, has never spoken of it to anyone, but she recognises now that it wasn't her fault. She'd had as little control over what was going on around her – the bullying, her mother's slow death, her siblings' desertion – as John Thomas had had over where he was housed after Daniel was killed.

Her hand lingers on one of his silky ears before she returns it to the steering wheel to negotiate the approach to the Harbour Bridge. They are both alone. He had lost his owner, she had lost her parents and Daniel.

Still, she thinks, surprising herself, she had been lucky too. At sixteen, reeling with grief from her mother's death and anxious to avoid the routine, ongoing harassment from her peers, Emma had taken refuge one lunchtime in an unlocked classroom. Two lunch hours a week she attended rehearsals with the orchestra; during a third she had a cello lesson. The remaining two were tricky to navigate. She had no friends to sit with, having been marked as a freak since the beginning of Year 9, and she usually retreated to the library rather than risk the taunts of the oval or the tuckshop, surreptitiously eating her sandwiches in a carrel at the back of the building, a book propped over the top of them to evade detection.

That week, though, the library had been closed for re-painting. It had been rainy that day, too wet to find a tree to sit behind on the fringes of the school ground, so Emma had headed to the top floor of the science block, as far away as she could get from her classmates, who were all sheltering in the undercroft. The first door she tried was locked. Thankfully, though, the second wasn't, and she darted inside, closing it behind her before she realised that there were already other people in the room. Eight or nine of them, seated in a circle on the floor, hands clasped and heads bowed, murmuring softly in turn. Emma had frozen. It felt wrong, somehow, to have stumbled upon them like this, so vulnerable and engrossed. She was tiptoeing back out when an older woman, her English teacher from three years earlier, glanced up, smiled and said, 'Emma – it's Emma, isn't it? Would you like to join us?'

So she did. Felt obliged to, really, having been caught out staring at them like that, but also because it was quiet and safe and she had nowhere else to go. They were a prayer group, the teacher, Mrs Case, explained. They weren't affiliated with any particular church, just people who believed in God and met once a week to pray with and for each other. 'I'm not religious,' Emma had blurted out, and Mrs Case had told her that was fine – they weren't particularly either, and she was welcome to stay. Two of the members moved apart, making a place for her to sit and she had lowered herself between them, uncomfortable at first, then gradually intrigued.

The girl on her left was from Year 12, but there were younger students too, a boy even smaller than her with shorts that came to his knees, one of the sporty girls from Year 10, a redhead with acne smeared across both cheeks. They were all so different, but they seemed at ease with each other, chorused 'Amen' each time somebody finished speaking and occasionally prayed directly for another member of the group.

When the library still wasn't finished the following week, Emma went back and they welcomed her in. She had been cutting herself for a while by then, could feel the scabs on her inner thighs rasp against each other under her school dress as she took her place in the circle. It had been a revelation, the accidental discovery while shaving her legs in the bath, how physical pain distracted her from her emotional anguish, erased it somehow, if only temporarily. No one had to know, she'd reasoned with herself. She'd just do it occasionally, and never anywhere it could be seen. It wasn't as if she actually *wanted* to hurt herself, but, oh, when she did, the cool release, the control . . .

The cutting wasn't something Emma ever shared with the prayer group, but she eventually ended up telling them everything else: that her mother had died two months earlier, incontinent and twisted in pain, that her father was mute and heartbroken, that her siblings, all much older, had retreated into their own lives. One lunchtime, stammering, she told them about the bullying too. Mrs Case had covered her mouth with her hand and asked, 'Why, why didn't you tell anyone?' but Emma had only been able to shake her head and stare at the floor. Where to start? It might have made things even worse at school. Everyone at home had enough on their plates. And maybe, just maybe, she deserved it somehow, for being too weak to stand up to it or manage it herself. She hated her weakness, was ashamed of it, detested it. Surely these people would too. Instead though, they gathered around her and prayed for her. One of the girls was crying, and as they laid their hands on her Emma had cried too. She had almost forgotten what it felt like to be touched.

The next week Mrs Case had taken her aside. There was a wedding coming up at the church she attended, the minister's daughter's, actually, and she could be a bit . . . particular. She wanted to walk down the aisle to Pachelbel's 'Canon' – didn't they all? – and St John's certainly owned a CD version, but the bride had somehow got it into her head that she wanted it played live by a string quartet. The minister was a friend of hers, and she knew that he and his wife would hire someone to do so, to make their daughter happy . . . so would Emma like the job? She knew how talented she was, had seen her perform at school assemblies. It would be paid, Mrs Case hastened to add. Plus there'd be rehearsals, of course, and she'd be paid for those too, a skilled musician like herself.

The Canon didn't take much skill, Emma wanted to tell her. The cello part was the same eight notes, repeated over and over, practically a dirge, but she liked Mrs Case and she liked the idea of performing for someone who actually wanted to hear the music, rather than her captive, fidgety peers, so she said yes. As it turned out, she liked St John's too. After the wedding, the minister thanked her profusely and invited her back anytime; the choirmaster swooped down and added that, actually, he'd been trying to get some decent musicians together to play at regular services for a while now, and had so far drummed up a trumpet and a violin. Might she think about joining them?

Yes, Emma thought, she might. St John's gave her the same secure feeling as the prayer group. People smiled at her and made room for her to sit down. No one locked her in the toilets. That she could play her cello there – that she was almost being begged to play her cello there – was a bonus. As was God.

God, she was gradually discovering, could be depended upon. God wouldn't die on her, or go quiet, or move out. God didn't care what size she was. God was a bit like Mrs Case: a bit old-fashioned, not someone you necessarily wanted to be seen with, but kind and always ready to listen. And God, most importantly, was steadfastly there, through Year 11, Year 12, her audition for the Con, through the sudden death of her father just three days before she found out that she'd not only been granted a place, but a scholarship too. Emma wept anew when she opened the letter. Her father would have loved that, would have burst with pride. But God was proud of her too, she told herself. God was all the father – and mother – she needed.

Emma pulls up outside the church, though church is Crossfire now, not St John's, and she no longer has her cello. She is early – Bridie was right, the traffic was bearable – and takes the opportunity to rehearse what she is going to say to the head pastor, Karl: *I didn't want to leave him all alone, I promise he'll be no bother, if he is I'll tie him up outside immediately.*

Karl, however, is all over John Thomas the moment she carries him through the doors, having first lingered on the nature strip for long enough to ensure that the dog didn't disgrace himself while she was trying to ingratiate him.

'Divine!' Karl exclaims, fondling the dachshund's ears. 'Christmas present?'

'Sort of,' Emma falters. 'He's still getting used to me, and I didn't want to leave him all alone. I promise . . .'

Karl cuts her off. 'Of course not! The righteous care for the needs of their animals. Proverbs, 12:10.' He blows a raspberry at John Thomas, who yips back in appreciation. 'Do you have a rug for him, something he can lie on while you work? No? Why don't we get him one of the beanbags from the creche? You'd like that, wouldn't you, handsome?' Karl finally glances back up at Emma. 'Such a gorgeous creature. What's his name?'

'John Thomas,' she replies.

'Perfect!' Karl replies, hurrying off to fetch the beanbag. 'So biblical! He's going to fit in great.'

Emma sets the dog down, trying not to smile. 'We won't tell him where it really came from, will we?' she whispers to him. John Thomas grins back at her.

The music team are similarly accommodating and, to Emma's immense relief, the dog lies quietly at her feet all day while they plan the next service, trotting happily outside to join them when they break for lunch. One of the guitarists throws him a ball for half an hour and he tears after it, hurling himself in the air, darting over Crossfire's expansive lawns like a mad thing. After that he sleeps all afternoon, curled so deeply into the beanbag that he can barely be seen.

'All good?' Karl asks as they return to Emma's car to make the trip home to Bridie's. 'Bring him back tomorrow if you like.'

John Thomas becomes a fixture at Crossfire after that, accompanying Emma to work each day, even attending services with her on Sunday. He seems to enjoy the lights and the noise, eyes darting around, tail waving as he scans the congregation, seated on what is distinctly now his beanbag in the wings. He definitely enjoys the attention from the musicians and other staff – the belly rubs between songs, the treats slipped to him that Emma pretends not to notice.

Bridie returns from LA, but it is tacitly agreed between them that John Thomas is now Emma's dog. Her sister probably planned it that way all along, manipulating them both, Emma realises, but she doesn't care. Neither does she mind all the walking he needs, an hour both before and after work each day. It gets her out; it gives her, quite frankly, something to do beside her job. The church agree that John Thomas can live with her in the flat as long as she pays for any damage, but that won't happen, she knows, because he is always with her, not left alone to chew skirting boards or bark all day. He is better company than anyone she has met online, which she gradually drops, rather than leave him alone in the evenings. He sleeps on her bed, draped across her feet on warm nights, under the covers nestled beside her on the cooler ones.

Waking one morning, John Thomas gently snuffling against her neck, Emma feels strangely, delightfully lighter. It takes her a moment to understand why: her loneliness, the solitude she has carried for so many years, is gone. She has no parents, no partner and barely speaks with her sisters, but she has this dog. Maybe, she reflects, this is all she needs – and God, and music. She has all three, the holy trinity. Really, her life is overflowing.

Clare

2004

'So how did you do this?' Clare asked, bending over the dressing she had been sent to change. It was almost the end of her shift and she was running behind, still had medications to dispense and an IV to check. She hadn't yet had a chance to read the file of this new patient.

'Chainsaw accident,' he replied.

Clare winced and glanced up, taking him in properly for the first time. He was relatively young, still in his twenties, probably not much older than she was.

'Seriously?' she asked. 'Are you a lumberjack or something?'

The patient laughed. 'You got me,' he said, 'hence the beard. They're compulsory in the business.' He reached up to stroke it, the springy brown mass bouncing back beneath his touch.

It was certainly lavish, Clare thought. There could be whole ecosystems living quite happily in that thing, though at least it looked clean.

'Nah,' he went on, as she bent once more to her task. 'I'm a landscaper. Landscape designer, if I'm trying to impress you. Which I might be.'

Clare smiled without looking up. Not many people tried to impress her. She eased the old dressing back, expecting the worst, but there were only a dozen or so stitches along the lower leg, neatly spaced and looking clean and dry.

'I was thinking *A Nightmare on Elm Street* when you said chainsaw accident. This is barely a daydream.' The joke was weak and she knew it, but to her gratification the patient laughed again.

'I know. I'm a disappointment. Girls are always telling me that.'

Clare changed her gloves and prepared to clean the wound. Was he flirting with her? That had never happened on her old ward. She missed paediatrics, missed the children, and had resented being transferred to general medical, but maybe it wouldn't be all bad.

'I was lucky,' the man in the bed continued. 'Stupid but lucky. I was cutting up a tree for my dad. It wasn't that big and I was in a hurry, so I didn't bother putting the guard on . . . The chainsaw hit a knot and kicked back. I could have taken an arm off.'

Clare nodded. 'You could have. Or your nose.'

'And ruined these good looks. What a loss to the world!'

Clare smiled. He was no oil painting – heavyset and slightly balding, despite the verdant growth on his face – but his eyes were kind. 'I'm sure it would have been,' she said, reaching for a new dressing. 'I'm Clare, by the way. How long are you in for, do you know?'

'Joel,' he replied. 'Only a few days, I think, just to make sure it heals okay. Apparently it's in a bad spot.'

'Yeah, the shin can be tricky,' Clare agreed. 'Poor blood flow, thin skin . . . It will definitely scar, I'm afraid, but maybe that will increase your chances. With the ladies, I mean. You can tell them you fought off a shark.' She flushed as she said it. *With the ladies*. That wasn't her usual bedside manner. Was she flirting back? Who even was she?

'Good plan. Or a bear,' Joel replied. 'Given the lumberjack thing, I mean. Hey, I like your hair.'

Clare's hand went to it unthinkingly. 'My hair? Thanks.' Stupid idiot, she thought. Now her glove was no longer sterile and she'd have to change it, look like a novice. For some reason that bothered her more than usual, but Joel didn't seem to notice.

'Yeah, I love purple. It's one of my favourite colours. Right up there with fuchsia.'

She peered at him, trying to determine if he was taking the piss. Fuchsia? He didn't look like the fuchsia type.

'And it goes so well with your eyes. They're amazing. What colour would you call them? Azure? Lapis?'

He *had* to be taking the piss, Clare thought. What man, other than Daniel, used words like *lapis*? Nonetheless, she was flattered, couldn't help but answer. 'Cornflower, my brother says. He's studying fashion design in London, so he's up on all that stuff. Colours, I mean.' She shrugged as if it was no big deal, her younger brother at Central Saint Martins, but her heart swelled with pride. Did Joel have any idea how hard it was to get in there, especially for international students? Maybe she should tell him. As she smoothed his fresh dressing down, however, he was watching her, not interested in hearing about Daniel.

'Cornflower,' he said thoughtfully. 'Of course. He's spot on. So pretty.'

Over her next few shifts Clare found herself looking forward to seeing Joel. It seemed the feeling was mutual: his face brightened as she approached and he always had an anecdote or a compliment ready for her.

'Sturt's Nightshade,' he told her as she arrived to do his observations on his second morning on the ward. 'It came to me during the night. That's what your hair reminds me of. It's a native plant, from Central Australia. Very striking, though I don't get much call to use it, sadly. Half the population want roses or lavender. No imagination at all.'

Clare giggled. She wasn't the giggling type, but it made her feel lighter, somehow, to picture him lying in his hospital bed overnight, thinking about her hair.

'Nightshade, huh?' she asked, fastening the blood pressure cuff around his bicep, being careful not to catch his arm hair in the Velcro. There was plenty of it, almost all the way to his shoulders. 'Isn't that poisonous? My NUM would think that was appropriate. She hates that I coloured it, but too bad. We're not at school anymore.'

'NUM?'

'Nurse Unit Manager – my boss.' Clare watched as the numbers clicked over, settled. '140 on 90. Bit high. How old are you again?' She checked his chart: twenty-seven.

'It's because I'm too fat,' Joel said, his hands going to his belly. His manner was so unselfconscious that for a moment Clare fell mute. Fat. He'd just said it. He wasn't defensive or apologetic, he didn't try to explain. Imagine, she found herself thinking, being able to just own it like that.

'You're not fat,' she replied automatically, though in truth he was quite overweight. 'You're big-boned. You're a big fella, just like those bears you fight off.'

'I'm a bear, all right,' he replied, and winked at her. She had no idea why.

The next day she found herself asking him about his job. Clare always talked to her patients; she enjoyed it and considered it part of her role, the human side of health care, but not all of them enjoyed it back. Joel definitely did.

'Oh, I've loved flowers ever since I was a kid,' he said as she was once again tending to his dressing. 'Don't know why.' He fell silent, and Clare worried that she was hurting him, but he was thinking. 'Colour,' he said eventually. 'Bright things. I've always been drawn to them. I must be part magpie. Like your hair. I noticed it straight away.'

'So you wouldn't have been so friendly if it wasn't purple?' Clare teased.

'Not a chance. I would have demanded another nurse.' He laughed – he was always laughing – then asked, 'What colour is it naturally?'

Clare felt her lips purse and kept her face down over the wound. 'Forgettable brunette. That's what I once heard my sister calling it anyway. She was telling my other sister that if there was a colour chart mine would be Blah Brown or Forgettable Brunette.'

'I'm guessing she's a blonde?'

Clare's eyes met his. 'She is. Golden blonde. The sort of hair people pay lots of money for, but she was born like that, of course.'

'Of course,' he concurred. 'And so your other sister must be too, if she was running down brunettes to her.'

'You're very astute,' Clare said. She liked Joel. He was interested and interesting. She could chat with him all day. 'Yeah. Hers is just ash blonde though. Nothing special, not like Bridie's. She's getting married soon – Bridie, the one who called it Blah Brown.' *The mean one*, she'd almost said, but reconsidered. Bridie wasn't mean, she was just . . . blunt. Frank to the point of rudeness. 'She'll look amazing. I actually can't wait to see her.'

'What sort of flowers is she having?'

'Tulips,' Clare said. 'Ivory. She's very minimalist. They're being flown in specially.'

Joel screwed up his face. 'Bor-ing. I bet you'd go for something much more unique.'

She reddened with delight, then steered the conversation back to him so he wouldn't notice. 'So did you ever think about being a florist, then?'

'I actually did.' He glanced over at her to read her expression. 'I know, I don't look like a florist, though I can actually do a mean bouquet. Nah, I like my flowers alive, not dead. I wanted to create beautiful things that last, aren't finished with in under a week.' He cleared his throat. 'And lest that all sound too gay, I enjoy being outdoors too. I couldn't bear being cooped up in one place all day.'

'Oh, same,' Clare said, standing up. The dressing was finished; she needed to get to her other patients, but she didn't really want to leave. 'I mean, obviously I'm inside here, but it's not like being in an office, stuck at a desk. And there's lots of variety. I've just finished two months on the kids' ward.'

'Did you like it?'

'I adored it.' She knew she was gushing, but too bad. He'd gushed about flowers. 'I'm trying to get a permanent spot there, but they're like hen's teeth. I love kids.'

'So do I,' Joel said. 'And you'd be great with them. I can tell.'

Four days later Clare came in for an afternoon shift and he was gone. Discharged the day before, she was told when she asked a colleague. Clare had been rostered off for the weekend and hadn't known. She pushed her disappointment down, scolding herself.

Of course Joel had been discharged. It was just a nasty laceration. It wasn't like he was going to stay on her ward for weeks.

'But he dropped in yesterday and left something for you,' the other nurse continued. 'It's in the tearoom.'

Clare made herself put her bag away and check in with a couple of her other patients before she allowed herself to go and see. No point getting excited. It was probably just a thank-you card. People sometimes did that. Sure enough, when she entered the tearoom there was a pale blue envelope with her name on it pinned to the noticeboard. The card inside bore a photograph of a deep purple flower with bright yellow stamens. She opened it.

This is Sturt's Nightshade – pretty stunning, huh? And this is my number. Give me a call if you ever want to catch up. Thank you for being a brilliant nurse.

Joel had signed it, his phone number scrawled beneath. It was completely inappropriate, Clare thought, to start a relationship with a patient. But he wasn't her patient anymore.

It took her a few days to work up the courage to ring him. At first she wasn't sure she even should. If they met up, he'd consider it a date, and Clare didn't date. Hadn't since uni, anyway – hadn't felt the need. Sex, she had decided four years ago, simply wasn't for her. She'd been twenty-two at the time. Surely you knew by twenty-two? She'd given it a shot, she'd been out with boys in her last year of high school and during her degree, but it left her cold. It was so . . . messy. Awkward. Boring. Just lying there while they thrust away, hoping it would end soon and she wouldn't get cystitis.

Admittedly, she hadn't had all that much sex – she didn't get asked out a lot – but the sex she'd had was undeniably under-whelming. A part of it, she acknowledged, was hating how she looked naked. Hating how she looked, period, but especially naked. Clare had been a chubby child, then a bulky teenager. A big girl, a chip off her father's block. 'You're made in my mould, Clare Bear,' he'd tell her, meaning it to be an alliance, a comfort, but it was anything but. Her father was fat. Everyone said so. And his was probably from the booze, but hers was just bad luck. She didn't feel like she ate more than her siblings, but nonetheless the weight found her, clung on and wouldn't let go. She'd lost some of it since she'd started nursing – being on her feet all day helped – but she was always going to have ample thighs, a solid arse. Scrubs covered a multitude of sins, for which she was forever grateful, and she never looked down when she was in the shower or getting changed, but still . . . she knew it was there, her dimpled skin, the too-prominent stomach. Why would she want to show anyone that? And why would they want to look?

But, but, but she thought later that night, alone in her flat. She really liked Joel. He listened, he paid attention, he made her laugh. It felt good when he complimented her, noticed her. Not good in the ache-between-her-legs way she'd heard her friends talk about in rela-tion to the guys they were into, but good in her heart, in her tummy. That other stuff could grow, couldn't it? Maybe she just hadn't met the right person before him. Maybe he'd be the one to show her what all the fuss was about. Clare tried to imagine him kissing her, fondling her breasts. Nothing, no ache, but the idea didn't make her want to throw up either. That was a start. She looked at the number again, held her breath and dialled.

They met a week later at a pub in the city. Clare was surprised by how tall he was, then realised she'd only ever seen him lying down.

Joel was large too, as he himself had pointed out, larger than her, and it helped her relax. She felt almost petite beside him as they waited at the bar for their drinks.

'How's the leg?' she asked when they returned to their table.

'Good as new,' he replied. 'Want to see?' He went to hitch up his pants, but she held up her hand.

'No! I'm off duty.'

'Fair call,' Joel said. He took a mouthful of beer, fidgeted with his coaster. 'Look, I hope you don't think it was weird that I left you my number . . . I only moved here from Perth a few months ago, and I still don't know many people. I'm usually pretty shy.' Another swallow. 'But you were so easy to talk to, and we all need friends, right?'

Clare nodded. 'Right.' What was all this about? Was he trying to reassure her that he wasn't going to jump on her, that his intentions were honourable? That was so old-fashioned, but then he was from the country. She liked him more every minute. 'Me too. Shy, I mean. I don't go out much, I'm pretty happy with my own company. Not like my brother. I think I told you about him? Daniel's never, ever home. Says he can't bear it. He's always at a club or a party or God knows where. I don't know how he does it. It must be exhausting.'

'He's the one in London, right?'

'Yes!' Clare smiled, touched that Joel had remembered. 'Though he'll be here for a visit in a fortnight, for Bridie's wedding. I think I told you about her too? They're the siblings either side of me. She's just as bad, can't ever sit still. I think they got all the social genes.'

'Are you going to be a bridesmaid?' Joel asked.

Clare laughed, sipped her drink and was surprised to find it was almost gone. 'Not a chance. Bridie's too sophisticated for anything as naff as bridesmaids. I think she's only going through with the wedding at all because it's a chance for a shindig. And maybe the presents.' The wine was warm in her head, lithe on her tongue. She suddenly had an idea. 'Hey, do you want to come? It's going to be huge. Half the arts scene in Sydney will be there. You can meet people, maybe make some work connections. There'll be lots of free beer, if nothing else.'

Joel was looking at her with his head cocked, lips twitching. *Oh God*, Clare thought, *I'm drunk. I've made a fool of myself. He thinks I'm insane, asking him to my sister's wedding within half an hour of our first date.*

'Sure,' Joel said. 'That sounds great. Thanks!'

They shared a pizza and a whole bottle of red. He didn't try to kiss her when they parted ways, but that was okay, Clare thought. He was a gentleman, she could tell. He was probably saving it for the wedding.

'So which of these people are your family?' Joel asked, shouting a little to be heard over the clamour. Bridie and Tom had chosen a winery as their wedding venue, and most of the guests were well on their way to getting very, very drunk.

Clare scanned the room, covertly allowing herself another quick glance at him. He'd scrubbed up nicely in a suit, the dark cloth accentuating his height and hiding his girth. 'Well, you've seen the bride of course. The golden amazon. Hard to miss. And that's Emma over there, near the bar, carrying the tray of hors d'oeuvres. She's the youngest. The outlier.'

'And working? At her own sister's wedding?'

'She probably volunteered. Emmie's not much into alcohol.'

Joel appraised her younger sister, his own glass raised to his mouth. 'She can't even be old enough, can she? She's teensy.'

'I know,' Clare said, trying to catch Emma's eye. She was hungry. The happy couple hadn't skimped on the booze, but there was barely any food to go with it. 'Hard to believe we're from the same gene pool. But she's nineteen, even though she looks about six, and not into spirits. Except the holy one,' she added. 'God.'

'Really?' Joel said, but she didn't answer him, staring around for her siblings.

'Oh, there's Allison.' Clare pointed her out. 'In the light blue, as if she's the mother of the bride. I suppose someone had to be.'

'You must miss them – your parents. Especially today,' Joel said gently and Clare felt tears rise in her throat. She really did need to eat.

'Yes,' she said curtly. 'Mum would have loved this. The first of us dispatched . . . and Dad would be holding court, toasting everyone and everything.' She swallowed. 'Let's not talk about it.'

'Fair enough. Tell me about Allison.'

'She's a doctor, training to be an obstetrician. Really smart. Lets you know about it too.'

Joel gave a low whistle. 'Okay, so an obstetrician, a film director and a budding fashion designer. What does Emma do?'

'She's studying music,' Clare said miserably. 'At the Conservatory. On a scholarship, of course.' She drained her glass. Was it any wonder she had purple hair? Her siblings outshone her in every way.

'You're an incredible family,' Joel said, turning to her. '*All* of you. And I bet none of them are as kind and thoughtful as you are.'

His tone was so sincere that Clare's mood lifted immediately. *Too right*, she thought. And none of the others had brought a date – except Bridie, of course – while here she was with a lovely man who clearly liked her back. She had that over them. 'Thank you,' she said, brightening. 'What about your family? Are they all still in Perth?'

Joel drained his glass and looked around for a waiter with another. 'Nah. My parents are gone, a few years ago now. That's something we have in common. I've got an older brother, but he fell in love with a backpacker and followed her to Germany when her visa ran out. It's partly why I came to Sydney – there's more work here, and nothing holding me there. It must be great to have so many siblings.'

'Clare!' They were interrupted by Daniel, who hugged her enthusiastically. A little too enthusiastically, she couldn't help but think. Yes, he'd been away in London for a year, but she'd seen him since he arrived back in Australia at a family dinner two nights ago, and again before the service.

'Daniel. Hi,' she said, but his gaze was on Joel.

'And who is this?' he asked with a distinct British accent. Funny, she hadn't noticed that at the dinner.

'This is my friend Joel, Joel Becker. My patient actually, but now friend.'

Joel held out his hand.

'Daniel O'Shea,' her brother said, shaking it. 'Would you like to dance?'

Clare thought he must be speaking to her, but before she could reply Joel had.

'Sure,' he said, smiling, those lovely kind eyes alight as Daniel pulled him towards the small floor at the front of the room. Clare watched, more astonished than angry, as Joel threw his arms in the air, Daniel shook his hips and grabbed Joel's waist, and they were swallowed up by the crowd.

Later, before leaving with Daniel, Joel would seek her out to apologise.

'But I *told* you I was gay,' he protested at her tears, looking stricken. 'I'm a bear, remember? And anyway, I thought it was obvious. Didn't the flowers give it away?'

'I'd never make that assumption. That's just a stereotype!' she shouted, humiliated at how naïve she'd been.

'But one I fit,' Joel said, downcast. 'I'm so sorry. I truly am. I never meant to lead you on. You're great, really great, and I wanted to be your friend. I still do.'

Daniel was waiting in the shadows, had the decency, at least, to look sheepish, embarrassed.

'He's bi, you know,' she told Joel spitefully. 'He can't keep it in his pants. Make sure you use condoms.'

They should have stormed away. Daniel certainly had a right to, but instead he stepped forward and kissed her on the cheek. 'I'll look after him, Clarey. Promise.'

Joel did the same, stooping to hug her. It was both touching and infuriating, as if they were children instructed to say goodbye to their maiden aunt. 'And I'll be in touch. We'll go get a pizza. Friends. I mean it.'

'Fine,' she said, despite herself. 'Go on. Have fun.' As they disappeared into the night she couldn't help but notice that they were exactly the same height. They looked good together. For some reason that made it worse.

Part Four

Allison

February 2019

Allison stands at the French doors opening out to her backyard and sighs. The bouncy castle procured at great expense for the twins' birthday party is still not inflated, a red and yellow puddle against the green of the lawn. The effect is quite pretty actually, but pretty is not what Allison wants. She wants it up, for God's sake. The guests are due to arrive in an hour. What the actual fuck are Jason and Joel doing out there? She opens the door, intending to give them a piece of her mind, then reconsiders.

She is always yelling at someone lately, it seems: the registrar yesterday who dropped the clamp he was passing her in theatre, the unseen driver of the Range Rover that cut her off in traffic, Eliot, who knocked over the glass of water next to his bed as he scrambled out from under the covers to give her a goodnight hug. Allison swallows, damp with shame. Her son, who hadn't seen her all day, had thrown his arms around her and she'd shouted at him. True, he shouldn't have left the glass perched on the edge of his bedside table – Jason shouldn't have let him have a glass at all, just one of the plastic tumblers – but he was in grade two. He still couldn't manage his shoelaces, and yet she'd snapped at him as if he had made a mess on purpose. She had momentarily felt her fingers itch with fury. Had she raised her hand? She hoped not.

The expression on Eliot's face had stopped her in her tracks: not just contrite, but afraid. Afraid of her. She'd apologised immediately and read the boys two chapters of whatever Harry Potter book it was that they were up to instead of the customary one, barely hearing the words, then kissed their foreheads, turned out the light and slunk away. Jesus.

The kitchen, she tells herself, turning from the backyard, *there is still so much to be done in the kitchen*. She needs to get the dips out of the fridge and arrange them on a platter, fetch the good glasses down from the top of the pantry, check that the jelly in the individual frogs in the pond has finally bloody set. She should have made them yesterday, but an emergency hysterectomy had run late and she just couldn't face it when she'd finally made it home, so numb with fatigue that after the scene with Eliot all she'd been able to do was shower and crawl into bed, hair still wet, dinner uneaten.

She'd constructed the ponds as soon as she'd got up that morning, parking the boys in front of *Bluey* to prevent them offering to help, but who knew jelly took so long to set? She sighs again. Entertaining is not her forte. Each of the boys' previous parties had been outsourced to somewhere she could simply transfer money, turn up, take photos and then go home again, and they'd been perfectly fine with that. This year, though, Jason had suggested the jumping castle to the twins without consulting her. He'd shrugged when she'd challenged him once they were out of earshot. 'Why not? No point keeping the place like something from a magazine if we don't get to show it off occasionally.'

But that was exactly the point, she'd wanted to tell him. Her home was her sanctuary, her retreat from the chaos and the mess she dealt with every day. The last thing she wanted to do was fill it with people and noise, people who would expect to be fed then grind crumbs into the carpet. By that stage, though, Marty and Eliot were leaping from couch to couch chanting 'Castle! Castle!' and the moment was lost.

Allison opens a packet of water crackers, tips them into a bowl, then changes her mind and painstakingly begins fanning them on a plate, neatly overlapping the edges. The effect is pleasing and momentarily soothes her. See? She can do this. Clare isn't the only hostess in the family. The knot in her stomach immediately returns. She has barely spoken with Clare since the lunch for Daniel, just a stilted call on Christmas morning and then another, a few weeks ago, to invite her today. She must have moved out by now, left the home she'd shared with Sophie. That can't have been easy. Allison should have called around with flowers, or sent Jason to shift the heavy stuff.

A cracker splits beneath her fingers and she snaps upright, dismissing her guilt. She is busy! They are all busy. And the O'Shea girls have never been the sort to live in each other's pockets. They are too different, and too spread out. What had her parents been thinking, staggering their procreation like that, dragging it out for years?

She opens the fridge feeling smug, extracts the dips. One and done, that was her. One pregnancy, two children. Efficient. Streamlined. She'd only missed three months of work. But Clare. She'd make it up to Clare today, she promises herself, returning to the half-constructed platter. Spend time with her, talk . . . Just as long as she didn't bring up the organ stuff again. That still makes her uneasy and is the reason, she tells herself, that she has avoided picking up the phone. It is all so . . . unnecessary. It makes her skin crawl. Death has already had enough from them. Why give it any more? Allison is not a superstitious woman, but it feels dangerous somehow, to dwell on their loss like this, as if they are tempting fate. Daniel is gone. Just let him go.

'How long now?' Eliot shrieks, tearing into the kitchen with a reptile clinging to his shoulder. Marty ambles in behind him and looks up at the clock hanging over the stove.

'Thirty plus ten plus one, two, three more minutes.' His little brow creases, then relaxes again. 'That's forty-three, isn't it, Mum? Forty-three minutes. I worked it out. You could too,' he says, turning to Eliot, 'if you ever learn to tell the time.'

'I can so tell the time!' Eliot appeals to her, cheeks flushed. They both know it's a lie.

'You almost can,' she soothes, just as Marty scoffs, 'No you can't! What time it is now, then?'

Eliot's eyes are red, a sure sign he is about to cry.

'Still a bit under an hour until the party,' Allison announces, defusing the situation. 'Have you fed Wilbur? He looks hungry. Better go do it before your guests arrive and you forget.' The water dragon appears more seasick than hungry but will, she imagines, be grateful to be returned to his enclosure regardless.

'It's my turn to feed him!' Marty protests. 'He did it last time. That's not fair!'

'Mum said I could,' Eliot replies. The dragon is in his arms now, hugged fiercely against his chest, staring up at her unblinkingly. If she wasn't so afraid of its claws Allison would be tempted to snatch it from him and set the damn thing free down by the compost heap.

'Eliot, you can feed Wilbur this time,' she says instead, placatingly, 'but Martin gets the next two goes, okay? And Marty, would you please go and see if you can help Daddy and Uncle Joel with the bouncy castle? You're so good at putting things together.'

Marty beams. 'I am, aren't I? Like Lego.'

'I'm good too!' Eliot whines, but Allison shoos him towards the side of the house where Wilbur is kept, her patience exhausted. The eternal push and pull of twins. Of all siblings, she supposes, but somehow it is magnified with twins, enlarged to the power of two. Her boys love each other, she is sure of that, but they have been competing since the moment they were born. Before they were born, in fact.

She had insisted on a vaginal delivery, wanting to experience what her patients did, knowing already that these would be her only children at her age. Her obstetrician had tried to talk her out of it, warning that most twin deliveries resulted in a C-section anyway, so she might as well just schedule one in, but Allison had stood her ground. She was more experienced, more senior, and the younger woman had known to defer. Eight hours into it, though, Allison was wishing that she hadn't. Her labour had been slow to progress. She had a logjam of babies in there, her obstetrician had told her almost gleefully, one lying perpendicular to the other. Eventually, with an episiotomy, with incisions in places she didn't want to think about, with ventouse and then forceps Eliot was coaxed into the world, his temples scratched and oozing. Martin, however, stubbornly remained behind. 'The baby's transverse,' the obstetrician had told her, as if Allison didn't already know. She taught this stuff, of course she knew. She'd possibly taught this girl. 'C-sec then,' she'd replied, and the obstetrician had nodded, any hint of I told you so carefully expunged from her face.

Forty minutes later Martin had been presented to her and she had more stitches, as she'd complained to Jason, than the Bayeux Tapestry. Stitches in her perineum, in the walls of her vagina; stitches across her abdomen, just above the line of her pubic hair. 'It's okay,' her obstetrician had told her, 'you'll still be able to wear a bikini.' Allison would have laughed if she hadn't been in so much pain. Still wearing a bikini had never been high on her birth plan.

It had been a good preparation for motherhood though, she thinks to herself as she starts setting out glasses. She had been cut and cut again, sliced and diced, she had earned those children in blood. Before she could even sit up they had been thrust at her, put to each breast, encouraged to suckle. 'I'm bleeding,' she had started to protest, but no one would have cared. That, she was soon to learn, was what mothers did. They bled, but they got on with it. It wasn't about them.

Bleeding. Allison stops, holds her breath. How long since she last bled? It is the end of February. Has she had a period yet this year? The champagne flute in her grasp is trembling, she notices with a separate part of her brain, and she sets it down before she drops it. There hasn't been a period. There hasn't been a period since, since . . . not since she and Jason had sex on New Year's Day. Unprotected sex. She groans. Why hadn't they used a condom? Because they'd got careless, because any such congress between them was so infrequent, because she was forty-seven. Forty-seven. She exhales, rationalising with herself. What were the odds of an unplanned pregnancy at that age? Less than one in a thousand, surely. It was more likely to be menopause . . . but then some women had a last-gasp surge in fertility right before they stopped ovulating. She'd seen it before, mothers who had long since packed away the pram and the change table, had had children finish high school, right back again at the starting line. Biology could be a cruel bitch.

Allison grips the edge of the island bench, heartrate accelerating. Pregnant or perimenopausal? She needs to know. She *must* know. In seconds she has gathered up her car keys, is leaving the house without telling anyone – they're all out the back, anyway – is reversing the Volvo down the drive and pointing it towards the local shopping plaza. Thirty-four minutes; she has thirty-four minutes. Easy. Okay, not that easy, but necessary. A baby would change everything, would upend her entire life. She has to know now.

Allison parks the car, not bothering for once to make sure she is precisely between the lines. Chemist Warehouse or Coles? Coles, she decides, in case she bumps into anyone. She can tell them she is getting some last-minute items for the party. Chips, tomato sauce, pregnancy test. It's almost comical. How many tests had she burned through when they were trying to conceive the boys? Thirty at least, but she'd got those from work, had tested obsessively, manically, in between seeing patients, practically willing the two blue lines into existence. Twins at almost forty without IVF . . . it had been quite an achievement, and she'd been proud of her fertility, donning maternity wear as soon as she began showing, eager to display her bump. Would that same fertility make her pay now?

Allison suppresses a shudder as she waits in line at the self-checkout, fidgeting with her purse. *Idiot. Fool.* One of Sydney's top obstetricians, panicking over an unplanned pregnancy. She is always, always in control. This is a big ball to drop.

Five minutes later she is in a public toilet cubicle with her knickers around her ankles. It's filthy, and Allison hovers precariously above the seat, anxious to avoid any contact with the grimy plastic. Testing at home would have been preferable, would certainly have been cleaner, but then Jason might have walked in, or one of the boys. None of them gave her any privacy. She was a mother, and ergo common property.

Gingerly she pokes the test between her legs, flinching as urine splashes her hand. She's out of practice. Allison wipes with one hand, clutching the warm test in the other, and stands up to wait, glancing at it nervously. All this time, the eight months since her last birthday, she has been worrying about dying, worrying that her late forties will be the beginning of the end, as they were for her mother . . . All that time, when maybe she should have been worrying about new life instead.

She closes her eyes at the impossible irony of it all, leans her forehead against the cubicle wall, heedless, now, of germs. They are the least of her issues. *If I'm pregnant I could quit work.* The thought flashes across her mind, surprising her. Surprising, too, are the emotions that accompany it: pleasure, relief. But she loves her job! Her work is who she is.

Startled, Allison opens her eyes. There is only one line on the stick. If she was pregnant she would be six weeks along by now; there would be, unquestionably, a second dark line. She exhales, feels for the first time the sweat pooling under her arms, adhering her blouse to her back. *Thank God*, she thinks, ignoring the tiny frisson of disappointment that ripples through her. *Thank God*. She pulls up her underwear, smooths down her skirt and looks around for a bin. Failing to find one, she drops the test onto the floor, kicks it among the tampon wrappers and the wads of wet toilet paper, then turns on her heel and goes home.

They will be looking for her. Her family will be needing her. The inflatable castle will be up, and all will be well.

Bridie

'It's the next one on your left. Maybe. I think.' Bridie screws up her face, trying to read the street sign, then quickly makes herself relax it again. No squinting, not if she wants to avoid botox, though she has a feeling that it's coming for her anyway. She stares out the window, careful to avoid straining anything except her eyes. 'Actually, it might be the one after that.'

Tom snorts and pulls over to the side of the road. 'Just give me the address, Bird, and I'll put it in the GPS, which is what we should have done in the first place, hmm?'

'No, really, it's the second left. I'm almost positive.'

'Sure you are,' Tom says, but he starts the car again. 'It's a bit weird, isn't it, that you don't know where your own sister lives?'

'Of course I do!' Bridie objects, reciting Allison's address to prove it. 'I just don't come over to this side of the city too often. Who'd want to?'

'North Shore princess,' Tom mocks her, but fondly. She smiles, not denying it, and slides a hand onto his thigh. The LA trip has been good for them. Tom's audition had gone well, which was the main objective, of course, but simply being there had made Bridie feel better. There was an energy in LA completely lacking in

Australia, a constant hum that invigorated and fed her. People were always working in LA: on a project, on their image, on a side hustle. Everyone she met had an agenda, things to do; none of this *She'll be right* or *No wuckas*. It was hardly a surprise, really, that the idea had come to her there rather than in self-satisfied Sydney, punch-drunk as it was on its natural beauty, all that sparkling water, all those harbour views. A little burble of anticipation rises up in her. The idea. She can't wait to tell the others, especially Clare. Clare will love it.

'You sure this is it?' Tom asks, peering up at a double-storey California bungalow flanked by silver birches. It's all right for him to squint, Bridie thinks. Wrinkles will only add character, add gravitas. He could walk around scowling all day and he'd probably end up on *Who*'s Sexiest People list. It's utterly unfair, or would be if he wasn't hers.

'Yeah, they extended a few years ago. I told you.'

'It's nice,' Tom says, opening his door. 'Very . . .'

'Suburban,' Bridie finishes. As she reaches into the backseat to retrieve her handbag there is a tap on her window, and she jumps.

'Hello!' Emma says. She is cradling John Thomas.

'Jesus, you scared me,' Bridie says, climbing out of the car. 'Oops. Goodness, I mean.'

'I saw you arrive just after I did,' Emma says, ignoring her faux apology. 'I thought we could go in together. Allison asked me to bring a cake, but I can't carry it and manage John Thomas. Would you do the honours, Tom? It's on the back seat.'

'Sure,' Tom says. He leans over and kisses her on the cheek, something Bridie has neglected to do. 'You look great, Em. I love that blue on you.'

'Why'd you bring the dog?' Bridie asks. Her tone is scolding, something she seems to default to with her younger sisters, just as Allison often speaks that way to her. Too bad. Luckily Tom is charming enough for the both of them. 'It's an eight-year-old birthday party. Don't you think there will be enough noise and chaos without introducing a dachshund into the mix?'

'I thought Marty and Eliot might enjoy seeing him. He was their pet, after all, after he was Daniel's.' Emma strokes the dog's head, which is tucked into the crook of her arm, and lovingly smoothes his glossy ears. 'And, to be honest, I didn't want to leave him alone. He frets, and I really enjoy his company.'

'I knew you would,' Bridie crows. 'You've got me to thank for that.'

'Don't push it,' Emma says, and follows Tom towards the party.

Allison greets them at the door, handing Bridie and Emma glasses of champagne. 'Cheers!' she exclaims, though they are still standing in the hallway and have not yet divested themselves of their bags. Two bright spots of colour dance on her cheeks; her Alice band is askew. Bridie returns the toast, intrigued. Has her normally so responsible, uptight sister already got into the grog? She takes a sip.

'Mmm. That's good. Bollinger, yeah? You're lashing out. What happened to your standard Yellowglen?'

Allison waves one hand distractedly. 'Oh, I was given the Bolly ages ago by a grateful patient. It's been in the fridge for yonks. I saw it when I was getting out the jelly and thought, stuff it. We should celebrate more often. No time like the present, right?'

'Right,' Bridie agrees. 'Cheers.' Who is she to argue if aliens have abducted her sister and replaced her with this much more agreeable facsimile?

'Cake, anyone?' Tom holds aloft the platter bearing Emma's creation, which is in the shape of a football. She has been heavy-handed with the icing, and Tom's hands are smeared with red and green.

'Tom! Sorry! I was too distracted by the bubbles,' Allison cries, whisking it from him. 'And Emma! You've outdone yourself! This is magnificent!'

Emma's eyes seek Bridie's, brows arched in surprise. 'It's just a sponge and lots of food colouring.'

'Well, you're an ANGEL. An angel, that's what you are. I can't wait to show the boys!' Allison turns rather unsteadily and parades the cake towards the rear of the house, calling for her children.

'Is Clare here yet?' Bridie asks. 'There's something I want to tell you all.'

Tom shoots her a look. *Not yet.*

'Marty! Eliot!' Allison continues, ignoring her, but when the twins appear they are far more excited by the dog in Emma's arms than the cake she has created.

'You brought John Thomas!' Martin shouts. Or maybe it's Eliot; Bridie has never been great at telling them apart.

'Did you?' Allison asks, head swivelling. 'Oh. So you did. I didn't notice in the hallway. It's rather dark.'

Or you're rather drunk, Bridie thinks, and giggles. This party is already far more entertaining that she had anticipated.

'I'm going to hold him,' Marty/Eliot says, grabbing for the dog's front half.

'No way. I am!' The other boy lunges for the back. John Thomas yelps and champagne splashes from Emma's glass as she struggles to lift him away from them.

Bridie holds her breath. Red alert! Red alert! Liquid down in the kitchen zone! The real Allison will surely return now. Instead, however, her older sister simply trills, 'Oh, boys. You're so silly! Tom, there's a mop in the laundry. Perhaps you could clean up quickly before the rest of the guests arrive?'

Tom looks as though he is about to protest – it is neither his dog nor his child that has caused the spill – but then Allison adds that the cold beer is also in there, on ice in the trough, and he trots off happily enough.

'I'll take John Thomas outside,' Emma announces. 'He probably needs a wee.' She turns to the twins. 'Maybe give him a bit of space, okay? He hasn't lived here for a while. He needs to remember where he is, and who you are. Otherwise you'll scare him, and you don't want to do that, do you?'

'No,' Eliot agrees solemnly. It must be Eliot; he has always been the more compliant of the two. Then his face brightens. 'We have a bouncy castle! Do you want to see it?'

'A bouncy castle! Sure,' Emma says, following the boys through the French doors, still clutching the dog.

'Right,' Allison says, heading to the fridge. 'That's got rid of them! More champagne?'

Bridie holds out her glass. She still hasn't put down her bag.

Bridie bides her time for the first ninety minutes of the party, feigning excitement through the tedium of pass the parcel, helping innumerable small children get their shoes on again after leaving the jumping castle, even cheerfully accepting a sausage wrapped in supermarket bread proffered by Jason from his position behind the barbecue. There's no way she's going to put it anywhere near her mouth though, and as soon as she can she surreptitiously feeds it to JT, who wolfs it down in two gulps, then trails behind her, tail wagging, as she scans the refreshments for sushi or something she can actually eat.

Finally Eliot and Martin are shepherded back inside to cut the cake. 'Happy Birthday' is sung, and the twins and their friends spill out from the living area at the rear of the house to spin in sugar-crazed circles on the lawn. The adults remain behind, shell-shocked.

Bridie watches Allison pour herself another drink, reduced now to Yellowglen. Clare slumps, eyes closed, against an overstuffed sofa as if wishing it would swallow her. She's been quiet today, Bridie reflects. Clare has always loved family gatherings, has presided over them, in fact, since their parents have been gone, but she has been withdrawn and distracted this afternoon, didn't even laugh when one of the guests completely missed the pinata he was targeting and took out one of Allison's pot plants instead. Never mind, Bridie thinks. This will cheer her up. She taps her wine glass with a fork.

'Hello, hello . . . Can everybody hear me?' Six faces turn towards her: Jason, Joel and Tom, Allison, Clare and Emma. Excitement fizzes in her stomach. It's been so long since she did this, stood up and commanded attention. Too long, by far. 'I have an announce-ment.' She pauses, lets the suspense build for a beat. 'Clare's decision, last year, that she was going to search for the recipients of Daniel's organs . . . I know I wasn't totally on board with it at the time'—she directs a wry smile at Clare, intended to convey regret and self-effacement—'but I've changed my mind since then. I've had some time to think about it. I even met one of them myself, a guy called Paul, who received some of Daniel's skin after a motorcycle accident and will probably be able to go back to work because of it. It blew me away. It's just amazing, what can be done, how many people Daniel has helped, and I want to share that with the world . . . so I'm making a documentary.'

Bridie stops, waits for them to clap or congratulate her, then rushes on when there is only silence. 'I've already started the research. Clare got the ball rolling, of course, and I'm hoping to film some of her meetings with the recipients, if they're agreeable.

But it goes even deeper than that . . . There're cases, in the medical literature, of people who took on characteristics of their donors post-transplant. Cellular memory, it's called. One man could barely draw stick figures, but then he became this incredible artist after a heart transplant. When he met with the donor's mother she told him that her son had loved painting ever since he was a toddler and had gone on to graduate from art school. Imagine if whoever was given Daniel's heart became a fashion designer? Other recipients suddenly found they craved food that their donors had loved, even if they'd previously detested it. And then there's a case study of a woman who became a lesbian after she received a transplant from, you guessed it, a lesbian donor.'

Jason laughs. 'That's nuts.' He takes a swallow of beer. 'Sorry, Bridie, but I don't believe it. You get a new kidney and it turns you gay? How can that possibly work? Much more likely that the recipient had been ill, close to death, and once she was suddenly well again it made her re-evaluate her life and how she wanted to live it.'

Bridie is incensed. 'Or maybe it's *true*. Maybe she really was altered. The very idea of transplantation is "nuts", when you think about it. Taking a piece from somebody's body and attaching it to someone else? That's freaky. It's still a new science. How do we know what's possible? Listen to this.' Another pause, all of their eyes fixed on her. She hasn't lost any of her instincts. 'There was a girl in India who lost both her forearms in a car crash. Another man died soon afterwards, falling off his bicycle, and his family offered the girl his arms. They were always going to look wrong on her – too big, too hairy, plus he was significantly darker-skinned than she was – but she accepted anyway. Better to have limbs again, to have hands, than just stumps. Do you know what happened?' She waits, scanning her audience. Emma looks white, as if she might throw up. 'Those forearms not only took, they changed. They adapted. Over the next few years they became lighter, smaller, less hairy – they transformed. True story. It was in the paper, I can show you the clipping. So how can we say what is or isn't possible?'

Jason's face remains sceptical, so Bridie rushes on. 'But that's not really why I want to make the documentary. That's just for interest, to get viewers in – and then just imagine the possibilities. It might inspire more of Daniel's recipients to come forward, so Clare can meet them. Even better, it will highlight organ donation, encourage it. Think how much good it could do!'

That's how she ends her pitch, hands outstretched, flushed and smug. Private gain, public good. The documentary is a brilliant idea, flawless. She'd felt it in her bones the moment it had come to her. It honours Daniel, it validates Clare, it will promote organ donation. It will promote her too, could well kickstart her stalled career, but Bridie doesn't intend to mention that. That is immaterial. What matters is that she finally has a project she believes in and can make her own.

Allison, though, is less impressed. 'This again?' she asks, swaying slightly on her heels. She grips the island bench for balance. 'God. And you want to make a *movie* out of it?'

Bridie bristles. 'TV. I've had some interest from SBS and ABC. It would be perfect for *Australian Story*.'

'You've already approached them? Without even talking to us? Of course you have.' Allison lurches off towards the kitchen. Seconds later, plates clatter as if they are being thrown into the dishwasher. Emma flinches.

'I *am* talking to you,' Bridie appeals to the rest of them. 'That's what I'm doing right now.'

Clare snorts. 'Once you'd already made up your mind. It's always been about you, Bridie, hasn't it? You just do what you want to do and don't worry about anyone else.'

'I thought you'd love this!' Bridie cries, stung. 'It was your idea.'

'To seek out Daniel's recipients, yes, but to speak with them privately, not put it all on show.' Clare is on her feet now, as angry as Bridie has ever seen her. 'And do you have any idea how difficult even that is? There were at least ten, but maybe up to twenty recipients. I've contacted them all, but only a handful responded. Two of those were interstate, and two declined to meet. Refused, really. Of the rest, so far I – or you,' she concedes, 'have met precisely three: the two men who received Daniel's skin and a kidney, and a teenage girl with his small bowel. That might well be it. We don't even know if those three will agree to be in your film, would want to be identified. It's not going to be much of a doco at that rate, is it?' Clare steps forward, fists clenched. 'But you – you've practically sold it already. Sold us. Sold Daniel. I bet you've even got a title prepared, haven't you? Well, go on. Let us hear it.'

'*Picking Up the Pieces*.' Bridie's voice is almost a whisper. She'd been so pleased with that, but now she isn't sure.

Jason laughs. Emma groans softly. Before anyone else can react the twins charge through the French doors. 'Mum!' one yells. 'Emergency! Come quick! John Thomas just threw up all over the bouncy castle!'

Clare

Clare leaves, just picks up her things and goes. Nobody notices. Jason and Emma have sprinted to the backyard, Joel is breaking the news to Allison, who has emerged from the kitchen at the slam of the French doors, Tom has his arms around Bridie, murmuring softly into her ear. Reassuring her, no doubt, telling her how wonderful she is, that she should forge ahead regardless, all that bullshit. Clare scoffs as she strides down the hallway and hopes they can hear her. The minute she is outside, though, tears rise in her throat. She's been doing so well, but suddenly she misses Sophie, the ache paralysing her like a swimmer with cramps.

Bridie, bloody Bridie. She'd sneered at the plan when Clare first announced it at Sake, but here she is, not even six months later, intending to turn it into box office fodder. Fuck. If it wasn't bad enough to have to front up to a kids' birthday party following the news she's just had from the clinic – all those kids, and none of them hers – to then have Bridie drop that on them. On *her*. She hadn't even consulted Clare, she'd just waltzed in and waited for them all to fall over themselves in admiration. At least the others seemed as shocked as she is . . . but they'll probably come round, she thinks to herself. Bridie will smooth talk them, dazzle them with promises of being on television. Bridie always gets what she wants.

Clare unlocks her car and sinks into the driver's seat, but her hands are so shaky she can't get the key in the ignition. Instead, she slumps forward over the steering wheel, face buried in her arms. Fuck Bridie. Fuck Bridie with her big house and her perfect husband and that ridiculous Barbie-doll body. Fuck Bridie, who couldn't even look after Daniel's dog, but wants to take over his legacy.

'Hey.' The passenger door opens and Joel slides into the seat beside her.

Clare looks up, blinking. 'Hi,' she says. 'What are you doing?'

'I saw you go. I thought you might want to talk. I thought you might want a drink, too. I brought wine.' He holds up a bottle of white, condensation clinging to its surface. 'Jason and Allison have their hands full. I don't think they'll miss it.'

Despite herself, Clare smiles. 'I don't think Allison's going to notice. I've never seen her so tipsy.'

'The dog vomit seems to be sobering her up.' Joel twists the cap, the seal breaking with a satisfying snap. 'Sorry. I couldn't risk glasses as well. I thought an alarm might go off if I tried to take them out of the house.'

'Fair enough,' Clare says. 'She's probably had them microchipped. What are you proposing we do? Neck it?'

Joel shrugs. 'Why not? I think the afternoon calls for it. But it's too hot in here.'

Clare stiffens. 'I'm not going back inside.'

'No, I know. It's okay. Let's just get out of the car, eh?' he coaxes gently, as if she is a stray dog he has found on the street, ears back and trembling. 'It's like a sauna. I'm too fat for this. We'll go up the road a bit, if it makes you more comfortable. There's a little reserve a few houses up. I saw it when I arrived.'

'So we can sit on the grass and pass the bottle back and forth like a couple of alkies?'

Joel laughs. 'Maybe. Who cares? I just don't want you going home right now.'

Tears threaten again, and this time Clare doesn't bother trying to fight them. 'Fuck her,' she says, swiping at her eyes. 'Fuck Bridie.'

Joel raises the wine. 'I'll drink to that. Come on, let's go.'

Thankfully there is a bench at the reserve, and they settle themselves on it in the shade of a gumtree. Clare takes the first mouthful from the bottle, head thrown back, and feels herself unfurl as the liquid snakes through her body.

'Oh, that's good. So cold.' She wipes her mouth and hands the bottle to Joel. 'Thank you. You were right. I needed that.'

Joel takes his own swallow and nods. 'They had plenty of ice, I'll give them that. Very organised.'

Clare smirks, retrieves the bottle from him. 'And you're surprised?'

'You're so different, you four, aren't you?' he asks, head cocked to one side, as if trying to figure it out. 'For sisters, I mean. Allison's so uptight and Emma barely says anything and Bridie's like a bulldozer . . . I love you all, don't get me wrong, but you're nothing like each other. And you don't even talk much, do you? Had Bridie told you about this idea of hers?'

Clare shakes her head. The wine is doing its work: calming her down, numbing her pain. She wishes she could live like this. How lovely not to *feel* so much, not to mind the sight of all those children at the party, their tiny faces lit up with excitement, or to baulk at the idea of going home to an empty apartment yet again. How lovely not to care. 'We've never been that close. Any of us, I mean, not just Bridie and me. You're right.'

'Did something happen?' Joel asks. 'I mean, tell me if it's none of my business, obviously, but I've known you all nearly fifteen years, and I just don't get it. Other sisters I know live in each other's pockets.'

'Not us. Bridie doesn't even have pockets, I don't think. They'd ruin the line of her clothes.'

Joel snorts.

Clare lifts the now half-empty bottle and holds it against her forehead. The sun is lowering, is warm against her skin. The party will be finishing soon. All those children will be going home, will be chattering to their parents about the castle and their lolly bags while they're bathed and cuddled and changed into fresh pyjamas. *Stop it*, she thinks, *just stop it*. She tries again. 'Nothing happened. There was never any big falling out, if that's what you mean. I think it's just that we're all so different, as you've said, and there're too many years between us. Once Mum and Dad died there wasn't much to keep us together.' She takes another sip of the wine, more slowly now, actually tasting it. 'Daniel, maybe. He got on well with all of us. He was a link. But after . . . after . . .' A sob breaks from her. 'I'm sorry,' she says, the anguish flaring, momentarily as fresh as the day she'd first heard the news. 'You never really get over it, do you?'

In response, Joel carefully lifts the bottle from her grasp, sets it to one side, and puts his arms around her. Clare relaxes against him. She is safe. She fits. The sensation astonishes her. She never fits. She always feels too big, too ungainly, but she slots inside Joel's arms perfectly.

'Why did Daniel dump you?' she mumbles. 'You're so lovely.' She feels his chest inflate with laughter.

'Now who's drunk?' he asks.

'No, seriously,' Clare says. Maybe she *is* drunk, but it suddenly seems a terrible thing not to know, to never have asked. Shameful. Joel must have hurt like she was hurting, but she hadn't noticed, hadn't cared, was too caught up in her own stuff. What a hypocrite she was, to be angry at Allison and Bridie and Emma for doing the same to her. 'You guys were so good together. Once I worked out you're gay, that is.' The memory still makes her flush. 'Daniel was an idiot to let you go.'

Joel inhales. She hears the breath start from somewhere deep inside of him and holds her own breath as it builds.

'I let him go,' he says eventually.

'What?' Clare twists in his arms so she can see his face, but he is looking away from her, staring out across the street. 'Really? I just assumed . . .'

'Yeah. Everyone did. He was hot and going places and I was the dumpy gardener. It makes sense. Why would someone like me break up with someone like Daniel?'

There is silence. She should, Clare thinks, but she can't. She doesn't know why, but she needs to understand this, to understand Joel. 'So why did you?'

'You're relentless,' Joel says, but he is smiling. 'And you reckon Bridie's bad? It's a family trait. Maybe you are alike after all.' He uncaps the bottle again and takes a long swig. 'Oh God. It's too boring for words, really. I wanted something serious, he didn't. Oldest story in the book.' Joel sighs. 'I was an idiot. It was all there from the start. We kept in contact, obviously, after we met at Bridie's wedding . . .'

'I remember it well,' Clare interjects.

Joel drops a kiss on the top of her head. 'Yep. Sorry about that. Anyway, I thought he was the greatest thing since sliced bread. He seemed to like me too, somehow, and even after he went back to Central Saint Martins we talked on the phone every few days, wrote emails to one another . . . It was lovely. I still have them. I just assumed he was seeing people – I mean, he was, what, twenty-three? And in London, at uni, and gorgeous. Of course he was seeing people, but I never asked him about it because I didn't want to know. I flew over on my holidays about a year after the wedding, told him I was meeting my brother in Europe and might drop in. That was rubbish, of course, and he probably knew it. I just wanted to see him. He met me at Heathrow, took me back to his flat and we barely left the place until I had to fly home again. After that I *really* didn't want to know what he was doing. Ignorance is bliss, right? Sometimes he'd go quiet for days, weeks, but I'd tell myself he was just busy with exams or preparing for his final showcase. He'd always get back in touch again eventually.'

Joel runs one hand through what is left of his hair. 'And then he finally finished his degree and returned to Australia. I thought he might have stayed in the UK, but it hadn't been that long since your dad died, or maybe it was just that Sydney was a smaller market, easier to crack . . . Anyway, I asked him to move in with me. Big mistake. I saw it as some sort of romantic commitment, but he saw it as somewhere to live while he got himself sorted.'

'Ouch,' Clare says.

'Yeah, ouch. After about six months he announced that he was moving into this old warehouse he'd just rented in Woolloomooloo.'

'His factory, or office, or whatever it was,' Clare says.

'Eventually, yes.' Joel swallows, but just air. The wine is gone now, and Joel sets the bottle down on the bench between them. 'So I said I'd move with him, share the costs, and he looked at me so sweetly and so sadly and told me that he loved me, but that life was too short for monogamy and I should stay where I was.'

A currawong calls in the branches above. Clare nestles in closer, her head above Joel's heart.

'Danny never lied to me, Clare Bear. He was always upfront. He never pretended to be anyone other than who he was. He told me we should stop seeing each other if it was going to hurt me, him being with others, but I couldn't let him go. I told myself I was cool, I could handle it, I was just like him. I wasn't though. I gave it a try, and I lasted about five minutes.'

'Yeah.' Clare allows herself a small smile. 'I can't see you on Grindr or Hinge or the like. You're not a player.'

'I'm not,' Joel agrees. 'And Danny was, but I still loved him. I loved him so much, Clare. So, so much. I just kept telling myself to ignore his flings and his crushes, that they didn't mean anything, that he kept coming back to me. I thought if I hung in there long enough he'd grow out of it . . . But you can't help how you're made. I understand that now. I always should have. You and me – we know better than most, don't we? And . . .' Joel's gaze falls away.

'And?' Clare prompts him.

'And I wanted children. I thought we might raise them together, but when I mentioned it to him Daniel just laughed. He wasn't being mean. I think he was surprised. The idea had never once occurred to him, that's what he said – not with me, not with anyone. He had so much he wanted to *do* and kids weren't part of it. Then soon after that he went into partnership with Morgan and before long they were sleeping together, and I just couldn't keep kidding myself any longer. Five years. Five years, it had been, and he was never going to be mine. Maybe a little bit, but not enough.'

'Morgan. Ugh. She's a piece of work. Worse than Bridie.'

Joel's lip twitches. 'Thank you. I appreciate that, given the current circumstances. But yes, she was. Is. She used to sneer whenever

I came into the warehouse to meet him, even long after we'd broken up, when we were just friends. She always made it quite clear she thought I was beneath him.'

'He was so lucky to have you, Joel,' Clare says, sitting up so she can look him in the eye. 'He didn't deserve you, if anything.'

'Nah, it wasn't like that,' Joel says. 'Danny was who he was, pure and simple. He never deceived me. We couldn't have stayed friends otherwise, later, when I'd got over my heartbreak.'

'Did you?' Clare asks. 'Get over it?'

'Not entirely,' he admits. 'It was always bittersweet, seeing him, but far better than breaking off contact altogether. Maybe you'll get there too – with Sophie, I mean.'

Clare flinches. She has forgotten about Sophie while she's been with Joel. The pain roars back, a dam wall breached.

'I doubt it,' she mumbles. 'I fucked her around too. Not like Daniel,' she hastens to add, 'not sleeping with other people, but with what I asked of her. Demanded, really. Kids. I wanted them so much I forgot all about her.'

'You can't help what you want, Clare Bear,' Joel says. 'I couldn't, Daniel couldn't, you can't either. Sophie understands that, I'm sure she does. Doesn't mean you can be together, but it doesn't mean she hates you either.'

Clare nods. The currawong sings again, silvery notes rising in the evening air. 'I'm glad you stuck around, Joel. For Daniel. And now for us.'

'He would have wanted it, you know,' Joel says. 'The TV thing. He was always determined to be famous, ached for it. It must have pissed him off no end, dying before he'd achieved world domination.'

A giggle forces itself over the lump in Clare's throat.

'Plus it could do a lot of good, like Bridie said. He'd have wanted that too.'

'You think?'

'I'm sure of it.' Joel is quiet for a moment, then adds, 'Danny would be so happy if it helped you as well, Clare. Not the documentary, but your search. Your finding him again. It is helping, isn't it? He'd love that.'

Clare picks up the empty bottle of wine, mulling over his words. 'The recipient I met last week – Amy, her name is. She's fourteen, and all her life she's had to be fed by a tube, but not anymore. She has a new small bowel thanks to Daniel. I hadn't even had a chance to tell anyone. I was going to, today, at the party, but Allison was a hot mess and then Bridie made her own announcement . . .' She pushes down her anger. 'I didn't want to talk about it after that. Amy was so lovely that I got a bit . . . protective, I guess. All I could think about was that now Bridie would want to get her grubby hands all over her, Bridie would be the one she spoke to, not me.' Clare tugs back a corner of the sodden label, rips away a satisfyingly long shred. 'But that's petty, isn't it?' she asks without looking up. 'Seeing someone like Amy on TV – all young and fresh-faced and, *well*, it would help, wouldn't it? It would encourage people to fill out the donor cards or say something to their families. And I still made that happen, and Daniel would be proud.'

Joel takes the bottle from her and squeezes her hand. Clare cries once more, but not for long. The sun is going down in a flurry of gold and red and lilac, and she doesn't want to miss it.

Emma

'Thank you, Emma,' Jason says for about the tenth time. 'Honestly, you've been fantastic. I really appreciate it. Al will too when she wakes up. Do you want me to walk you out to the car?'

'No, it's fine. It's barely dark. And I've got John Thomas to protect me, don't I?' She scoops up the dog and scratches him under the chin.

'He still looks a bit green,' Jason says dubiously. 'For a black dog, that is. Do you want to take an old towel to put down on the seat, just in case?'

'I think it's all out of his system now,' Emma says. 'Maybe save it for your wife.' It's not like her, to make a joke at somebody else's expense, but she can't resist. She has never seen her big sister – her biggest sister – even tipsy before, never mind had to hold her hair back while she threw up. Emma wonders if she's gone too far, but Jason laughs.

'Hopefully she's got it out of her system too. God, she hasn't done that in years. Not since we were dating.' His face is wistful. 'It was kind of nice to see, actually, her all giggly and carefree like that, at least before the vomitathon. Can't believe she chose the boys' birthday party to get pissed at, though. What's that all about?'

He looks to Emma as if she might have the answer, but she shakes her head. Her sisters are a mystery to her. Where had they even gone, Bridie and Clare? One moment they were all standing together, hearing Bridie outline her documentary plans, the next John Thomas had been sick. She'd rushed outside to take care of him and when she returned the living room was empty, Bridie, Tom, Clare and Joel as absent as if they'd been vaporised.

'Thank God you stuck around,' Jason says, as if reading her mind. 'I couldn't have faced the clean-up myself, plus getting the boys into bed. You were fantastic with them. Why haven't we had you over to babysit?'

Emma laughs. 'Because you've never asked, maybe?' She'd enjoyed it too, she wanted to add, but was that a bit pathetic, admitting that dealing with two eight-year-olds, admiring their presents, supervising their teeth-brushing and reading them a story had been the best Saturday night that she'd had in months?

'And maybe because we never go out,' Jason says. 'But perhaps we should, give Allison a chance to let her hair down more often. Do you think you'd want to if we did? Sit for us, I mean.'

'I'd love to,' Emma says. She has never really thought about having children – she doesn't have a boyfriend, never mind a husband, so it's cart before the horse stuff – but as she'd gazed at Eliot and Martin once they'd finally fallen asleep, Marty with a football tucked under one arm, she'd felt an unexpected twinge. How lovely it must be to have a family. Maybe, she considers, she should give online dating another try. It is tedious and humiliating, but how else will she ever have this – somewhere she is loved, somewhere people need her and notice when she is gone? Things like that don't just fall from the sky.

John Thomas squirms in her arms and she lifts him against her shoulder, patting his back. 'Better get this one home,' she says. 'He's had a big day.'

'Haven't we all?' Jason rolls his eyes. 'Sure you don't want me to walk you out?'

Emma fishes in her handbag for her keys. 'No, honestly, my car is just up the street. Stay with the twins and Allison. Give her my love in the morning.'

'Sure,' Jason says. 'I will. And aspirin.'

Emma is almost at her car when a figure looms out of the darkness and onto the pavement in front of her. Alarmed, she drops her keys and tightens her grasp on John Thomas, unsure if it is her heartbeat or his she feels accelerating.

'Emma?' a voice says. 'Is that you?'

'Clare!' she replies, relieved. 'You gave me a fright. I thought you went home ages ago.'

'I've been talking with Joel,' Clare says. 'He just left, and I was about to. What are you still doing here? The party must have been over for a while.'

'I stayed to help Jason,' Emma says. 'All the rest of you had gone, and Allison was a bit out of sorts.' She crouches down to retrieve her keys, placing the dog on the nature strip.

Clare is immediately beside her, seating herself on the gutter. 'Seriously?' she asks. 'How out of sorts? Tell me all about it!' She tugs at Emma's arm, pulling her next to her.

Clare, Emma realises, is a little tipsy. It's clearly the night for it. 'You would have seen if you'd stayed,' she says waspishly.

Clare ignores her. 'Did she chuck? Please tell me she chucked.'

Emma smiles. She can't help it. 'Yeah, she chucked. In her ensuite, though, not in front of the kids, fortunately.'

'God, that would have been great though, wouldn't it? All over those perfectly tended rose bushes. *Bluuuuurgh!*' Clare hugs herself. 'A lasting memory for the lucky guests. What happened? Was it the dog vomit that set her off?'

'Nah, she coped with that pretty well. Made Jason hose it off the bouncy castle, but then all the kids piled back on it while it was still wet. It was like a gigantic Slip 'N Slide. They were all careening off each other into the walls and out onto the grass and Allison was yelling at them to stop, that someone was going to break something, but no one was listening, just getting up and throwing themselves back on again.'

Clare wheezes with laughter, tears in her eyes. 'Fuck, that's funny. I wish I'd seen it. She must have been having conniptions.'

Emma relaxes against her, pulls John Thomas into her lap. It doesn't look like they're going home just yet. 'Her eyes were almost spinning in their sockets. The boys were like human pinballs, hurtling into each other, then bouncing off. It must have made her dizzy just watching them, because she suddenly started gagging and raced inside.'

Clare hoots with delight. 'I thought she was a few sheets to the wind.'

'Yeah, she was. She didn't go back out after that, just took herself to bed with a bucket.'

Clare wipes her eyes. 'And here was I thinking that a children's birthday party was going to be boring.'

'Nothing boring about today,' Emma says.

A hush falls between them; the easy camaraderie is lost.

'Listen,' Emma ventures as the silence lengthens. 'What you're doing, looking for Daniel's recipients – you know I'll help you, don't you? I haven't really been involved since that first meeting with the

Organ and Tissue Donation Service because of work, and, well, because you haven't asked me, and that's your call of course . . .' She is rambling, she thinks, and forces herself to slow down. 'I just wanted to make sure you know that I think it's wonderful. I'm on your side.' Emma takes a deep breath, proceeds with caution. She does not like conflict, usually distances herself from it, but she's been thinking about this all afternoon as she cleaned up the party leftovers and held back Allison's hair, and if conflict is necessary, so be it. 'What Bridie suggested today – I can see why she wants to do it. But I also get that this is personal, that it's your thing. If you want to keep it private you should.'

Clare turns to her, face pale in the gloom. 'What are you saying?'

'I'm saying that if you don't want her to make the show, the documentary, she shouldn't. I'll back you up. I'll tell her not to.'

Clare's eyes glisten. 'Wow,' she whispers. 'The mouse who roared. Thank you, Emma. That means a lot.' Then she looks away and stares down at the road. 'I probably shouldn't have taken it so hard,' she says finally. 'That's what I was talking with Joel about, but he thinks it should go ahead. He thinks Daniel would have wanted it, and that's the bottom line, really, isn't it? Not me. Not what I want.' She sighs, the force of the exhalation ruffling John Thomas's fur. 'It just got to me how Bridie does whatever she likes without thinking about anyone else. And I was already in a bad mood.'

The statement hangs in the air between them, a question begging to be asked.

'You were?' Emma delves gently. Feelings. They never talk about feelings. 'Why?'

Clare sighs again, reaches for the dog. 'May I?' she asks.

Emma nods, and Clare transfers John Thomas onto her lap, caressing his ears. He barely stirs.

'I miss him,' she says. 'Even more since Sophie left. I never wanted him to go to Allison's. If I'd known Soph was going to dump me I might have got in first, then at least I could have kept him.'

'Maybe we could share him,' Emma suggests bravely, but Clare shakes her head.

'No pets in the flat. Plus he's your dog now. But thank you. That was kind of you.'

Their eyes meet. Emma watches as Clare swallows, looks away again, then suddenly blurts out, 'The clinic . . . I had an appointment yesterday. I was meant to be starting a cycle, but one of the doctors came in to talk to me. She wanted me to think about it, said that with my history it probably isn't a good idea. She told me'—Clare makes air quotes—'that I might just be washing it down the drain.'

'Washing what? What clinic?'

'IVF,' Clare mumbles.

'I don't understand,' Emma says. 'Who was doing IVF?'

'We were,' Clare replies wretchedly. 'Sophie and I, before we split up. Ten cycles, all up, and some of them took, but none of them stuck.'

'Meaning?' Emma asks. She is struggling to keep up.

'Meaning that every time I got pregnant it would all be okay for a few weeks – for six, or even eight weeks – but then I'd miscarry. Every single time, like clockwork, one after the other after the other. I never once made it out of the first trimester.' Clare's fingers are twined around the dachshund's ears, squeezing and releasing. John Thomas wakes up and shakes his head in protest.

'You were trying to have a baby?'

Clare snorts. 'Yep. A baby. Or babies. Hence the IVF.'

'Sorry,' Emma says. 'It's just . . . I just, I didn't know. Why didn't you tell me? Tell us?' She puts her hand on Clare's forearm and finds it is trembling.

'I don't know.' Clare pauses, thinking it through. 'The first time we agreed that we'd wait and announce it at twelve weeks, like you're supposed to, when it's safe.' Air quotes again. 'When I lost that one there didn't seem much point telling anyone. It was gone; why announce it? And we started trying again almost straight away. I got pregnant after about six months, but then when we lost that one too Sophie wanted us to stop, to put it behind us. It was never her idea, the children thing. She only did it for me.'

'So you used donor sperm? And it was always you who was going to carry the child, not Sophie?'

Clare nods. 'Yes. Donor sperm, my eggs, my womb. We were both going to be the parents, of course, but I was going to be the stay-at-home mum. Sophie couldn't take the time off work, not even for the pregnancy and having the actual baby. She didn't want to, anyway, and I did. I loved being pregnant, even when it was only for a month and I was sick every morning. It felt like I was doing something I was meant to be doing.'

'Oh, Clare.' Emma reaches for her hand. 'That must have been awful. I'm so sorry. I wish you'd told me.'

'Why?' Clare asks, pulling away, relentlessly stroking John Thomas once more. 'It wouldn't have made any difference. I still would have lost them.'

'But you tried again? Did anyone know? Bridie? Allison? Any of your friends?'

'Only Sophie. I thought about asking Allison for advice – it's her area, isn't it? Not IVF, but babies and the having of them – but it took me two years to talk Sophie into the next attempt. To nag her into it.' She shakes her head ruefully. 'And that one barely lasted a fortnight. It was heartbreaking, and it was embarrassing. I felt like such a failure. I couldn't bear the idea that Allison might think so too.'

'Oh, she would never—' Emma begins, but Clare cuts her off.

'Then I turned forty, last year, and time was really running out, so we had another go. It was our tenth attempt. I was sure it would be the charm, that the universe would see how desperate I was and take pity on me.' She laughs mirthlessly. 'Same outcome, except with the added bonus of Sophie getting jack of it all and moving out. There was still one embryo in storage, though, leftover from a previous cycle, and she said I could use it. I met with the clinic just before Christmas, and we organised that I'd start the meds as soon as I got my period. Well, all the stress of the move must have delayed things, but I finally got it Thursday night, so I went in yesterday for the blood tests and to collect them, but there was a new specialist, a woman I hadn't met before, and she pretty much told me that I was wasting my time. That I was too old, too overweight, that my body had already shown it couldn't do it. She suggested I look into surrogacy instead if I was that determined to use the embryo.' Clare's voice wavers. She leans forward and buries her face in John Thomas's scruff. 'But surrogates are so hard to find. You can't pay them, you're not even allowed to advertise for one . . .'

She is weeping, Clare is weeping, and Emma reaches out to rub her back. The gesture is intended to comfort, nothing more, but as she lays hands on her sister an idea occurs to her, an idea so pure, so *right*, that it can only be divine.

'I'll do it,' Emma says. 'I'll be your surrogate.'

Emma

2011

The first bouquet had arrived for her on the opening night of *La Bohème*. It was beautiful, if a little conventional: six red roses arranged in a haze of baby's breath, their buds only recently unfurled.

'Pretty!' Liu exclaimed as Emma, blushing, took delivery at the dressing room door. 'Who are they from?'

'I don't know,' Emma said, setting them down on her seat to hunt through the foliage for a card. 'Probably my brother.' Daniel had sent her flowers on the opening night of her very first event with the orchestra of the Melbourne Opera, almost two years ago now. Gerberas, she recalled, clashing pink and orange and trembling with vivacity. She had been trembling too, about to take her place in the pit with the other cellists for *Cavalleria Rusticana*, almost sick with nerves, terrified she'd muck it up and be sent home in disgrace. She hadn't though. She'd got through, even enjoying herself by the final pages of the score, and when the orchestra had taken their bows and returned backstage the first thing she had done was ring him. 'That was so lovely,' she'd told him. 'No one else remembered.'

'I'm sure they did,' Daniel had soothed her. 'They just forgot to do anything about it.'

A spray of irises and tiger lilies were delivered on the first night of *I Pagliacci* four months later, then an enormous bunch of hydrangeas for *Madame Butterfly* at the end of the year, their purple heads so heavy they sagged on the stems. Daniel again, both times, the cards attached bearing simply his name and a line of crosses. He'd fallen out of the habit since then, hadn't sent anything for at least eighteen months. And fair enough too, Emma thought, extracting a white envelope from between two roses. It was her job now, playing with the MOO, not the grand and terrifying undertaking it had been when she first left Sydney. So why had he started sending flowers again? Roses weren't even his style.

'Good luck tonight, Bella.' Liu read the card aloud over her shoulder.

Emma quickly crumpled it in her hand, flushing anew. 'It's a mistake,' she said, humiliated. 'They're not for me.'

'What do you mean?' Liu asked. 'Of course they are! The courier called out your name, didn't he?'

'Which isn't Bella,' Emma said. She strode to the corner of the dressing room and dropped the card in a bin.

Liu ran after her and fished it out, laughing. 'It means "beautiful", you stupid girl.' She smoothed out the paper, studying it as she did so. 'And it isn't signed! You have a secret admirer.'

The concertmaster appeared in the doorway. 'Five minutes,' he called over the clamour.

'I doubt it,' Emma mumbled. Liu was right, she *was* stupid. How was everyone she knew so easy in the world, while for Emma it was a constant surprise, a perpetual battle?

Liu squeezed her shoulder. 'Ah, my sweet little *naif*,' she said, though Emma was only a few years younger than her. 'You're such an innocent. I love that about you. Do you still think the roses were from your brother?'

Emma shook her head, colour rising once more to her face.

'Keep blushing like that and your toes will drop off from lack of circulation,' Liu said, gathering up her instrument. 'So who was it then? Any ideas?'

'None at all,' Emma replied, her own cello in hand, following her friend out into the wings. 'Seriously. None.' Who else, other than Daniel, would want to send her flowers?

More flowers arrived on closing night a few weeks later. Pink roses this time, full blown and blowsy, already waiting on her chair, the most junior of the cello section, when she filed into the pit. Liu nudged her, eyes delighted, and Emma shoved them quickly under her seat so she could take her place before anyone else noticed. She was distracted all through tuning. How had they got there? No courier or delivery boy would be allowed in the theatre. And was there a note again? Surely they were from the same person. She slid one heel back to check they were real, that she hadn't dreamed them up, and was rewarded with the rustle of tissue paper. The bassoonist next to her frowned and Emma immediately straightened and readied her bow. Was it just her imagination, or was the conductor staring straight at her? She prayed he hadn't heard too, that he didn't think she was distracted, wasn't in every way prepared for the journey they would take together over the next few hours. So focused was she from then on that at the end of the performance Liu had to remind her to retrieve the bouquet.

No more blooms appeared over the next few weeks, which were taken up with a regional tour of the Bellarine Peninsula and then rehearsals for the orchestra's next collaboration with the Melbourne Opera. The second set of roses had not contained a card and in the flurry of the tour, together with learning her part for *Carmen,* Emma gradually forgot about them. She did note, though, that she was feeling lighter, more settled. The move down to Melbourne had been difficult, had challenged her in every way, but maybe, she thought, it was finally paying off. Professionally, of course, it had been nothing but a blessing. After finishing her degree at the Con she had freelanced for the next few years, picking up casual positions in orchestras whose cellists were sick, pregnant or in rehab, patiently bowing her way through Pachelbel's 'Canon' at more weddings than she cared to remember. She'd attended auditions too, dozens of them: the Sydney Symphony Orchestra, Opera Australia, Sydney Youth Orchestra – anywhere, basically, that would listen to her play. And she'd been offered nothing until Daniel encouraged her to cast her net wider, to look beyond her hometown. When the email had landed from the Melbourne Opera Orchestra, her first impulse had been to suspect that someone was tricking her. A proper orchestra. A real repertoire. Farewell Pachelbel! It would mean black dresses and opening nights and her name in the program, but far more importantly, she would take her seat among serious musicians; she would learn, she would improve, she would be mentored and nurtured, and one day, maybe, she would be a serious musician too.

'Melbourne?' Bridie had asked when Emma told her the news, screwing up her nose and peering at her as if she were suddenly a stranger. 'God. Wow. All by yourself? Do you think you're up to it?'

Emma had drawn herself up to her full height – which, admittedly, was only somewhere around Bridie's irritatingly impressive rack – and replied that she was twenty-four, not fourteen, and it was an important career move. Besides, she'd added, it wasn't as if she was jetting off to Vienna or Prague. She would only be an hour's flight away. How hard could it be?

Very hard, as it turned out. Emma had visited Melbourne twice before, as a child on a family holiday and to audition for the MOO, but those trips had in no way prepared her for actually moving to the city. There was so much, she quickly realised, that she simply had no clue about: how to find a rental, having previously lived in university accommodation or the spare rooms of her fellow students' sharehouses; which suburbs she should be looking at; how to use the public transport. Trams, especially, frightened her, the way they rang their bells so aggressively if you were anywhere near the tracks, the agony of knowing you had to signal your stop and being so frightened of getting it wrong that whenever she did she disembarked anyway, just for show. Emma couldn't find tangelos at the supermarket and didn't know to check the forecast before leaving home, no matter that it looked sunny enough. Especially if it looked sunny enough. The MOO performed at the Athenaeum Theatre in Collins Street but frequently held its sectional rehearsals off-site – at the Arts Centre or over at Southbank, sometimes at the VCA, and Emma seemed to spend her first weeks turning up at the wrong place or desperately hailing taxis to get her and her cello somewhere on time. She was lonely. Oh, she was so lonely. She had always felt herself to be a solitary creature, by circumstance if not choice – that missing playmate, the high school years, her parents' deaths – but at least in Sydney she'd had her siblings, had people she knew from the Con, from St John's, from the various quartets she subbed in and out of. In Melbourne she knew no one, could go whole days without speaking a word. Anxiety coiled in her gut, pressed down upon her as she lay in bed, like an animal crouching on her chest. If she died in the night would anyone miss her? How long would it take them to find her body? Her sisters called sporadically in the first month after she moved and Daniel sent his flowers, but they were not a family who lived in each other's pockets, who were constantly in touch. After a while the calls dried up and Emma wondered if she might too, just evaporate into the ether, leaving no trace.

Thank goodness, then, for Liu. She had returned to the MOO seven months after Emma had commenced there, having completed a year on an exchange program with the Orchestra di Padova e del Veneto in Italy, and just as Emma was wondering if she could endure a single day longer in Melbourne. Liu was a local and liked to talk. She took the chair next to Emma's, whose previous occupant had been the other half of the exchange, a solemn girl who had never once said a word to Emma, or indeed anyone. Emma had assumed it was because the Italian was a far more proficient performer than she was and had thought Emma was beneath her, but she realised with hindsight that maybe the girl simply didn't speak English very well. How awful, she'd reflected, to not only be away from home, but unable to understand the language either, an alien in all senses of the word.

'How could you bear it?' she'd blurted out to Liu not long after they'd met, and Liu had looked at her and laughed but then very distinctly taken Emma under her wing. She'd shown her the city – her favourite dumpling bar in Market Lane, the best op-shops in Fitzroy, the cycling trails out along the Yarra past the Convent and the Children's Farm. Liu, it transpired, was the key to unlocking the whole cello section, constantly inviting the other five members to drinks after performances or barbecues in the Museum gardens near her flat in Carlton.

Gradually, wonderfully, Emma felt herself uncurling. The other cellists smiled and asked her how her weekend was at Monday rehearsals; the lead, Percy, invited her to his home for dinner and to meet his wife and children. Emma plucked up the courage and joined a church in Kew, a large one with a music program where she could offer her services. Their worship style was contemporary so there wasn't much call for her cello, but when she was asked to conduct the children's choir she accepted with alacrity. She didn't know much about conducting but the children didn't either, and it gave her somewhere to be every Sunday morning and Thursday night, meant she could enter the building with purpose, with a role, instead of creeping in, worrying that she looked like a loner. Work, too, started coming more easily, the techniques she had struggled with after joining the MOO now second nature, her sight-reading exponentially better than it had been before the move. Two years it had taken for her to start to relax. Melbourne still wasn't home, but it wasn't so frightening either.

And then the flowers started again. Always roses, though now just a single bloom, yellow, orange, white, at first appearing on her chair before a performance, then turning up at rehearsals too. Only those where the whole orchestra was involved though, Emma noticed, never at practices with just the other cellos or the larger string family.

'It's clearly one of us, someone in the MOO,' Lui pronounced. 'Who else has the access? But not from our section. Have you noticed anyone from brass or woodwind making eyes at you?'

'I'm looking at my music!' Emma protested, but no, she hadn't. The only time she ever felt particularly scrutinised was when the visiting conductor took the podium. Lorenzo was in his mid-forties and from the Turin Philharmonic; he had been with the MOO for around six months. Every so often she would feel his eyes on her, dark and intense, and her bow would quiver in her hand. At the dress rehearsal for *Carmen* she covertly watched him back and was relieved to see his gaze linger on two other musicians, a third violinist named Thuy and the brand-new piccolo player she hadn't yet met. That made sense, she thought. The three of them were the youngest, the least experienced in the orchestra. Lorenzo was making sure they were up to the task, keeping a fatherly watch over them. The notion endeared him to her. It had been a long time since she had had a father.

Lui, though, had other ideas. 'It's him,' she hissed, inclining her head towards Lorenzo as the audience cheered after the opening night's finale. 'See how he's looking at you? He's devouring you whole.'

Emma hadn't seen, hadn't noticed, too transported by the music and the death of Carmen on the stage above them, killed by the man who then sang of how he adored her. 'Don't be stupid,' she'd hissed back, but as she was packing away her cello Lorenzo approached.

'Emma,' he said, her workaday name exotically accented. 'It's Emma, is it not? I wanted to congratulate you. I've been watching at rehearsals. You work so hard, you improve so much.'

Liu cleared her throat as she zipped her music case. Emma could tell without turning her head that her friend was smirking.

'Thank you, Mr Avante,' she stuttered, blushing. She was always blushing. 'But everyone works hard.'

'Lorenzo,' he said, smiling. 'Si, they do. But you,' he paused, 'had more ground to make up.'

Alone in bed that night, the Toreador song and Lorenzo's words echoing in her head, Emma wondered if it wasn't a backhanded compliment. Had she been so green that she'd stood out, capturing his attention because of her ineptitude rather than anything else? Maybe, she thought, but did that matter? After offering his praise he had taken her hand, her bowing hand, and held it briefly to his lips, staring into her eyes. Behind them, Liu had coughed so much you would swear she had consumption.

Two nights later Lorenzo asked for her phone number. The audience had filed out, the houselights were up and only a few musicians were left in the pit. It would be useful, he said, to talk after each performance. He could offer some tips, some insights. It would improve her playing.

'What about me?' Liu asked, overhearing. She had already zipped her cello into its case and was waiting for Emma to do the same before they caught the tram home.

'You have studied in Italy!' Lorenzo exclaimed, throwing his hands out. 'There is nothing more I can teach you.'

'Whereas Emma has a lot to learn,' Liu said, nodding. 'And not just about music.'

'That was a bit creepy,' Liu remarked later as the almost-empty tram trundled towards Carlton. 'Approaching you like that. Offering tips.' She enclosed the last word in air quotes, pronouncing it with scorn.

Emma was surprised. 'Do you think? I thought it was nice of him. He's just trying to improve the orchestra.'

'Sure he is,' Lui said. 'Just don't say yes when he suggests some work on your fingering.'

Emma reddened. Lui could be crude sometimes, crude and wrong. She was grateful for Lorenzo's interest in her. As a guest conductor, he must know what it felt like to be a newcomer, an outsider. It was sweet of him to want to help.

'I doubt he'll call anyway,' she said. The tram turned a corner, flinging them against each other, the cellos they were both holding between their legs rocking together like partners in a dance.

'We'll see,' Liu said, steadying hers.

But he did, an hour later, after Emma was already in bed. The ringing jolted her from sleep and she groped for her phone on the bedside table. It was plugged in, charging. She hadn't bothered turning it off because no one ever called at night.

'Hello?' she answered cautiously.

'So, we start this evening, eh?' Lorenzo's voice was warm and familiar, seemed very, very close in the darkness. Emma snuggled back under the covers, clutching him to her ear. They spoke for almost an hour, initially about technical matters, but eventually exchanging stories of how they had each come to the MOO. He rang almost daily after that, always after they had been in concert, but increasingly on their off-nights too. Emma found herself anticipating the conversations, unable to sleep until they had rung off around midnight.

'Back when we were doing *La Bohème* . . . did you send those flowers?' she asked during one call. It was so much easier to be brave while talking like this, cocooned in bed, without her flushing face to give her away, without having to meet his eyes. She still found herself growing heated when he watched her during rehearsals, caught him smiling as her own gaze skittered back to her score.

Lorenzo laughed. 'You have me,' he said. 'I did, I admit it. You always looked so serious, even scared. I wanted to cheer you up.'

Disappointment prickled her skin. Is that all it had been? Not because he liked her, or thought her pretty, but because she seemed glum? *Idiot*, she chastised herself. *Pretty. How ridiculous.* She winced at her own presumption.

'Thank you,' she replied stiffly. 'That was very kind of you.'

'I did some digging,' Lui informed her at an afternoon rehearsal. She'd asked Emma the previous week if Lorenzo had ever called, and Emma had coloured before she could deny it.

'Once or twice,' she'd admitted, though the number was five times that, and though texts were now starting to appear on her phone at random intervals. *How goes your day?* the first one had asked. *Sleep well, Bella* had arrived the previous night, the endearment causing her to do anything but.

'One of the violinists I was with in Padua knows him,' Liu continued. 'They were part of the same orchestra a couple of years ago . . . She told me he was a bit of a Don Juan. A flirt, a player,' she clarified, observing Emma's face. 'Has a girlfriend, but never takes her on tour. Likes to invite female colleagues for private lessons, that sort of thing.' She arched her eyebrows suggestively. 'There were even some rumours . . .'

'He's just being friendly,' Emma cut in, annoyed. 'He's European, and an artist. That's how they all are. It's in his blood.'

'Not all of them,' Liu replied. 'I've lived there, remember? And I've seen his type. I don't trust him. Don't let him get into *your* blood. Or anything else, for that matter.'

Emma turned Liu's warning over in her head as she lay in bed that night, waiting for Lorenzo to call. He had asked her never to ring him, explaining that she might disrupt his work or a rehearsal, and she'd acquiesced readily. She didn't want to annoy him. Was Liu right? Was Lorenzo flirting with her? He'd called her Bella, after all. Twice. Maybe it wasn't just purely professional, this interest of his. The thought both alarmed and delighted her.

Sex wasn't something she had much experience with. Okay, any experience. Her teenage years had been lost to bullying and self-harm, not spent thinking about boys or making out in cars. Towards the end of them she'd joined the church, where anything carnal was forbidden, of course – and that had suited her fine. There were her scars, for starters. No one would ever want to look at those, and how would she explain them if they did? It was more than that, though. Emma had been so grateful to finally have somewhere to belong that she had no desire to upset any applecarts, was happy to toe the line. If God wanted her to save herself for marriage, that was exactly what she would do. He must have His reasons.

She'd dated during and after uni, but only other Christians, boys who knew the rules too. Some had wanted to bend them, but when they had she'd quickly ended things. It wasn't that it had been unpleasant, their erections rising against her as they kissed her goodnight. Quite the contrary. She had enjoyed it, had to fight the urge to arch back, but she couldn't do it to God. God was all she had, God and music. She didn't want to disappoint Him – and besides, there were other ways to be intimate.

When Lorenzo conducted her, when they worked together, him setting the tempo, her following his lead, trusting him, opening herself up to the music and the moment . . . that was far more intense and profound and satisfying than anything she had ever done with a boy. Lorenzo must have felt it too. That was why he'd reached out to her, for the music. To improve the music, to be the best they could be. But then maybe . . .

Her phone rang, and she snatched it up greedily.

They met backstage at the Athenaeum the next day. During their phone call Lorenzo had suggested that they practise a section of *Carmen* that he sensed she was finding particularly difficult. Emma, embarrassed, had agreed. The production had been running for a fortnight now, and she thought she was on top of it, but what did she know? Lorenzo was the conductor, had decades more experience than she did. If he felt she needed more work, she must do.

How generous he was! How lucky for her to have attracted his attention.

When she turned up that afternoon at the rehearsal room he'd booked he was already waiting, had set up her stool and the music. While she tuned her cello he fussed around her, adjusting the stand, curly black hairs bursting from the open neck of his shirt. Emma had to look away. He was almost too virile, too masculine. She could smell him as he stood behind her tapping his foot, a mixture of cologne and fresh sweat, pungent in their close confines. Lorenzo made her play through the offending section, suggested some modifications, then directed her to start over. Emma complied, but before she had reached the end of the first few bars his mouth was on her neck, one hand sliding over her breast. Startled, she dropped her bow. Lorenzo bent to retrieve it, returning it with a smile and a flourish. 'Again,' he commanded, and again she played, again, he swooped, lips hot and determined against her skin. This time she made it to the end of the habanera, but her technique, she knew, was shot.

He touched her, after that, every time they met. Sometimes it was a kiss, hard and hurting, pushed against a wall in a dressing room. Other times his hands were crueller and raised bruises – a nipple tweaked while he stood behind her in one of the many private rehearsals he insisted upon, his hand thrust between her legs in a lift at the Arts Centre. Emma couldn't bring herself to even acknowledge the advances, far less reciprocate or refuse them. Lorenzo was her senior, a maestro; she was the lowest chair in the cello section of an antipodean orchestra. He was clearly attracted to her, she told herself. He was just a little rough because that was his nature – passionate, unrestrained. Maybe, she sometimes fantasised, he'd ask her to accompany him back to Italy at the end of his tenure.

He'd arrange an audition for her with the Sinfonica di Roma, sing her praises, pull some strings. On other days, though, she felt dirty, cheap. The evening phone calls had ceased. Lorenzo grabbed at her body whenever he could, but looked away when conducting her, focusing on the woodwinds instead. The piccolo girl, Emma noticed with a pang, had left the last performance with an armful of apricot roses.

'Have you heard?' Liu asked breathlessly a few days later when Emma took her place beside her at rehearsal. 'Lover boy's been stood down.'

Emma was concentrating on positioning her stopper, but looked up sharply. 'Who?'

'Lorenzo. The Italian Stallion. Thuy made a complaint against him, apparently.'

'She did? What for?'

Liu held up both hands, making squeezing motions. 'He got a bit gropy with her. Tried to cop a feel in a rehearsal room, pinched her on the arse when she was going up some stairs in front of him. I told you he was bad news.'

'Yeah,' Emma mumbled, averting her face.

Lui set down her bow. 'Emma,' she said. 'Has he touched you too?'

Fool, Emma thought. *You brainless little fool.* She clamped her lips shut and refused to answer Liu, then completed the rehearsal staring at her score and blinking back tears.

She handed in her resignation the next day.

'You don't have to go!' Liu protested. 'You did nothing wrong. And he won't be back. They'll send him home – he's got a bit of a track record, apparently, like I'd heard. No one will be giving him a second chance. You'll never have to see him again.'

Emma just shook her head. It didn't matter. She'd have to see Thuy again, and the piccolo player; she'd have to see Liu. Was it possible to die of humiliation? It certainly felt like it. Why had Emma been so blind? Because she was pathetic, she thought. Pathetic, idiotic, inane. Because she had been so desperate for attention, so starved of it, that she'd let him molest her and hoped it might be love.

'Just chill,' Liu went on. 'He didn't rape you, did he? He didn't scam you or take your cash?'

Emma turned without replying. She couldn't explain it to Liu. True, Lorenzo hadn't relieved her of her maidenhood or her money, but what he had taken from her was almost as bad. Her confidence. Her trust. Her hopes. How stupid of her to imagine, even for a moment, that just once she might have something for herself.

Leaving Melbourne was a lot quicker to arrange than moving there had been. Emma hadn't acquired much in the three years she'd been with the MOO; what she couldn't pack she gave away. A recently recruited percussionist took over the lease of her flat, and after that it was only her cello she had to organise, but she couldn't quite bring herself to do so. Every time she looked at it she felt ill, remembering Lorenzo with his arms around her, adjusting her grip on the fingerboard, recalling him fondling her thigh while she tried to play a scale. Because she was petite the instrument had been custom-made, crafted to suit her proportions. She was flying back to Sydney in three days, then two, one, and it couldn't just go in the hold, but still she hadn't booked shipping, didn't want to think about it. The cello, her constant companion for so many years, suddenly revolted her. Lorenzo had ruined it. She never wanted to see it again.

On the morning that she left, with the taxi idling outside, Emma lugged it down the stairs from her apartment and propped it in the street against a Salvation Army donations bin, then clambered into the cab before she could change her mind.

Part Five

Part Five

Bridie

April 2019

'I still can't believe she asked me,' Bridie says to the screen.

'Of course she did,' Tom replies. 'It's a brilliant idea! You know that.'

'I thought it was,' Bridie says somewhat doubtfully. 'But, you know . . . She was so *angry*, after I told everyone at the twins' birthday party. She could barely look at me. Clare's never angry. She just goes along with everything. And then she disappeared, left Allison's place without saying goodbye, before it was even over.'

'Well, she's clearly come round, so don't worry about it. Tell me again what she said.'

Bridie reaches out and touches her husband's image on the screen. They are FaceTiming: she in Sydney, he in LA, where he is shooting a film, the one he'd auditioned for before Christmas. *Don't worry about it*. Oh, Tom. Everything is so simple in Tom-land. You want a role, you get it. You alienate half your sibship, no biggie.

Bridie strokes his jaw, imagining the rasp of his stubble beneath her fingertips. She misses him. Their big house is too quiet without Tom around. She should fill it up a bit, ask some friends over, but for some reason she doesn't have a lot of friends. Industry contacts, yes;

friends, not so much. Bridie had never noticed it when she was work-ing; she hadn't needed them. Work was her friend.

'It was a few days ago,' she tells him. 'You know I texted her after the party, but she never replied. That was, what, six weeks back? I hadn't heard from her since, then out of the blue she calls up and tells me that the woman who received Daniel's corneas has agreed to be part of my film if I'm still interested. *Your film.* That's what she said, cool as a cucumber, as if it was something we'd agreed upon all along. And now we're going together to see her today.' Bridie shrugs. 'It's . . . surreal. I haven't quite got my head around it.'

'Good on her,' Tom says. 'Clare, I mean. She's obviously come to her senses. And you must be excited, to be directing again.'

'It's more filming than directing,' Bridie says, then considers. 'I guess it's both, actually. Filming *and* directing. And sound too, I suppose, and editing. God. I hope I remember how to do all that stuff. I'm used to having a team.' Her laughter, even to her own ears, sounds nervous.

'You'll be fine. Like riding a bike. Like Tropfest, remember? You did everything for that too.'

'Not really. Dad and Daniel helped. But yeah.' She smiles at the memory. 'That worked out okay.'

'Sure did.' Tom is smiling too. 'Your legs, when the wind blew your dress up. I couldn't get to the after-party quickly enough to track you down.'

'Because you were so impressed by my cinematography, right?'

'Among other things.' Tom's voice is low and suggestive; his eyes twinkle as if on cue.

This is why he keeps getting cast, Bridie thinks. It's a winning combination, the boy next door with a hint of the jungle. 'I hope you're not making faces like that at your co-star,' she says.

He laughs. 'Only if the script calls for it. But honestly, I don't think she can make any faces back. Too much botox. I'm glad you don't go in for that.'

'Not me,' Bridie demurs, knowing full well she will have some the moment she needs to. It's what this industry demands of women, both on-screen and off. Pilates and a good moisturiser just aren't going to cut it.

'So this is the first one?' he goes on. 'For the documentary. First recipient?'

'The first I've locked in,' Bridie says. 'I already filmed the guy who received some of Daniel's skin, remember? That's what got me interested.'

'And there'll be more?'

'I hope so. We need at least four, I think. It's an hour's TV. Clare's pretty sure that one of the kidney recipients will come to the party. She's already met him, like this one, and then we just have to find one more. We could actually wrap it up quite quickly.'

Tom beams from the monitor. 'That's fantastic, Bridie, it really is. You're making it happen. I love it.' His obvious pride disarms her.

'I'm shitting myself,' she admits.

'Why?' His eyebrows crinkle in surprise.

'I'm all out of practice. Ugh. It's such a great idea and it could be amazing – I know that – but just say I fuck it up?' She glances away to the clock, not meeting his eyes. Clare will be here soon. 'Plus doing it in front of her – in front of Clare. I'm so nervous. I'm sure she already hates me. She'll hate me even more if I make a hash of it.'

Tom chuckles. 'Seriously? You're worried about Clare? Oh, Bird. Do you have any idea how scared she is of you?'

*

'Her name is Maria. Maria Zanetti. She has keratoconus. Had, now, I suppose.'

'Right,' Bridie says. 'What's that?'

'It's an idiopathic condition where the cornea gets progressively thinner and starts bulging outwards, into a cone shape, impairing vision.'

'You've done your research, haven't you?' Bridie asks.

'Well, yes,' Clare says, staring straight ahead, eyes not leaving the road. 'Of course I have. But I'm a nurse too, in case you'd forgotten. Have been for almost twenty years. I already knew a lot of this stuff.'

'Yep. Sorry,' Bridie says. They are driving to Canberra, three hours away, where Maria lives. It is going to be a long trip. Bridie had offered to drive – she hates being a passenger, yielding control – but Clare had been adamant. 'No way,' her sister told her. 'You always run late.'

Bridie tries again. 'So this woman, Maria, she got both of Daniel's corneas, yeah? At the same time, or separately?'

'Separately. The transplant needs time to take, and for the swelling to go down, so everything is still pretty blurry for the first month or so. If you did both at once the patient would have no functional vision at all.'

'Got it. So there's no *a-ha* moment then?'

Clare looks at her quizzically, a short, puzzled glance before her attention returns to the freeway.

'You know,' Bridie elaborates, 'the bandages come off and trumpets sound, the blind can see, it's a miracle, that kind of thing. Excellent television.'

'Oh,' Clare says. 'No. It's not like that. It's much more gradual. I hope it won't be too boring for you.'

'Of course not,' Bridie says, stung. 'I'm really grateful that we're doing this, Clare. That you organised it. Honestly. Anything we get will be fantastic.'

Clare sighs. 'I hope so. Maria's pretty shy. She told me when we first met that she doesn't do a lot of socialising, because it's too embarrassing when she can't tell who someone is or she trips over stuff because of her eyes.'

'Has she had it all her life?'

'Not quite. It came on about ten years ago, during puberty, which I think is fairly common. Tough, though. No one likes standing out when they're a teenager.' She glances across at Bridie again. 'Well, you might have. I certainly didn't. She's twenty-six now, and she still finds it hard to talk about.'

Great, Bridie thinks to herself, but presses on. 'But it's been a success? The transplant. Transplants?'

'I think so. She only got in touch last month, though I sent out the letters almost six months ago, in November. People seem to have to work up to it. When we met she'd just had the second transplant – the bandages were still over her eye – but she said the first had made a distinct improvement.' Clare pauses. 'She didn't actually talk about it much, the transplants, to be honest, and I didn't ask her. She was far more focused on thanking me – thanking us – because she couldn't thank Daniel. She was so grateful for the chance of being normal. That was her word – normal. Poor kid. As if she was some sort of freak because she couldn't see properly.'

Bridie peers out the window, at trees and paddocks endlessly spooling past like the background of a cartoon from her childhood. This might be harder than she'd expected. 'If she's so shy, if she doesn't want to talk, how on earth did you get her to agree to take part?'

'Easy,' Clare says. 'She had a *Black Box* poster pinned up in her room.'

Something shifts between them after that. Is she imagining it, Bridie wonders, or is Clare extending an olive branch, acknowledging that Bridie may have something to contribute after all? It feels like a lifetime since she made it, but the mention of *Black Box* reassures and encourages her. *I can do this. I've done it before.* In return, Clare seems to relax slightly too, hands unclenching on the steering wheel. The kilometres slip by in silence, but this time it is companionable.

'Are you hungry?' Clare asks. 'We could stop for lunch, if you like.'

'I'm fine,' Bridie says. She fiddles with her seatbelt. 'Why'd you organise it? Today. Me filming Maria.' The question bursts from her, unplanned. 'Please don't get me wrong. I'm *so* grateful, Clare, I really am . . . I just thought you hated the idea.'

'I did.'

Their eyes meet. Clare's are beautiful, Bridie thinks. Such a clear, restful blue. Why has she never noticed this before?

'I still do a bit, to be honest, but Joel thinks Daniel would have liked it.' She returns her gaze to the road. 'The more I thought about it, the more I realised he was probably right.'

'Well, God bless Joel,' Bridie says. 'I need to buy him a drink. And you.'

'He's a good man,' Clare agrees. 'A good soul. He made me want to be . . . generous. That's what it's all about, isn't it? Giving.' She struggles for words that won't come. 'Putting something out there into the universe. Then maybe you'll get something back.'

'Maybe,' Bridie says. She has no idea what Clare is talking about.

'That's the theory, anyway.' Clare's face contorts. For a moment Bridie thinks she might cry, but then she seems to collect herself.

'So do you know if any of the other recipients might be interested in being part of this?' Bridie ventures.

'Have I asked them, you mean?' Clare shoots her a look, then relents. 'Yeah. Jeremy, the kidney recipient, has agreed to take part, and Paul's definitely up for it. You've already got some footage from him, I know, but he said he'd be happy to oblige if you wanted any more, like at home with his family, or on a building site once he's back at work.' Her mouth twitches. 'I got the distinct impression that he's hoping you'll call. Told me he can't wait to see himself on TV.'

Bridie exhales. She hadn't realised she'd been holding her breath. 'That's fantastic! Thank you, Clare – though I hope Paul knows there are no guarantees. It might not get picked up.'

'I think it will. The woman who received Daniel's pancreas said no though. She won't meet me either. I think some people just want to put it all behind them, get on with their lives.'

'I suppose that's fair enough. Their call. That's three at least. I'd rather four, but I can make it work with three if I have to.' Bridie's stomach clenches as the words leave her mouth. It is so strange to talk about her brother like this, so wrong, as if he were just an inventory of pieces rather than someone she still misses so much she regularly scrolls through his old Instagram account just to catch a glimpse of his smile, his slate-blue eyes.

'Good.' Clare hesitates, then speaks in a rush. 'Look, I haven't told anyone this – I don't know who I would tell – but just yesterday I had a voicemail from the wife of another recipient. The man who received Daniel's hand.'

'His hand?! Fuck.'

'I know,' Clare says. 'It surprised me too when I first went through the paperwork. I'd just assumed all the transplants were internal organs – kidneys, lungs, heart, that sort of thing. I'm still waiting to hear from the heart recipient, by the way. There's been no reply to my letters. Anyway, the wife said that her husband, the hand recipient, would be happy to meet, but they didn't want a lot of fuss, so they probably wouldn't take part in the documentary. Still, you never know . . .'

'A hand transplant. My God. That's amazing.' Bridie's mind is spinning. 'I hadn't even thought . . . Do you think any other limbs were transplanted?'

Clare shakes her head. 'No. It's all documented. Just one hand, his right.'

'Even so . . .' Bridie suddenly has a thought. 'What about sperm? I mean, when he was alive, obviously. Just say Daniel was a sperm donor? That could be part of the film too. It's the same sort of thing, the gift of life, all that. We could track down the recipient. The child! Children!' Her stomach clenches again.

'Settle, Bridie.' Clare laughs. 'Firstly, it would be completely unethical. Secondly, we have no reason to believe that Daniel ever donated his sperm in any other way than the conventional manner, though I have no doubt he did a lot of that.'

'Ick,' Bridie says. 'That's my brother you're talking about. Don't make me think of it.'

'You started it. You wanted to unearth his mystery offspring and expose them to the world!'

'Yeah, yeah. It would be *such* good TV though. Can you imagine?' Bridie stretches in her seat. They've been in the car for almost two hours. 'And it would have been nice if Daniel had had a kid.

We haven't really produced many between us, have we? Mum and Dad would be disappointed.'

'I don't think he ever wanted children,' Clare says. 'Like you.'

'Like me,' Bridie agrees. 'Can't see the attraction. Allison did the right thing, of course. What about you? Were you ever tempted? And there's still time for Emma, I guess.'

Clare looks away. 'Yeah,' she says eventually. 'There's still time for Emma.'

Almost as soon as she is introduced to Maria, it is clear to Bridie that the young woman really doesn't want to be in front of a camera. It is hard to imagine why she has agreed to the shoot – possibly so that Bridie will autograph her poster, something she requests as they shake hands; possibly out of some sort of gratitude to Daniel or Clare, whom she looks to constantly as Bridie is explaining how things will run. Bridie takes her time, soothes and cajoles, but the second the red light comes on and she asks her first question Maria freezes, shields her eyes, is dumbstruck. They do take after take with the same result.

'Is it too bright?' Bridie asks, careful to mask her frustration. 'Do you want to stop?'

'No,' says Maria. 'I'm sorry. I'll try harder. I get embarrassed . . .' Her voice trails off.

'Maria's eyes used to be quite . . . protuberant,' Clare explains from the rear of the room. 'I don't think you like being looked at much, do you?'

The girl dips her head, hair hanging over her face. 'They pointed in different directions too. People were always nudging each other and trying not to laugh. They didn't think I could see them, but I could.'

'They're perfect now,' Bridie says, and it's true, they are, but Maria lifts her hands to cover them again.

'I'm sorry. Maybe this wasn't such a good idea. I really wanted to do it, but I can't.'

'Let's try something else,' Bridie says, thinking quickly. 'I'm going to make everything dark, okay?' She motions to Clare to close the door, but remain nearby, next to the light switch, then lowers all the blinds. 'Can you see me?' she asks Maria.

'Only faintly.'

'Good. Now close your eyes. We're going to do the interview this way, okay? It's your story that matters. Your words. Nothing else.'

Maria remains hesitant to begin with but soon loosens up. Out it all comes: the gradually blurring vision, the falls, the teasing, the boy who had dumped her because she looked like Popeye, the loss of her place on the volleyball team, the stuffed toy guide dog that kept turning up on her desk in her final year of school. Bridie steps her through it, lets her talk it all out, then gently shifts her questioning, guiding her towards the transplant: the suggestion from the ophthalmologist, the research she'd done, the waiting for a donor.

'Open your eyes,' she suggests to Maria as they chat, and Maria does so, engaged now. Bridie signals to Clare and, using the dimmer, Clare raises the lights, increment by tiny increment, as they continue the interview. The surgery, the bandages afterwards, then the weeks that followed as each eye learned to see again. 'This,' Bridie asks, 'was it like this?'

And Maria smiles, her face fully visible now, smiles and says, 'Yes, exactly, as if the world slowly came back into focus.'

When Bridie plays it back later the effect is exactly what she had hoped to achieve: Maria, emerging out of the darkness and into the light, her voice growing stronger, more confident, as her story reaches its conclusion.

'Brilliant,' Clare breathes, looking over her shoulder, and Bridie flushes with delight: because she is working again, creating, but also – who knew? – because her sister approves of what she has made.

Clare

July 2019

'Can my sister stay in the room with us?' Emma asks as she sits on the edge of the table, clutching the paper gown around her. Her legs swing in mid-air, miles from the floor. Stripped of clothes and make-up, she appears about twelve.

'Yes, of course,' the ultrasound technician says, eyes flitting to Emma's left hand, her bare ring finger. 'Is she your support person? That's nice.'

'Yes, she is,' Emma replies, 'and the mother.'

This time the technician doesn't even pretend not to stare. 'Really?' she asks, taking Clare in for the first time. Clare nods. 'So your sister is having a baby for you? Wow. That's pretty generous.'

'And it's not even my birthday,' Clare says lamely, trying to make light of the situation, at the same time as Emma declares, 'No, it's her baby. Her egg. I'm just carrying it for her.' Her words are so certain, so matter of fact, that a lump rises in Clare's throat. *Thank you*, she mouths to Emma, but the technician has moved between them and Emma doesn't see.

'Goodness. Okay,' the woman is saying. 'Can you lie down now? On your back, legs flat, arms by your sides. That's right. Well, it's still very generous. You have to go through pregnancy and then labour, and neither of those are a walk in the park. Do you have children of your own?'

'No,' Emma says, staring at the ceiling.

'I see.' The technician reaches for a bottle of gel, lifts the gown to just below Emma's breasts and anoints her stomach. 'It might be a bit cold. Sorry.' She finishes what she is doing but remains by Emma's side, hands on her hips. 'I'm surprised. Most clinics won't accept surrogates who haven't completed their own families. In case something goes wrong, you understand,' she continues, her back to Clare, 'and you can't have your own children, or you get too attached. It's a little bit risky, really.'

'Too late now,' Emma says cheerfully, as if she is talking about having ordered dessert, not bearing Clare's child, and the technician *humph*s a bit and returns to her machinery at the foot of the table.

It is all Clare can do not to laugh out loud, in glee and gratitude and sheer surprise. Emma, tiny, timid Emma, talking back to someone, lying there half-naked and covered in goo, but standing her ground.

'Here we go,' the technician says. 'You can watch on that monitor in the corner if you like.'

If you like? Clare's entire body swivels towards the screen as it crackles to life. She holds her breath. She has been here before, more often than she cares to remember, and she knows what she is looking for. Grey pixels falter, resolve . . . then there it is, the frantically flashing cursor that is the baby's heartbeat.

'Emma!' she exclaims involuntarily, startling her. 'Look!'

'What? What's the matter? Is everything okay?' Emma half sits up on the table, and the technician tsks at her.

'Can you lie down again please? I need to take the measurements.' She squints at Clare. 'And the nuchal translucency screening, I'm guessing?'

Clare meets her gaze. 'Yes,' she says. 'I was thirty-seven when the egg was harvested, so you should. But I'm keeping it either way. I've had four prior miscarriages.'

The technician nods, her features softening. 'Fair enough. Good for you. We'll still have to wait for the results, but as far as I can see everything looks perfect, if that helps.'

'What are you talking about?' Emma asks. 'Should I be worried?'

'Checking for Down syndrome,' Clare says. 'Because of my age. Just so I know though, and you do too. I wouldn't'—she pauses—'do anything about it.'

'I know,' Emma says. 'But the baby will be fine. God wanted me to have it for you.'

'Her face!' Clare laughs once the technician has left the room, the scan completed. 'She thinks we're complete idiots. She'll probably report us to Community Services before you've even given birth.'

Emma peers down at her abdomen, carefully wiping it of gel. 'I don't see why,' she says mildly. 'I'm sure she's had worse. There,' she adds, dropping the tissues into a bin next to the table. 'I think I got it all.'

Clare watches as she zips her skirt over her still-flat stomach. 'How do you feel?' she asks, sitting down next to her on the examination table. 'After all that, I mean. The scan. It's pretty amazing, isn't it?'

'I didn't really know what I was looking at, to be honest,' Emma admits. 'It still doesn't seem quite real. Maybe when I start showing, or feel it move . . . I haven't even been sick yet.' She turns to Clare, brow creased. 'Do you think that's a bad thing? Should I tell the doctor?'

'I don't think it matters,' Clare says. 'I got sick every time, but it didn't make a difference. I still lost them.' Once on the toilet, she remembers, bright red blood splattered against the glaze of the porcelain. Once at work, as she was reaching to hang a drip: a sudden cramp, then the foetus, the embryo, the whatever it was slipping out of her as if making its escape.

Something brushes against her arm, warm and soft. Emma's hand, seeking out hers.

'You must be terrified,' her sister says. 'I'm sorry. You've been through so much.'

Clare swallows. 'That thing you said earlier, about God. Is that why you did it, why you offered? Because he told you to?'

Emma tilts her chin, considering. 'Not told,' she says. 'Not directly, not actual words as such. It's more a feeling.' She corrects herself. 'A *knowing*. A certainty. Being sure of something. I can't really explain it . . . it sounds a bit woo-woo, I guess, but it's real. It's God.' She squeezes Clare's hand, fingers long and supple.

Musician's fingers, Clare thinks, remembering her sister as a child, that enormous cello propped between her thighs, dwarfing her.

'And I'm sure about this,' Emma continues. 'I don't expect you to believe me, but I am. It's going to be all right. The baby's going to be fine. That doctor said it, but I knew it anyway.' She squeezes again. 'And I'm past twelve weeks. It's time to tell people.'

Emma's words stay with Clare as her sister finishes dressing, as Clare pays the account and they walk out to her car together. *Tell* someone? The very idea feels presumptuous, like it will be inviting disaster. Clare has been pregnant four times and has never yet told anyone. Well, Sophie, she thinks, but Sophie had always been right there, standing outside the bathroom while Clare urinated on a stick, or holding her hand while they awaited blood test results at the clinic. In the first years of IVF Clare had fantasised repeatedly about making such an announcement – to her family at Christmas, given that was the only time they were ever together; to her colleagues, less formally, over biscuits in the tearoom on the ward. She had imagined accepting their congratulations, one hand on her stomach, blushing and smiling at the attention . . . But then the miscarriages had started, and the failed cycles and the debt and the arguments, and after a while she had stopped thinking further ahead than *please please please let there be a heartbeat*. But there *had* been a heartbeat today, strong and healthy, 150 beats per minute according to the technician. She turns to Emma.

'Who should we tell?'

Emma fastens her seatbelt. 'Well, Allison and Bridie, first off, of course. Maybe Joel?' She answers herself. 'Yes, he'd definitely want to know. It will be Daniel's niece or nephew, after all. Then I'll have to let Crossfire know, and you can tell your friends.' She peers over her shoulder into the backseat. 'You'll need to get a car seat in here. And a pram, the sort that folds up, so it can go in the boot. Plus maybe one of those Baby on Board signs, like every other parent on the road seems to have.' She smiles at Clare, teasing, and in response, Clare bursts into tears. A car seat. A pram. It's almost too much, an embarrassment of riches.

'Are you okay?' Emma asks, alarmed. 'What's wrong? Do you want me to drive?'

Clare swipes at her eyes and shakes her head. 'I'm fine. I'm sorry. It's all just . . . just . . .' She can't explain, can't tell Emma that she is both ecstatic and petrified, that hope is a terrifying thing. A car seat? In all her years of yearning for a child, she has never once dreamed of buying a car seat.

'You're overwhelmed,' Emma diagnoses, studying her. 'I get it. Swap spots.' She undoes her seatbelt, walks around to the driver's side of the car.

Clare does what she is told, still sniffling. 'Would you like to have lunch, or do you need to get back to work?' she asks Emma once they are both settled again.

'Neither,' her sister replies, peering into the rear-vision mirror as she reverses out of the car park. 'I think we should go see Allison.'

Thirty minutes later they are on the other side of the city, negotiating a second hospital car park for the day.

'Maybe this isn't a good idea,' Clare worries aloud. 'She'll probably be busy. She's always busy. I should just text her.'

'We're here now.' Emma points out. 'Might as well give it a shot.' She takes the keys from the ignition but turns to Clare before leaving the car. 'You know I'll see whoever you want me to. It's your baby. Of course you want the best possible care for it. Did you ever consider Allison?'

Clare fiddles with the strap of her handbag, running the leather through her fingers. 'No,' she admits. 'St George is closer to you than RPA. And I think Allison only takes on complex cases, multiples and at-risk mothers, that sort of thing. This would be too straightforward for her – I hope anyway.' She hesitates. 'And it's Allison, you know?'

Emma nods. 'I know. I sort of thought that. She means well, obviously, but you didn't want her taking over.'

'Yeah.' Like Bridie, Clare thinks, foisting her documentary on what had been Clare's project, her two older sisters like forces of nature, pushing in where they weren't wanted, bossing her around. Yet the documentary actually looks like it is going to be pretty good, she reflects. Very good. And Bridie has been respectful and courteous, has let Clare call the shots every time they've met with a recipient. Confused, she opens the car door.

'Come on,' she says. 'Let's get this over with.'

They linger in the vast foyer of the Royal Prince Alfred as Allison is paged.

'I bet she'll ask you if you've been taking prenatal supplements,' Clare mutters to Emma. 'And staying away from cats.' Her stomach clenches. It's like waiting to be called in to the headmistress's office. When Allison appears ten minutes later, however, it is she who looks anxious.

'What's happened?' she demands, eyes swinging between them. 'Why are you here?'

Emma steps forward. 'I've got some news. Actually, it's Clare's news. Both our news.' She pauses, eyes alight. 'I'm pregnant.'

'Fuck.' Allison's hand goes to her chest. 'I called reception when I got the page, and they told me my sister was waiting to see me. Sisters. You've never been here before – I thought someone must have died. I didn't know what you were going to tell me.' She sinks into a plastic chair and leans forward, catching her breath. Allison's blouse is crinkled, the top button missing. There are grey streaks in her blonde hair.

So you're not infallible, Clare thinks and then feels ashamed. 'I'm so sorry,' she says. 'We didn't mean to scare you. Honestly. It was a spur of the moment thing.'

'We really are.' Emma's voice is contrite as she lays a hand on Allison's forearm. 'Can I get you something? A glass of water?'

'No, it's okay,' Allison replies, sitting back up. 'I just got a shock. It reminded me of that day . . . Daniel . . .' She draws a shuddery breath, then suddenly focuses. 'You're *what*?'

'Pregnant!' Emma exclaims. 'And it's Clare's baby. Her embryo.'

'How on earth . . .' Allison begins.

'Left over from an IVF cycle I did with Sophie. Emma's my surrogate.'

'Oh, that's wonderful!' Allison leaps up and embraces her, then does the same with Emma. 'How far along?'

'Twelve weeks. We just had the scan.'

Allison is immediately all business. 'Here? Who's your obstetrician?'

'No – at St George,' Clare answers. 'It's closer to Emma. Makes more sense for her appointments and the delivery.' Was she mistaken, or did a flicker of relief cross Allison's face?

'It wouldn't be ethical for me to be your doctor anyway,' Allison says. 'But you'll keep me informed, won't you? And ask me if you have any questions. Did you have the NT measurements done?'

Clare nods. 'I'll send you the results when I get them, if you like.'

'Thank you.' Allison looks once more between the two of them. 'Baby Emma! I can't believe *you're* having a baby! Or that you are, Clare.'

She is genuinely delighted, Clare realises, and something inside her uncoils, relaxes. Maybe Emma is right. Maybe it was going to be okay, after all. Maybe this time, after all these years . . .

Allison's pager sounds. She checks it, then snaps it back onto her waistband, sighing.

'I've got to go. Sorry. Emergency C-sec. I want to hear more though. Everything! How this all came about, and what your plans are, Clare, and where you're going to live and when you're due,

Emma . . . Let's have dinner soon. The three of us. Actually, Bridie too. Though she'll probably want to film it.'

'Film it?' Emma says. 'Why?'

'Well, it's another sort of organ donation, isn't it, surrogacy? Temporary, but it's a donation all right. Emma's giving you her uterus. Bridie will love it.' Her pager sounds again, but Allison ignores it. 'What did she say when you told her?'

'We haven't,' Clare says. 'We came straight here from St George.'

'So you told me first?' To Clare's surprise, Allison flushes with pride. So much of this visit has surprised her. She is so glad Emma suggested it. 'Call her,' Allison urges. 'Call her now, quickly, before I really have to go. I want to know what she says.'

Ignoring the sign on the wall, Clare takes her mobile from her bag, thumbs through her contacts and waits while it rings.

'Hello?' Bridie says.

'Bridie, it's Clare. There's something I wanted to tell you.' Watching her, Emma stifles a giggle; Allison's eyes sparkle. Blue eyes, Clare thinks. They all have them, in some form or another. Her child probably will too. 'I'm pregnant,' she says, 'but Emma's having the baby.'

There is silence on the other end of the line. For a second Clare thinks that the call has dropped out, but then Bridie speaks, loud enough to be heard by the others, though she isn't on speaker: 'What the actual *fuck*?'

Allison

September 2019

'Clamp. *Clamp!*' Allison hears the panic in her voice and bites her lip, bites down hard. She is in charge here. She needs to keep it together. Her patient is relying on her. Her team is relying on her, and now they are tense, alarmed, looking to each other, eyes wide in the small slit of skin between their scrub caps and their masks. She curses herself. Fear is contagious; hasn't she learned this? But the second baby's heartbeat is stalling, dropping faster than she can work and *clamp, clamp, where the fuck is that clamp*?

Afterwards, she has to tell the parents. Her registrar offers and for a second Allison is tempted, but then she peels off her gloves and squares her shoulders. It is her job. It was her mistake. Or was it? She has no idea, mulling it over as she washes speckles of blood from her forearms, as she removes her shoe covers. Did she mess up? She didn't think so, but then what the hell had happened? It had been a straightforward pregnancy, for twins, anyway. The mother had done everything right, had got to thirty-six weeks, and the first baby, a girl, had been delivered by C-section four hours after labour had commenced. That was fast, particularly for a primigravida, but it still didn't explain what had come next: the second twin dying before she too could be extracted from the womb. There had been no warning, no placental abruption or uterine tear or pre-eclampsia, just the previously steady heartbeat suddenly slowing down, slowing, flickering, then extinguished for good, a candle going out.

Allison had plunged her hands into the mother's abdomen, ripping the child out of her – no time for the standard procedures and incisions now – and had tried CPR, a defibrillator, but all to no avail. The baby was dead. Perfectly formed, but dead. There will have to be an autopsy. The parents need to know why. *She* needs to know why. Did she miss something, fuck up, or is it just one of those things, Mother Nature reminding her that at the end of the day it is she who holds the cards, not Allison?

Her nails bite into her palms. She pulls her cap from her hair and hurls it at the linen skip, but it misses, flutters to the floor. All those years of study, of experience, of 24-hour shifts and ruined dinners and missed birthdays . . . All her achievements, her fancy title, her fancier office, and still the baby is dead. Friends and family of the parents will no doubt point out that at least they still have one child and won't be going home empty-handed, but Allison knows that is no salve; she knows it in her gut. They had made themselves ready for two babies, had prepared their house and their hearts just as she and Jason had done eight years ago for their own twins, and the survival of one will never be a consolation for the death of the other.

Allison stands in the OR, defeated. There is blood on the floor. There is always blood. Allison smears it with her toe. A nurse approaches her, pushing a Perspex crib. The baby inside it flails around as if looking for her sister.

'She's a livewire,' the nurse says. 'Thank God. Would you like to take her out to her parents? The mother's in recovery. She'll be waking up soon.'

A bath, Allison thinks. That's what she'd like. She just wants a bath, and a glass of wine, and maybe half a Valium to take the edge off and help her sleep. But it is only four pm, and the rest of the day stretches out ahead of her like an obstacle course: breaking the news, answering the parents' questions, writing up the file, filling out the autopsy paperwork, checking in on her other recent deliveries – and then, when she can finally leave the hospital, she will start her second job, being with her family.

It's not a job, she tells herself. She enjoys it. But there is no sense of anticipation for it, just fatigue, fatigue and sorrow and the nagging fear that what has just happened is all her fault, even though she has done everything she could.

'Of course,' she tells the nurse, and hauls the crib towards the recovery room.

The next morning Allison doesn't get out of bed. It is a spur of the moment decision: her alarm goes off and she throws back the covers the way she has trained herself to, but then she impetuously snatches them back again. 'I don't feel well,' she tells Jason when he mumbles something beside her, his own alarm still an hour away. Somehow she goes back to sleep until it wakes her, then she calls the hospital. 'Sick,' she tells them without getting into specifics, but it's true, she is sick. Heartsick. Ninety-nine percent of births at the RPA go smoothly, successfully, but as Chief Obstetrician she invariably sees the ones that don't. And that's her job, she knows this, but it skews things; it has her confronting death at every delivery. Not today though. Today she is having a break from death.

She remains in bed while Jason gets the boys up and makes their breakfast; she is still lying there as the front door bangs behind them when he takes them to school. Marty and Eliot don't say goodbye. They are not used to seeing her in the mornings.

Allison dozes for a bit, but wakes unrefreshed. It is strange, still being horizontal at ten am, and not as gratifying as she has expected. She is relieved to have a day off work, the first she has ever taken without submitting a leave form at least a fortnight in advance, but now she feels guilty. Guilty, and a bit . . . bored. *Relax*, she tells herself. *You've earned this. It's stress leave after yesterday. Have that bath you wanted. Paint your nails.* But what is she going to *do* while she's in the bath or her nails are drying? Restless, she wanders downstairs to look in the fridge, picking up her phone as she goes. It rings almost the moment that she drops it into the pocket of her robe. The caller ID shows Clare.

'Hello?' she says, curious. They are not the sort of sisters who call each other for a natter. They are not the sort of sisters who call each other, full stop. If something has to be arranged, they do it by text or email – Allison doesn't have time to talk, but here she is now, in her empty house, picking up.

'Allison!' Clare exclaims. 'I didn't expect you to answer. I'm so glad you did . . . Emma's not well. She's having contractions.'

'Contractions? That's way too early. She must only be, what, twenty-three, twenty-four weeks?'

'Twenty-four.'

Allison switches on the kettle and selects a mug from the cupboard, phone tucked between her shoulder and her chin. 'They're probably just Braxton Hicks. Relax. Quite normal at her stage. Early, but normal.'

'That's what I thought,' Clare says, 'but Emma says they're regular. She's timing them. And she's had some bleeding too.'

The kettle boils, clicks off, but Allison doesn't pick it up. 'Regular? How regular?'

'She said they were fifteen minutes apart, but now it's closer to twelve.'

'Hmmph. Does she feel well? Is she nauseated? Any pain?'

'I don't think so,' Clare says. 'I'm not with her. She just called.' Her voice slides upwards. 'Should I be worried? Are you worried?'

'No, no,' Allison soothes her. 'Very few pregnancies are completely textbook. Most have their niggles. I'm sure everything's fine.' Mentally, though, she is already working through a checklist. Pre-eclampsia? Cervical insufficiency? Oligohydramnios? 'How much bleeding was there? Just spotting or a gush?'

'I don't know!' Clare wails. 'I'm not there. She only called me five minutes ago.'

'Have you told your obstetrician?'

'Emma's on the phone to her now. That's what I told her to do. I'm waiting for her to ring back.'

'Good. Okay. She's well into her second trimester, Clare. It's probably nothing.'

There is silence on the other end of the line. Clare, Allison realises, is trying not to cry.

'Where are you? Do you want me to come over? She should see her own obstetrician of course, but if it would help . . .'

'I'm on a train. I feel so bloody helpless, Allison. What if she's miscarrying? I couldn't bear it. I'm not even with her.'

'Shhh. She'll be fine. It's unlikely she'll miscarry now.' *Keep her talking*, Allison thinks. *Calm her down.* 'A train? Where are you going? Have you got the day off work?'

'Yes,' Clare hiccups. 'I'm heading into the city, to meet someone. A recipient, actually, and his wife. They're down from Queensland for his annual check-up and staying at the Sheraton, but there's never any parking, so I thought I'd get the train and now I'm bloody stuck here and Emma's having contractions . . .'

'It's okay. It's okay. Is it someone for the documentary? Is Bridie going too?'

'No, he doesn't want to be filmed. I asked. He's an older man. Sixty-four, I think. A farmer. No fuss, you know the type. I've been hoping he'd reply for so long. And now . . .' Clare breaks off. 'Emma, that's Emma calling. I'll ring you back.' The line goes dead.

Forgetting her coffee, Allison heads back upstairs to get dressed. She will go to Emma, she decides. Clare is panicking, and Emma must be scared too. They have their own obstetrician, of course, but Clare has called her, must want her there, for comfort, for a second opinion. Chances are it's nothing, but she's not busy . . . It's a god-send, really, that she can be available for them. Just as the phone rings, though, she has another thought.

'Clare?' she asks, snatching it up. 'How is she? What's happening?'

'Dr Parker told us to meet her at St George. She said the same as you, that it was probably nothing to worry about, but she wants to monitor Emma, just in case. Emma's heading there now. I'm getting off at the next stop, and I'll get an Uber.'

'Good,' Allison says. 'Good. That's the right thing to do.' She takes a breath. 'Listen, I can join you there, if you'd like, if you need me. Or otherwise . . . otherwise I could go and see the recipient. If they're not here for long, I mean, and it makes you feel better.'

'You'd do that?' Clare asks. In the background, an automated voice makes an announcement. 'But you hate the whole idea. You've always hated it.'

'I'm feeling left out. You've got Bridie roped in now, and Emma.' Allison laughs to show she's joking, but she doesn't really know why she has offered, to be honest. It's to help Clare, as she's said, to take one worry from her, but maybe it's for herself too: because the empty day stretching ahead is more daunting than her usual hectic schedule, because it will take her mind off yesterday and the lone twin flailing in her plastic box.

'Thank you,' Clare says. 'Thank you so much. I really appreciate it. I'll text you the details from the Uber. Patrick, his name is. Just ask him his story, find out if and how it's helped. Maybe get a photo, if you can.' Allison can barely hear her over the background noise: the train braking, the clang of a level crossing.

'What is it?' she asks. 'What was transplanted?'

'Pardon?' Clare says. 'Sorry – here's the station. I've got to go.'

'The recipient.' Allison is almost yelling now. 'What did he get?'

'Oh,' Clare says. Allison hears the carriage doors slide open. 'Didn't I tell you? It was a hand transplant. He has Daniel's hand.'

They meet in The Gallery at the Sheraton Grand on Hyde Park, as per Clare's instructions. Patrick, in his moleskins and boots, is instantly recognisable, a country boy come to the big smoke. He and his wife are already waiting for Allison when she arrives. He stands stiffly to greet her, and it takes her a moment to realise that, beneath his pants, both his lower legs are prostheses.

'Pat Webster,' he says. 'This is my wife, Mary.'

'I'm Allison,' she says, shaking his proffered hand. His grip is warm and firm. Without meaning to she glances to his other hand, curious, and is disappointed. It is little more than a stump and half a thumb, the skin puckered, raised and red. Her heart sinks. *Not a great job*, she thinks. *Not good at all*. She has no familiarity with hand transplants, but she'd hoped for better than this. Clare must have too. Maybe it's just as well Patrick doesn't want to be filmed.

'Would you like a coffee?' Mary asks. 'We were just about to order. And maybe some cake. It's so fancy here! I just want to be served something on one of those silver stands.'

Allison laughs. Her hips will not thank her for it, but why not? There are worse things than wide hips. She slides onto a banquette seat opposite the Websters.

'Cake sounds wonderful. My treat. I'm so sorry that Clare couldn't make it. Thank you for seeing me anyway.'

Mary unfolds a serviette and places the crisp fabric over her lap. 'It's a shame. I was looking forward to meeting her. She's been so lovely, and so polite. Some sort of medical emergency, she said? I hope everything's all right. We know all about those.'

'I think she will be.' Allison's eyes dart again to Patrick's stump as a waitress takes their order. There is nothing of Daniel in it, nothing at all.

Mary follows her gaze. 'Pneumococcal sepsis. Did Clare tell you?'

Allison shakes her head.

'Six years ago now. One minute he came in from the tractor with a bit of a temperature, the next he was hot as Hades and could barely breathe.' She shakes her head. 'They had to call the RFDS to get him to Brisbane before he died. The Flying Doctor,' she explains for Allison's benefit. 'We're pretty remote.'

Patrick chuckles. 'You can say that again.' It is clear he is happy for Mary to do the talking.

'He was lucky. They thought he was going to die, told me to prepare for it, but he's a fighter. Still, it was awful. Lost all four limbs, or part of them, anyway. Both legs, below the knee. His hand, his wrist, then all the fingers on the other hand. For a while I think he probably wished he'd died, didn't you, love? It's no life, being a farmer without your hands or feet.'

Their coffees arrive, followed by a selection of delicate cupcakes and eclairs arranged in tiers. Mary exclaims with delight, but Allison barely notices. Her mind is ticking over . . . *All the fingers on the other hand*.

'That's not the transplant, then?' she says suddenly, indicating Patrick's left hand.

Mary hoots with laughter. 'I would have asked for a refund if it was! Not that they billed us, I'm being silly, but you know what I mean.'

'It's this one,' Patrick interjects, holding out the hand she'd shaken when they met. 'I'm right-handed. You need a right hand.'

Allison reaches for it again, her mouth an O. It is darker than she would have expected, darker and rougher, but Patrick is a farmer, of course he works outdoors. The irony of it all – Daniel's hand doing manual labour! *Clare*, she thinks, *you've got to see this*.

'Pretty good, huh?' Patrick remarks.

'Yes. It's amazing! May I?' she says, turning it over, stroking the fingers. Daniel's fingers. Daniel's long, creative fingers. 'I'm such a fool. I'm a doctor, did you know? But I still didn't get it. It felt so strong when I shook it . . . I just assumed that couldn't be the one.'

'That's the one, all right,' Patrick says mildly. 'Not a bad fit. Bit smaller than the original, but I'm not complaining.' He pushes up his shirt sleeve with his bad hand, and there is the join, fifteen centimetres above the wrist, a V-shaped indent marking the spot.

'It's amazing,' Allison says again. Everything about it astonishes her: the surgical skill this has taken, the vision and the courage of the first team to attempt it; that she is holding her brother's hand almost four years after his death.

'It really is,' Mary agrees. 'We're so grateful – to you, of course, but mostly to the doc. Paddy was really down before he got it. I had to do everything for him – his shoelaces, brush his teeth, dry him after a shower, even wipe . . .' She pauses. 'You get the idea. It's given him his life back, his independence. He's old, for a transplant recipient, but the surgeon knew he'd make the most of it. He had to see all these psychologists before they'd even put him on the waiting list, but when this came up and they rang us . . . well.' Her eyes shimmer with tears, with a moment recollected.

Patrick smiles at her, gently takes his hand from Allison and pats his wife's arm.

'What can you do with it?' Allison asks. 'Everything?'

Patrick shakes his head. 'Not quite. Not the fiddly stuff, yet, but there's still time. It keeps getting better. The surgeon said that the nerves need years to knit. I can drive again – that's a big one – and use a fork, write a letter . . .'

'And the birds. You can do the birds,' Mary interrupts.

'The birds?'

'He volunteers at a local place, a raptor rehabilitation centre. Has for ages. They take in injured eagles, falcons, owls that have been hit by cars, or after bushfires, make them better, then release them back into the wild.'

'I can feed the birds again,' Patrick says, a shy smile creeping across his face. 'That's the best bit. I can pick them up and give them their medicine, or keep them calm for the vet. They know you're trying to help them. I've never been scratched. Magnificent creatures, they are.'

'I'm so happy to hear that,' Allison says, and she is. Her day, her world, has expanded somehow. She hasn't thought once about yesterday's events. Did Bridie know this would happen? Had she envisaged such a story? She remembers her sister, in the kitchen at the boys' birthday party, announcing her documentary, justifying it.

She'd had a vision too. And Allison thinks of Daniel, finally allows herself to feel the ache of his death, the stupid, pointless waste of it all, the hole he has left in all their lives. But he isn't gone, not completely, and the hurt is salved a little, shot through with wonder.

'Patrick,' Allison asks abruptly, 'have you noticed any changes in yourself since the transplant? I know that probably sounds weird, but . . .'

'I have!' Mary butts in. 'Your sister told us that your brother was a fashion designer, right? Well, he'—she gestures at Patrick—'actually thinks about what he's wearing now, rather than just throwing on whatever he left on the chair the night before. I swear he's even trying to match things, like his shirt and tie today.' She laughs and shakes her head in disbelief. 'Next he'll be wanting me to take him to Country Road.'

Emma

October 2019

'Too soon!' Emma calls over the din of the Crossfire band rehearsing. 'Harry! Nathan! You're coming in too soon.' Julian halts, but Harry, on electric guitar, continues playing, eyes closed, blissfully unaware. Emma takes a deep breath. 'TOO SOON,' she bellows.

It does the trick, but the effort makes something twang inside her. She steps down from the box she stands on when conducting, clasping her stomach.

'Are you okay?' Julian asks, before turning to Harry and yanking out his lead.

'Thank you,' Emma says. She gingerly straightens up, alert for any further pain, but everything seems fine. 'I'm just going to sit down for a minute,' she tells them. 'You two don't come in until the eighth beat, not the sixth. Maybe practise that while I catch my breath.'

She leans back in her seat, belly jutting out in front of her. John Thomas, napping in his beanbag, rouses himself, stretches and then noses her leg, asking to be picked up.

'I can't,' she tells him regretfully, caressing his ears instead.

'You won't fit in my lap. I don't *have* a lap anymore.' It is astounding to her just how big she is, though maybe it's also because she's so short. As Clare has observed, there is nowhere for the baby to go except straight out in front of her. It worries her a little. She isn't due until January, another twelve weeks hence. How enormous will she be by then?

There is a knock on the door of the rehearsal room. Emma struggles to her feet, motioning to Julian and Harry to be quiet.

It is Karl, the head pastor. 'Emma,' he says, 'I'm glad I caught you. Could we have a quick word?'

'Sure,' she agrees, surprised. Karl never interrupts rehearsals. Music is how Crossfire hooks people; he's used the word himself. 'Do you want to come in?'

'I think my office would be better. Julian, can you take over for a bit?'

'Don't let Harry start before the count of eight, all right?' Emma adds. 'I'll be back to check on you.' John Thomas trots beside her as she follows Karl past the music rooms, the creche, the soup kitchen. Crossfire, she reflects, is like a Christian Google.

'How are you feeling?' he asks once she is seated in front of his desk. 'Have you been well?'

'Yes, thank goodness. Thank the Lord,' Emma amends. The onset of contractions four weeks ago had given her a scare. Two days she'd been in hospital, with a drip in her arm and Clare beside her, pale and sleepless, jumping up and reaching for the call bell every time Emma so much as winced.

'It's too early!' she'd cried as Emma was admitted. 'Why's it happening?'

But Dr Parker had shrugged. 'Sometimes it just does. The medication should stop it.' And thankfully it had, but ever since Emma had been wary, on high alert. Clare too, judging by the frequency of her texts and calls.

'Good.' Karl nods. 'Good, that's good. I did, ah, want to speak with you about your pregnancy.'

'All going well, I can work until Christmas,' Emma says. What else could Karl be talking about? 'I'm sure you'll need me for Advent.' She smiles at the thought. It is the busiest time of the year, and her favourite. Five services every Sunday, instead of the regular four; carols mixed in with their usual repertoire. She enjoys arranging the music to create just the right atmosphere: festive, but holy too, a shout of joy in the darkness, a celebration of the most important birth there has ever been.

Karl, though, isn't smiling with her. 'Emma,' he says, steepling his hands. 'There have been some . . . concerns from the congregation about your condition. You know I believe you about the surrogacy, everyone who works with you does, but some people have been saying'—he coughs, a dry, embarrassed sound—'that you actually conceived the regular way, which would of course be an affront to God, given you're not married.'

'But I didn't!' Emma protests. 'You can ask the clinic. It's all documented. I'm doing it for my sister.'

'I know. I believe you. But there's still the matter of how it looks, to have you right up the front every service, clearly expecting, but not wed.'

'How it looks? It's a big church, Karl. It's huge! Most people in the congregation don't even know me, and the ones who do understand the situation. We put something in the newsletter, remember?' He must, she thinks. It had been his idea, not long after she'd broken her news, a discreetly worded announcement congratulating her on carrying her sister's baby.

'That was a couple of months ago though now,' Karl says. 'We have new members arriving all the time. The Eldership is concerned that it's sending the wrong message.'

More concerned about new members than their director of music, a staff member of almost five years? Emma wants to ask. *More worried about how it looks than how I feel?* The words form on her tongue, but die there. She doesn't like conflict. She doesn't want to argue with Karl, who is her boss, but also a man of God. He must know what he's doing.

'Maybe I could address the congregation directly before each service?' she suggests instead. The idea appals her, to stand up in front of over a thousand people, her belly almost in a separate post-code, and explain herself, but what else can she do?

Karl clears his throat again. 'We had an alternative plan. Perhaps you should start maternity leave early. It might be good for you. You've already been in hospital once . . . You can take your time to recover after the birth, then come back when you're ready. We'll still pay you, of course, and you can stay in the flat . . .'

'Early?' Emma interjects. 'How early?'

'Before next Sunday.' Karl, at least, is embarrassed enough to look away.

'Right.' Emma's head is spinning. 'So no one will see me and my shameful stomach.' She stands up. 'I may as well leave, then. Julian can take over.'

'You can see the week out. Or at least today. Do a handover, get organised.'

'No, I'll just go now,' Emma says. 'I'm sure you'll manage.' She is being petty, but then so are they. Suspended from her job, asked to step down, for the sin of being pregnant, something offered in love.

She strides across the room, JT at her heels, then turns, one hand on the door knob to Karl's office.

'Jesus would have done it too, you know,' she says.

Karl is still in his seat, hasn't tried to stop her. 'Jesus,' he replies, 'was a man.'

The contractions start again while she is asleep. Emma wakes with a gasp, and John Thomas is immediately beside her, licking her face. The dog, always close, has shadowed her since she swept out of Crossfire the previous day; he seems to know something is wrong. Perhaps not so much swept as scuttled, Emma thinks, seven months pregnant and trying not to cry. When they'd arrived home the flat had seemed even smaller than usual and she'd stood in the doorway, clutching John Thomas to her chest, a lump in her throat. It was so wrong, being asked to leave like that, as if what she was doing was a crime. She should make a fuss on social media, sell her story to the press, but she knows she won't. Jesus, she reminds herself, was also an outcast, and Jesus is the only one she has to answer to.

Another contraction. Emma whimpers and clutches her abdomen. When it eventually subsides she switches on the light and checks the time: 4.22 am. Far too early to call anyone. *Please Lord, make it stop*, she prays. *It's still too soon. Please let the baby live.* But the next contraction rolls in with ever greater force, skin rippling beneath her fingertips, her body jack-knifing with the pain.

John Thomas snuggles against her, head beneath her chin, and she whispers, 'It's all okay, it will be okay,' over and over into his fur, comforting him, comforting herself. The spasm wanes. Emma holds her breath, waiting. One minute, two. When ten have passed she turns off the light and wills herself to relax, tries to fall asleep. It's all okay, it will be okay, but then, oh God, a tremor so violent her back arches with its force and she is terrified she will be cleft in two. John Thomas barks, alarmed by this invisible presence; Emma grits her teeth and picks up her phone.

This time she is in hospital for three days. Clare called an ambulance and although Emma had protested, she'd been glad when it arrived, the flashing red lights a comfort even as she worried they would wake her neighbours. Despite her pleas, the paramedics had refused to let her bring John Thomas, and he'd been locked inside, howling, as they carried her away.

'I'll go and get him,' Clare assured her as Emma was triaged in the ED and hooked to a drip. 'Just as soon as you're stabilised and it's safe for me to leave.' The contractions, however, hadn't abated until midday, and as Clare reluctantly reported that evening, by the time she'd got to Emma's flat John Thomas had chewed off a skirting board and defecated twice on the carpet.

'I've called Joel,' Clare announces the next day. 'He's going to take JT while you're in here. I wish I could, but I can't keep him at my place, you know that – my landlord will kill me. I'm out most of the time, anyway, either on a shift or here. Joel says he can take him to work with him though. One of the benefits of being a landscaper, I guess.'

'Thank you,' Emma says. 'He just needs to be with someone. He can't bear being alone. Hopefully it won't be for long.'

The crisis has passed, but Dr Parker has declared that Emma has an irritable uterus and must remain in hospital, under observation. Allison had concurred over the phone.

'There's a good chance the baby will survive if it comes now,' she'd remarked, 'but it's not ideal. It's still only about the size of an eggplant. You need to try and keep it in there.'

The comment had annoyed Emma. Of course she is trying! What does Allison think she is doing? Playing roller derby?

'Joel sounded really happy to be asked, actually,' Clare continues. 'Maybe he gets a bit lonely. It's sad he never re-partnered after Daniel.'

Just as long as he doesn't get too attached, Emma thinks. She will need the company too.

Clare drives her home the next day, via a detour to Joel's to pick up John Thomas, and they end up staying for lunch.

Joel smiles as he opens the door. 'Come in! How are you feeling? All okay now?'

'Fine,' Emma says, looking past him, scanning the room for her dog. John Thomas appears in the doorway of the kitchen, claws clicking on the tiles, and she hurries to him as quickly as her swollen body will allow.

'I'm so sorry!' she apologises as she scoops him up. It had been awful, leaving him behind when the ambulance took her away. She can still hear his cries, cannot bear to imagine his distress. John Thomas yaps with excitement as she smothers him in kisses, his sinuous body contorting in delight, but once they sit down at the table he runs off quite happily to nose around Joel's garden.

'He settled in really easily,' Joel says, slicing a loaf of sourdough. 'I thought he might fret a bit, but he was as good as gold. I'll have him back anytime.'

'That's great,' Emma says, not meaning it as much as she thought she would.

'I guess he's used to moving around,' Clare says, reaching for the butter. 'He's quite the frequent flyer, isn't he?'

'He's not staying here though,' Emma says. 'It's just a visit. He knows his real home.'

Even so, when they get up to leave half an hour later the dog regards her for a moment, seated at Joel's feet, and has to be called three times before he follows them out to the car.

A walk, Emma decides, once Clare has deposited her at her flat, fussed around asking over and over if she can get her anything, then finally departed. That's what they need – a long walk through all John Thomas's favourite doggy haunts, to make up for her having abandoned him and to remind him where he really lives. She will enjoy it too after three days in bed, and for the first half hour Emma does. Turning for home, though, she realises she has bitten off more than she can chew. They had taken it slowly, she had stopped to let John Thomas sniff at every clump of grass that takes his fancy, but now she feels a dull ache in her pelvis, a tightening of her belly. *Not again*, she prays, yanking at the leash. Maybe if they hurry home and she can rest it will all be all right, but by the time she puts her key in the door the contractions are crowding upon her like teenagers at a rock concert.

'Fuck!' she screams in frustration and sinks to the couch.

John Thomas cocks his head and waits to see what will happen next.

'Rest,' Dr Parker tells her firmly as Emma is discharged yet again forty-eight hours later. 'Lots of rest. You don't have to stay in bed, but I don't want you on your feet. No working, unless you can do it on your laptop from the couch. No driving, no going to Coles.

Certainly no exercise. We need to get this baby to thirty-two weeks at least, so its lungs are fully formed. Do you understand?'

Emma nods. *I was only taking my dog for a walk*, she wants to tell the obstetrician, then realises that that too is now off the agenda. No more walks.

'Otherwise we'll have to admit you until you go into labour,' Dr Parker continues. 'It's great that the medication has worked thus far, but I'm sure you don't want to have to be attached to a drip for the next month, do you? You'll be much more comfortable at home, but you must take it easy.'

'I'll make sure she does,' Clare says, patting Emma's hand, and Emma stiffens. She knows her sister means well, but it's so condescending. They've always been like that, Allison, Bridie, Clare. They've always treated her like the baby she once was, as if she'd never grown up.

Emma pulls her hand away. 'I'll behave, I promise.' Petulance twists her words. 'You have to go back to work, anyway. Maybe you'd like to set a camera up, so you can monitor me from there.' Clare is fast running out of leave, having taken time off through Emma's two previous admissions; she needs to reserve as much as she can for when the baby is finally allowed to be born.

'Emma!' Clare is stricken. 'I don't mean it like that. You know I don't.'

Emma does know it, allows herself, ashamed, to be led out of St George and strapped, once more, into the passenger seat of Clare's car.

'I can quit work,' Clare says the moment they have cleared the hospital car park. 'I could even move in, if you like, or you could move in with me.'

Emma shakes her head. She knows that Clare is extending an olive branch, but she can't quite bring herself to grasp it. 'There isn't enough room at either of our flats. And you should be working.

You need to get some money behind you, so you can stay home with the baby for a bit.'

Clare sighs. 'I know. I just feel so dreadful about all this, everything you're having to give up. What about your own work?'

'Thankfully that one sorted itself.' Emma stares out the window. Bloody Karl. He'd be unbearably smug if he knew what was happening, would probably claim that letting her go was all part of God's plan. She hopes he never finds out.

'What do you mean?'

It is Emma's turn to sigh. 'Crossfire suspended me. Or put me on early maternity leave, or something. They've got an issue with unmarried mothers.'

'Seriously? Is that even legal? And it was all right for Mary, wasn't it?'

Emma snorts. Fair point. And she was a virgin too. 'They're still paying me, I still have the flat, they just don't want me hanging around looking all unwed and fallen.'

Clare exhales. 'Wow. Not very . . . Christian of them, was it?' She pauses at an intersection, brow furrowed, and waits to pull out before speaking again. 'Well, I'm glad at least that it's one less thing for you to deal with right now, and that you're still getting paid. And maybe it will be nice to have a rest. You can read, and watch Netflix, or play your cello.' Her eyes leave the road to seek out Emma's. 'I haven't seen your cello in ages. It's not something that's easy to hide, not where you live anyway. Do you leave it at Crossfire?'

'I ditched it, years ago, when I left Melbourne. None of you noticed.' Emma is suddenly furious, incandescent with rage. Her sisters, her own flesh and blood, and none of them know *anything*: about the bullying, or her cutting, or what had happened in the MOO. They had always been too old, too grown up to be interested, too immersed in their own lives. Emma was forever the straggler, the afterthought, eternally alone. True, she had never told them, but had they ever asked? The four of them were like planets in the solar system, occasionally hoving into view of one another, but always, always fixed in their own immovable orbits.

'Why?' Clare implores, but Emma refuses to answer. The silence settles between them, flooding the car. Eventually, Clare tries another tack.

'Shall we go and get JT? It was great Joel could have him at such short notice again, but I know he'll be thrilled to see you.'

'No point,' Emma says. 'I can't walk him. I can't look after him. I'm barely even allowed to stand up. He'll go nuts. And just say I need to go to hospital again? I can't be forever calling you in the middle of the night to deliver him to Joel's.'

'You can—' Clare begins, but Emma stops her.

'It's not fair to John Thomas, getting dragged from pillar to post. And he's happy at Joel's. You saw that.' A tear slides down her cheek and falls into her lap. Emma turns her face away, determined that Clare will not notice. It is the right decision, she knows that, but why, for her, has sacrifice always been the largest part of love?

'We'll get him back later, once the baby is born,' Clare promises, her words cracked and urgent, but Emma can't respond. She is holding back sobs. John Thomas will be Joel's dog by then, she knows it. They are orphans, the two of them, insignificant things that nobody wants, with no real place in the world. She will not hold it against him if he finds somewhere he can stay.

The weeks at home pass slowly. Emma misses the lunch at Sake marking the fourth anniversary of Daniel's death; she is on home arrest for her own thirty-fourth birthday. Clare visits as often as she can, as does Allison, even Bridie once or twice, but they are all busy, they all have their work. Emma's friends from church call occasionally, but do not come around. She is tainted, she thinks. She is too complicated now, a gravid grey area in their black-and-white lives.

Whole days elapse where Emma is alone from the moment she wakes until she falls asleep again, exhausted with isolation, marooned in her too-big bed. A husband, she finds herself thinking. She wants a husband. What was it that St Paul had said in his first letter to the Corinthians? *It is better to marry than to burn.* But she isn't burning, she is drowning. Little by little she starts talking to the baby, who is almost always present, cartwheeling across her midriff, tiny fists pushing out from under her ribs. It soothes her, the chatter; it passes the time. And who else would she talk to? She has no job, no partner, no pet. Even God seems distant, as if He is looking away – not forsaking her, but distracted, somehow, busy with other things. Occasionally, on waking, it takes an hour or so before she remembers it is Clare's child she is carrying, not hers. In such moments she strives to recall why she had agreed to this in the first place – offered it, in fact. God had called her to, or so Emma had believed, but maybe, she reflects, she had just been lonely. She wishes she was having twins, because then she could keep one. But that was wrong, so wrong. This wasn't for her. She was merely a vessel, a conduit. She was a servant, just as Jesus had been, but Jesus feels far away too.

Emma dozes during the day, then can't sleep at night. Reality contracts and expands; she is little more now than bloat and blood. The story of Abraham comes to her as she lies there waiting, standing over his son tied to an altar, unsheathing his knife at the demand of his Lord. Such faith, Emma thinks. Could she do it? She only has to hand this baby over, not kill it, but more and more the outcomes seem equally impossible.

Part Six

Allison

November 2019

'Working late, Dr Cunningham?'

Allison jumps, startled. She's been miles away, daydreaming, instead of bringing her files up to date. She smiles sheepishly at the nurse hovering over her.

'Yes. Well, sort of . . . I've got something on tonight, and there didn't seem any point going home first. By the time I got there I'd pretty much have to head out again. And there's always things to catch up on.' She gestures at the medical records spread out on the desk in front of her.

'Oh, I know,' the young woman says, reaching for one. 'Can I have this for a minute? Ms Sackville, bed twenty-four. I need to do her obs.'

'Sure. How's her mastitis?'

The nurse grimaces. 'Still pretty bad. I feel awful asking her to feed – but the baby, you know. And she'll recover quicker if she can. No pain, no gain.'

Allison nods, but the woman has already left, scrubs softly swishing together as she heads down the hallway away from the nurses' station. Allison loves this time of night on the ward, though she is rarely here to appreciate it. Dinner over, visitors ejected, the faint squawks and protests of neonates being settled to sleep. She leans back into the pool of light she is working under and picks up her pen, but is immediately distracted once more. Hands, she thinks, examining hers. She has taken them for granted, but imagine not having hands to deliver babies, or perform surgery, or hug her boys. Hands, Daniel's hand, Daniel's hand on Patrick's body . . . She has thought of it near constantly in the two months since they met, equally awed and moved. Daniel's *hand*, still able to write, as she is now, and hold a toothbrush, caress a grandchild, though the rest of Daniel is dead and gone. She is a surgeon, but she cannot get her head around it. Daniel's hand on Patrick's body, a transformation far more personal than she had expected.

Neither, too, had she expected to stay in touch with the Websters, yet a week after they met she had found herself ringing them. Mary had given her their number following the morning tea at the Sheraton, inviting her to call if she or Clare ever had any questions and Allison had thanked her with no intention of doing so. They had already been so kind, she said, she appreciated them meeting her, all the best for the future, yadda yadda . . . and then a week later – not even; four days – there she was dialling. Technical questions, initially, about the surgery and the process of rehabilitation. Because she was a doctor, she told herself. Because she was interested in anatomy and innovation, because it was such an audacious idea to conceive of, replacing somebody's hand, never mind actually pull off.

She'd kept calling, though, after those questions had been answered, and had suggested they chat over Skype. 'Did you want to see this?' Patrick had asked the first time they did so, raising his arm into view, and she had, she did. Her eyes had feasted on the hand, Daniel's hand, for the duration of the conversation. At the end she'd apologised, a little ashamed at her greed, and he'd shrugged and drawled, 'No worries. Visiting rights, eh?'

Mary, seated next to him, had laughed, so Allison had too, but it wasn't funny, it was true. They continued the calls fairly regularly after that, maybe every second week. Patrick told her about his work at the raptor centre, about the feather transplants they were trying; Mary enquired about other recipients and Allison had mentioned Bridie's documentary.

'Can you let us know when it's on?' Patrick asked, surprising her. 'I'm not big on cameras. *60 Minutes* did a story when I had the transplant, and that was enough to put me off for my life – this young chickie always nosing around or shoving a microphone in my face, but maybe it's good for people to know about. Maybe I should have gone in your sister's thingo.'

Allison was about to reply, but then the boys tumbled into the study and onto the screen, and Mary asked them if they'd like to ride on a tractor or shear a sheep, and the next thing she was inviting them, Allison, Jason, Eliot and Martin, to come and stay in the summer holidays, and Allison said yes before even thinking about it. She is looking forward to it; she has already booked her leave. Jason had been surprised when she told him, and she'd gone on about wanting the twins to see the real Australia, the land, the people, not just inner-city Sydney, but that had been only half the story. Not even half. They are going, she thinks to herself, so she can see it again. The hand. Is that weird? It is a little, but too bad. All of a sudden, just in these last few days, she has finally understood Clare's intention in tracking down the recipients: to reclaim Daniel's life, reclaim all life, to declare a victory over death, the very thing that Allison herself has been railing against.

Allison puts her pen down again, no further through the progress notes she must make. *I owe her an apology*, she thinks. *And a thank you. I'll tell her as soon as I see her tonight.* Tonight. She checks her watch. Damn.

Tonight is twenty minutes away, when her sisters will gather to watch Bridie's documentary being screened on the ABC. Allison stands up and starts putting the files away but then abandons them, breaking into a trot as she heads out of the ward and towards the hospital exit. A stitch immediately blossoms across her abdomen but she ignores it, forcing herself to go faster. No pain, no gain. She doesn't want to be late, and she still has to get across the Harbour Bridge. It will be fun, she thinks, smiling despite her discomfort. It will be good to sip champagne as they toast the premiere – the expensive variety, knowing Bridie. It will be good, she admits, to watch the show, to watch everything she had argued against. It will be good to sit back and see Daniel's life, going on.

She pulls up outside Bridie's waterfront home at the same time as Joel. 'Hey,' she says, greeting him with a hug. 'Bridie told me she'd asked you. I'm so glad you could make it.'

'Make it? I wouldn't have missed it for the world.' He disengages himself and leans into the car. 'Out you come, little man.'

'Oh, you brought JT!'

'Had to,' Joel says. 'Emma was right. He *really* doesn't like to be left alone. Ask my carpets. I hope Bridie will be cool with it.'

'She can hardly complain. She gave him away.' Joel raises one eyebrow at her.

'Okay, okay, I did too. But there were reasons. Hello, John Thomas. How are things?' The dog wags his tail, but his eyes are wary.

Bridie barely notices him when she opens the door, cheeks flushed from excitement or alcohol. She leads them through to the media room, barefoot but wearing a plunging silk dress, as if she couldn't quite decide whether to dress up for the occasion or not. The enormous TV is already on, dominating an entire wall, a cacophony of light and sound. Tom fusses with glasses; Clare and Emma are seated together on one of the long low sofas facing the screen. Emma is so pregnant that Allison can barely make out her face behind her enormous bump.

'Are you feeling okay?' she asks, bending to kiss her cheek. 'Should you be here?'

'Yes,' Emma replies, struggling to sit up so she can reciprocate. 'I needed some mental health leave. I'm going nuts at home. Besides, all I do there is sit on the couch in front of the TV. It's no different.'

'I checked with Dr Parker,' Clare interjects. 'She said it should be fine. There haven't been any contractions for over a week now, and it's not as if she's exerting herself. I picked her up, and I'll drive her home.'

'Hey, I can hear you, you know,' Emma says tetchily. 'My ears still work, even if I seem to have misplaced my legs.'

'You're doing brilliantly,' Allison reassures her. 'What are you now? Thirty-two weeks?'

'Almost thirty-three.' Clare beams. She is radiant in her excitement, pretty even, and Allison can't help but grin back.

'I should get out the boys' old stuff for you. It's up in the roof – the baby bath, and the change table, the walker. I don't know why I didn't think of it before now.'

'That would be wonderful,' Clare says. 'I'm just starting to get some of the basics together. I was too scared before now. It felt like I might be tempting fate.'

Behind Clare, Emma has averted her face, is staring at the still-blank screen at the front of the room. She should say something,

Allison thinks, include her in the conversation, but before she can her phone vibrates.

All good? Got there safely? reads the text from Jason. She sends him the thumbs-up emoji in reply, then adds *E&M asleep?* This she has also taken for granted: a second parent, a conventional arrangement, the assurance of backup. They'd decided that with school tomorrow it would be too late a night to bring the boys over to Bridie's, and thus Jason would remain at home with them. A simple decision, the obvious one, but Allison is grateful for it. How will Clare fare without this? Maybe Emma will stay involved, help her out, but is that wise?

'It's about to start!' Bridie says. 'Top-up, anyone?' She pours champagne while Tom dims the lights. Allison sits down next to Clare, Bridie squeezing in on her other side.

'This is like that time when we were kids,' Allison reminisces. 'Do you remember, B? You asked Mum what it was like, being an air hostess, and she lined us all up on the chesterfield and brought out drinks on a tray and served them to us.'

'I don't remember,' Emma says.

'You weren't there,' Clare replies. 'I don't think you were even born yet.'

'I was never there.' Emma abruptly leans forward, her face screwed up. 'Ouch.'

'What?' asks Allison.

'Nothing,' says Emma. 'The baby's kicking.'

'Shhh,' Bridie admonishes them, pointing the remote towards the TV to raise the volume. The *Australian Story* logo appears and then dissolves into a second title: *Daniel's Gift*.

'Oh, I like that,' Allison says. 'Much better than "Picking Up the Pieces." It should really be gifts, plural, though, shouldn't it?'

'Are you going to talk through every minute of the show?' Bridie hisses, eyes fixed on the screen. John Thomas yaps and Joel clamps a hand across his muzzle, trying not to laugh. Bridie rolls her eyes and reaches for the remote again, but suddenly there is Daniel at the launch of one of his collections, glorious in an impeccably cut navy blue suit, hair flopping across his eyes of the exact same shade, smile so magnified by the ridiculous screen it is like a thousand flash bulbs going off, a starburst.

Allison sinks back against the sofa, a lump in her throat. Her brother. Her baby brother. His hand rises to flick back his hair – their father had once remarked he'd get RSI, he did that so often – and Allison's eyes are drawn to it, riveted.

Then another image appears, a younger man, broad-set, blonde and sunburned. 'My name is Paul Rossi,' he says. 'I have Daniel's skin.'

Allison doesn't notice the dog after that. She doesn't notice Bridie, tense and fidgety beside her; she forgets to sip her champagne. Paul tells his story – the accident, the transplant, how he has been able to resume his life – and then it is Jeremy, the kidney recipient. By the time a before-shot of Maria flashes up, goggle-eyed, squinting, Allison is spellbound, utterly immersed. So immersed that she jumps when Emma topples out of her seat, onto her hands and knees, with a cry.

'No!' she shrieks.

Clare is immediately beside her, crouched on the floor. 'What is it? What's happening?'

'It hurts,' Emma moans. 'It really fucking hurts.'

'Where does it hurt?' Allison asks, snapping into professional mode. 'Has it only just started?' She places her fingers on Emma's neck, tries to gauge her heartrate.

'I had a few contractions earlier tonight, when I was in the shower,' Emma gasps. 'But they stopped. And I thought it would be okay to come. I had to come! Then they started again just before . . . just before . . .' Her eyes close as she rides out the spasm, sways with it. Above her, Daniel is once more on-screen, teenage Daniel, pins clamped in his mouth, frowning as he adjusts the costumes in a school production. Their mother had had the photo in a silver frame on her dressing table.

'Should I call an ambulance?' Clare asks. She fumbles in her handbag for her phone, hands shaking.

'It might be quicker if we just take her ourselves,' Allison says. 'Or it might be a false alarm.' She turns back to Emma, who has now curled into a ball and is lying on her side, panting. 'Emma, is that one over? I have to examine you. Can I do that? I know you probably don't want to be touched, but—'

'*Aaaaaah*!' Emma screams. 'Fuck. Fuck!'

'What's happening?' Bridie asks. The dog barks again, and at the edge of her vision Allison is conscious of Joel leaving the room, carrying him outside.

'Should I get towels?' Tom asks. 'Boiling water? Scissors?'

Allison ignores him. 'Emma,' she tries again, more firmly now, her doctor voice. 'You have to listen to me. I need to examine you. Can you roll over, onto your back? Come on, Emma. You have to try.'

Emma whimpers, but does as she is told. Allison quickly runs practised hands over her sister's straining abdomen. The baby is head down, low, in the correct position. This, she realises, is no false alarm.

'The baby wants to be born, Emma,' Allison tells her as calmly as she can. 'We're going to get you to hospital and see if we can stop it, like we've done before, get you something for the pain. I think we'll go in my car, okay? It will be quicker. Tom and Joel can carry you out. Clare will drive. I'll be with you all the way, checking on you. I won't let anything happen to you, I promise.'

In response Emma sits up, screams again, and Allison's knees are soaked with amniotic fluid as Emma's waters break.

'Jesus!' Bridie exclaims, then quickly adds, 'Saves. Jesus saves,' as if it matters at this point.

'I told you I should have got towels,' Tom says.

'It's coming NOW,' Emma grunts. 'I can feel it. NOW!'

Instinct takes over. Allison wipes her hands on her blouse, delves beneath Emma's dress, pulls her underwear out of the way and, sure enough, there it is. The baby's head is crowning.

'You're right,' she says, all business. 'Tom, go get me those towels. Bridie, find some cushions for her back, to help prop her up. Clare, you call Dr Parker. Actually, wait,' she amends. 'Call NETS first. Give them the address, tell them we have a preterm primigravida in advanced labour, and I'm expecting to deliver unless they can be here in five minutes.'

'She's going to have it *here*?' Bridie asks, then turns to Emma. 'Shall I film?'

'Ahh, ahh, ahh, fuck, *ahhhhhh*,' Emma groans, a ululation of pain.

'It's okay,' Allison says. 'You can push. Your little one is in a hurry.' She accepts three towels from Tom, then tells him to go outside to await the ambulance.

'You too, Bridie,' Clare barks, reaching for Emma's hand. She and Allison exchange a look. 'I'm staying though.'

Allison nods. 'Emma, Emma, we're here,' she says, sliding a towel beneath her, pushing her dress up, easing her underwear off and her legs apart. 'We're here, Clare and I. You're having the baby, but we're right here with you. It will all be all right.' Even as she says the words she sees the scars, hundreds of them, a spiderweb of scars, a silvery filigree etched into Emma's thighs. What the hell?

Oh, Emma, she thinks, suddenly understanding, *Why did you do it? What did we miss?* For a moment she is distracted, leans in to inspect them more closely and vows to herself that someday soon she will talk to Emma about the scars, find out who her youngest sister really is and what she's been through. Then Emma moans again, flesh bulges and tears, and Allison retreats, her well-drilled hands gently receiving the child that is staring straight up at her, emerging from her sister's body. Blue eyes, she thinks stupidly. Welcome to the family.

Bridie

Bridie peers at her reflection in her laptop screen, automatically smoothing her hair, then just as quickly lets her hands fall to her sides. The connection is loading. The last thing she wants is to be caught grooming herself. Besides, her hair is perfect – at least it bloody well should be. She has spent a small fortune having it and her make-up done professionally this morning, rising at five to be ready for the eight am call. Nothing too fancy, of course – this is a business meeting, not the Oscars. She needs to look natural, but she knows from experience that LA natural is very different to the Sydney version.

Tom appears in the doorway. 'Smile, Bird. You look as if you're about to be executed.'

She shoos him out of the room, frantically waving her arms instead of yelling at him, because her microphone is on and who knows when it will kick in? He grins, understanding, mouths *Good luck* and leaves, closing the door to her office behind him. Sweat pools in Bridie's armpits, though the day is so far only mildly muggy. Her tongue is sticking to the roof of her mouth. She quickly reaches for her glass of water, careful not to leave her lipstick on the rim, and as she puts it down the connection is made, her screen lighting up. Bridie sits up straight, plasters a smile on her face. She is on.

'Thank you so much for making the time to meet with us, Bridie.' The two women who have materialised on-screen in front of her are both impeccably dressed, carefully styled and at least twenty years younger than her.

'No problem,' Bridie says, and it isn't. What else would she be doing at eight o'clock on a Wednesday morning? A Pilates class at best, but otherwise she'd probably still be in bed. The days have felt long, too long, since she finished the *Australian Story* documentary, the fleeting months of work reminding her how much she has missed it.

'I'm Kate,' the first woman continues. 'She's Cate too, but with a C.' Her offsider gives a little wave. 'We know you must be very busy, but we have a proposal we're hoping you'll consider.'

Bridie feels her stomach tighten.

Cate with a C takes over. 'As I'm sure you're aware, the market for screening content has accelerated significantly over the past decade. Exploded, really! Here at Netflix, we're always on the lookout for exciting new work. A colleague showed us *Daniel's Gift*, and we really enjoyed it.'

'We did!' Kate number one interrupts. 'It made us cry.'

'In a good way,' number two clarifies. 'A *meaningful* way.'

'What was it like?' number one asks abruptly. 'Meeting those people, I mean, who have . . . bits of your brother? Was it weird?'

Her colleague frowns and looks down at her notes. Bridie senses this wasn't part of the script, but she can't ignore the question.

'A little, yeah,' she says. Weird is the wrong word, but something in her had shifted during the making of *Daniel's Gift*. When Clare had first outlined her plan to track down recipients Bridie's reaction had been one of annoyance, of scepticism. Flesh was simply flesh. It wasn't Daniel, it was just tissue and cells and gristle. Why chase after it? It made no more sense to her than treasuring an old school uniform he once wore or a book he might have read; it didn't change the fact that he was dead. But spending time with Jeremy, with Paul, with Maria, had softened her stance. Their improved lives had moved her. She hadn't expected that. It didn't mean Daniel was still alive, just because they had his bits, as Kate One put it. He patently wasn't. The alchemy of transplantation though – *that* was real, and something she had tried to capture in her documentary.

Cate Two clears her throat, brings them back to business. 'So we looked into it, and yours was the only name we could find associated with the production. Is that right?'

'Yes,' Bridie says.

'Just you?' the first woman probes. 'You weren't commissioned by, or working for, a company? No financial backing?'

'No, I did it all myself,' Bridie says, hoping they can't see her heart hammering beneath the expensively casual t-shirt she has selected for the meeting. 'Direction, production, editing, voice, what script there was . . . all me. I prefer to work independently.' *That's one way of putting it*, she thinks to herself. Better than admitting that no one has wanted to touch her with a bargepole for the past five years.

Cate Two nods. 'Impressive.'

'Very,' her partner agrees, head bouncing along in sync.

Bridie fights the urge to giggle. It is like being interviewed by two Bratz dolls.

'We applaud independence. We value being able to work directly with content creators.'

'And maybe you'd like to work with us.' Cate Two cuts to the chase. 'Here's what we were thinking: *Daniel's Gift*, but bigger. An eight-part series, each episode focusing on one specific recipient, before and after their transplants, the difference it's made to them and their loved ones. Family audience, nothing too graphic, but lots of emotion.'

'Lots,' Kate One agrees. 'As heart-wrenching as you can make it. We might premiere it around Mother's Day. Or Thanksgiving.' She turns to Cate Two. 'Actually, Thanksgiving would be lit, wouldn't it? Everyone gathered together for the holidays, but they need something to do, to *watch* . . . The ratings would be through the roof.'

Cate Two claps her hands. 'Perfect! And that gives you almost a year. That will be enough, won't it?'

'Sure,' Bridie says, head spinning. *Daniel's Gift* has had some glowing reviews in the local press after screening the previous week, but it has otherwise failed to make much of a splash. When the email from Netflix arrived, requesting a meeting, her only thought was that they might want to license it for streaming, and even that seemed too much to dream. An entire series? All directed by her? It is impossible to take in. Could she do that in eleven months? She has no idea, but only a fool would admit as much.

'I can just see the promos,' Kate One gushes. 'A very special television event . . . a holiday viewing spectacular.'

'Spectacular?' Two queries. 'It's not on ice. But maybe it should be!'

They collapse against each other in laughter, then simultaneously compose themselves and turn back to Bridie. 'We're joking. Sorry,' Kate One says. 'This could really do well though, which of course has benefits for all of us. Now, you had four recipients in your original film, didn't you? Kidney, skin, eyes, liver.'

'Corneas,' Bridie says, 'not eyes. But yes.'

'Corneas, sure, same same. You could get some others though, couldn't you, to make it up to eight? What else is there? Maybe a lung recipient? Or a heart? A heart would be fabulous.'

A part of Bridie is appalled, repulsed. This is her brother they are talking about, her brother's organs – his death that has made this possible. Surely the Bratz twins realise that, could show a little more empathy? Yet another part recognises exactly what they are trying to do and is, despite herself, excited by it. 'I directed *Black Box*,' she blurts out. They need to know that this is not her first rodeo, that if what they are proposing is to go ahead she will be a partner, not a pawn.

'Oh, we're well aware of that,' Cate Two says. 'Among other things.'

The women exchange a glance.

'Tom Flanagan,' Kate One says. 'He's your husband, right?'

'Uh huh.' They have done their due diligence.

'We want him too. He's got something big coming out with Paramount soon, doesn't he? The talk is it might make him a star.'

He's already a star, Bridie wants to say, but nods instead. Maybe in Australia, but Australia doesn't count.

'So it wouldn't hurt if you got him involved. And if his film flops we can edit him out.'

They cackle together as Bridie smiles along politely. So much of this, she thinks, is offensive. *A holiday viewing spectacular*. The quibbling over which organs to feature. Their blatant attempt to cash in on Tom. But she wants to do it, yearns to accept. With the right promotion, with the Netflix reach, this could be huge. This could get her back on track. More than back: in front, in demand.

'Well, then, are you interested?' Cate asks.

Bridie swallows. Is she selling out? *Daniel's Gift* was one thing, but this is quite another. For all the talk of admiring her independence, she knows she will have far less control over the finished product; it will be significantly more commercial, less nuanced. But an entire series, accessible globally . . . Daniel would have loved it. Daniel would have signed on the spot. It will be the feature they had never been able to collaborate on.

'I'm in,' she says. 'Once I see your terms, of course, but provisionally yes.'

Both women beam. 'Fantastic,' Kate says. 'Just one further thing . . . We need a new title. We don't want it getting mixed up with the original documentary, if people are searching online or whatever. Something punchy, poignant, memorable.'

'Did you have any thoughts?' Bridie asks.

'None,' Cate Two says airily. 'We'll leave that with you.'

They are wrapping up now, but for some reason the words stick, cohere, as if Daniel has personally delivered them to Bridie.

'That could be it,' Bridie says. 'The title. *I'll Leave You With This*.'

Kate One whistles appreciatively. Cate Two notes it down.

'Nice,' she says. 'We'll forward the contracts.'

The door to Emma's room is closed, and Bridie taps at it nervously. Tom had surprised her with a bottle of Bollinger as soon as she left her study after the Netflix meeting, and Bridie had knocked back three glasses, heady with exhilaration. Nine am had seemed a little early, but what the heck? As Tom had said, it wasn't every day you were handed an entire series. By evening though, her delight had been replaced by a creeping anxiety. *Clare*, she'd realised as she tossed in bed, unable to sleep. She had to get it past Clare. The contracts arrived in her inbox that morning, but Bridie hasn't looked at them yet. Instead, she is at the maternity ward at St George, ostensibly visiting baby Violet O'Shea for the second time in her short life, but actually preparing to pitch. She taps again, more loudly.

'Bridie!' Clare says happily as she answers the door. 'I didn't expect to see you so soon. You were only here a few days ago.' Clare is glowing, alight; her eyes, though deeply ringed, have a sparkle to them that Bridie has never seen before.

'You look great,' she says, meaning it, as she hands Clare a spray of pink balloons purchased in haste from the foyer. 'Motherhood must agree with you.'

'Oh, you shouldn't have! You already brought us those beautiful flowers last time. Emma?' Clare calls back over her shoulder. 'Bridie's here. Can she come in?' *She's feeding*, she mouths to Bridie, and Bridie nods as if she has any idea what that entails. 'Emma?' Clare asks again. There is no response. Clare retreats into the room, balloons bobbing after her.

'She's fallen asleep,' she half-whispers when she returns. 'Come in and see Violet though.'

'Won't that wake Emma up?' Bridie hisses back, but Clare shakes her head.

'No. She's out to it. She's been doing it pretty tough.'

Bridie follows her in, watches as Clare crosses to the bed and gently lifts the baby, who has finished suckling, from Emma's chest. An elongated nipple slides out of her mouth. Bridie looks away, but not before she has noticed that it is flecked with blood.

'Clare?' she says, concerned. 'I think Emma's bleeding. From her, um, boob.'

Clare, though, is unfazed. 'Here we go, little one,' she croons, settling Violet into the crook of her arms. 'Oh, breastfeeding does that, at least until her nipples toughen up. Because Violet's stomach is so tiny she has to be fed every hour and a half. It takes a toll.' She pulls the curtain across at the end of the bed, then eases herself into one of two chairs for visitors, gesturing to Bridie to take the other.

'Do you think that's, uh, a good idea? The breastfeeding?' Bridie can't help but notice that Emma looks grey with fatigue, her eyes sunken beneath their lids, arms curled and frozen, as if she was still clasping the baby. 'I thought she'd just, you know, hand over Violet and that would be it.'

'That was the plan,' Clare says, making faces at her daughter, not looking up. 'But Violet came so early . . . She couldn't feed at all for the first few days, and then the NICU doctor said it would be best for her to have breastmilk once she could, at least for the first month. Emma volunteered. I wouldn't have asked her, she's already done so much. But we both want what's best for Violet . . .'

The baby wails, a surprisingly large sound for such a small being, and Clare reaches into the bassinet next to the bed, drawing out a stuffed hippopotamus.

'Peekaboo!' she cries, waving it above Violet's face. 'Where's Violet? There she is!' The infant, distracted, stops squawking. 'Violet loves Mr Hippo,' Clare says, finally looking up. 'Joel gave it to her. He's besotted! He's already been in three times.'

'So you're staying here too?' Bridie asks.

'Uh huh. I've got a fold-up bed that I get out at night. Emma's doing all the feeds, but I take care of everything else – bathing Violet, settling her, changing her nappies. We're knackered, aren't we, sweet pea?' she says, speaking to the baby again. 'But it's all worth it.'

'Sounds like Joel isn't the only one who's besotted.' Bridie fiddles with her bracelets, steels herself to press on. 'Clare, listen, there's something I need to tell you. Netflix have asked me to extend *Daniel's Gift*, my documentary, turn it into a series. They really loved it, they want to do something more, with eight recipients this time, not just four, an episode for each. They think it could be big.'

Clare blows a raspberry on Violet's stomach. 'That's exciting,' she says. 'Congratulations!'

'Are you serious?' Bridie asks.

'Of course,' Clare replies. Another raspberry. 'Let me know if you need any help finding the extra people you need. A few of them have contacted me since *Australian Story* screened, did I tell you? The woman who received Daniel's pancreas and wouldn't take part – she said it was wonderful, and wishes she'd agreed. And the lung recipient, who never answered my letters. They're all coming out of the woodwork.'

'You're kidding,' Bridie says.

Clare shakes her head. 'Nup. You clearly hit a chord. Still no word from whoever got Daniel's heart though, which is a shame. I'm really curious about that one.'

'And you'd put me in touch with them all?' Bridie asks, relief wrestling with disbelief. 'I thought you'd hate the idea. I was terrified of telling you.'

Clare snorts, the sound muffled against Violet's stomach. '*You* were terrified? Bridie the brave? Can I get that in writing?' She sits back up, cuddling Violet against her. 'But you would have gone ahead anyway, right?'

'Probably,' Bridie concedes. 'Still . . .'

'I did it for me,' Clare interrupts her. 'To mend my heart. I was in a bad place, an awful place, when I first had the idea to find the recipients. But it's bigger than that now. I realised that, when we were shooting your film with Maria, with Jeremy. It's not just mine anymore.' She smiles down at Violet, her face tired but peaceful. 'And I don't need it to be. It's funny how things turn out, isn't it?'

There is the click of heels in the hallway, a knock at the door.

'Shall I get that?' Bridie asks.

'Please,' Clare says.

The baby has fallen asleep. Bridie bends to kiss her cheek, surprising herself. 'I'll leave you to your visitors,' she says to Clare. 'Tell Emma I was here.' She slides back the curtain, and there is someone hovering at the entrance to the room, half-hidden behind an enormous bouquet of cornflowers and gerberas.

'Oh,' Bridie says, taken aback. 'Sophie. Good to see you. I was just leaving – but please, go in.'

Emma

December 2019

Not mine, Emma tells herself. *Not mine, not mine, not mine.* She resolutely turns her back on Violet, asleep in her bassinette, and begins emptying her bedside locker in preparation for leaving the hospital. Underwear, pyjamas, t-shirts. Emma shakes each one out, then meticulously folds it again before laying it in her overnight bag. Overnight. Ha! She has been at St George for exactly four weeks and one day, since she was brought in by ambulance after giving birth on the floor of Bridie's media room on 23 November. Had she gone to term and Violet had arrived when she was supposed to in the middle of January, Clare and Emma had agreed that Emma would remain in hospital until she recovered, could see the baby whenever she wished, but wouldn't feed her. That would be Clare's job, her first real opportunity to bond with her child after the nine months Violet had spent growing in Emma's body, and the infant would have been robust enough to commence on formula immediately.

But we make plans and God laughs, Emma thinks, balling some socks together, then immediately castigates herself. God would never laugh at her. He loved her, and He must have had His reasons for Violet's premature arrival, which had upended everything.

Instead of going home within a few days of the birth, getting back to her old life, Emma had remained in hospital for weeks, the baby constantly by her side. Instead of taking meds to suppress lactation, the paediatrician had encouraged her to work to increase her supply, to the point that now Violet barely needs to mewl and milk flows from Emma's breasts, her nipples like faucets she can't turn off. Simply thinking about it has produced the familiar tingling sensation in her chest.

Emma gives up on her packing and goes to stand at her daughter's crib. Not her daughter, though. *Not mine, not mine.* Would it have been better to start her on formula straight away? Some premmies did; they had to. Or even donor breast milk, which the paediatrician had also suggested.

'What would be best, though?' Clare had asked almost before the words left his mouth.

'The mother's breastmilk is always best, for all babies, but especially premature ones,' he'd replied. 'It's got the right fatty acids, the enzymes they need, the antibodies; it's much more easily digestible.' Had she imagined it, or had his gaze flickered then to Emma, not even two hours post-partum, dazed and bleeding in a recovery room? The paediatrician had cleared his throat, looked away. 'It's a little different in cases of gestational surrogacy,' he'd said. 'You're the biological mother'—he'd nodded at Clare—'but you won't produce milk. Your sister here will, however. Her body, her hormones – they don't know it's not technically her own child she's been carrying, so will concoct the perfectly tailored food for little . . . Do you have a name yet?'

'Violet,' Clare had replied. 'Violet Emma O'Shea.'

Is that why she had offered to breastfeed? Emma wonders. Because she hadn't expected that, her name attached to Violet's, had neither asked for or imagined it? Because she was so deeply touched that something of hers would remain with this small girl forever? 'Oh, Emma. Of course I gave her your name,' Clare would say later, eyes wet, when Emma brought it up. 'She wouldn't be here without you. It's the least I could do.'

Emma's eyes were wet too. 'I'll breastfeed,' she'd said impulsively. 'I want to. For her.' And Clare had nodded and hugged her and not long afterwards a nurse had come in and showed her how to position baby Violet's downy head against Emma's heart, skin to skin, her big purplish eyes staring unblinkingly into Emma's own as she latched on.

Milk is dripping now, warm and slippery, soaking the breast pads in Emma's bra, threatening to overflow and spread across her top. Emma glances over her shoulder. They are all alone: the nurses are busy elsewhere, Clare has gone to collect the car. Violet is still soundly asleep but Emma plucks her from her bassinette, sits down on the edge of the bed, places her against her and lets her nurse. *Just once more*, she thinks. She is supposed to be weaning, but just once more. She craves it. Breastfeeding has complicated everything, or maybe it would have been complicated anyway. The tiny fingers curled against her flesh, the pull of the fluid leaving her body, the ache of it all, oh, the ache! Emma closes her eyes, leans into the pain of their imminent separation. Soon pain is all she will have. *Not mine*, she schools herself, *not mine, not mine, not mine,* but the child who drinks from her, is nourished by her, has no understanding of this distinction, cries aloud when Clare returns and Emma has to break their contact and lift her away.

Three days later it is Christmas. Bridie has invited them all for lunch, the first time they have celebrated it together anywhere other than Clare's. Emma is torn about attending – on the one hand, it will be preferable to spending the day alone, which is the only other option given she isn't working at Crossfire, as she usually is, and has no desire to attend a service and face their stares and questions, or worse, concern. On the other, though, Christmas lunch with her family will mean hours spent in close vicinity to Violet. She has not seen the baby since she left the hospital, but has thought of her constantly, obsessively: as she eats, as she showers, even as she sleeps. Clare has texted photos and Emma pores over them, memorising every detail. *She looks like me*, she catches herself thinking at one point, and the wave of sorrow that follows is so overwhelming that she deletes the picture immediately.

Still, here she is, seated between Joel and Allison, picking at the food in front of her. It's probably delicious – Bridie being Bridie has had everything catered, happily admitting that her favourite kitchen appliance is her credit card. Emma, though, has no appetite. Clare bounces Violet on her lap at the other end of the table. *Put her down*, Emma thinks. *She's only four weeks old, let her nap,* but Clare holds tight, proudly showing off her daughter, and Emma has to look away.

'She's a good size for a premmie,' Allison observes, scooping prawns onto her plate.

'Isn't she?' Clare beams. 'She was such a great feeder, just stacked on the weight. It's why we were able to be discharged before her due date. We're so grateful to Emma.' She smiles at her, but Emma can't seem to remember how to smile back and beheads a prawn instead. Her breasts, though tightly bound, are red-hot and painful; her stomach roils with nausea. Something bumps against her ankle, and she glances down to find John Thomas, wagging his tail, looking for food. She slips him her dinner roll and he devours it in one gulp, then moves away to beg elsewhere. *Everything leaves*, Emma thinks. Everything she has ever loved leaves her.

'A toast!' Tom proposes, pushing his chair back, lifting his glass. 'Merry Christmas! And thank you all for coming. It's good to do this again. I missed it last year.'

'Merry Christmas,' everyone echoes, but Tom isn't finished. 'To Clare!' he says, tilting his champagne flute towards her. 'I'm not sure I've ever thanked you for all the years you organised this. It's a big job.'

'Yeah, and you didn't even cook,' Jason calls out.

'Dad!' Eliot says, and Allison shushes him, laughing.

'And to Violet,' Tom continues. 'The newest, most beautiful O'Shea girl. Welcome!' He swivels suddenly to look Emma in the eye. She isn't expecting it, watches helplessly as champagne sloshes out of her still-full glass and onto the tablecloth. 'To Emma, too, for bringing her here.'

Blood roars in her ears. Emma has to look down so that no one sees her cry. She has done a good thing, the right thing; she has done, she firmly believes, what God wanted her to. Why, then, does it hurt so damn much?

'And to Daniel,' Joel interjects, 'To absent friends. We miss you.' He reaches for Emma's hand under the table as he speaks, and she squeezes it back, grateful to him for diverting everyone's attention.

'To Daniel,' she repeats. Oh, how she wishes he was here, wishes she could show him Violet, that he could see what she had done.

'To the Rabbitohs!' Martin cries, getting in on the act.

'To poo and bottoms!' Eliot shrieks, not to be outdone.

'That's enough,' Jason says, removing Eliot's glass of soft drink. 'I think it might be time for you two to go and have a run around outside before the presents. Take JT.'

The twins scramble up from the table, but Tom still isn't done. 'One more,' he says. 'To my brilliant wife, Bridie. Congratulations on the Netflix deal. You're amazing.'

His eyes are soft and proud and loving. How must it feel, Emma wonders, to be looked at like that? To be adored, to be cherished . . . Her gaze drifts unthinkingly to where Violet lies, now asleep, against Clare's shoulder.

Bridie stands up. 'Seeing as you've mentioned it, I've had an idea.'

Allison groans. 'Here we go.'

Bridie ignores her. 'Having you all around the one table, it's inspired me. Wouldn't it be great, for the Netflix series, if there was a scene right at the start, or the end – or both – of all of us and the recipients doing the same thing, sharing a meal, talking together? Like a merging, a binding, of Daniel's old family and his new, showing life going on, closing the circle.'

Emma hasn't met one of them, she realises. She'd supported Clare's idea right from the start, the only sister who had expressed any enthusiasm initially; she'd gone with Clare to speak with the Organ and Tissue Donation Service, yet here she was, a year – more – later and she was still yet to meet a recipient. It wasn't her fault, Emma thinks guiltily. She'd been busy at Crossfire, then on bed rest . . . Clare knows that. Nonetheless, it feels like yet another way that she has missed the boat and her older siblings have left her behind.

Bridie turns to Clare. 'I didn't mean to spring it on you. It only just came to me. Would that be okay?'

Clare inclines her head, smiles. 'Don't ask me. You can do what you like. It's your baby now, not mine.'

Emma winces, pulls herself to her feet. 'I've got an announcement too. I'm leaving Crossfire. I'm not going back, not after the way they treated me. They can shove their job.' She has been pondering it for a while, but has no idea why the decision has suddenly erupted out of her like this, and so publicly. All she knows is that she cannot bear any more talk of babies or families, must shut it down before she is destroyed.

'Good girl,' Allison says softly.

'But where will you live?' Clare asks. 'You won't be able to stay in their flat.'

Emma hesitates. She hadn't considered that. She hasn't thought it through at all, other than knowing, more strongly each day since Violet was born, that she *has* to go, she cannot return there.

'You can come and live with Tom and me if you like,' Bridie says. 'Even if it's just while you get back on your feet, sort out what you're going to do.'

'Really?' Emma asks. 'That's so nice of you.' She has been alone for the past three days since leaving St George. Alone when she wakes, alone when she sleeps, alone through the endless afternoon hours, the evenings that stretch forever. They have never been close, she and Bridie, but this is the second time Bridie has had her to stay, and the thought of being somewhere, anywhere, where other people are, fills her with gratitude.

'It is,' Bridie agrees. 'Particularly after the mess you made last time you were here.' She winks and drains her glass.

'What about you, Clare?' Joel asks. 'You're not going to be able to stay where you are forever . . . All those stairs to get up to it, and there's not much space.'

'I know.' Clare sighs. 'Believe me, I'm already tired of sharing a bedroom with Violet. She's so noisy!' She turns to Bridie. 'Maybe you've got room for one more? One and a half, really.'

'Uh-uh.' Bridie doesn't even consider it. 'No babies. I need my sleep.' She gestures at Emma. 'Besides, first in, best dressed. You'll work something out.'

It takes her a minute or two, but Emma suddenly realises that Bridie is protecting her. There is plenty of room in her mansion – she could have them all to stay, twins included – but somehow she must understand that Emma can't be near Violet, can't live with her, if she is to get on with her life. And Joel, too, the way he'd intervened with his toast just as she'd been about to burst into tears. He must have sensed it – he was right next to her – and stepped in immediately. Maybe, Emma thinks, she is not as alone as she had feared.

'Meanie,' Clare says, pouting.

'Angel,' Emma says. She lifts her glass. 'Cheers.'

She moves in two days before New Year's Eve, having given Crossfire her notice and spent the intervening time cleaning and packing up the flat. Bridie and Tom are kind to her, but busy with their work and either away or plugged into their Airpods. Tom is swept up in the publicity for his new film, a Boxing Day release, while Bridie seems to be forever in her study or on the phone, pulling things together for the Netflix series, which she hopes to start shooting in January. Their schedules only make Emma more conscious of her own lack of purpose, their easy, playful partnership contrasting with her solitude. She enjoys the space and the light of their home, their expansive garden, but it is quiet, too quiet. There is no music in it. There is no music in her. She drifts through the gleaming rooms, aimless, unsure how to fill her days, her life.

She loads Christian Connection onto her phone, Tinder, Bumble, then deletes them all again without even opening the apps. It is all too hard. Who would want her anyway, adrift, unemployed, scarred inside and out?

On New Year's Eve she, Tom and Bridie sit out on the decking watching fireworks explode over Sydney Harbour. 'Make a wish,' Bridie says, but nothing comes to mind. There is no point wishing for what she knows she can't have.

The doorbell rings, and Tom gets up to answer it, Bridie trailing after him. They must have had invitations, Emma thinks. They could have gone out, but they have stayed home with her and she is grateful for it. Tom returns carrying one end of a huge box, Bridie struggling with the other.

'It's for you!' she tells Emma excitedly. 'Open it!'

Emma does, fighting her way through the cardboard, through layers upon layers of bubble wrap. Something black nestles beneath them. A case, she thinks, and her breath catches in her throat. A cello case.

She does not open it. She cannot. There is no card, no return address, but she knows who it's from, and it feels like a bribe, like thirty pieces of silver. Clare means well, she has no doubt of that, but a musical instrument can never be a fair exchange for a baby, for the ripping out of her heart.

Eventually Tom lifts the case from the packaging and places it in her room, propped in the corner near the door. The year 2020 begins, a week goes past, and then another before a summer thunderstorm shakes the house and sends the cello sliding to the floor. Emma reacts instinctively, is out of bed and picking it up before she can stop herself, then snaps back the latches, suddenly curious, and throws the case open.

The cello that nestles inside glows with warmth, with life, must have cost a small fortune. How, Emma wonders, has she resisted it so long? She had hated all that her cello had come to represent at the MOO and there had been no place for such an instrument at the synth-laden Crossfire, but she is not at the MOO now, she is not at Crossfire. Slowly, tenderly, she lifts it from its bed of velvet, gauges its length, its heft. It is perfect for her. It is as if it was made for her. And it is good, so good, to hold something in her arms.

Clare

February 2020

'More salad, Clare?'

Maria, the recipient of Daniel's corneas, holds the bowl out towards her, but Clare shakes her head. 'I'm full, thanks,' she replies, and she is, though not in the conventional way.

'I hope you still have room for dessert,' Maria says. 'I made loukoumades. Donuts, Greek style, with honey and ouzo.' She smiles shyly. 'I haven't done that in years, since I was a teenager when my mother taught me how. They're fiddly, the little balls, and measuring out the ingredients – it was too hard, I kept messing it up.'

'But now you can again?' Clare asks.

'I can,' Maria nods, and Clare's heart swells. It has been doing so all day, ever since she arrived at Bridie's for the lunch her sister has organised. It is why she cannot eat: because she is replete with joy, suffused by it.

'I wasn't sure about coming today,' Maria confides. 'I'm more than happy to be in the series, like I was for the documentary, of course. It's changed my life, having my vision back.' She hesitates, choosing her words. 'But that was just with Bridie, at home, and with you. I thought it might feel weird, all of us here together, everyone

Daniel helped, plus his family. Like a freak show.' Her mouth purses. 'That's pretty rich, isn't it, given I used to be a freak?'

'And?' Clare prompts gently.

'And it doesn't. It feels fine. It feels special, actually, as if we're all members of an exclusive club. We've got something in common. We all share something . . . Blood, I guess. Cells. A second chance.'

Clare follows Maria's gaze around the large table set up on the decking. Joel was right, she thinks, with both pleasure and pain. Daniel would have loved it. Paul is at one end, deep in conversation with Jeremy and Bashir, the liver recipient. Allison is seated next to Patrick, who holds his phone out to her with Daniel's fingers, the two of them poring over something on the screen. Off to the side, Bridie is filming discreetly, Tom standing next to her. The twins run around on the lawn with John Thomas and Amy, the fourteen-year-old whose bowel was rebuilt using Daniel's small intestine; Patrick's wife, Mary, chats with Malcolm, who has Daniel's lungs, and Li Mei, who received his pancreas. The two of them had only come forward since *Daniel's Gift* was screened, as had Alan, who'd had his fibia rebuilt after an accident using Daniel's bone. He'd been unable to attend the lunch, but was locked in to be filmed next week.

Eight, Clare counts, with satisfaction. Bridie has done well, will have enough for her series, though she had thought that her sister had told her she might actually have nine recipients all up, had joked gleefully about having a spare, or maybe pushing Netflix to let her include an extra episode. Clare's eyes light on the empty seat next to Emma, whose plate is untouched. She is too thin. She has lost more than the baby weight.

Clare glances away uncomfortably, the sleeping Violet suddenly heavy in her arms. *I'm sorry*, she wants to say, but this isn't the place, and she's not sure it's even appropriate. After all, Emma had offered to carry Clare's embryo. Clare hadn't asked her, hadn't even thought of it. They both knew what they were getting into, and if it had been harder than Emma had anticipated, Clare hoped that the cello – a Tetsuo Matsuda, constructed of spruce, maple and ebony – had expressed how grateful she was. It had wiped out her savings. She had had to organise a bank loan to buy it and doesn't know how she is going to pay next month's rent, especially given Violet is still too young for her to think about going back to work. But Bridie has told her that she has heard Emma playing the instrument – late at night, and only ever in her room, but that is enough.

Clare holds her daughter closer, leans over and inhales the scent of her scalp. A million cellos, a million bank loans . . . she would have done all it took for this one small girl.

'I think I'll go and fetch the loukoumades,' Maria says, rising from her seat. 'Can I get you anything? A drink?'

'I'm fine, thanks,' Clare says. She gazes out over the harbour, taking it in. It is a perfect late summer's day. White sails flutter like snowflakes against the navy water, sunlight bounces and sparkles from every surface, momentarily blinding her. As her vision clears she sees Joel on the lawn, smiling and walking towards her, but before he can take Maria's now-vacated chair Allison slips into it instead.

'Glorious, isn't it?' she asks, indicating the view. 'Do you think Bridie even notices it anymore?'

Clare laughs. 'Probably not. She hasn't taken her eyes from behind that camera all afternoon.'

Violet stirs, hiccups, and Allison stretches out her arms. 'Can I hold her for a bit?'

'Sure,' Clare says, passing her over.

'Gosh, she's a good weight for, what, three months now?' Allison asks. Clare nods. 'She's really catching up. You can hardly tell she was prem. You should be proud, Clare. You're doing an incredible job.'

The unexpected compliment makes Clare blink. Has her oldest sister ever praised her? Competent, efficient Allison; Allison the doctor, whom Clare has always assumed looks down on her, a lowly nurse.

'Thanks,' she begins, but Allison is not yet done.

'And today,' she says, peering around. 'That's what I came over to tell you. I should have told you a while ago – this is your work too. I know Bridie organised it, the lunch, the film, but none of it would have come about without your original idea. Your vision.'

It is probably lucky Clare is no longer holding Violet, she thinks. She might have dropped her out of shock. 'I never dreamed of this,' she admits. 'I was just trying to . . . stay alive, I think. To have something to go on for. I was at a pretty low ebb at the time.'

Allison peers at her over her sunglasses. Their gazes lock, hold. 'I wish I'd known,' she says. 'There's so much we don't know about each other, isn't there? All of us, I mean. Emma, for example . . .'

'What were you looking at with Patrick?' Clare interrupts. She does not want to talk about Emma, is only too aware of her, empty-armed, alone, at the far end of the table. 'On his phone, I mean.'

'He was showing me some of his birds, how they're doing. They're looking amazing.'

'His birds?'

Violet, waking briefly, has started to fuss, and Allison gently rocks her back and forth. 'He volunteers at a rehabilitation centre for injured wildlife. Raptors, specifically. You know we went up there, to their farm, over summer? Well, Patrick took Marty and Eliot to the centre and I tagged along. It's fascinating stuff. There was a sparrowhawk that had got caught in a fence and broken its wing, and a kestrel that had lost almost a third of its feathers in a bushfire. Pat was showing me how they're doing now, another month on.'

Clare shakes her head. 'I don't know what I find more surprising – your sudden interest in birdlife, or that you took a holiday.'

Allison snorts. 'I take holidays!'

'Not interstate ones, you don't. You hate being too far from the hospital.' Clare is not in the habit of challenging her older sister, but Allison concedes.

'Yeah, you're probably right. That's going to change, though. And I'm so glad we did go. The boys loved being on the farm. And what the centre is doing with the raptors – it's astonishing. I could have visited every day. Microsurgery, feather transplants . . . Did you know they can take feathers from dead birds to help injured ones fly again? Imping, it's called. They insert them into the shafts, or implant them surgically . . .'

'What do you mean, that's going to change?' Clare asks.

Allison strokes Violet's head, gazes out, away, over the decking, the garden. 'Stopping, having a break, being with the boys and Jason . . . I really needed it. I don't think I've stopped since Mum got sick.'

'You haven't stopped since you were born,' Clare murmurs, not unkindly.

'And those birds, watching their recovery over the weeks we were there, seeing them on Patrick's phone just now, all healed and glossy – it made me think. Lots of things have made me think. Emma, the night I delivered Violet, and this little girl at work, and nearly having a baby.'

Clare can't make sense of it. 'Emma? And what baby?'

Allison closes her eyes. 'It doesn't matter. It's too hard to explain, but I need to change things. I'm going to stand down.'

'You're quitting your job?' Clare's voice skids upwards – Allison *is* her job – and Violet startles, awakes, begins to cry.

'Not completely quitting,' Allison says, trying to soothe her. 'Resigning my post as Chief Obstetrician. Cutting my hours back.'

'To be with Martin and Eliot?'

'To be around more, with everyone,' Allison says, patting Violet's back. 'And maybe to do some voluntary work, like Patrick. Not with birds,' she clarifies, 'but there's plenty of places my skills can be used.'

'Wow.' Clare is genuinely surprised. Of all that has transpired from her original idea to find Daniel's recipients, Allison leaving her job is not one she would have ever foreseen.

'What does Jason think?'

'I haven't told him yet.' Allison finally meets Clare's eyes, her expression embarrassed, even vulnerable, and as such completely unfamiliar. 'It's only really clarified it for me, being here today. I was talking to Malcolm earlier. He had cystic fibrosis – you probably know that – and he was preparing to die. Now he's preparing to live, rethinking everything, so why shouldn't I?' She looks down at Violet, who is still wailing. 'You have.'

'Do it,' Clare says, 'but you better tell Jason.'

'Yes.' Allison hands Violet back to Clare. 'There you go, sweetheart,' she says. 'Sorry I can't make it better. Maybe Mummy can.' To Clare's gratification the baby settles immediately, relaxing against her. 'I'll go talk to him now, while the boys are occupied. Wish me luck.'

She is gone before Clare has the chance to do so, moving across the deck to where Jason is cleaning the barbecue. They are well matched, Clare reflects, watching them. Always working, doing their duty, but maybe that can change.

'My turn,' Joel says behind her. 'I've been wanting to talk to you all day. May I?'

He seems strangely formal, even nervous. 'Sure,' Clare says. 'Have a seat. I don't think Al's going to be back in a hurry.' She expects him to ask about Violet, or say something about the lunch, the Netflix series, but what comes out of his mouth instead is totally unexpected.

'I had a question for you. Sophie. Are the two of you getting back together?'

Clare is lifting a glass of water to her mouth, splutters into it instead of sips. 'God. No. Why on earth would you think that?'

'Bridie told me that she came to see you at the hospital. I remember you telling me, the night of Martin and Eliot's birthday party, that you'd broken up because you were too driven about having a baby.'

Clare smiles. 'Driven is a nice way of putting it. Obsessed to the point of insanity, maybe.'

'Yeah, well, I just wondered, with that resolved, if maybe she thought, or you thought, that you might give it another crack.'

'No. Not at all. Sophie visited because she was happy for me, because she's a good person.'

'Right,' Joel says. 'Okay. But have you thought about it at all? Would you?'

'That ship has sailed,' Clare says. 'I wore her out. She's with someone else now, but even if she wasn't . . . no. I don't even think about her.' It's true, she realises, has been for a while, even before Violet was born. Sophie had broken her heart, but hearts can mend. So much can mend. Today only proves that in spades. 'Why do you ask?' she queries, suddenly curious.

Joel clamps his hands together, studies them intently, clears his throat. 'It's silly,' he says.

'I won't laugh,' Clare promises.

'Danny was the love of my life,' Joel says, inspecting a thumbnail. 'You know that. I never got over him. Never wanted to, still don't. I see so much of him in you, in all of you – in Bridie, in Allison, in Emma too, even in the twins – that I guess you hold that space now.' He pauses, blinks.

'Go on,' Clare says.

'We've always been mates, haven't we, Clare? Better than mates. Real friends. Allies.' He glances up, searching for a reaction.

Clare nods.

'Yeah. Well, I wondered – maybe you'd like to live with me? At Tideways, with Violet. Your place is no good for a baby, and we can help each other. You can work while I look after her and vice versa, and John Thomas will love the company. It might be better for all of us than being alone.'

Clare feels herself smile, the warmth spreading out across her chest. 'Are you proposing?' she asks.

'Not like that!' Joel hurries to assure her. 'Not in a conjugal way. You'd have your own room. Violet will too, we all will. But yeah, I guess I am,' he says. 'I'm proposing that we become a family.'

'That's what I hoped,' Clare says. 'Still, I think you should get down on one knee. Neither of us will probably do this again in the rest of our lives.'

Joel grins, sinks into the position in a flash. There is a lull in the conversation around the table. Out of the corner of her eye, Clare sees Allison and Jason turn towards them from the barbecue, watches Bridie lift and focus her camera, senses Emma leaning forward, craning to hear. This will not be a traditional match, she thinks, but there is nothing traditional about any of it, and why should there be? Her sister has had her child for her; her brother is absent but present in equal part. Eight visitors form an impromptu audience, strangers with whom she shares blood.

'Clare O'Shea,' Joel booms, making JT bark with excitement, 'will you do me the honour of moving in with me, of sharing your life, of sharing my home – Danny's home – with me, of raising your daughter with me, so long as we both shall live?'

'I will,' Clare says. 'I shall. I will.'

Emma

Everyone is so busy crowding around Clare and Joel that nobody except Emma notices the dark-haired man appear at the side of the house, glancing around as he crosses the lawn.

'Can I help you?' she asks, walking over to him.

'Is this the lunch for the . . . the organ recipients?' he asks, flushing. 'Sorry, I know that sounds weird.'

Emma smiles. 'It does, but it is.'

'Oh, good.' He relaxes. 'Are you Bridie?'

'No, I'm her sister, Emma.'

The man holds out his hand. 'Hi, Emma, I'm David. Good to meet you. Sorry I'm so late. I told Bridie I might be – it was a long drive – but she said not to worry, just to get here when I could. No one answered when I rang the bell, but I could hear people, so I came through the side gate. I hope that's okay.'

'Of course,' Emma says. 'Are you helping her with the filming?'

'Sort of.' He flicks his hair out of his eyes, a gesture so familiar that something catches in Emma's throat. 'I'm, um, in it. The show she's making. At least I think that's the plan. Apparently the Service has been trying to find me for a while, but I moved to Melbourne – I forgot to tell them – and they didn't have my new contact details.

I ended up contacting them instead, after a friend told me about that show on the ABC, and they asked if Bridie could call me.' He shrugs. 'So here I am.'

He is a recipient, it is finally dawning on Emma. After all this time, she is the one meeting a recipient first. 'And you've driven up from Melbourne just now? Today? To be in Bridie's series?'

David nods, his hair flopping back into place. 'It was all a bit last minute. I couldn't get a flight, and I really wanted to be here. Her brother saved my life. Your brother too, I guess. I would have driven to Darwin.'

'Saved your life?' Emma asks. 'How?'

'I have his heart,' David says. 'Mine started failing in my late twenties. Congestive cardiomyopathy. I prayed five years for a transplant, and now it's been four more, a bit over, since the surgery.'

'Prayed,' Emma echoes. 'Prayed. Really?'

'Every day,' David says. 'On my knees, in the car, at church, at work, while I was watching TV, and God delivered. I knew He would.' He is studying her face, drinking it in; he has not released Emma's hand since shaking it, and his is entwined, warm and vital, with her own. 'That probably sounds a bit weird too. There's not many people I'd tell that to, actually. They don't get it.'

'I get it,' Emma says. *Mine*, she thinks, she knows. *Mine. Mine. Mine.*

If you are interested in registering as an organ donor, you can find more information here:

https://www.organdonation.nhs.uk/

Acknowledgements

I'll Leave You With This is my sixth published novel, but for quite a few years I didn't think I was going to make it past five. With sincere and enormous gratitude to those who helped me get it over the line:

Beverley Cousins at Penguin Random House for having such a belief in the work, for giving me one of the kindest structural edits I've ever had, and for being so easy and delightful to deal with. Similarly, Amanda Martin for further edits and unstinting enthusiasm – you've both been fabulous. Thank you!

Pippa Masson, my agent, who has had my back for seven books and over fifteen years now. Thank you, P, for always supporting and championing me, for answering my emails so promptly, and for your transparency and honesty in all our dealings. I lucked out when you picked me up off the slush pile in 2006!

I received very helpful feedback on an early draft of this novel from the wonderful Julia Stiles as part of an Australian Society of Authors (ASA) mentorship I was awarded in 2021. Thank you both – the mentorship awards change writing lives. So too does Varuna, the National Writers' House. I completed final edits on *I'll Leave You With This* there as the recipient of a Residential Fellowship in 2022 and couldn't have had a happier or more productive two weeks. Much gratitude to both the ASA and Varuna for your support of Australian writing.

Madeline Bowmer, previously of the NSW Organ and Tissue Donation Service, who answered lots of my questions while researching this book. Any errors or literary licence are mine, not hers.

Peter Walsh, the first hand transplant recipient in the southern hemisphere and his wife, Marg, for not only agreeing to meet with me but for being so friendly and so helpful and for answering all my nosy questions. I have used some of Peter's medical details in the book with permission, but the rest of the character of Patrick Webster is fiction. Also Barb who put me in touch with them after my internet sleuthing. Thanks!

One of my oldest friends and noted producer Anna McLeish answered questions about the film industry for me, while on Twitter Sonja Louise set me straight about Christian dating sites. Joel Becker, OAM and ex-CEO of the Australian Booksellers Association, entered a Love Your Bookshop Day raffle to have a character in one of my books named after him at Fairfield Bookshop back in 2019 and will probably be very surprised to see it finally eventuate. Ongoing thanks to Heather and Dick at Fairfield Books for all your support across the years, too.

And finally, *I'll Leave You With This* was started during the second of Melbourne's many Covid lockdowns of 2020 and 2021 and finished in the sixth, a time that also coincided with my daughter having to do most of her Year 12 online. Dark days! Abundant thanks to the people who got me through it, who were always there for a chat or a whine or a virtual wine: Kerri Sackville, mainly and often; Cam, who talked me through some plot points, which almost made up for her taking over my study; Laddy for trying to make coffee quietly for the year that I worked at the kitchen table (thank you xxxx); my dad, John, who also helped me talk through the book as we walked around and around our 5 km radii; Katrina Gow, who always gets it; GJ (go the Bunnies!); Dec, for the photos; early readers Sally Hepworth, Meredith Jaffe, Fleur McDonald, Maggie MacKellar and Joanna Nell; my wonderful writing network, particularly Darren Groth, Fiona Higgins, Graeme Simsion, Lisa Ireland, Nicole Hayes, Meg Dunley, Tess Woods, Bension O'Reilly, Michelle Barraclough (who also does amazing websites), Eliza Henry-Jones and the rest of the Botches (where would I be without you?) – Kylie Orr, Lisa Joy, Katelin Farnsworth, Caroline Gilpin and Charlotte Callander – and, when we were allowed back in them, the Shepparton, Northcote, Balwyn and Ivanhoe pools, where much plotting was done. Also Taco. Always Taco, devoted companion of the longest lockdown in the world. John Thomas is for you.

Book club notes

1. What do you think of Clare's idea to track down the recipients of Daniel's organs?
2. Is flesh just flesh, as Allison contends, or does it hold meaning even after death?
3. Why do you think the sisters aren't closer? Do you believe this will change in their future?
4. Is Bridie out of line in suggesting her documentary? Why or why not?
5. Joel's friendship is one of the few things the O'Shea sisters have in common, and he attends all the family events in the book. Why has this connection endured? Were you surprised by his proposal to Clare?
6. Like Joel, John Thomas once 'belonged' to Daniel, and thus the four women all feel attached to him, yet none is able, or willing, to keep him. What does this say about each of them?
7. Is Emma over-reacting when she leaves the MOO? Explain your reasons.

8. How do you feel about organ recipients and the family of the deceased meeting? Do you think this is dangerous, as Marion from the Organ and Tissue Donation Service warns, or should it be facilitated?

9. Do you believe that recipients can ever take on characteristics of their donors?

10. Have you registered as an organ donor, or thought about it?

Kylie Ladd is a novelist, psychologist and freelance writer. Her five previous novels have been published in Australia and overseas, and *The Way Back* has been optioned for film. She has also co-edited and co-authored two non-fiction books, and her essays and articles have been published in *The Age* and *Sydney Morning Herald*, *Griffith Review*, *Meanjin*, *O Magazine*, *Good Medicine*, *Kill Your Darlings* and *Reader's Digest*, among others. Kylie holds a PhD in neuropsychology and lives in Melbourne with her husband and two children.

www.kylieladd.com.au